DR. LUMUMBA'S DREAM OF INCEST

BY

ANNA PURNA

Bloomington, IN   Milton Keynes, UK

authorHOUSE®

AuthorHouse™
1663 Liberty Drive, Suite 200
Bloomington, IN 47403
www.authorhouse.com
Phone: 1-800-839-8640

AuthorHouse™ UK Ltd.
500 Avebury Boulevard
Central Milton Keynes, MK9 2BE
www.authorhouse.co.uk
Phone: 08001974150

Revised Edition, first published by AuthorHouse 3/26/2007

ISBN: 978-1-4259-9468-6 (sc)
ISBN: 978-1-4343-0279-3 (hc)

Printed in the United States of America
Bloomington, Indiana

This book is printed on acid-free paper.

Danger and delight grow on one stalk.
—John Lyly, 1580

"The stalk, of course, is the penis," said Lumumba.
"Danger and delight are its attributes, and on this
happenstance does civilization rest."
—Africa, 1999

Cast of Characters

Herbert Hickey, Professor of Anthropology, Yale University

Kathryn Hickey, his wife

Soddhu Phalen, former dean of School of Medicine, Yale University, Kathryn's father

Bob Grisham, Chair of Herbert's department

John Slaughter, Professor of Philosophy, Yale University

John Wiggins, Dean of Divinity School, Yale University

Dorothy (Dotty) Wiggins, his wife

George Baxter, rich philanthropist, alumnus of Yale University

Lydia Baxter, his wife

Greg Vandenberg, graduate student working for Herbert

Louise Wallaroo, Kathryn's mother

Gordon Wallaroo, her husband

Apes: Research subjects at Yale: Bill, Tom, Albert, John, Freddie, Brian

Apes: African jungle: Lumumba, Tchibanga, Yendi, Okovango, Kumasi, Yalinga, Nedele, Kribi, Oyem, Mohele, Bata, Doba

Professor Xeno, researcher at Yale School of Medicine

Jorge Cortina, Cuban/concert pianist

Grizzled Dwarf

Dr. Crumb, researcher at Yerkes Center for Primate Studies

Bangassu Jamu, Assistant at Mahale Wildlife Research Center, Africa

Robert Goldschmidt, staff member at US Embassy in Nairobi

Mabu Odongo, Chief Customs Officer, Kenya International Airport

Constable Mwabiki, policeman at Kigoma Police Station

Marty Johnson, senior analyst at Bechtel

Vivian Johnson, his wife

Royce Dodd, senior analyst at Bechtel

Betty Dodd, his wife

Mr. Vreeland, music critic for New York Times

Jacques, a pilot

Masuru, Maasai game warden at Mt. Kenya Safari Club

Bagamoyo, a rabbit

Abdel Zahr, Egyptian tour guide

Dr. Tom Baker, head of Patriot Act Neurological Intervention Corps (PANIC)

Mr. Ntimama, associate of Dr. Baker

Victor Muñoz, Professor of Molecular Biophysics at Yale University

Mohammed, a waiter at the Nefertari Hotel in Egypt

Mohammed Amal Nawal Asad, first officer on the Happy Pharaoh cruise ship, Mohammed's uncle

Joe, alumnus of Yale University, friend of George Baxter

Pamfilo and Refugia, tourists in Egypt

Pedro, steward on Iberia Airlines, chauffer for Juan Carlos, king of Spain

Juan Carlos, king of Spain

Queen Sofia, his wife

Dinner guests of Juan Carlos: Duchess of Caceres, Countess of Monte Cristo, Princess Hortensia of Bulgaria, Prince Mark of Macedonia, Countess of Salamanca, Lady Grandee of Cordillera, Duchess of Badajoz

Cardinal Gomez, Cardinal, Madrid

Mr. Brown, US Congressman

Basque terrorists: El Lobo, El Gato, El Pollo

The Osborne Group: Miguel, Angel, Luís

Terrorist Group in Egypt: Shining Path of Allah's Virgins (SPAV)

Wambussi Gang, Africa

General Arriba, Commander of the Northern Forces, Spain

Commander Cox, officer in charge of US Navel operations, Tarragona, Spain

Karonga, a martyred elephant

Prologue

"Okovango, Okovango! Where are you, Okovango?"

Yalinga the ape called loudly to her son and signed the words to Bata who was sitting above me in the branches of a miombo tree. I watched with guarded interest as the second ape shook his head and shrugged indifferently.

"Ask Mrs. Hickey," he signed, pointing in my direction. "She's still hiding in the nest Nedele made for her to sleep in last night."

In a fruitless effort to disappear I pressed deeper into the woven leaves and branches of what I preferred to call a hammock. Yalinga spotted me and signed disdainfully:

"That she-bitch wouldn't know a chimpanzee from an orangutan."

"Nor would she care to," I replied. The words were signed with the slowness of a beginner, and Bata screeched with laughter.

But Yalinga glared angrily.

"Okovango, you little monkey! If you don't come down now I'm going to throw you from a tree!"

Where the hell is Herbert, I thought. As I flattened myself even deeper a male chimp named Tchibanga suddenly appeared and grabbed Yalinga from behind.

"Relax," he said,* pulling her against his hairy torso. "Okovango is at the fig tree playing with old Kumasi."

Yalinga looked relieved.

"This is a new part of the mountains," she said, "and who knows what strange creatures could be lurking behind the bushes!"

---

* Note to reader: This is the first of many places in my narrative where I've substituted the word "said" for the verb "to sign" although this is how the chimps and the humans communicated. (K.H.)

"You're beginning to sound like Mrs. Hickey," Tchibanga replied. "What you need is a good fuck."

Without further ado Tchibanga mounted her and the two went at it unmindful of my presence. As they thrashed about wildly I had a sudden vision of them tumbling into my hammock and commencing a merry threesome.

It was Herbert's fault of course that all this was happening. Had he listened to my father and declined the now dubious honor to head up Project Mark I'd still be safely ensconced in my home in New Haven. But no, the prospect of fame and glory had been too great, so here we were, in the middle of nowhere, the captives of a mad ape and his dangerous troop of followers.

On the other hand, wasn't this whole thing rather incredible, being here in this wild tangle of rain forest having a first-hand glimpse of how these wild creatures lived? That's the sixth time, I thought, unable to take my eyes away from the activity above.

But at last they were done and the two disappeared. I considered going to find Herbert, then decided against it. Let him find me, I thought. Anyway, I didn't feel like asking Bata to help me to the ground some twenty feet below.

The hammock creaked as I stretched and yawned. The sound of clamoring birds was everywhere. By now I could recognize what some of them were: parrots and canaries, bee-eaters with blue feathers and red wings, an African cuckoo making soft 'hoop-hoop' sounds, a green-colored woodpecker knocking loudly on the dark red bark of a hagenia tree with reddish flowers falling in long pendants like thick bunches of grapes.

The gaps left by the birds were filled in by the whirring of insects. There was something seductive about the sound, and as I listened to its relentless drone my mind began to wander. The events of the last few days seemed unreal. How had it happened? How had we come to be prisoners of a maniacal ape? He was maniacal all right. Passing himself off as a graduate of Yale! The nerve! I didn't believe it for a moment. His story was full of holes. For one thing, how could an ape ever pass himself off as a human? And even if he could, how could he do it at Yale, the most prestigious school in the world? It was absolutely ridiculous!

Oh he had a good story all right, how he'd murdered Dr. Xeno and escaped from his lab. But wasn't he just making use of a well-publicized story and using it to his advantage? Everyone and their mother knew about the case, how Professor Xeno, a brilliant researcher at Yale Medical School doing work on chimpanzees, was found decapitated in his lab. At first it was thought that some animal rights groups had been responsible for the crime. But then the evidence began to point to a disgruntled grad student who felt slighted when Dr. Xeno failed to credit him in a co-authored paper entitled "A Study of the Resettlement of Arteries in the Arachnoid Membrane of Deactivated Chimpanzees."

"Dr. Xeno never gives you credit for anything," the student had said as he was led away in handcuffs. Later he was released for lack of evidence, and now this mad ape was telling Herbert that it was *he* who had decapitated the professor. Impudent ape! I hated him for his lies.

As the momentary idyll of the afternoon faded into the deep forest twilight, I sat upright. The din of insects and birds now began to press in on me and I looked instinctively for Herbert.

Instead I saw Okovango hanging to the back of the old ape Kumasi.

"You are a bad little boy," said Yalinga as she pried the little chimp off. "Perhaps I should send you to bed without supper."

But in the same instant she pulled him to her breast and, leaning against the trunk of a tree, closed her eyes contentedly as the little chimp began to nurse.

A crashing in the bush startled no one but myself. Okovango's eyes opened wide as Herbert emerged from the thick growth of forest, surrounded by an army of flies. He had the look of a happy idiot, a broad smile across his handsome face. With childish peevishness I decided not to let him see how relieved I was.

He came toward me holding a stem covered with delicate flowers that looked like pale stars. His pants and shirt were covered with slugs, but he paid no attention.

"Look, my darling, a *rhodosticta* for your glorious hair," he said triumphantly.

"You call that glorious?" Yalinga scoffed. "I've seen better hair on a sun-scorched hippopotamus or a dung-beetle's bottom."

She made a sudden lunge and snatched the flower from Herbert's hand.

Herbert looked crestfallen.

"C'mon Yalinga, I went through hell to find it."

"A pity you didn't stay there."

She tossed the flower back, I watched as he made his way slowly up the tree to the great merriment of the apes.

Their screeching annoyed me and as Herbert leaned toward me holding the flower in his mouth I gave him a push. A look of surprise crossed his face as he lost his balance and fell backwards, landing with a crash. Dazed but in one piece he got up and slowly brushed himself off.

"Jesus, Kathryn, you could have killed me!"

"I'm sorry, darling, but you're starting to smell like an ape."

"This is a side of you I've never seen."

"It must be the jungle, my dear. It brings out the beast in me."

"I'll say!"

The *rhodosticta* lay crushed at his feet. He glanced at it and walked away. A sigh escaped me as I watched him disappear. Was I right to feel so angry, so unforgiving? Was our present predicament really the final page to a catastrophe which had started at Yale a year ago? Or was I judging too harshly? Was Project Mark no catastrophe at all but something good, something brilliant, something, as Herbert had said, which would change the world forever, make it a better place?

As Bata chewed on a leaf, his black fur glistening in the sunlight which filtered through the treetops, I lay back and closed my eyes. The events leading up to this moment passed through my mind one by one amidst the drone of insects and chirping of birds.

PART I
HERBERT

Chapter One

The Coming of Khvetukdas
Or
Et Tu Khvetukdas?

"Oh sweet Jesus!"

It was early morning, the first light of dawn had barely crept into the bedroom. Herbert was making love, and as wave after wave of ecstasy swept over me Jesus came into focus and turned into a man of flesh and blood: well, in such godlike moments, what else but think of god?

When the religious moment was over Herbert went back to sleep. But I was too excited. Hardly more than 12 hours ago a freight truck had pulled up behind Kline Hall and Herbert called out to me:

"They're here, my love! Come and take a look at the little creatures."

It was Sunday afternoon and the campus was deserted. He kissed me as the truck backed up and came to a stop.

"Too bad Pagálu and the dean can't be here," he said as he signed the invoice. "This is one of those moments that will go down in history."

"Signing an invoice?" said the driver.

"No, no, my good man. Teaching religion to our closest relatives, the apes."

It was only to be expected, I suppose, a natural progression of one thing leading to another, first the groundbreaking experiment in the sixties when a chimpanzee named Washoe was taught to communicate with humans in American Sign Language. Later the astounding news that chimpanzees shared 98 percent of the same DNA as ours. So now what else was left but to teach them religion, or at least to try?

"Sounds nuts to me," said the driver.

These were the exact sentiments of my father: "Ah yes," he had said, "the chimpanzee has 98 percent the same DNA, and yes, it has been taught to communicate in sign language. But to teach it about God? To give it a Christian conscience? Why, it's pure poppycock, my dear Kathryn, balderdash and poppycock!"

There was no point in arguing. Daddy knew everything, and his own involvement in a recent scandal had done little to humble him. But there were others who were just as convinced otherwise: John Wiggins, dean of the Divinity School, for one, and Soddhu Págalu, Professor of Anthropology for another. Granted, both men had a stake in the project: the dean had agreed to be the primary mover while Págalu, along with Herbert would form the rest of the team.

But they had their own following, not least of whom were the Baxters, George and Lydia; a prominent couple at Yale (George was a Fellow of Yale College), they were also the masterminds behind the idea: "Isn't it time," said George at one of the Yale Corporation meetings, "to extend the Yale mission beyond our own human experience?"

The genius of this notion had been recognized at once, and all 19 members had voted unanimously in his favor.

I closed my eyes. Whatever happened, I thought, no matter who was right, Project Mark was bound to be interesting.

Later that morning the chimps were taken on a tour of their new surroundings. Several small labs on the 10th floor had been converted into a single room. This is where they would sleep and have their classes. But it was decided they would take their meals in the North Dining Room two floors above.

"If they're going to think like us," said Bob Grisham, chairman of the Anthropology department and Herbert's boss, "they might as well eat like us."

As the chimps continued their tour of the floor, Dean Wiggins tried to appear serene. But it was obvious his trip to Atlantic City over the weekend had not been a success, and he reprimanded the chimps often for venting their natural curiosity.

"The biology students will get angry if you touch their experiments," he signed slowly. And again: "If you break that vial you will probably die."

He spoke as he signed*—one of the primary goals of the project was to teach the chimps to understand spoken language—but his voice was harsh and impatient and the chimps put their head in their hands and began to whimper.

"Now see what you've done?" said Professor Págalu, his eyes red from jet lag. About every eight weeks he made a flight to India. Dean Wiggins shot him a dirty look.

"Listen here, you fire-worshipping idiot, if I had my druthers. . . ."

"Your druthers?" said Soddhu sarcastically. "Oh how shameful, he forgot to put on his druthers!"

He winked at me and smiled. It was hard not to like him, he was such a handsome fellow. But Wiggins wasn't impressed.

"I *know* he's going to try and teach them his pagan religion," he muttered.

"*My* pagan religion? What about yours? Anyway, if it weren't for mine you Christians wouldn't have a leg to stand on."

"That's bullshit," the dean replied. "There's not the slightest resemblance between Christianity and Zoroastrianism."

"Are you kidding?! Why, it would take a couple of days just to name all the similarities."

"Unfortunately we don't have the time," said Herbert, checking his watch. "Unless you want to pass on lunch."

"I'd rather be tortured by the Reverend's Sunday homilies than do that," said Soddhu rubbing his stomach and looking hungrily in my direction.

"Kathryn?" he said, offering me his arm as the dean ran off to take care of some business.

With the help of four grad students we walked up the two flights to the dining room and led the chimps to a table which had been reserved for us by the window. A panoramic view of the campus and city spread in all directions. The rugged bluffs and tangled woods of East Rock Part rose off to our left.

The chimps screeched excitedly as their bowls of warm oatmeal were placed infront of them. They ate greedily but with good manners. I was amazed to see them using a spoon.

"Perhaps the Baxters know what they're doing afterall," I said.

---

* Because the dean had only just learned to use sign language, he eventually relinquished the task to Herbert and Soddhu who were already adept at it. K.H.

5

"Just because they can grasp a spoon doesn't mean they'll be able to grasp the Epistles of Paul," said Greg Vandenberg. He was a grad student working on a master's degree in Anthropology.

"Listen," said Herbert. "If all they do is learn the Lord's Prayer I think I'll have tenure."

As we talked the chimp's eyes went from one face to the next. It almost seemed as if they were carefully recording our conversation so they could review it later in the privacy of their cages. All except the smallest ape who kept looking away, toward the bluffs.

"I think he's homesick," said Págalu. "He's the only one from Africa. All the others were bred in captivity."

"How can you tell them apart?" I asked. "Except for the little one they all look alike."

"Dear lady," Soddhu replied. "That's because you are not yet a mother."

"Hurray for that," I replied.

"Ah yes, American women like to wait. And why not, when they are as beautiful as you? Motherhood, as saintly as it is, does take its toll on a woman's body."

As his eyes bored into me, I felt the blood rush to my cheeks.

"What are the chimps' names?" I asked quickly.

The chimps were asked to introduce themselves; they gave their names as Bill, Tom, Albert, Brian, John and Freddy. Each one politely shook my hand.

"You are from Africa?" I said to Albert. The little ape nodded and made a "y" sign with his right hand, which meant yes.

"I hope you're not feeling homesick," I signed.

"I miss my sister," he signed back. Herbert shrugged helplessly.

"We didn't want any distractions," he said "There's a time limit on this project, you know. Speaking of time. . . ."

He got to his feet.

"Hurry up, boys," he said to the chimps, "it's time to start your lessons."

As Págalu held my chair I found myself staring at him curiously. Up until now our acquaintance had been casual, I'd seen him at parties, sometimes in the hallway. We always said hello, but that was about all. Rumor had it that a secret wife lived in India, which is why he was always traveling there. Indeed his latest trip was the eleventh or twelfth one in a period of just as many months.

"Did you have a good time?" I asked as we left the dining room.

"In India? Actually I did. It was a little more productive than usual."

6

The day was warm and Soddhu's shirt was half open. As I entertained the thought of him coupling with his wife my eyes were drawn to his undershirt which appeared to be made of fine muslin.

"I'm doing research on a book I'm writing," he continued.

"Is it about the fire temples?"

"Ah, so you know about them?"

"Only a little, this much maybe."

I held my index finger about an eighth inch above my thumb.

"I can see I'll need to educate you."

"Start with yourself, Professor. Everyone says you are married."

"If only it were true, but I'm still waiting for the right woman."

"Herbert says that Zoroastrians never marry outside their religion."

"Unfortunately that *is* true, which is why there aren't many of us left, only about 200,000 maybe. Our blood is purer than Evian, we are the original Aryans, Mrs. Hickey. The word Aryan means people of Iran, and Iran was originally Persia, which is why we Zoroastrians are also called Parsis since we and our religion originated in Persia."

"*You* are the Aryans?" I exclaimed.

"None other. How Hitler got his blond, blue-eyed people mixed up with us is beyond me."

"You should do a book on that."

"The one I'm working on is much more important."

"What's it about?"

"I should like to tell you, Mrs. Hickey, but only when I know you better."

His hand went reflexively to his undershirt.

"You may be the only man on campus who still wears one," I remarked.

"This is not your ordinary undershirt," he replied. "It's called a sadreh, or a next-to-skin shirt. It's part of our ancient tradition, and to wear it means I've committed myself to a life of Good Thoughts, Good Words and Good Deeds. The only time I take it off is when I shower. Here, look. There is a little bag just below the neck of the sadreh which I fill up daily with good deeds."

I could see there was something in it, which looked like dried leaves. But before I could comment we entered the lab, and the grad students sat the chimps down in chairs. A few minutes later John Wiggins came in with his wife Dorothy. As he held the door, three workmen pushed in an upright piano. The dean was beaming.

7

"God has shown us the way," he said. "We will teach them their first lesson through song. Isn't that how young children learn in Sunday school?"

"Why, that's brilliant!" said Herbert. "You know, taming the wild beast through music and all that."

The dean nodded and signaled to his wife. Her large behind barely fit onto the bench as she sat at the piano. She was about to play when the dean stopped her.

"Let us take a moment to pray," he said. "Please, Lord, help us to lead these fellow creatures from the darkness of their ways into the divine light of thy great wisdom. Bless us this day with a miracle."

"Should anything happen overnight I would be very much surprised," said Soddhu matter-of-factly.

"The Lord works in mysterious ways," Wiggins snarled.

"Is that how you got your job?" Soddhu retorted.

"Why, you insolent creature!" said the dean's wife. "If you don't apologize to my husband I shall not play."

"It's all right, Dotty," said Wiggins. "Such is to be expected from a man who worships fire and other forms of magic."

"Turning Christ into a wafer isn't magic?" Soddhu retorted.

"It's the other way around," said Dotty. "The wafer turns into Christ."

"Forgive me, dear lady, I always forget the intricacies and nuances of Christianity."

"It's hardly a nuance," she replied haughtily. The chimps who had followed everything began to whimper.

"Hit it, Dottie, while there's still time," said the dean.

"What shall I play?"

"Try 'Jesus Loves Me,' it's one of my favorites."

His wife turned her ample bosom toward the piano. As her large hands pounded the keyboard, Herbert and Págalu signed the first verse, which went like this:

Jesus loves me, this I know,
For the Bible tells me so.
Little ones to him belong.
They are weak but he is strong.

When Mrs. Wiggins finished, the apes looked at each other and scratched their heads.

"Do you boys have a problem?" the dean asked, looking directly at Brian. There was an edge to his voice and Brian squirmed uncomfortably.

"Who is Jesus?" Brian signed.

"He is the son of God," Dean Wiggins replied.

"Who is God?"

"He is Jesus' father."

"Oh, now we understand!" said Brian nodding to the other apes.

"Are you putting me on, or what?" said the dean.

"C'mon, Dr. Wiggins, they're just little chimps," said Greg. "Maybe it would help if they could see a visual representation of God."

He left the room and returned with a picture book of the Sistine Chapel. Turning to the famous painting of God and Adam he showed it to the apes. Albert looked surprised.

"God is a very old man?" he signed. "If he were a chimp we'd chase him away from the females."

The dean cleared his throat.

"No more stalling," he said. "This is serious business. Dorothy, hit it again."

She banged through the song a second time, and for a second time the chimps sat and stared at the signs with frozen expressions.

"Perhaps a song wasn't such a good idea afterall," said Greg.

"God gave my wife a sign," said Dean Wiggins. "We'll try it one more time."

Three was the charm. With a sudden lurch the chimps began to bend their fingers and touch their palms. Amongst the many words I recognized the sign for Jesus. Dean Wiggins made a sound in his throat like he was choking.

"I think they've got it! Dotty, keep playing!"

The chimps began to sign faster, but when they tried to sign 'love' all they could do was cross their wrists.

"Your wife's going too fast," said Greg.

"Yes, yes, you're right. Dotty, take it slow, like this:

Jesus.....loves.....me.....this..... I.....know.....For.....the.....Bible .....tells.....me.....so.....Little.....ones.....to.....him.....belong..... They.....are.....weak....but.....he.....is.....strong.

With the new tempo the apes signed the song back without making a single mistake. Then they did it again and a final time on their own. Herbert hugged me deliriously.

"Tenure, tenure!" he whispered. Dotty glared at Soddu. "And you said there'd be no miracles!"

"I didn't think it would be this simple," he replied. "Maybe it's a fluke."

"It's no fluke," said the dean. "God has led us to a new category of converts, the Lord be praised!"

At three o'clock the lessons ended, and after a few more handshakes and congratulations, Wiggins and his wife departed. The chimps yawned and stretched.

"C'mon boys, let's go to the park," said Herbert. "The chair of our department thinks you should have daily exercise. Good for the mind and good for the soul."

"Perhaps they'd rather rest," I said.

"Orders are orders."

"Must they always be obeyed?"

"I love that rebellious streak in you," Herbert said.

"Yes, it turns me on too," said Soddhu smiling.

Outside Kline Hall, half way across the lawn Albert stopped to look at a large abstract sculpture made of metal.

"What is it?" he signed twisting his head underneath to get a better look.

"Damned if I know," Págalu replied.

Several cars stopped to gawk as our procession continued down Hillhouse Avenue over to the little park behind the Anthropology building. Stately trees still graced the lawns of what had once been elegant mansions. Now the houses were part of the campus. The one to our right, for instance, belonged to Dr. Levin, the school president. It had a beautiful sunken garden paved with bricks and lined with flowers. A large planter sat in the center, and off to the side stood a brick wall with arches and reflecting mirrors.

Fall was coming but the days were still warm. For a long time we sat on the grass watching Págalu and the grad students play with the apes. They ran this way and that, and it wasn't long before the men took off their tops.

"I must tell Soddhu," said Herbert, "that undershirts went out in this country about seventy years ago."

"It's not an undershirt, darling, it's called a sadreh, and it's part of his religion."

"When did he tell you that?"

"Actually just today, right after lunch. Don't be jealous, darling, it was all done in the interests of science."

10

Just then the chimp named Bill ran down a small flight of steps into the garden belonging to the president. Before we could stop him he jumped into the planter and threw a stone at himself in one of the mirrors. There was a loud crack.

"What have you to say for yourself?" Herbert asked when Bill was brought before him. After thinking for a moment, the recalcitrant chimp smiled broadly and replied in sign language: "Jesus loves me, this I know, for the Bible tells me so." When he finished he ran off to join the others, where a game of hide and seek was going on.

"I guess you'll need to teach him about sin," I reflected. My eyes searched for Págalu.

"Yes, it's a pity but I suppose we'll have to," Herbert replied with a sigh. He put his arm around me.

"Happy, darling?"

"Deliriously," I replied as I watched Soddhu trying to climb a tree and catch Freddy. It was hard to take my eyes off the sadreh now that I knew what it stood for.

"I think we should celebrate," said Herbert. "Project Mark is going to be a great success, I can feel it in my bones."

Greg came running toward us.

"Have you seen Albert?" he asked.

"He's over there inside that hollow tree," I said, gesturing behind the president's house.

"I think that was me," Greg replied. "It was my turn to hide."

"He can't be far," said Herbert. But after combing the immediate area there was no sign of him. The other chimps were hurried back to the lab and a search party was formed: Herbert, Págalu, Greg and myself.

I had a sudden inspiration.

"Do you remember how he was looking at the bluffs today?"

We took off for the park. A police car with flashing lights passed us at the river. Soddhu reached into his sadreh and pulled out some leaves.

"I didn't know you chewed tobacco," I said as Herbert took one and threw it in his mouth.

"Only when I'm nervous, darling, it helps me to relax."

A monument dedicated to war soars about sixty feet in the air near the edge of the bluffs. There are four statues about twenty feet from its base, and it was on this level where we saw Albert. We heard his screeches before we saw him. Each time he tried to get a handhold on the slippery mortar above his head he had to drop back. His fecal matter had soiled the statues and the police had drawn their guns.

"Don't shoot," Herbert cried racing up to the captain. "He belongs to the university."

"What's he doing up there then?" the captain asked.

"He got away, isn't it obvious?" said Soddhu.

"Captain," said another officer, "I think we should shoot him. By the time they get him down there'll be shit all over the place."

"Oh come on," said Greg. "Haven't you ever peed or pooped in your pants when you were scared? Look, I'm doing it now."

Sure enough, poor Greg's pant legs were all wet and there was a pool of water next to his foot.

"Maybe we'll have to shoot you too," said the second officer.

"Look, Captain," said Herbert. "That chimp—his name is Albert— understands American Sign Language. If you give us a minute we can get him to come down."

"We can get him down quicker than that," said the captain.

Another officer had come to join us. "This just came in sir," he said handing the captain a dispatch.

The policeman read it and turned to Herbert. "Your Albert has some powerful friends," he said. "We're not supposed to harm a hair on his body."

Herbert tried to see whom the dispatch was from, but the captain quickly stuffed it into his pocket. Without much enthusiasm the men put their weapons away and a few minutes later the squad cars left the park.

It was late that evening when we fell into bed. We were too tired to celebrate but not to make love, and as always, Jesus came on cue.

Instead of bringing Dotty the next day, Dean Wiggins brought two children's books which had simple pictures on each page. Locking his eyes onto Tom he said:

"Which would you rather read, 'Jesus and the Family Trip' or 'Jesus and the Grumpy Little Man'?"

"Are you the grumpy little man?" Brian signed innocently.

Págalu laughed, and two of his shirt buttons popped off exposing what appeared to be the end of a string wound around his waist. Tom grasped it and began to pull.

"No, no!" Págalu exclaimed, pushing the chimp away. "Leave my girdle alone, you little rascal!"

"Ha!" said Wiggins triumphantly. "Into cross dressing, eh, Professor?"

"Not at all, dear Dr. Wiggins," Soddhu replied. "Actually this is part of my religion."

12

"A *girdle*?"

"A *sacred* girdle. We call it the Kusti; we put it on each morning to remind ourselves of our sacred commitment to live a morally responsible life."

"From what I've heard, it hasn't helped you much."

"Spoken like a true Christian."

"Gentlemen, *please*," said Herbert. "The chimps are waiting." But Págalu continued to lean into Wiggins' face.

"Perhaps I shall take the chimps to New Rochelle one of these days. A true Zoroastrian has no conception of bigotry."

"If they ever set foot in one of your heathen fire temples," the dean exploded, "you'll be back in Bombay so fast you won't know what hit you!"

"I think George Baxter might have something to say about that."

"To hell with George Baxter!"

The chimps began to whimper.

"See, you've done it again," said Soddhu.

The words struck home. Poor Wiggins hung his head in remorse and would have stayed that way had Albert not slipped up to him and taken one of the books from his hand. The ape signed to Herbert:

"I already know about books. Is this a good one?"

The dean quickly recovered his wits and moved in on the chimps.

"The best there is," he replied. He turned to page one and began to read.

The ease with which the chimps took to these books was a shock to everyone. But it was the pleasantest of shocks, the kind that anyone would like to experience. That humans could impart their greatest achievement, religion, into the brain of an animal was a heady experience all right, and I was feeling the delirious effects of all this when a few days later I went to Soddhu's office looking for Herbert. He wasn't there, but I ran into Greg. He looked startled and quickly put a book on the shelf behind Soddhu's desk.

"What's that?" I asked curiously.

Greg looked around mysteriously.

"One of Soddhu's secret books from India. He gets furious when nonbelievers look at them."

"Well, you should respect his wishes," I said.

That being said we picked up the book and began to turn the pages.

"Wow, look at this!" said Greg. "It's a ritual sacrifice to the gods of the sacred fire. Or how about this? A guide to purification before marriage with your sister."

"Let me see that!"

I started to reach for the book when Soddhu's voice boomed out behind us.

"Heathen Christ worshippers! Put that book down before I'm forced to cover you in gomez."

He knew it was us and his voice was playful.

"Perhaps you should tell us what gomez is before we put it back," I said feeling excited and glad that we'd been caught. "Perhaps we'd like to be covered in it."

"Uh, I don't think so," Greg said, running his finger down the page. "It says here that gomez is the sacred urine of bulls, and men and women who've contracted something called Khvetukdas."

"It's also the prescribed punishment for unbelievers who profane the sacred texts," said Soddhu putting the book back on the shelf. "But I'll settle for an extra shift in the lab."

He reached into his sadreh.

"Only one," he said slapping Greg's hand as he tried to take two leaves. "My supply is low this month. Kathryn, may I buy you an ice cream?"

"Only if you tell me what Khvetukdas is."

"My dear Kathryn, as much as I'd like to indoctrinate you into its joys, the power of a goddess can only go so far."

I ignored his prater but curiosity got the better of me; I found myself a few days later standing in his office, alone, on the pretext of looking for Herbert. On the wall was a picture of Zarathustra. He looked like Jesus only more mature and robust. There was the same halo around his head and he had the same color hair, beard and eyes as our Lord and Savior.

With a cursory glance at the door I went to a pile of papers on Soddhu's desk. By chance, the strange word Khvetukdas stared up at me right away. Apparently it was a manuscript that Soddhu was writing on the subject.

With a sense of adventure I began turning the pages incautiously. Suddenly a hand appeared out of nowhere, a large beautiful hand, and pulled mine to dark waiting lips.

"Mrs. Hickey, are you ready for the gomez?"

As I looked at Soddhu's beaming face I wanted to say yes. Instead I said:

"Is this the book you are writing?"

"Yes, I cannot tell a lie."

"On Khvetukdas?"

14

"On marriage in ancient Iran. Nothing you'd be interested in."

"I'm interested in anything you write."

"Really?"

He gave me an appraising look, then said: "I can see I shall have no peace until I tell you. Oh all right then. Afterall you are my goddess. But keep this strictly confidential. If word got out what I was working on Wiggins would have my hide tacked to his chapel wall."

"My lips are sealed," I said, moving closer. The sense of conspiracy was delirious.

"I'm trying to prove," he said, "that the practice of consanguineous marriage (marriage within the first degree) in ancient Iran—Persia if you will—was the central motor of Western civilization and the impetus behind the Crucifixion. The term for these unions is Khvetukdas" (he pronounced it kwee-doh-dah), "and while many of my fellow Parsees would go down fighting before admitting to the practice there is just too much evidence to the contrary. I myself believe that our prophet Zarathustra was killed just for advocating it. But men carried Khvetukdas on for many more centuries, thanks to the cleverness of a class of priests who were powerful and conniving; I'm speaking of course of the Magi."

"The Magi! My God, I can see why you don't want the dean to get wind of this!"

"Or anyone else for that matter. There's a lot of things I have to work out. But once I've published it ought to knock the dean's socks off."

"How will he or any other theologian come to terms with the Three Wise Men making love to their daughters?"

"Yes, it's scandalous isn't it?"

"Very."

We were standing so close our bodies were touching. I made no attempt to pull away as his lips touched mine. Was it his sadreh, the Kusti or the knowledge that Mrs. Baxter was coming into Herbert's office a little too often these days? Whatever it was I was unable to pull away, not this time or all the times that followed.

In a smattering of time the apes went from watching Donut Man videos to reading tracts from the Bible. Their grasp of Jesus' love was profound, and when Christmas rolled around they spent hours on end gazing quietly at the miniature figures of a Nativity scene which the dean had set up in the classroom. Poor daddy, he was almost as stunned as he'd been six months ago when an indiscreet affair with a pretty med student had cost him his position as Dean of the School of Medicine. ("Damn it, now I'll never have my portrait hanging is Sterling Hall," he lamented when asked

15

to resign.) But he remained on the faculty, and his professional opinion on Project Mark was as highly regarded as his professional opinion on such topics as myocardial infarction and acute muscle contusion in a rat, for instance, or the hippocampus response to glucocorticord in pre-natal women. Until now, that is; with the smashing success of Project Mark his influence began to dwindle.

Not so the bickering between Soddhu and Wiggins. The dean had just put the finishing touches to the Nativity scene, and was fussing over the figures of the Magi, when Soddhu entered the room.

"Did you know that the Magi used to fuck their daughters?" he asked incautiously. Apparently he'd forgotten his own admonition for discretion.

"I wish I knew what it is that Baxter sees in you," the dean replied crisply. "It surely cannot be your intelligence."

"Why is that?"

"To try to denigrate the birth of our savior—surely there are better ways to do it than this cock-and-bull story about the Magi."

"Would you like to see proof?"

"I would like to see what you consider to be proof."

Soddhu left the room and came back a few minutes later with a book. It was called the *Dinkard*, one of the sacred books of his people, he said, written thousands of years ago in the days of the Zoroastrian priests, the Magi. He handed it to Wiggins and pointed to the following passage which was highlighted in yellow:

The consummation of mutual assistance of men is Khvetukdas, that union with near kinsmen and, among near kinsmen, that with those next-of-kin. And the mutual connection of the three kinds of nearest kin— which are father and daughter, son and she who bore him, and brother and sister—is the most complete that I have considered.

The dean snapped the book shut.

"Lies and slander," he said. "Probably written by commies. Now if you'll excuse me I have to give alms to the poor."

"You can lead a horse to water but you can't make him drink," Soddhu called after him as the dean hurried from the room.

As the months passed the chimps began to internalize not only the teachings of Jesus but also the most complicated aspects of religion itself.

They were acquiring not only the spiritual and emotional attitude of those who believe in a superhuman power, but also an unrelenting awareness of sin, culpability, fault, error, transgression, wrong-doing, badness, regret, remorse, self-reproach, self-condemnation and guilt—all the qualms of conscience that come from a strong religious formation. Everyone was elated.

Oh yes, there were a few minor glitches. Sometimes when the chimps got too rambunctious they would throw their Bibles at each other or make airplanes from its pages. Probably the worst blunder was when Bill was caught pleasuring himself and using the pages like a Kleenex. But these transgressions occurred only occasionally and once corrected were never repeated. No better students could have ever been found, was the general consensus, than these six chimps.

Herbert and I were having dinner at the Copper Kitchen. Usually we came with Págalu for the macaroni, but tonight he was at the *Darb-e-Mehr* or fire temple in New Rochelle. He was celebrating something called the Jashne Sadeh or the 'discovery of fire' festival. The restaurant seemed lonely without him, but my attention was soon drawn to a noisy table near the back of the room. The conversation was animated and everyone was laughing. They were mostly students, but a couple of men whose backs were toward me appeared to be older. One of them turned around to summon a waiter.

"Why, it's daddy!" I exclaimed. He saw me and a minute later squeezed into my side of the booth.

"Congratulations, Hickey, you're the new star of Yale. Frankly, my boy, I didn't think you had it in you."

"No?"

"No. Frankly, I thought you'd end up classifying bone fragments for twenty years and publishing articles on primate femur development that no one would ever read. When you remembered to say "I do" to my daughter at the alter, I was frankly surprised. By God, Hickey, I always thought the chimps were smarter than you! I always thought of you as intellectual lint, but maybe I'll have to reconsider. My word, Hickey, how do you expect anyone to take you seriously with a dissertation on the effects of hemorrhoids on the religious sensibilities of Tasmanian devils?!"

"I'm glad I've proved you wrong, Fred."

"Who says you have? By the way, Hickey, I hear that your chimps have refused to pray."

"Who told you that?"

"Word gets around. Anyway, compared to everything else they've learned—Christian ethics, theology, liturgy—you'd think praying would be relatively simple."

"We've come to the conclusion that it might be a physical thing, getting them on their knees, you know, something to do with their prehensile toes, maybe."

"As good a reason as any, my boy. Speaking of prehensile toes, Katheryn, how is you mother and her new boyfriend doing, Gordon something-or-other? Wallaroo, isn't it?

"Oh, daddy, you know they're married."

"Yes, yes, I just can't seem to get it into my head that she left *me*, Fred Phalen, Professor Emeritus, Dean, er, ex-dean, of the Medical School at Yale, for an aborigine from Australia. Tell me, children, what is the world coming to?!"

Chapter Two

The Propitiousness of Prayer

The strains of a Viennese waltz met our ears as we drove up the narrow lane to George Baxter's house. He lived on a large estate in Madison about twenty miles outside New Haven. A rambling Cape Cod-style house sat on a lonely stretch of private beach looking out onto Long Island Sound. It was surrounded by an English countryside of open fields, meandering streams and shade trees. There was a private tennis court, and off on a rocky point an outdoor pool in the shape of a figure eight. A full moon completed the picture of elegance and privilege.

As we entered the large drawing room crowded with the cream of New Haven, George Baxter hurried over. He was a man of about sixty, his face had the look of tanned leather, his body was massive, the veins bulged in his hands and forehead. He wore his gray hair in a crew cut. His latest exposure to the sun had taken place just a few days ago in Africa where he and Lydia had gone on safari.

"Herbert, Kathryn," he said, "you two should really be guests of honor tonight. Your husband has made my wife a happy woman."

"He succeeded where you failed?" I asked.

"I'm talking about Project Mark, young lady," he replied testily. "As a matter of fact, Hickey, there are people in Africa who are talking about Mark already."

"But we haven't published any of our findings!" said Herbert.

"News travels fast when you're on to something big," Baxter replied. He saw how anxious Herbert looked and clapped him on the back.

"Don't worry, the missionaries aren't going to infringe on your territory. Not yet, anyway. All I've done is mention Project Mark to

19

Tom Baker, a friend of mine. Ever heard of the Patriot Act Neurological Intervention Corps—PANIC for short?"

Herbert looked blank and Baxter said: "Tom sets up clinics to rewire people damaged by war in third world countries. He's over in Africa now setting one up in Kizumbi."

"Kizumbi?"

"That's in Tanzania."

"I didn't know there was a war in Tanzania," I said.

"It's strictly a precaution," Baxter replied, "should there ever be one."

He looked around the room as if he were searching for a rare bird hiding in the jungle. Just then Lydia Baxter appeared and hooked arms with her husband. Despite her flawless elegance she had the look of a cannibal—someone who would eat you raw. She was about thirty years younger than George, about the same age as myself.

Her eyes wandered over me as she flashed a smile which was too perfect to be real.

"Do you mind if I borrow George for a few moments? There's a little business he needs to attend to."

"My dear," said Baxter, standing firm despite his wife's tugging. "It better be important. Hickey and I are talking about Africa."

"Well, what a coincidence," she replied. "It's that man you've been expecting from Africa—Nutty Mama or something."

"How many times must I tell you, Lydia, that it's *Ntimama*?"

Excusing himself he disappeared down the hallway. A minute later I could hear loud voices coming from the foyer.

"How many times have I told you not to come here?!"

"A dozen maybe, I'm not counting."

"Then it's time you started. And take that damn hat off, this is America, not Africa."

The voices became inaudible as Baxter disappeared into a room off the foyer. Walking stiffly behind him was the striking figure of an African man of about thirty. He was dressed in an overcoat and wore dark glasses. A leopard skin hat was perched on his head, and under his arm he carried a large briefcase. It was also made of leopard.

"I myself just love that hat," Lydia purred.

"You'd look good in it too," said Herbert.

Lydia looked at me, a mirthless laugh broke from her lips. It sounded like shattering glass.

"Do try the zebra, you two. George shot it himself. Where are those damn servers, the ones with champagne, I mean?"

I glared as she went off to find them.

"Sweetheart," he said, "I was only kidding about the hat. Come on, let's try the zebra and see what stripes taste like."

"You go, I'm suddenly not hungry." I pulled away and went up to the deck overlooking the bay. Was he really kidding about the hat? Consumed with jealousy, a tap on my arm almost made me jump. It was Dotty Wiggins, the dean's wife.

"Kathryn, may I have a word with you? It's quite important, and you're the only one I can talk to."

Her ample figure moved menacingly inside her evening gown. Her hair, usually so well coifed, was falling out from the diamond tiara which sat precariously atop her forehead.

"Please, Kathryn, I'm in a terrible state, but I didn't want to talk to you infront of George Baxter, I don't trust the man."

"I trust him more than his wife," I replied. Dotty appeared not to hear me.

"Oh Kathryn, I've been so stupid! Here we are teaching these chimps to be Christians, and for what? They'll never get into heaven, they're animals, they don't have souls! I don't know why I didn't think of it before!"

"Even if you're right, Mrs. Wiggins, I don't think anybody will want to stop the project. It's too big, too important. Herbert's going to get tenure and maybe the Nobel Prize. C'mon, let's go downstairs and get drunk."

"That's not going to help the chimps, Kathryn. Poor things, they're just being sold a bill of goods, making them believe in a place they'll never enter, it's just terrible!"

"You must be talking about the shrimp Bombay," said John Slaughter coming over to join us. "It's got enough cayenne to make it a candidate for Saddam Hussein's biological weapons program."

Slaughter was a professor of philosophy. With him was Bob Grisham, chair of Herbert's department.

"Mrs. Wiggins doesn't believe that any animal, even one that has converted to Christianity can be saved," I said.

"They don't have souls," Dotty said though clenched teeth.

"Nonsense," Slaughter boomed. "You've been reading too much Aquinas, Dotty, or paying too much attention to his edict that animals can't get into heaven. The truth is they have no money, that's why he came out with that stuff. And you know what? Animals were treated a lot better before he did."

Dotty's expression changed.

"You mean they have souls afterall?" she asked.

"Of course," Slaughter replied, "although I have to say that I agree with the dean's wife; it's quite wrong to make an animal think it's a Christian."

"But we are all animals," said Grisham, "when you get right down to it."

"Oh no we're not!" said Mrs. Wiggins. "We have left bestiality behind and become noble human beings. Religion is man's highest achievement. Without religion we would be no different from the animals. There would be no culture, no morality—civilization itself would cease to exist. Sex is carnal, religion is spiritual. The two can't—no, mustn't—ever meet, and if you keep teaching religion to those chimps, something evil will come of it. From what Professor Slaughter says they can't separate the spiritual from the carnal. And don't tell me that's not like dragging the Word of God through the muck and mire."

She turned abruptly and walked off in a huff. Herbert and Págalu narrowly missed running into her. "Has anyone taken a look at Baxter's collection of etchings?" said Soddhu excitedly. "He has some great Summerian depictions of the river goddess making love to a bull."

Herbert pulled me aside.

"Let's make love," he whispered. "I think there's something aphrodisiac about the zebra steak."

"Professor Págalu and I were about to go down to the bar," I replied.

"It has to wait," said Grisham. "Págalu, Slaughter and I have some business to attend to."

The business had to do with Soddhu's tobacco, but they waited until they thought we were out of sight.

"Are you sure you wouldn't rather make love to Lydia?" I asked as we made our way through the drawing room.

"You're even more beautiful when you're angry," Herbert replied. "C'mon, I'm as horny as a toad."

We walked across the lawn toward the pool house. But the area had already been invaded, so we headed toward a small forest of trees just behind it. To our surprise we discovered a building without windows hidden amongst the trees. It appeared to be deserted, but as we approached we could hear strange sounds coming from inside.

"Maybe we should go back," I said. "This place is creepy."

"All the better to eat you, my dear," said Herbert pushing open the unlocked door. The light of the moon illuminated the room. It looked like Ground Control in Houston. There were radio sets, computers and electronic equipment of an unknown nature flashing with lights. The floor looked like the stock exchange, knee-deep in paper.

Suddenly one of the machines began to beep loudly. As paper began to roll Herbert held it to the moonlight:

"Ntimama arriving tonight. Stop. Will brief you on the latest movements of Angola rebels in Zaire. Also rebels in Congo, in Nigeria, in Senegal, in Ethiopia, etc. etc. Stop. Inother words, all red armies. Stop. Thanks to State Department we have clinics everywhere in Africa. Stop. The heart of darkness. Stop. Regards to Lydia, Tom Baker. PS: Latest CNN story on PANIC was terrific. Thanks! Membership has increased twofold. Barnum was wrong, a sucker is born every second not minute. Tom."

"We'd better make it a quicky," said Herbert as he tore off the transmission; then, looking thoughtfully at the floor, he picked up several more.

"Insurance for Project Mark," he said, folding the papers and putting them in his pocket, "in case we ever need it."

The rest of the papers served to cushion—but ever so slightly—the hardness of the floor.

Daddy's remarks about prayer had cut Herbert to the quick, and he became determined to overcome whatever obstacles he had to, to get the apes to pray. A meeting of the chimps was convened in the dean's office, Págalu reluctantly attending. There were many knick-knacks on the shelves, souvenirs from Wiggins' trips abroad. One of them, a plaster caste of Oedipus made in Greece, stared at us blindly from the corner of his desk.

The meeting began, questions were asked, answers given, the dean himself demonstrated different attitudes of prayer (Christian type on knees, Moslem type prostrate on the floor, and Jewish type butting head against the wall.) But nothing seemed to shed any light on the problem, and after an hour or so the dean sank down wearily in his chair.

"I think it's hopeless," he said. "And what a shame, too, since prayer comes in so handy at times."

"Such as?" Brian asked with attitude.

"Such as when sin cuts men off from God," the dean replied sternly.

What sorts of things would do that, Albert wanted to know.

The dean looked thoughtfully at the plaster statue. It would be the sort of thing, he said, that happens if a son sleeps with his mother. Albert wanted to know why that was a sin, and Wiggins told him about the incest taboo and how nobody is supposed to sleep with anybody who is a close relative. As he spoke he turned an angry look at Soddhu, but Albert became very agitated.

When questioned he said that he had a sister in Africa named Nedele and that he needed to go over there right away and talk to her about Christ. Of course the dean told him it was out of the question.

"God has great plans for you, Albert, right here at Yale."

It was the wrong thing to say. The little ape screeched and began to hurl himself about the office, run hither and thither, tossing things on the floor, covering and uncovering his eyes with his hands. Suddenly he stopped infront of the plaster caste.

"Oh don't do it, Albert, that's my prize possession!" the dean cried.

But it was too late. Albert raised the caste above his head, then dashed it to the floor where it broke into a thousand pieces. The dean began to weep, the chimps began to scream, and for the first time in ages their handlers had to be called in to subdue them. When the mayhem was over the dean's office looked like a war zone. There were books, papers, paperweights, and shattered glass from broken photographs scattered everywhere. Truly it was the rampage of a wild animal. But the next day Albert prayed.

The news traveled fast, I dropped what I was doing and hurried to the Divinity School. As I entered the chapel I saw Albert kneeling on the floor. Hooting softly, his hands were pressed together just below his face, pressed with such force, infact, that you could see them tremble. He seemed to be trying to push his knees into the floor.

"Albert," said Herbert, shaking him gently on the shoulder. "You needn't put so much force into it."

"Oh but I must," Albert replied. He face was filled with a beatific light. "The more I press my hands together, the less chance I have of touching myself where I'm not supposed to. (And touching anybody else, for that matter, especially my sister.) Prayer is a wonderful thing, isn't it, Dr. Hickey! You see, if I keep my knees pressed together like this there is no way I can do anything to Nedele because my penis is tucked so tightly between my legs."

"Nedele?"

"My sister. Ah yes, Dean Wiggins was right, prayer is a real Godsend. It makes me completely incapable of sinful behavior. Pressing my hands and knees like this—it's as good as being tied up!"

This so impressed the dean (the other chimps had soon followed suit) that at his insistence they were relocated in a large room off the Divinity School's quadrangle. It didn't take a brain surgeon to see how happy they were in their new quarters; a sprawling area of grass and trees stretched between the walkways, and when the chimps weren't studying they were allowed to play in the trees and swing from the brick columns lining the green. They took their meals inside the Divinity School refectory, and sat in on classes taught by the faculty: *Gender in Early Christianity, New Testament Ethics, History of Western Christianity I* and *II, History of Christian Thought, History of Christian Theology,* and *The Writings of Josephus* were but a few of the offerings in which they excelled. A conference room with a fireplace became their private classroom, and when it was time for worship they hurried to Marquand Chapel, and knelt in its white pews to offer their prayers to God.

Never again did Dean Wiggins stop to scold them; any infractions were taken care of quickly by scrunching themselves up in prayer. But even more surprising was the fact that Albert had now begun to profess an interest in the Ministry.

Dean Wiggins was delighted. He publicly forgave Albert for the recent rampage, and made sure the little ape was given instruction in these courses: *The Principles and Practice of Preaching, Sermon Writing and Delivery, Pastoral Counseling, Expository Preaching, Structure and Power in Christian Ministry,* and *Pastoral Care and Counseling with Young Adults.* The classes had gone exceptionally well.

"Do you accept Jesus as your Lord and Savior?"

A baptism was about to take place at Albert's request.

Dean Wiggins leaned into the faces of the six apes as Herbert and Págalu did the signing. The apes nodded their shining black heads in tandem.

"Jesus is a bridge between us and God," said Bill.

"God is too holy to approach, so Jesus came down and died so that man and chimps could get close," said Freddie.

"Our God is so big, so strong and so mighty, there's nothing our God cannot do for you," said John.

"The mountains are His, the rivers are His, the stars are His handiwork too," said Brian.

"Without Jesus Christ, man and chimps are doomed to darkness," said Tom.

"The wages of sin is death; but the gift of God is eternal life," said Albert.

The dean picked up a bucket of water and was about to dip in his ladle when Albert started up again.

Praise God, from whom all blessings flow!
Praise Him, all creatures here below!
Praise Him above, ye heavenly host!
Praise Father, Son and Holy Ghost!

25

Dean Wiggins beamed. "In the name of the Father, Son and Holy Ghost I baptize you all." With great solemnity he ladled water onto each of the shiny heads. Afterwards, Lydia Baxter placed a gold crucifix around each chimp's neck. They screeched with delight, then put the crosses to their lips and smacked them loudly.

Later, when he left the room Pastor Wiggins looked like a man who had seen God.

I was starting across the green when Dean Wiggins spied me from the steps of Center Church. With a light step he fell in beside me. As usual every silver hair on his head was perfectly in place though the day was blustery.

"There's not a better spot on earth," he said making a sweeping gesture toward the green with its majestic old elms and row of churches: Trinity Episcopal Church, the Center Church and the United Church. "Even the school—the entire campus looks like a church. What better place than Yale for these less fortunate creatures, the apes, to be taught the ways of God."

"Quite right," I answered. But I was thinking of something else and began to rummage through my purse.

"I understand you and Dotty are going to Egypt," I said

"Yes, in June. The old girl deserves a vacation, she's put up with a lot. What's the matter? Did you lose something?"

I was rummaging in panic.

"I can't find the tickets Daddy just gave me at lunch!"

"Perhaps you left them on the shuttle."

I dug a little deeper.

"Oh thank God, here they are."

The dean looked unhappy.

"You are going to see Jorge Cortina?"

"Next month at Carnegie Hall."

"This Cortina may be one of the greatest pianists of all times," said Wiggins, "but until his government changes it's my belief that there should be no cultural exchange program between the United States and Cuba."

"Well, you need to write to your congressman or better yet, get in touch with somebody at Skull and Bones."

"I have, and they said it was too late, that the State Department has authorized the Ringling Brothers Barnum and Bailey Circus to go to Havana in the fall. My lord, they must be blind! Even the chimps have learned that Christianity cannot exist without capitalism. Me oh my, what is the world coming to?!"

I found Herbert in the Day Missions Library, a solemn room of books and wood paneling in the Divinity School. He was leafing absently through an ancient book on Japan. There was a note lying next to it, and at the sound of my footsteps he instinctively tried to hide it.

"A love letter from Lydia?" I asked caustically.

"Oh darling, it's you! Here, you'd better read this."

The memo read as follows:

Yale University
Inter-Office Correspondence

To: The Directors of Project Mark
From: Bob Grisham, Chair

Re: Security Alert

Recent information received from campus security indicates that fringe elements of animal rights organizations may be planning raids on labs using animals for research. All faculty involved in such projects are encouraged to review security procedures. Please contact campus police immediately if you notice anything suspicious. All rumors are to be taken seriously.

"Well, it doesn't worry me," I said. "It's not like the chimps are being tortured or anything."

"Yes, but how are the activists to know? Anyway I wish Págalu hadn't taken Albert over to Center Church this afternoon."

"I just came from there, I didn't see anybody."

"Oh my God! Should we call the police? But then I'll be late for class!"

"Darling, don't panic. I don't mind walking back, Daddy and I ate too much lunch, I can use the exercise."

Retracing my steps to the green I arrived at the corner of College and Elm just in time to see two policemen on horseback writing up tickets for a couple of vagrants. I guessed they'd had too much to drink, but so had most of the people I passed as I crossed the green and walked up to the church. Much to my relief Albert was sitting inside. He was gazing at the stained glass window just above the pulpit. It was called the Davenport Window, and it depicted the Reverend John Davenport conducting the first Christian service in New Haven in 1638. Albert got up when he saw me.

"Dr. Págalu is down in the crypt," he said. "I'm supposed to let him know if anyone arrives."

"Anyone he doesn't *know*, Albert. Now you stay here and don't go anywhere, I'll be back in a minute."

How divine, I thought, to meet Soddhu in the crypt, a large chamber beneath the church marked with tombstones and large slabs set upon supports. A vision of sacred rites performed with gomez ran through my mind, but when I entered the crypt I saw that someone was already there, and for some reason I decided it would be prudent to stay back, behind one of the brick columns which stood in rows throughout the chamber. The conversation echoed loudly.

"Don't you think that one good turn deserves another? Getting Wiggins to okay you for Project Mark took a lot of doing."

"Ahura Mazda, but this is asking too much!"

"Why is that?"

"It's one thing to buy a little khat whenever I'm in India; it's quite another to be the middle man for a big payload coming in from Africa."

"But think of all the money!"

"I'm trying hard not to."

"Well I think you should. That temple of yours in New Rochelle—yes I've been there—is rather an eyesore, don't you think?"

"It's an old house, if that's what you mean."

"Old and dilapidated. Imagine what it would look like if you fixed things up; or better yet, if you tore it down and built a brand new temple, maybe something patterned after the temple of King Darius. You could have winged figures of Ahura Mazda all over the place."

"That would be a dream come true, and everyone in the Assembly would say so."

There was a pause, then Soddhu said in an anguished voice, "Ah, gee, George, can't you go yourself?"

"Sorry, I'm too busy raising funds for the Republican presidential committee."

Just then something brushed past me. A moment later I was staring into the glaring eyes of George Baxter. Soddhu stood next to him holding Albert's hand.

"Ah, Mrs. Hickey! What a delightful surprise to find you here. Soddhu and I were just ironing out a few things."

"In a crypt?" I asked indiscreetly. Baxter leaned into my face.

"Can you think of a better place," he said, "to work out the details? The dead add a kind of solemnity to business dealings. They remind the living of the serious consequences that ensue when people act without thinking, or reveal secrets that belong behind closed doors."

He walked away with a final menacing look; the veins in his temple bulged just below his crew cut. As soon as he left I turned on Albert.

"You're just like Judas," I said angrily. There was an unmistakable smirk on his face as he clung to Soddhu's hand.

"Kathryn, dearest, it's all my fault. When Albert told me you were here I repeated his words without thinking. Baxter doesn't know sign language any more than a mollusk."

"Oh well, nobody's perfect."

"You are, my darling."

He leaned me against the column and began to undress me.

"Tell me about the gomez," I whispered.

But before long I began to feel uncomfortable. The little ape was breathing down our necks, watching every move we made. It proved to be too much, we pulled ourselves apart and put ourselves together. As the three of us left the crypt, Albert's face decidedly bespoke of triumph.

It wasn't long afterwards that George Baxter visited the lab. With him was an old college buddy named Joe. They had crewed together on the rowing team at Yale, and Joe, like Baxter was a member of Skull and Bones.

But while Baxter prattled on about the good old days, Joe kept his eyes glued on the chimps.

"So you think these apes of yours are pretty good?" he said to Herbert.

"Ask them anything you like," Herbert replied.

"Can they recite the Lord's Prayer?"

"Backwards and forwards," said Págalu.

"Try it backwards," said Joe

"I think that's just an expression," said Baxter.

"Don't worry, they can do it," said Págalu. He gave the instructions and they signed the words as follows:

Amen. ever for, glory the and, power the and, kingdom the is thine For: evil from us deliver but, temptation into not us lead And. debtors our forgive we as, debts our us forgive And. bread daily our day this us Give. heaven in is it as, earth in done be will Thy. come kingdom Thy. Name thy be hallowed, heaven in art which Father Our.

"Of course they know it forward too," said Dean Wiggins quickly. At his behest the chimps recited the prayer forward, signing the words in perfect unison.

29

"I'm telling you these chimps are as versed in theology as the pope!" said Baxter grinning broadly.

"We shall see," said Joe in a curt voice. With Págalu's help he began posing questions to the chimps. Did they, for instance, believe in causes, would they fight against evil, would they have joined Richard the Lion-hearted and fought in the Crusades, were the Crusades justified, was Saladin a bad man, what did they think about Osama bin Laden, Saddam Hussein, Fidel Castro? Did the ends justify the means?

"This is worse than a doctoral qualifying exam," Herbert muttered.

The room became tense as the grilling continued.

But the chimps, bless their hearts, stood up admirably to this unusual line of questioning. When it finally came to an end Joe shook everybody's hand and left with Baxter.

"Whew! Did you feel we were on trial or what!" said Greg. But the dean was excited. "We're all going to win the Nobel Prize, Hickey for innovative research and me for finding a new source of revenue for the church. Did I tell you that Reverend Nicholson wants to give them communion on Sunday? Dotty has their choir outfits all picked out."

But the old saying about the best-laid plans of mice and men was about to come home with a vengeance. The ancient Greeks would have understood it only too well.

Arriving at the Divinity School early next morning, Greg found the cages empty and all the files on the project gone. A frantic search was made in the rooms off the quad, then the Divinity School itself. When nothing turned up the police were called and the entire campus was searched. An all-points bulletin went out and people who didn't look like they belonged on campus were stopped and searched. (For some people this was nothing new.) It was late afternoon when the captain came into Grisham's office. It was the same officer we had met on the bluffs.

"I think we've found something," he said. Everyone followed him back to the Divinity School and up the stairs to a little room over the refectory. On the glass was written the following message in red lipstick:

We are against school prayer, even for monkeys.
Signed: Atheists for Animals United.

The dean stomped his feet, his face red with rage.

"Damn their dirty hides!" he cried. "May they rot in hell and burn for all eternity!"

Daddy called that evening.

"If your husband needs a job we've got an opening here in the janitorial department."

"Dad, that isn't funny."

"Who says I'm joking?"

Daddy's glee was tempered slightly by the universal belief that the chimps would be recovered. But as the weeks passed and not a hide nor hair of them turned up, this belief began to fade. Eventually it faded altogether, and those who were closely involved in the project had to sadly admit that the chimps were never coming back.

It was the morning of the concert. Though summer was almost here the days had turned cold again. But the sight of trees in their new growth helped to foster a feeling of cheerfulness in the house that was totally lacking otherwise and had nothing to do with the weather.

Herbert was in the kitchen reading the Yale Daily News and working on his second pot of coffee.

"Daddy says you'll get an ulcer if you keep drinking all this coffee."

"Please tell daddy to mind his own business. By the way, did you know that he perfectly matches the description of the guy who's been killing all these people on Amtrak? He has a goatee and black ruthless eyes."

"If you're trying to get a rise out of me you're not going to succeed. I don't want to spoil the concert tonight. What's new with the pandas?"

I could see the headlines. It was a big story, how a plane carrying two pandas from China to the United States had been diverted to a secret game park in Kenya to be hunted by Saudi royalty. Word had slipped out, a huge world outcry had erupted, and President Moi, buckling to the pressure, was vowing to make a thorough investigation and all but guaranteed the safe return of the pandas.

Instead of answering me Herbert said: "You know I don't think I want to go tonight." He flicked the newspaper with his thumb. "Not as long as this guy is still killing people. They just found his ninth victim in Penn Station."

I tried to stay calm.

"Darling, it's your favorite music—Sheherazade and The Emperor Concerto. And we have reservations at the Russian Tea Room, remember?"

"I'm not taking the train and I don't feel like driving. Maybe you could go with a girlfriend. Or better yet, take Daddy. He got the tickets, didn't he?"

"Yes, he got the tickets. So what? Is he not supposed to ever do anything nice for us? Anyway, I didn't see you going to get them."

"In case you've forgotten, I was busy with the chimps."

"Oh yes, the chimps. Which reminds me. How long are you going to go on like this? I have feelings too, you know, and I'm getting tired of reaching over every night and being repulsed. It's not just teenage boys that have raging hormones, you know."

"I'll go to the store tomorrow and buy you a dildo."

"Don't bother, I have other means."

When Soddhu arrived at the house it was late, and by the time our train got to Central Station there was only enough time to grab a Coke. A handful of demonstrators stood outside the theater holding up anti-Castro signs, but their message was lost on the well-heeled crowd. It was a sold-out performance.

As we went to our seats I noticed people looking at us. Soddhu smiled at everyone.

"We make a handsome couple," he said. "I wish we could always be together."

"I don't think it would much bother Herbert."

"What a fool he must be!"

Suddenly Soddhu put his hand on my arm and looked into my eyes with a combination of boyhood earnestness and sultry oriental desire.

"Kathryn, come away with me! Who needs Yale anyway? We'll go to India, buy a beautiful house—champagne and roses and dinner on the terrace—I'll work on my manuscript and you'll inspire me, you'll be my muse."

Before I could answer the Workers National Symphony Orchestra stood on their feet, the conductor came on stage and after the enthusiastic applause died down he raised his baton and the exotic strains of Sheherazade began to fill the auditorium.

The music unfolded seamlessly into a fantasy in which Soddhu made love to me in an alabaster palace surrounded by jungle temples with altars carved in the shape of Kama Sutra poses. I felt myself drifting off in a cloud of incense and spices until my reverie was interrupted by the crowd rising to its feet to give a standing ovation. The conductor bowed humbly and in his tailcoat it was hard to imagine that he was a communist revolutionary come to overthrow our culture.

The intermission was filled with Soddhu's entreaties to run away with him. I felt relieved when the chimes called us back to our seats. A voice came over the loudspeaker.

"Ladies and gentlemen. The management has an announcement to make. A short while ago Mr. Cortina received a death threat from an anonymous caller who identified himself as a member of a group called 'Communists No, Be Capitalists' or CNBC. Although there is no record of this organization we are taking the threat seriously."

"Son-of-a-bitch is going to cancel!" said a man sitting next to us.

But everyone sighed with relief when the announcer told us the show would go on. Cortina, he said, would appear as scheduled, but to ensure his safety the FBI had insisted he wear a full body suit made of Kevlar; it was 100 percent bulletproof. The audience responded with grateful applause mingled with whistles and boos aimed at the anonymous caller.

"Are you sure you want to stay?" Soddhu asked. "Maybe it will be another grassy knoll."

The man next to us heard the remark and decided to leave. A few others also got up.

"Where can we go?" I asked.

"Dinner and my apartment."

"Well, why not."

We started to get up when there was a gasp from the audience as a man came on stage disguised as a monkey. His furry costume looked so realistic that everyone started whispering at once, wondering what was going on. The conductor accompanied him looking rather dazed.

"May Ahura Mazda be praised!" Soddhu exclaimed. "He looks like Albert!"

A second later all bedlam broke loose. The audience roared with laughter and shouted "Bravo, Cortina!" The sight of a monkey about to play Beethoven was beyond belief. But Cortina remained calm. Bowing to the audience, he took his seat at the piano. When the noise died down he nodded to the conductor and the music began.

It was difficult to settle down. But as Cortina's long fingers wrapped in Kevlar swept across the keyboard the Hall became quiet. His prodigious talent was all too apparent, and his flawlessly executed runs seemed to be all the more incredible because of the way he looked. If the FBI had done it to humiliate Castro, they had greatly miscalculated. The audience sat spellbound, and when Cortina kicked off his shoes and played a perfect run with his toes (yes, they too were wrapped in Kevlar!) people stood up and began to chant: "Jorge, Jorge!"

Encouraged by this adulation, Cortina stood up and executed some arpeggios with his rump.

"This is the greatest pianist of all time!" exclaimed a woman who was dripping in diamonds. She was almost in tears.

As for Soddhu, the tears were already streaming down his face.

"Albert," he murmured. "My little Albert!"

There was an orchestral interlude, Cortina got up and unnerved the conductor by looking over his shoulder. A minute later he was breathing down the neck of the first violinist.

"Jorge! Jorge! Jorge!"

The electrifying performance reached its climax, and Cortina, charged up by the crowd, played the final bravura passages with his hands, feet and rump. As the conductor hurried off the stage Cortina stood up to take his bows. The audience went mad; shouting and screaming and stomping their feet, within seconds the stage was littered with everything from money and jewels to brassieres and panties. The woman with diamonds threw them on the stage. I started to unclasp my own necklace but Soddhu stopped me.

"Herbert told me how much he paid for that."

"But I must give him something!"

"Here, take my Kusti."

He reached under his shirt, yanked it off and I threw it toward the stage. The strange garment caught Cortina's attention, he looked at it curiously, then put it in his pocket. A twinge of excitement ran through me, and I knew that tonight was the night I'd let Soddhu make love.

"May Ahura Mazda rejoice!" Soddhu cried as we fell into each other's arms. The sadreh which he left on did little to hide the fact that he was a magnificent specimen.

"Yatha ahu vairyo," he exulted. "The will of the Lord is the law of holiness!"

Of course for me it was not Ahura Mazda but Jesus Christ I saw as my own excitement grew to a florid climax. I loved it when Soddhu chanted in my ear:

"All the shores of the sea Vouru-Kasha are boiling over, all the middle of it is boiling over, when she runs down there. . . ."

But it wasn't the boiling seas of Vouru-Kasha I was thinking of as I lay in bed the next morning. It was the idea that a Yale professor had married a full-fledged floozy. What would Daddy think if he ever found out? Eventually the smell of coffee drew me into the kitchen. Herbert kept his head in the newspaper, and as I poured a cup of coffee he extended his own cup for a refill.

"I hear that you and Soddhu scored last night," he said in an off-handed manner. My face turned scarlet.

34

"Did Soddhu tell you?" I stammered. The cup shook in my hand.

"It's right here in the paper: 'Several women fainted in the aftermath of Cortina's performance.' I will eat humble pie and confess I wish I had been there."

"I wish you had too," I said feeling contrite.

He continued to read aloud: " 'Never before have the comic arts and the classical arts merged so sublimely. Overcoming enormous odds—the discomfort of a cumbersome suit which we hope was proffered by the FBI in a sincere attempt to keep Mr. Cortina safe—the artist took his craft to new heights. We disagree with the assessment of some of our colleagues that Mr. Cortina took the concept of freeness in playing to absurd lengths. Our belief is that, since technical virtuosity plays a great part in an artistic performance, what is wrong with using the rump as long as the notes are clear and the music is attacked precisely? The real question is, will all piano playing in the future be measured by this performance?' "

The phone rang. It was Bob Grisham.

"Hang on to your pants," he said. "We think we've found Albert."

Now it was Herbert's hand which began to shake.

"Where?" he asked in a trembling voice.

"In Mahale, of all places. Somebody dumped him off at the preserve."

"But that's where he came from!"

"Yes, it's odd, isn't it? Anyway, I need somebody to go there and bring him back, assuming it really is Albert."

"Don't look at me, Bob. There are things here I need to attend to."

As he spoke he turned toward me. I felt myself blush.

"Look, Hickey, I need someone I can trust. You can take Kathryn, the trip will be good for both of you."

"Will we need visas?

"I've already got them and the tickets too. See you in an hour."

Chapter Three

A Heated Discussion while Dining on Zebra

We arrived at Kenyatta International after an all-night flight from London. As the plane descended through a mass of clouds and made its approach across the brown plains I saw an amazing sight—giraffes and zebras running below us in all directions. My expectations of Africa were being fulfilled even before we landed.

Inside the terminal Herbert went to find a cart. The airport swarmed with people. There were Africans and Europeans, college kids with backpacks, men with briefcases in business suits. I stared in fascination at the African women dressed in bold colorful cotton dresses which I later learned were made of pieces of rectangular cloth called kangas.

As I continued to stare I felt a slight touch on my arm.

"Mrs. Kathryn Hickey? I am Bangassu Jamu from the Mahale Research Center. Your arrival is quite timely. Your Albert has been doing very badly of late. We are all quite concerned."

Perhaps it was something in his eyes or his voice, but I liked him immediately. He was dressed in a crisp short-sleeved sport shirt, Jordach jeans and Nike running shoes.

"We're not sure it *is* our Albert," I replied. "That's why my husband is here, to identify him. Here he is now. Darling, do you think that cart is going to work? The wheels are not turning."

"It's the only one I could find" he replied. "I thought a good kick might get it started."

Bangassu Jamu introduced himself again. He said:

"But we know it is Albert because he was brought here by a gentleman from Yale. 'Here, take him,' he said. 'He is too much a loose canon.'"

"In that case, why the hell are we here?!" said Herbert.

As he began throwing our luggage into the cart a sturdy white man dressed in khaki and wearing a pith helmet came bounding toward us. Bangassu stiffened.

"No no no!" the man exclaimed. He tried to pull a bag away from Herbert. Aiming his remarks at Mr. Jamu, he said: "Bangassu can do that, can't he?"

"Sure, Bwana, why not?"

As the African began handling the luggage the other man held out hand.

"Robert Goldschmidt's the name, from the American Embassy. The Consulate told me about your problems with Albert and asked me to keep an eye on you."

"It seems everybody knows about Albert except me," said Herbert.

"'Skull and Bones grapevine' you might say. By the way, where is your colleague, Professor Págalu?"

"Didn't they tell you? It's just the two of us, myself and Kathryn."

"Bwana needs new grapevine," said Bangassu.

"Yes, apparently so," said Goldschmidt looking disappointed.

"Do you two know each other?" I asked.

"Bangassu used to work at the Embassy," Goldschmidt replied. His mind seemed to be elsewhere.

Herbert said: "Well, we'd better get going. We're catching a flight out of White Airport today and going directly to the Center with Mr. Jamu."

Goldschmidt snapped back to attention.

"I'm sorry, Professor," he said, "but there are no flights going out of White today. Some kind of high alert, apparently. I came here to steer you to a hotel."

"I have not heard of any high alert," said Bangassu, surprised.

"Bangassu not hear *many* things, I expect," replied Goldschmidt.

"I heard you didn't get a boy last night."

"Bangassu hear wrong, Goldschmidt get two boys. Oh, sorry, Professor, Mrs. Hickey!"

"Damn!" exclaimed Herbert, slamming one of his carry-on's to the ground. "That means we have to spend money on a hotel room!"

"I expect your department will pick up the bill," said Goldschmidt.

"Are you kidding? It's hard to get a box of paper clips out of them."

"There are some very proper hotels in Nairobi that will have a minimal impact on your budget," Bangassu said.

"Yes, but they're full of Africans," said Goldschmidt. "They'd probably prefer a room at the Norfolk."

"But of course," said Bangassu. "Perhaps Bwana can get them in on the spook special."

Goldschmidt shrugged. "Bangassu thinks the Norfolk is a CIA branch office—but it's just a good place for imperialists to meet and figure out how to exploit the natives." He smiled blandly at Bangassu.

"The Norfolk," I said. "Isn't that where Ernest Hemingway used to stay?"

"Hemingway, Robert Ruark, Baroness Karen Blixon, Teddy Roosevelt—all the great hunters of their time."

"I'm glad those days are over," I said.

"Why, who says they are? Air Force Two is coming over next month full of senators and congressmen just raring to plug an animal."

"How lovely."

"It is lovely. Wait 'til you've seen an elephant crash to the earth after an explosive bullet's been pumped into his brain. Africa is the land of hunters, it's the one thing this hellish country has going for it. There's nothing like being on safari. Man against beast. The thrill of the kill. I can get you on a safari, Mrs. Hickey, where you can shoot lions, leopards, even elephants—anything your little heart desires."

"Thanks, I'll keep it in mind."

"Take Hickey's bags, Banga. Time they go through customs."

"Don't be ridiculous," Herbert said. "We'll get another cart."

"Nonsense," said Goldschmidt. "Bangassu's better than a cart and besides, he's free."

Fortunately for Bangassu there were only two medium-size suitcases; time had not allowed us to pack very much. I paired up with Goldschmidt as we walked over to the customs counter.

"Why do you dislike Mr. Jamu?" I asked.

"Because he is a trouble-maker of the first order. Unless you think it's okay to steal top secret documents from the Embassy."

"Was he arrested?"

"No, we couldn't prove the charges. But even so, you can't start treating blacks as equals or the next thing you know you'll have gays in the military and a woman in the White House. And that, Mrs. Hickey, would be the end of civilization."

By now we had come up to customs. The lines were very long but Goldschmidt escorted us into a side office where an enormous uniformed immigration officer was sitting behind a desk with a large pistol placed conspicuously infront of him. He was drinking a Diet Coke and sweating profusely.

"How's it going, Mabu," Goldschmidt said as if he were an old friend. "Have you been doing an efficient job tormenting the tourists?"

"Always," the man replied. "Tourists need to be tormented. It gives them a thrill. Let's them feel like they've braved the savages of the Dark Continent."

Then, running his eyes up and down me as if I were a suitcase he had a mind to open, he said, "I am Mabu Odongo, Chief Customs Officer at this airport. What have we got here?"

"This is Dr. Hickey and his wife Kathryn," said Goldschimdt. "I'm taking them to the Norfolk so they can rest up before they head for Tanzania."

"Oh, yes, the talking apes," grunted Mabu.

"You know about them?" Herbert asked.

"I'm afraid so," said Mabu, picking up his pistol and checking the ammunition clip. "It's much more difficult to shoot a chimp and eat it now that we know they can talk. It's almost like committing a crime. Thank goodness this is Africa and not the United States." He ended his speech with a deep laugh.

"Anyway," Goldschmidt interrupted, "the lines were long and I thought a couple of good Cubans might expedite matters, if you know what I mean." He handed Mabu a small box wrapped in brown paper that he produced from the pocket of his safari jacket.

"Good smoke always helps in customs," said Mabu with a wink, placing the package carefully in a drawer in his desk. "Are you carrying any wild animals, contagious diseases or subversive ideas?" he asked Herbert.

"I'm from Yale, not Berkeley," Herbert retorted.

"Then I let you through!" said Mabu grandly, gesturing to the back door of his office. "Enjoy your stay in Kenya—and don't listen to anything those Tanzanian monkeys might have to say—just in case you have to shoot them later."

His laughter continued as we exited the room and headed toward the street. An embassy car was waiting to take us to the Norfolk. Bangassu followed in his jeep. As we left the plains behind the traffic grew heavy; in the distance the skyline of Nairobi looked like Manhattan.

A corpulent African dressed as a Beefeater helped us unload.

"Where's the little monkey from America?" he asked.

"We're sneaking him in in a suitcase," Goldschmidt replied with a slap on the back. "You know the hotel rules—no pets."

Herbert went to register.

"How about I pick the two of you up for dinner?" said Goldschimdt. "You can't visit Nairobi without eating at the Carnivore."

"Only if Mr. Jamu will join us," I replied.

"I think Banga needs to find place sleep tonight, right Banga?"

"And refuse Mrs. Hickey's kind invitation? I should be delighted."

Goldschmidt picked us up at seven. Sleep had refreshed us, and we stared in wild-eyed wonder as our driver moved through traffic like a demon; soon we cut through a field on the outskirts of the city and arrived at the restaurant.

We waited for Bangassu in the Simba Saloon, a large palapa adjacent to the restaurant. A good sampling of humanity crowded inside—Africans, Europeans and Indians all mingling in a friendly informality quite different from New Haven.

We drank a round of dawas, Goldschmidt asked questions about Soddhu, which made me feel homesick. I wished Bangassu would show up.

"You can't count on natives to be on time," said Goldschmidt. "Some of them don't even know how to tell time."

"I guess Mr. Jamu's not one of them," I said as Bangassu entered the restaurant.

He greeted many people as he made his way over. He seemed to know all the waiters and many of the customers. As he sat down at our table Goldschmidt looked at his watch. "Banga two minutes late. How he expect overthrow government if he can't be on time?"

Bangassu turned to us and smiled. "Mr. Goldschmidt has invented the idea that I am a revolutionary and I have invented the idea that he is an agent for the CIA. Isn't it silly, the ideas that pop into one's heads?"

We walked over to a floor-to-ceiling menu board. Among the offerings were zebra, hartebeest and crocodile. Since we had already tasted zebra Goldschmidt suggested we order the Carnivore Meat Platter, one kilo's worth, and split it amongst the four of us.

"Unless Banga want his raw," he said.

Bangassu laughed and sipped his dawa laconically as a fire crackled in a huge roasting pit nearby. The smell of meat was overwhelming.

"*Jambo*," said the waiter coming up to take our order. He wore a straw hat and a long striped apron.

"*Habari za jioni*," Bangassu answered. "Good evening."

As they spoke in Swahili, Goldschmidt squirmed uncomfortably in his seat.

40

"You never know what they're saying," he said.

"You don't speak Swahili?" I asked.

"Certainly not. It's too barbaric for my taste."

"Some people might say the same about English," said Bangassu.

"Such a person would be a fool."

"There are fools in all cultures."

"Some more than others."

"And your definition of culture?"

"Culture," said Goldschmidt, "is man's barrier against the wilds of nature and the beast within all of us. You Africans are on the brink of annihilation."

"Are you saying we have no culture?" Bangassu asked.

"I'm saying that Africans are too close to nature and nature is culture's enemy. Culture evolved in order to stamp out nature and bring her to her knees."

"Perhaps being closer to the beasts makes us more civilized than you think," said Bangassu. "We kill for food, you kill for profit. We band together to protect our kin, you create bureaucracies to isolate people and control them. We dance to express the joy in our souls, you dance to look stylish for your hollow friends. Which of us do you really think is more civilized?"

"Mr. Goldschmidt," said Herbert to change the subject, "what's your job at the Consulate—aside from getting people through customs?"

"Oh, that's just about it," Goldschmidt replied. "Customs and desk work and keeping an eye on Bangassu, making sure he doesn't kidnap any of our honored guests. My official title is Assistant Communications Officer."

"Well, we appreciate all the help you've given us."

"Not at all. It's an honor to meet the brains behind Project Mark. I'm only sorry I couldn't have met your colleague, Dr. Págalu."

"I'm afraid the real credit should go to the dean of the Divinity School, John Wiggins. Albert took to his classes like a duck takes to water. Even Billy Graham was impressed.

"The history of your church," said Bangassu, "with its witch burnings and torture chambers ought to have made you stop to think." He spoke with surprising vehemence.

"Bangassu sound like communist," said Goldschmidt. "Maybe he should go live in Russia."

"I understand Mr. Jamu's misgivings," said Herbert. "But our chimps are the most well-adjusted Christians I've ever seen."

"That's too bad," said Mr. Jamu cynically. "As hopeless neurotics you could have had a whole new market for Prozac."

"I never thought of that," said Herbert.

"Well I for one am sorry the project ended so abruptly," said Goldschmidt. "Religion would have been a good way to keep the chimps in line. Just let them know they're all sinners. Nothing like a little guilt to get the troops to obey the rules."

Our dinner came.

"I like to see a woman eat," said Herbert as I dug hungrily into the crocodile.

"Here, have some hartebeest before Banga eats it up," said Goldschmidt. He passed me a platter of sputtering flesh.

Bangassu chewed his crocodile thoughtfully. "Why are you so afraid of the breakdown of culture?" he asked Goldschmidt.

"You see?" Goldschmidt said, pointing his fork in the air for emphasis. "The typical response of a revolutionary: getting rid of culture is the answer to everything."

Bangassu looked at Goldschmidt. "Nature is under siege, scientists have warned the world about the frailty of ecosystems and the extinction of life, yet the developers continue to raze the land and destroy its habitats inorder to build more homes and plant more crops. This behavior is a product of culture and culture tells man that he owns the earth. Even as a poorly paid assistant at Mahale I can still think, and I am suspicious of culture."

"Behold the new Marxist who puts nature and the environment over human needs," said Goldschmidt sarcastically.

"And what are human needs, afterall? More plastic gee-gaws and a license to kill so Mr. Goldschmidt can live out his secret agent fantasies. Perhaps you should just pave the entire planet and get it over with."

"Now you're talking!" said Goldschmidt. "Waiter, another drink for my friend."

As soon as we got to our room I collapsed on the bed. The dawas had taken their toll, so had the food, the heat and jarring traffic.

"I'm going to sleep well tonight," I said.

"Maybe not," said Herbert, picking up a complimentary newspaper that had been placed on the table. "Listen to this:

The body of world-renowned pianist Jorge Cortina was found late Sunday off a practice room at Carnegie Hall. The death is being investigated as a homicide. In a statement from police, robbery appears to be the motive, since Mr. Cortina's wallet and watch were missing. Still it has not been ruled out that anti-Castro forces were involved. Many have not forgiven Cortina, whose last appearance rocked Carnegie Hall, for appearing in an ape costume. The president of Cuba has charged the United States government with involvement in the affair, and has threatened to expel all Americans from the country. A request by Cuba's deputy foreign minister to return the body to Cuba is expected today.

Herbert looked at me. "There's something to tell your grandchildren someday. You were at his last concert. Poor fellow. That bulletproof suit didn't keep him from getting his neck broken. The murderer must have been strong."

Chapter Four

The Pelvis Unveiled

Or

The Lumumbian Theory of Evolution:
"It All Has To Do with Fucking."

"It's Albert, all right."

Herbert recognized him sitting with a group of chimps on the other side of a chain-link fence separating the camp from the forest. But neither of us was prepared for the change which had come over him. At Yale, Albert had been mild-mannered and timid, a scholar eager to learn. Now he swaggered about with an exaggerated air of importance, a Bible clutched between his fingers. The other chimps watched with annoyed expressions.

"Hello, Albert."

Herbert signed and spoke at the same time.

Without looking at us Albert replied in sign language, "I'm very busy right now ministering to my flock. If you would like to come back later, I think I'll have some time for you. Confession is at four."

"Well I'll be damned!" said Herbert.

"I'm sure you will be unless you repent," Albert replied. This was a total surprise, since Herbert had spoken out loud.

Just then a large male gave a hoot and landed at Albert's feet.

"You silly baboon," he signed. "Nobody came to confession yesterday, and nobody will come to confession today because nobody gives a twit about the insect taboo."

"This is Albert's cousin, Yendi," said Bangassu. "In the short time Albert has been here he has managed to teach sign language to most of the apes in this area. They in turn have taught it to some other apes in more distant parts of the reserve."

"You mean the wild chimps have been teaching each other to sign without help from humans?" Herbert asked.

"It appears so," said Bangassu solemnly.

"If that's true," Herbert said, "it will be the biggest discovery in biology this century. Independent language use among wild apes! What a fantastic development!"

Herbert looked at me in triumph.

"If this is not Nobel Prize stuff I don't know what is."

Yendi looked at us suspiciously.

"Come on," he said to Albert, giving him a shove. "Let's go find Nedele and get some poontang."

Albert screeched in horror. "Let the wicked forsake his way," he said, "and the unrighteous man his thoughts. Isaiah 55:7."

"Oh shove it," said Yendi and loped away.

Herbert took me in his arms and twirled me around.

"We've done it!" he exclaimed. "We've succeeded in planting a permanent sense of morality in a chimpanzee. Our Albert remains a full-fledged Christian even in the wild!"

Bangassu's expression was less exuberant.

"It may look good on paper, Dr. Hickey, but we are bracing for disaster. At the very least, the chimps will kill him."

"And the worst?"

"They'll try to kill us, which means of course we'll have to kill them, and there goes our tourism."

Albert had come up to the fence. At my bidding Bangassu opened the gate and I stood with open arms.

"Here, Albert, come and give me a hug."

"Woman, I know thee not!" he signed disdainfully. "Now I must do the Lord's work."

He went quickly over to another group of chimps and began signing the Sermon on the Mount.

"Unbelievable!" said Herbert.

Bangassu shook his head.

"Every day he is either here or there"—Bangassu indicated the forest-covered hills that stretched into the distance—"teaching, teaching, teaching. A few of the apes find it amusing, but who knows how long that will last?"

The afternoon went by quickly. We slept and made love until we were called to dinner.

It was a delicious meal prepared by the camp staff—homemade bread, fresh vegetables and zebra steaks washed down with French wine, which made us feel optimistic. No mention was made of the trouble brewing beyond the compound, and the conversation centered around various subjects including Cortina's death and the disappearance of the pandas. While Bangassu speculated on the various parks where they could be, we emptied another bottle.

Outside the moon was full and the warm night air was filled with a cacophony of sound. We decided to take a walk.

"Don't go beyond the perimeter," Bangassu warned. "There are many dangerous animals."

"Don't worry," said Herbert, "I have no desire to be a lion's late night supper."

"I love Africa," I said as we strolled along the pathway.

"And I love you," said Herbert.

The moon, the stars, the croaking of frogs, the sounds of strange birds, and Herbert standing in the softly moving shadows of the trees illuminated by the moon—it was perfect. My dalliance with Soddhu I decided was over.

As we walked toward the chimp sanctuary only the insects and birds of the night seemed to be stirring.

We stopped infront of the gate which was now padlocked. Beyond it was an extraordinary tree. Its tangled roots reached upwards, leaving dark caverns large enough for a man to squeeze into. A canopy of branches extended overhead, and climbing through it all was a vine of remarkable flowers with large white petals that looked like wet wool gleaming in the moonlight.

I reached for the padlock and pulled on it. To my surprise it was open.

"Don't be silly," Herbert said as I started to push the gate. "Those chimps can hurt you as much as a lion."

"But Bangassu said they always sleep down by the food house."

I pulled free of Herbert's grasp and let myself in.

"Damn it, Kathryn!"

He hurried after me muttering loudly. As he peered nervously into the forest I stood on tiptoes next to the giant roots and reached up for one of the vines. The flowers exuded a pungent, sultry smell.

At that moment there was a crash. A group of chimpanzees—about twelve—were moving slowly towards us. Out infront was a large chimp

46

walking almost upright and looking around warily. In the light of the moon his eyes seemed to blaze.

"Hide!" said Herbert, pushing me inside the tree.

As he spoke one of the apes looked in our direction. But a moment later they all began to chatter and use their hands in sign language. The moonlight sharpened the edges of their gestures making it possible to see what they were saying.

"We thought you were coming sooner, Brother Lumumba," said a chimp who was next in size.

"I had a little trouble in New York," said the ape who stood upright.

He cut a striking figure. The hair on his chin was shaped like a goatee. His forehead was not nearly as furrowed as the others, and his nose not as flat. The chimps who gathered around him ministered to his needs, and for a few moments he appeared to be enjoying the attention. I had the strange idea I'd seen him before.

"I'm glad you didn't fly into Gabon. The reports are true. Our dear cousins in the Forest of the Bees have all been wiped out. The bush-meat trade is going gangbusters. There are poachers everywhere looking to supply the logging companies with meat. Some of them think that chimpanzees taste as good as beef."

"You were smart to move here, Brother Oyem," said the large ape. "In Mahale there are no real dangers."

Oyem shook his head dubiously.

"That was before my son came back," he signed. "He is driving us crazy with his incessant talk about the insect taboo."

Another ape nodded rapidly.

"Africa is the land of insects," he signed. "How are we going to keep them away? You'd have to dig a hole and go underground!"

"Kribi's right," said Oyem. "I know it's only a matter of time, dear brother, before someone lets him have it. Maybe it will be me. Not only am I tired of hearing about this taboo, but I am also tired of hearing about this Jesus fellow who was crucifried for our sins. By the way, what is a sin?"

"And what is crucifried?" asked another ape.

A female who was nursing an infant signed awkwardly.

"Dear Uncle Lumumba," she said. "He's already turned Nedele into a basket case. She used to be so happy, and now all she does is sit around and mope. Worse than that, nobody can mount her, she runs away as if she's being chased by a leopard. I tell her, 'Nedele, you know what the males do to a female who refuses to get fucked? Remember what happened to Massinga? They killed her for that very reason.' But it doesn't seem to matter, she's only interested in mourning dead animals or keeping them alive, even if they're only bugs."

"Yalinga's right," said Oyem. "The other day I found her trying to rescue an ant that had fallen into a stream. When I asked her why, she said that she could not bear to see it die.

" 'But it's only an ant,' I said. 'That may be,' she replied. 'But look closely, Uncle. Do you see how it struggles to stay alive? I know how scared it is, I am struggling to stay alive too.' Her words have left me with an uneasy feeling."

"As well they should," said the large ape called Lumumba. "Because the trouble is that Albert now thinks of himself as being human and is trying to make others feel that way too. And that's the worst thing that could happen to anybody. You'll have to stop him before he spreads the human contagion to all the chimps in the area."

"How do we do that?" said Oyem.

"A blow to the skull might suffice," said Lumumba.

"A bit extreme, brother. His mother Mohele would never forgive me."

"Then take him to the museum, the one at Olduvai, about seven hundred kilometers from here. Someone found the oldest human skull there. A professor at Yale told me about it."

At mention of Yale, Herbert moved slightly. Once again Lumumba looked in our direction.

"What does all that have to do with Albert?" Oyem asked.

"Perhaps when he sees how similar the skull is to ours, when he sees they are monkeys just like we are you can prove to him that their supposed superiority is rooted in a bunch of hocus pocus—in hallucinated lines which became laws that don't exist anywhere except in the imagination of crazed primates who call themselves humans. Once you bring him to understand the truth underlying all the illusions he'll be okay again. I guarantee he'll want to recover his animal dignity."

"The Serengeti Plains," Oyem signed fretfully. "It might as well be on the moon. What do you think, Kumasi?"

"What isn't near may not be far," replied the ape called Kumasi. He appeared to be very old. His brown fur was heavily sprinkled with white, and his long, gnarled fingers twisted grotesquely around a stick.

"Do they have hippos there, Uncle?" one of the smaller chimps asked.

"My dear little Doba," Lumumba said. "Not only are there hippos, there are rhinoceroses too."

48

"But how will we get there?" Oyem asked. "From what I hear there's not much cover once you leave the mountains. It's better you take him."

"I'm afraid that's out of the question," Lumumba replied. "I have a rendezvous in Spain and my plane leaves in two days."

A look of anguish swept over Oyem's face.

"We'll all be killed by the Maasai before we get a hundred meters from the trees," he said.

Lumumba shook his head. "You are forgetting how much time I spent roaming about in America disguised as a human."

"But that was America," Oyem said. "From what I understand anything's possible over there. An ape could run for president and no one would notice as long as he had good PR and good makeup."

Lumumba looked pleased. "You've been reading the newspapers, haven't you?"

Oyem nodded. "I took your suggestions. The people at the camp still haven't figured out where their papers are going."

Lumumba reached out and pulled something from Oyem's head, then flicked it in the air.

"Don't worry," he said. "You'll be surprised what clothes and a little pancake makeup can do. When I was hiding out at Yale I got laid every weekend. Humans—especially 19-year-old Ivy-league girls—are remarkably unperceptive. If you flatter them enough they see what they want to see. If they noticed my fur, I told them I was a wild beast and all they did was get more excited."

Just then there was a thrashing in the underbrush and Albert appeared waving his Bible.

"Uncle Lumumba," he exclaimed. "Are you here for midnight mass? Christmas is a ways off, but I thought I'd hold one anyway. It's such a beautiful evening."

Lumumba patted Albert affectionately on the head. "Wouldn't it be nice instead of holding mass to hold Nedele's hand beneath this big, beautiful moon?"

"Oh, no, Uncle. That would not be nice at all. Females are dirty and turn all us males into sinners. Besides, Nedele is my sister and if I did anything with here I would be breaking the insect taboo."

"You see, you see?" Oyem said, hopping up and down. "He keeps talking about that damned taboo. What I want to know is what do insects have to do with fucking?"

Lumumba pulled his goatee and looked at Albert thoughtfully.

"Albert, how would you like to go on a journey tomorrow?" he asked.

"I don't have time for traveling, Uncle. There is much work to be done here converting the chimps in the mountains to Christianity. The sin and depravity they are living in is unspeakable—mothers and sons lying together, brothers and sisters casually fondling each other's genitals or trading sex for a few termites. I may be the only hope they have of receiving the Word of God and saving their souls from eternal damnation."

"My dear Albert. You cannot convert the heathen until you yourself have been purified. Before you minister to the chimps you must prove that your faith is strong enough to resist the temptations of the world. Think of the journey as a kind of quest that will make you worthy of so great a task as bringing salvation to the mountains of Mahale."

"Could we go to Rome?" asked Albert excitedly. "It would be a sinful indulgence, but I'd do anything to see the old holy sites I've read about and see the vagina hat the Pope wears on his head when he celebrates mass."

Lumumba eyed him curiously.

"Why do you call it the vagina hat?" he asked.

"Because it has two lips on top and rather looks like one," said Albert.

"Perhaps there is hope for the chimp yet," Lumumba mumbled to himself. To Albert he said:

"Don't think of the journey as an indulgence. The route will be filled with peril. You'll need all your Christian faith to make it through."

The other chimps crowded around Lumumba and Albert. "What about us?" they signed. "We want to see the vagina hat too!"

"And I want to see the hippos," said Doba.

"And if Albert is right about God," said another of the smaller apes, "it's not fair to leave us behind to be damned. But if he's wrong, we should all be there so we can give him a good gang-banging."

"I'm sorry, Bata," Lumumba said. "Only Albert and Nedele can make the pilgrimage."

It was obvious from the commotion that the other chimps were upset. It was also obvious that Lumumba was not to be dissuaded, and eventually the troop of chimps disappeared into the forest. We emerged from our hiding place, grateful to be alive.

"That was a close call," I said, "sorry, darling."

"Sweetheart, I wouldn't have missed it for the world. Those were *wild chimps* and they were using sign language at a level never seen in captivity. My guess is that being in their natural habitat must somehow amplify their natural language capabilities. But who would have guessed!

But I need to document this. Do you suppose that Albert could get me an interview with this Lumumba fellow?"

Suddenly there was a loud rustling above us and the sound of crashing branches. A dozen black shapes came hurtling down from the tree, making shrieking sounds as they landed. It was impossible to escape, they had us surrounded.

A moment later Lumumba appeared and the apes parted to let him through. Although he was a few inches shorter than I, his gaze was so intense that I felt he was looking down on me from some great height. What was most remarkable was that he stood straight as an arrow, one arm hanging loosely at his side, the other stroking a red goatee flecked with gray. As he contemplated our presence, Herbert introduced us and explained how we had come to be inside the enclosure. When there was no response, Herbert took out his handkerchief and wiped his forehead.

"Tell him you're from Yale," I said, trying not to laugh at the absurd idea that Lumumba had actually been there. But the information seemed to have the desired effect.

"What year?" Lumumba signed.

"Actually I'm not an alumnus," Herbert replied, breathing easier. "I'm a professor of anthropology."

"Are you here to put your nearest relatives under a microscope?"

"I would like to document their use of ASL in their natural habitat."

"And it would be a feather in your cap to interview me, I imagine."

"Your perceptivity is amazing," said Herbert grinning broadly.

Just then there was a noise in the underbrush and Albert appeared carrying a tablecloth, a bottle of wine and some cookies he had pilfered from the kitchen. When he saw us he stopped abruptly.

"Why, Dr. and Mrs. Hickey!" he signed. "Are you here to celebrate mass this evening?"

"You know them?" Lumumba asked his nephew.

"But of course! Dr. Hickey is my mentor. If it weren't for him I would never have found Jesus Christ."

Lumumba drew himself up ominously.

"So you were the devil behind this lunacy!" he signed. He opened his mouth, his canines gleamed menacingly.

"No, no," said Herbert quickly. "It was Professor Págalu and the dean of the Divinity School, John Wiggins. I was only there to assist."

"I think he's lying," said one of the larger apes.

"Tchibanga's right," said Kribi. "Let's kill them now and be done with it."

"Yes," signed his friend Tchibanga. "They know about the museum trip and will probably alert the authorities."

"Which means," signed Yendi, "we'd have to hear more of those damned psalms!"

"And all that stuff about the insect taboo," Tchibanga added.

"A little meat would taste good tonight," Kribi signed, looking at my thighs. "It's been a long time since we ate colobus monkey."

As the apes began to crowd in, Herbert tried to protect me. Shielding me with his body he made a final plea.

"If you let us go, Lumumba, we'll take Albert home with us!"

"*Dr.* Lumumba," the ape replied, drawing himself up. "I did my dissertation on Kant's ontological definition of the aesthetic object which I compared to the categorical epistemology of the transcendental imagination in the *Critique of Pure Reason*. It actually made quite a stir in philosophy circles. Unfortunately I had to leave the university after a certain misfortune befell me."

"They discovered you were an ape?" I asked.

"Much worse, dear lady. I had tenure stolen out from under my very nose."

The apes drew even closer.

"*Dr.* Lumumba, I am appealing to your higher self," said Herbert. "Is this any way to treat a fellow colleague?"

"Think of it as inter-departmental rivalry, my dear professor. We're fighting for tenure and may the better man win."

"But I'm willing to take Albert off your hands!"

"My plan is better. It offers Albert a chance for recovery whereas yours, at best, will make a clown of him."

"What's wrong with that? I can get him a job as an assistant to the dean of the Divinity School. John Wiggins is very fond of him."

"I'm sorry, professor, but I think Kribi's plan is better, although I've come to detest the taste of flesh myself."

He nodded to the others, and with Albert in tow turned to go.

"Did you ever think the end would be like this?" I said as Herbert and I drew closer in each other's arms.

"If a Rockefeller can be eaten by a shark I suppose we can be eaten by a monkey."

His words comforted me a little, but the great comfort came with Bangassu's appearance at the gate and several men from the camp.

A shot rang out and one of the apes fell to the ground.

"They've killed Oyem!" Kribi signed frantically. There was a sudden tug under my arms as I was lifted off my feet and transported aerially from tree to tree. We were far from the compound when without ceremony I was deposited on the ground. Herbert dropped down next to me a moment later.

"Sleep well, Dr. and Mrs. Hickey," said Lumumba as he alighted gracefully. "Tomorrow will be a day of reckoning."

There was no point in trying to escape, the apes were everywhere. Anticipating that this would be our last night on earth we made passionate love, then dropped off to sleep on a bed of soft ferns.

Doba woke us up with a kick.

"Uncle says you're allowed to choose your last meal. Which would you prefer, termites or figs?"

As we ate our figs Lumumba sauntered over.

"My dear friends," he signed. "I have good news and bad. The good news is that Oyem is not dead, the bullet only grazed him. The bad news is that since he can no longer take Albert and Nedele to the museum I've decided to delay my trip and go there myself."

"And we get to go too," said Doba, jumping up and down excitedly.

"That's right," said Lumumba. "As long as we have these humans with us its not safe to return to the preserve."

"You're taking us along?!" asked Herbert.

"As collateral," Lumumba replied.

"I'll need my cosmetics case," I said.

Lumumba smirked. "Dear lady," he replied, "no one in Africa uses deodorant, or haven't you noticed?"

As the sun grew warmer the apes finished eating and began to groom. Nedele sat on the ground playing with Yalinga's baby, while Yalinga sat nearby chewing on leaves and fending off the advances of Kribi, Yendi and Tchibanga as they rolled in the leaves and displayed their erect penises.

Kumasi sat off by himself, watching the others with a sad and faraway look. Bata and Doba groomed one another, while Albert kneeled in the open and prayed. Eventually, everyone was ready, and with Kribi and Tchibanga at our sides we followed the troop as obediently as sheep.

The hills sloped off at a gentle angle. The apes seemed to have a knack for picking a path through the forest, for in places where all I could see was an impenetrable wall of underbrush, they would reveal a continuation of cavern-like openings between the trees. As the occasional view of Lake Tanganyika became less and less frequent, Herbert guessed we were heading for the crests of the mountains to the east.

"Over my dead body," I said.

He stopped to tie his shoe.

"Sweetheart," he replied, "as soon as we're out of the forest and somebody sees us we'll be rescued. Lumumba can't disguise the entire troop, I'm betting on that."

"Stop talking, you poor excuses for animals," signed an angry Tchibanga. He gave us a push and we moved on.

To tell the truth, what caused the most discomfort that first day was the simple idea of being a captive, the idea of not being able to do what I wanted. Strangely enough Lumumba seemed to know what I was thinking.

Free will, he said, was just a diversion from the real issue—a man's desire for his mother.

Herbert was amazed and asked what free will had to do with incest.

"You have to go to the root of the word to understand," Lumumba replied. "Do you think that the words you speak today with their twisted and complicated meanings are the same words your ancestors used when they first began to speak? To the mind of a hominid breaking away from the howls of an animal there could be no more than one meaning to a word."

"But what does that have to do with free will?" Herbert asked.

"The expression 'free will' is derived from human emotions rooted in sexual desire. 'Free' comes from the Sanskrit 'beloved' and is linked to love and desire. The word 'will' comes from an ancient root meaning to wish strongly for something—to desire or will it. The true definition of free will, in other words, is 'the desire for the beloved'."

Herbert looked at me sideways.

"Maybe he did go to Yale," he said. "It sounds like he took one of Dr. Vandevort's classes."

"Don't be ridiculous, darling. Daddy would have known about it. Please don't humor him by asking any more questions."

"But I have to, I still don't see the connection to incest."

"That's because the words have taken on an inverted meaning," said Lumumba. "By believing in free will (by the way, the word 'believe' also comes from a Sanskrit word meaning 'desire'), a man *believes* he can stay away from that sexual object which he desires most—his mother.

"Free will, which was originally a name for this controlling drive, gradually evolved into a ploy to divert consciousness away from its obsession with voluptuousness (another word, by the way, which has the same root as 'will'.) The early Christians, for instance, thought of sexual abstinence as a way of using their free will to purify themselves in the sight of God. But this freedom was merely an illusion. In reality, they were simply hiding from the dictates of the incest taboo. They weren't

54

escaping from it. They were pushing it down where its influence was invisible. When men claim they are acting out of free will, they are really obeying the law of the incest taboo in its most insidious form."

"You seem to be implying that men will go to the ends of the earth to observe this taboo."

"Ah, yes. Because there must be *something* behind this metamorphosis of 'will', 'freedom' and 'power' into their exact opposites. You have to ask yourself *why* a man would choose—supposedly out of his own free will—to do the exact opposite of what he ought to want to do. Why else would a man volunteer for deprivation and hardship?"

"Well, perhaps because he thinks it is the right thing to do," said Herbert.

"Precisely my point," said Lumumba. "He doesn't do so because *he* wants to but because the law—that is, ultimately, the law of the incest taboo—says he should do it. When men think they are most free they are actually the most enslaved. Take it from me, the human lexicon is rooted in the genitals."

"Please, Uncle," said Albert, who had been listening, "no more talk about the insect taboo. It's making me feel sick to my stomach."

"Ah, yes," Lumumba replied, "the age-old human retreat into illness prompted by one's forbidden desires. And now it manifests itself inside the stomach of a Christianized chimp. The question is, will he want to take the verbana plant or a bottle of Pepto-Bismol for quick relief?"

We came to a stream and stopped by a small clearing shaded with palm trees. Some of the apes climbed up to eat fruit while others drank from the stream. Nedele lowered herself next to the edge and began to rescue insects which had fallen into the water. Kribi was lying in the grass, bouncing Yalinga's little son up and down on his stomach.

"That's what Daddy used to do when I was little," I signed to Albert who was also watching. "Perhaps your cousins aren't so bad after all."

"Oh yes they are," he signed back. "In a couple of minutes Kribi's going to start molesting him. They all do that, the dirty bastards! Just you wait and see."

As Kribi began to quiver and move his hips suggestively, Okovango looked frightened and began to cry.

"Let him go," said Albert, coming to the rescue. "Do you want his little soul damned in hell before he even has a chance to avoid the mistakes we made?"

"And what mistakes are those?" Kribi replied in a belligerent tone.

"Breaking the insect taboo," said Albert pontifically. "Let him go or he'll spend the next billion years marinating in a sulfur pit."

At a sign from Yalinga whose expression seemed to say, "There's nothing to do about Albert except humor him," Kribi put Okovango down and the little ape ran quickly to his mother.

Albert looked at me sadly.

"They used to do that to me too when I was little, and I thought it was fun," he said. "Can you imagine that? Oh what a sinner I am. Thank God I found Jesus!"

I went over to Herbert who was sitting on a moss-covered log.

"I'm almost sorry we're going to be rescued," he said, his gaze focused on Lumumba a few feet away. Search planes had been circling overhead all day, crisscrossing the same areas over and over, but the density of the forest cover kept us hidden from view. It was as if the pilots thought we could not have gone beyond the general area of the Mahale preserve. Lumumba decided to increase our speed, and by late afternoon the planes had been left far behind. Whenever the going got tough Albert was there with a comforting homily such as "God will watch over you" and "never fear, God is near."

As the day began to fade, the forest took on a mysterious air. We dined on figs and dates, and afterwards Lumumba signaled to Albert and began to poke in the sandy loam with a long piece of twig.

"He's probably searching for termites," said Herbert.

But it was obvious he was doing something else and Herbert, always curious, got up to see. A moment later he came dashing back all excited.

"I knew they used twigs for getting at termites and ants," he said. "But as an implement of art? This is incredible! You must see it."

The diagram looked like this:

[Note to reader: Lumumba's drawings of man and ape come from *The Missing Link* by Raymond A. Dart, Harper & Bros., 1959.]

56

"Not too bad for primitive art," I said to Herbert.

Lumumba's eyes flashed and I had the distinct impression he understood what I was saying. But to Albert he said: "With these drawings I intend to show you that the supposed superiority of a human is nothing more than a fluke, a whimsical confluence rooted in geometry, and that the intelligence of an animal is directly proportional to the angle of inclination of the spine."

"Please keep it simple, Uncle. All I really learned in school was religion."

"Well, now I'm going to teach you a little science."

"Why do I need science when I have the Lord?"

"That, my dear nephew, is when you need science the most. Now pay attention. Animals, dear Albert, are governed by nerve impulses that control what they do and define their experience of the world. But those nerve impulses obey the laws of physics. A man named Newton showed that changing the trajectory of a particle traveling in a straight line requires energy. Thus, when you increase the number of curves in a pipe carrying liquid, it reduces the total flow rate because the particles have to change direction.

"It's the same thing with nerve impulses in the body. The straightening of the spine in humans caused an enormous increase in the flow of electrical energy from the pelvis to the brain. The result was a kind of madness: early men ran amuck, fucking everything in sight. The larger human brain evolved as a way to control the chaos unleashed by the new architecture of bipedalism—the new relationship between gravity and sexuality."

"Excuse me, Dr. Lumumba, but what does gravity have to do with the nerve impulses?"

It was Herbert, and Lumumba looked pleased.

"Do you remember how Galileo showed that the acceleration of a ball rolling down an inclined plane increases as the angle of the plane increases? Well it's the same thing here, only in reverse. As the angle of the spine moves toward a perpendicular axis to the earth, the pull of gravity on the electrical particles increases."

"But shouldn't that slow them down?" Herbert asked. "If they are moving away from the earth at a steeper angle, they ought to go slower— that is, they should become less energetic."

"But actually the reverse is true," Lumumba replied. "In the process of overcoming the force of gravity, the nerve impulses become even *more* energetic. It's like a weight lifter increasing the weights on his barbell. The more he puts on, the bigger his biceps become.

"An animal whose spine runs parallel to the earth—and of course I'm speaking of four-legged animals—will have less energetic transmission than one whose spine is more steeply inclined. This one"—Lumumba pointed to the human figure—"will have the most steeply inclined spine and therefore the most forceful transmission. After thinking about it, I've come to the conclusion that it's this steep inclination which lies behind the entire evolution of the human species."

"What does an ape know about evolution?" I said to Herbert.

"I would have expected a more open mind from the wife of a scientist," Lumumba said.

Then he could understand! From now on I would have to be more careful!

"I must differ with your hypothesis," said Herbert, speaking out loud instead of signing. "The theories of human brain evolution focus on the adaptive advantages of greater intelligence, not the force of nerve impulses generating a primal electrical chaos."

"Your brain evolved, my dear professor, from the primal electrical chaos that resulted from the altered inclination of your spine—that and nothing else."

He pointed to the drawing of the chimp and said: "Look at the relationship between the chimp's spine and the pelvis that houses its gonads. It's the angle between the two that makes all the difference. It's the angle that shields the chimp's brain from the full force of the electrical energy generated by orgasm.

"The whole process can probably be explained by a mathematical equation having to do with gravity and other forces. With the upright spine, the pelvis became the center of human gravity, a phenomenon found only in humans. This change led to a vast increase in the amount of electrical energy transmitted to the brain during orgasm. This new surge eventually became the catalyst of human evolution."

"I told you he was smart," Yendi signed to Herbert. "He'll get us across the Serengeti, you'll see."

"When did all this happen?" asked Bata. He and several others had come over and were watching with thoughtful expressions.

"Twenty-five million years ago," Lumumba replied, "a common ancestor to modern apes and humans, probably *Dryopithecus*, roamed the forests of Africa. Like all non-human primates today, this creature was a quadruped and used his hands to propel himself.

"At some point, perhaps ten million years later, there appeared an ape-like creature who walked on two legs. The reason he evolved is not crucial to our argument. Perhaps it was the need to leave the forest in search of food—as many of you anthropologists maintain, Dr. Hickey. Or it may have been some other reason. What is critical is the fact that once erect, the structural changes which occurred in the pelvis caused unforeseen consequences in the nervous system. For now the electro-chemical shocks which you humans refer to as orgasm had a direct route to the brain and produced a sensation of pleasure so great, so irresistible that it resulted in nothing less than a revolutionary change of the entire planet."

The small chimp named Doba signed, "What you are saying, Uncle, is that when the first apes stood up they began fucking unlike any creature had ever fucked before?"

"Exactly so," said Lumumba.

Turning to Herbert, he said: "You modern-day scientists like to use terms like 'reproductive advantage' and 'selective advantage,' the idea being that walking upright allowed early humans to look over the underbrush and see the lions a little sooner, thus allowing more to survive and produce more offspring. But the truth is, it was all in the fucking. The fucking itself was the reproductive advantage. Great orgasm, more sex. More sex, more offspring. Your ancestors were caught in the jaws of an orgasmic delirium. They were too busy fucking not to survive. It wasn't that their upright posture allowed them to stay ahead of the lions by running any faster—what difference would that make out in the Serengeti? They outsmarted the lions because they were desperate to get laid."

"What does 'reproductive advantage' mean, Uncle?" asked Bata.

"It really means nothing," Lumumba answered. "It's their way"—he shot us a dirty look—"of veiling what they don't understand. And fucking is something they don't understand because they are so afraid of it.

"On the other hand, reproductive advantage means something that gives you an advantage in reproducing. What greater advantage can there be, what greater enticement, than having a great orgasm?

"As you can see," he said, pointing to the diagram of the human, "this pelvis is shaped like a basin. Which one has more room for orgasm—that boiling of hormonal soup and electrical charges? The ape's or the human's? I would more expect to see a fireworks display in this one"—he pointed to the basin. "I'm sure I'd get more for my money."

"I must protest, Professor," said Herbert. "Our species evolved through a process of random variation and natural selection."

"There go the big words," said Bata derisively.

"Big words for little people," Kribi chimed in.

"Yes, you're right, Kribi. But if Dr. Hickey wants to continue in that vein, random variation and natural selection all boil down to one thing—fucking. And reproductive advantage is nothing more than a cover-word

59

for fucking. The species that fucks the most is the one that proliferates the most, and fucking is what humans do best. Other than insects, humans win this feat hands down. Why do you think they look the way they do? It's because their bodies have been transformed into sex machines. They've lost their fur, their sense of smell, their defensive teeth. The only thing they're really designed for now is fucking. If it weren't for the incest taboo, people would spend the whole day in bed. Which would be nice because then there wouldn't be any time for killing each other and destroying the planet by erecting thousand-foot-high monuments to the phallus. I'm speaking of skyscrapers, of course."

Later when we were alone I complained to Herbert: "He could never get that past peer review, let alone get a serious hearing from the scientific community."

"But it's elegant," Herbert replied, using the vernacular I heard so often from the lips of professors. "We stood up, our posture overwhelmed us with orgasm, and the evolution of the human species began as a result of its being overwhelmed. I think I rather like it."

The next day was a repeat of the first. The chimps fed on leaves and shoots along the way, and by the time we made camp in the late afternoon, I was feeling famished. Dinner again consisted of figs and clumps of red fruit which the chimps tossed down to us from the tops of the trees.

"I hope you're going to feed us something other than this," said Herbert to Lumumba.

"That would be most difficult," Lumumba replied. "Despite the vast commercial potential of selling Big Macs to mountain gorillas, McDonalds hasn't gotten around to putting in a franchise."

"Well, what about having that colobus monkey? I know you like to eat them."

"There will be no animal sacrifices on my watch," Lumumba replied.

"Hold on, Professor," said Kribi. "I'm not going to Olduvai if I can't have me a little fun."

"My dear Kribi," Lumumba replied. "Your idea of fun is not the same as mine. Spend a year or two inside a Yale lab and see how much fun it is playing the victim."

"What does that have to do with catching a baboon and smashing his brains out?"

"Boy, are *you* a dolt," said Bata piously. "Uncle is trying to teach us about the insect taboo, and all you want to do is engage in carnage."

"As if you're any better! The last baboon we killed, if I remember correctly, you were first in line to rip him apart."

60

"That's because I caught him," said Bata proudly.

"Ah yes," said Lumumba. "The first glimmering of humanity in the great ape, if you will. A foretaste of the sexual frenzy that engulfed human beings when they first stood upright. But if we wish to be better than them—and we do—we will leave all animals alone and model ourselves after the great poet Ovid who said:

Oh, what a wicked thing it is for flesh
To be the tomb of flesh, for the body's craving
To fatten on the body of another
For one creature to continue living
Through one live creature's death.

Herbert looked annoyed.

"If you're planning to enforce your ideology on us," he said, "I think we shall probably become quite ill. We can't feed on figs and dates every day, let alone leaves and shoots."

"Well, perhaps we can add some tapioca root and wild cashew nuts."

With the approach of evening, the chimps turned to the business of building their platforms high in the trees away from predators. But for us it was the cold we feared more than a leopard: once the sun had set the forest showed no mercy.

On the third night we decided to try our hand at building a hammock. But as Herbert started to twist some low-growing vines together Yendi climbed down and pulled them away.

"Trees are for apes," he signed. "Ground is for humans."

"But my wife is very susceptible to the cold," Herbert replied.

"There are a dozen apes here," Kribi answered, "who can do for your wife what you can't. And if you don't shut up and go to sleep, I'll be the first one."

"Just you try it," said Herbert with uncharacteristic bluster.

"Will somebody please put them in a hammock," Lumumba signed with great annoyance."

Nedele climbed down from her hammock and, choosing a broad bough with a horizontal fork, bent the limbs over it, holding each in place with her feet. Then she snapped several branches in two and arranged them into a leafy mattress.

"I know it's not like the beds you have at home," she said as she helped us into it. Her eyes were full of sadness.

"Why it's ten times better," I replied. "Thank you, dear, you're a wonderful friend."

She blinked unbelievingly, then slowly returned to her hammock. The forest was filled with the sounds of creatures—frogs, insects and birds who sang to the waning moon a lullaby set in the key of a strange song.

"This is really incredible," said Herbert pulling me close. "I can't wait to tell Págalu."

Págalu! At the mention of his name, what did I think of? His beautiful body? Our passionate night of love? No, it was gomez and Khvetukdas. How strange, I thought, how very, very strange. As I drifted off to sleep, I heard Herbert say, "So the upright spine was the catalyst, eh? How very interesting."

Lumumba's lecture had little effect on Albert. He continued to pontificate, and the next day berated all the males (save old Kumasi) for taking Yalinga by turn that afternoon when we stopped to rest.

"Thou shalt not succumb to the temptations of the flesh," he thundered. "If you wish to partake of the spirit of God, you must foreswear the perdition of woman. They are vile creatures. They brought the downfall of men in the Garden of Eden, and they are the reason that apes have been excluded from the kingdom of heaven. Repent and Christ will show mercy. Persist in your depravity and you will be cast into the pits of hell."

"You mean like this?" said Kribi, picking Albert up by the scruff of the neck and tossing him into a nearby pile of leaves. As Albert scrambled to his feet and began brushing the leaves from his fur the apes screeched with laughter.

"No sermons today. It's not Sunday," Yendi said.

"A man of God brings the Word of God to the heathens every day," said Albert.

"But you are not a man, you are a monkey," Yendi replied.

"You can take the man out of the monkey, but you can't take the monkey out of the man," Kumasi signed as he hobbled along.

Kribi dragged the little chimp over to a pool of water and forced him to look at his reflection. He pointed to Herbert and said, "That is a man over there. And this is a monkey over here."

"But this," said Albert, holding his Bible triumphantly in the air, "is the great equalizer. Both of us are Christians."

Lumumba's pace was not bad. The chimps stopped frequently to eat and play. On these occasions Lumumba would talk to Albert, and with growing boldness Herbert began to listen in.

One afternoon the conversation went like this:

"My dear nephew," said Lumumba, "if your feelings of guilt hadn't blinded you to certain insights into the universe that are the birthright of all animals, you would know that your body is a receptacle of energy and that reproduction is less a method of procreation than a transference of energy. I myself spend much of my time contemplating the nature of this energy. For instance, when atoms and molecules are rearranged into different combinations, chemical reactions occur and some of these may be orgasmic in nature."

"Can that be proven?" Bata asked.

"If the rings of a coffee stain can be proven mathematically, why not the rings of an orgasmic reaction? But the mass must be found first, since the mass of the product is the same as the mass of the reactant."

"Has anyone found the mass for orgasm?" Herbert asked.

"No, but they might be on the verge of it. Something they call 'dark matter' has all the ear-markings of an orgasmic event."

"Isn't that what's inside Yalinga's vagina?" Yendi asked innocently.

"Since these particles are so elusive, who knows?" Lumumba replied. "But is it just a coincidence that scientists are searching for this elusive particle inside the deepest recesses of the planet, in places that mimic the interior of the pelvis such as caves, tunnels and mine shafts? And isn't it a funny choice of words, this dark matter? Is there anything darker than the realm of sexuality? Could dark matter be made of something so strange that it hasn't yet been theorized? Something so elusive it may never be detected? Does that not answer the description of orgasm? Has anyone yet dared to detect its interacting particles? Without dark matter, they say, the universe does not make sense. But if the universe is orgasmic in nature, and everything from nebulas to gamma rays are energized by the orgasmic burst of particles, then why not choose this unseen material as a starting point to explain the nature of all living organisms?"

"Did you ever express this theory at Yale?" asked Herbert

"Yes, it's one of the reasons I had to leave early."

"I would have thought they would be more open minded."

"At the central nerve of the incest taboo? My dear professor, how naïve can you be? Your school might appear to be progressive, but try to get peer review on a taboo and you'll be kicked out on your ass."

(He was not telling the truth, as we were to learn later.)

During Lumumba's discussion Albert had started puckering his lips and making sounds to annoy the professor. But instead of getting angry, Lumumba took on a thoughtful expression.

"Perhaps," he said, "orgasm is nothing but the refraction of sound waves within the particles. For if sound travels faster in warm air than cold, and is then refracted to the ground, perhaps a heated particle might make its own sound waves, and the refraction thereof cause the sensation of orgasm."

"The second law of thermodynamics seems a better choice," said Herbert. "It's the latest rage, you know, for explaining all sorts of things from Immanuel Kant to the Ming dynasty."

"So I've heard," said Lumumba. "But the idea of sound intrigues me. Instead of using frequencies emitted by hydrogen to search for radio signals from outer space, why not use them to search for signals inside the body? The human body is 60 percent water, and almost all space not occupied by atoms is filled with water. Surely there's a formula for orgasm just waiting for the right person to discover."

"Yes, if he's willing to be hauled off to jail for indecent exposure," I said quickly. I didn't like the look in Herbert's eyes. It reminded me too much of Project Mark.

"But it might be worth it," said Lumumba, "just to get the lowdown on what the different forces inside a water molecule do during orgasm. Who knows what happens when an intra-molecular force meets up with an intermolecular one. Or when clouds of negatively charged atoms meet with positive ones. Or water-loving (hydrophilic) polar molecules meet with water-fearing (hydrophobic) non-polar molecules. Is orgasm the result of this clash of forces? Does gravity play on the interaction of these forces? Since water is the source of life, surely its role in the release of orgasmic forces is incalculable.

"What I don't know is whether the system absorbs heat or releases heat. In principle it should be possible to model the changes produced in the body during orgasm. Scientists have created computer models that simulate the interaction of protein molecules with water over a particular arc of time. The essence of the problem is the dynamic interaction between hydrophobic reactions and hydrophilic reactions. Now if orgasm really does permeate the molecular substructure of the universe, it should be possible to detect changes in these molecular interactions during orgasm. All you have to do is tinker with the input variables and buy enough time on the supercomputer. A couple of days on a teraflop machine and the answer ought to print out as clear as day."

"And after that," said Herbert enthusiastically, "it's the Nobel Prize."

"Why not? And think about this too," said Lumumba. "A sea turtle can find its way back to the beach where it was born by identifying the magnetic inclination angle of its nesting site—that is, the angle between the earth's magnetic field and the earth's surface. Not only that, it can distinguish between different magnetic inclination angles and different field intensities found along its migratory route

"Now since there are concentrations of magnetic material in the human body, with the heart tissue having the highest concentration, who is to say that some similar phenomena might not be taking place during orgasm? Who is to say that the angle between the earth's magnetic field and the earth's surface does not play a role in the phenomena of orgasm, particularly when you take into account the 90-degree angle of the upright spine? If birds are guided by this geomagnetic field, it must be a very powerful field indeed."

"I agree with you," said Herbert. "Your old friend Dr. Xeno was actually studying the presence of magnetic material in human brain tissue at the time of his death. A colleague of mine told me just recently about a paper Xeno was writing on the interaction of magnetic fields with the human central nervous system."

"I know all about that paper," said Lumumba.

He turned around and pointed to a large incision at the base of his skull.

"You're lucky to be alive," said Herbert.

"Yes, Xeno's death was quite fortuitous. What was it? An unhappy grad student? Anyway, during the turmoil I managed to escape."

"Rather a pity," I said. "We still don't know if there's a connection between brain tumors and microwave ovens."

"Don't forget cell phones," Herbert added.

Once again Lumumba showed his gleaming canines. But a moment later he regained control and said:

"A more critical connection, and one that would certainly do your species a lot more good, is between magnetism, gravity and orgasm.

"For instance, studies of the human hippocampus have revealed crystalline particles of magnetite. The question is, what goes on within the crystals? It is so easy to forget that the brain is the biggest sex organ in the human body.

"On the other hand even bacteria produce magnetite. Might they have an inclination angle too? And what little jollies might they experience, if they do!"

We had come to the edge of the forest. The gently rolling plains in the distance were dotted with circular huts which Lumumba called bomas.

Nedele gazed off toward a small herd of cattle.

65

"Uncle says that the tribesmen like to drink their blood," she said. Her face twisted with pain.

"You love all the animals, don't you?" I asked.

"It's more a case of knowing how helpless they are and terrified when people come to hurt them."

"Like now?" said Tchibanga suddenly landing between us. "Come on, Nedele, let's have a bit of fun. You're always so serious."

Nedele's eyes grew wide and she moved close to me. "I can't," she replied. "Mrs. Hickey and I are talking."

"Screw Mrs. Hickey." He pulled her into the forest.

Damn that Project Mark, I thought as I listened to Nedele's terrified screams. I wondered what pious ideas Albert had put in her head. The ancient and brutal laws in Leviticus I knew to be part of it, and that could make anybody feel guilty. But Albert didn't seem to care, and that he'd put her life in real danger seemed to mean nothing; his sanctimonious agenda apparently absolved him of all guilt in the world he now lived in.

Within minutes of leaving the forest, we stumbled upon a herd of scrawny cattle tended by a young boy wearing shorts and a T-shirt. A dozen copper bracelets dangled from his arm. When he saw us he dropped his shepherd's stick and took off at a run. But a moment later Kribi caught up with him, dragged him back and broke his neck.

"That is hardly the correct behavior for the protégé of a Yale professor," said Herbert after recovering from the shock. "The poor boy did nothing to deserve this."

"It's the new rules of the game," Lumumba replied. "You kill us, we kill you. Besides he would have set off the alarm and spoiled our trip to the museum."

"Are you planning to kill everyone who sees us?"

"My dear Professor, let's just call it a little population control. Now move."

Despite his bravado Lumumba made it a point to avoid any more contact with bomas and humans. But the new resolution wasn't easy to accomplish, and by the end of the day another young boy had bitten the dust.

That night we camped near a village. When it was dark Lumumba sent Kribi and Yendi down to steal food. They came back with sacks of bananas and biscuits.

Herbert was clearly annoyed.

"Kathryn and I can't live on this stuff!" he said.

"My, aren't *we* picky," said Yendi.

"If you can kill the boy you can kill a cow."

"Why are people so obsessed with eating meat?" asked Doba.

"We're not obsessed," I said. "We need the protein."

"Not necessarily," replied Lumumba. "The first hominid, Australopithecus, ate plants because that was his inheritance. But later on the particles of orgasm accelerated beyond what his brain could withstand and he went crazy and began eating his own species. That is your inheritance, my dear Dr. Hickey. Look at it and learn. Only a few thousand years ago the Anasazi Indians were making soup out of each other. And of course there are still cannibals around today."

"You have to be pretty hungry to eat your own species," Bata said.

"It has more to do with the laws of physics than with hunger," Lumumba replied. "When men first stood upright, they were so tormented by their unmanageable sexual drives that they went into an orgy of killing and cannibalism. Before language could evolve and the concept of relationships, brothers killed brothers, sons killed fathers and fathers killed sons. Male rivalry was out of control. The spinal column was accelerating electrons between pelvis and brain with too much momentum. You might say it was the first subatomic particle accelerator on the planet. The question is, was the increase in brain size merely a product of this acceleration? Or was it due to the ensuing carnage? To my thinking, learning to make weapons was the watershed event. The brain's growth really took off at that point. That is the secret legacy of your species. Big brains are just an unintended consequence of this primitive arms race."

"Dr. Lumumba," said Herbert, "while your desire to minimalize us is understandable, I have to protest. Our cerebral cortex is a brilliant achievement that could certainly not be rooted in the diabolical scenario you have painted. It arose from the entire complex of adaptive responses such as language, tool-making, cultural transmission of experience, and much, much more."

"My dear Dr. Hickey," Lumumba said. "You needn't be so pained by the thought that your ancestors evolved from a universal orgasmic orgy. As for your 'complex of adaptive responses', they were all part of the second phase of the brain's growth, which came from the need to deal with the universal chaos. To stop the intra-species slaughter, early humans had to control the gonads. This essentially is the explanation for the evolution of the cerebral cortex. The second brain expanded into the third in order to accommodate language, religion and eventually civilization itself, all of which evolved as mechanisms to repress the gonads and end the eating of human flesh. Where do you suppose your taste for meat comes from anyway?"

67

"Probably from the same place as yours," I replied.

"Yes, we have our psychic needs too, and eating a colobus monkey has much less to do with supplementing our diet with protein as with a dire need to control our testosterone: every now and then we need to tear something apart and devour it. This helps to keep the peace. Better a colobus monkey or a baby bush pig than one of our own. Fortunately for us, the testosterone never got out of hand like it did with you humans. Our spines still slope, and our experience with live shock waves, which you call orgasm, never got the better of us. If it had, we would be driving cars and sending rockets into space, just like you. Indeed, any animal with the same vertical spinal column would have evolved into a human-type being. Any species that went through the same chaotic experience of being bombarded by electrons at 90-degree angles would have become exactly as you have become. If horses and pigs had learned to walk upright, horses would be sitting pompously in judges' chambers and pigs would be solving the mysteries of quantum mechanics."

Old Kumasi stopped frequently to rest. Sitting stiffly on an old tree trunk or leaning against his walking stick, he signed to us several times that the only real thing about life was death, probably to make us feel better about the boy. Yalinga and Yendi loped along with Okovango while Nedele divided her time between us and Kumasi.

Albert walked with Bata and Doba. I could see that he was talking once again about the "insect taboo." His two companions remained unconvinced.

"Your uncle says that the insect taboo is a figment of the imagination," Bata said. "He says it's an imaginary line, nothing more than a circle drawn in the dust."

"Uncle will burn in Hell for his thoughts," Albert replied. "I hope I can save his soul before it's too late."

"If it's not an imaginary circle, then what is it?" asked Doba.

"The insect taboo is the word of God," Albert replied. His eyes burned like a fierce prophet of the Old Testament. "And the Word of God is everywhere."

"Is it here now?" asked Doba.

"I'm afraid not," said Albert. He turned around and looked at Yalinga and Yendi who was pumping her furiously from behind.

"They have let Satan into their hearts," said Albert, "and the Evil One has poisoned their thoughts against Him."

"Do you mean to say that God doesn't want us to have fun?" Bata asked.

"Do you think it will be fun to burn for all eternity in the sulfurous pits of Hell?" said Albert. "Those few moments of dirty pleasure will cost them an eternity of torment."

Doba looked distressed. "Perhaps there is another God—perhaps a chimpanzee—who will let us have some fun once in awhile."

"There is only one God," said Albert. "And one of His most important commandments is not to worship other gods."

"How can we worship other gods if there are no other gods?" asked Doba.

"There are false gods," said Albert, "created by men as a way to avoid serving the real God. The false gods are gods of orgy and depravity. They are nothing more than personifications of our own sinful lusts and desires—desires that God commands us to control."

"Why would God order us not to have sex and then make having sex so much fun?" Bata asked. "It sounds like we get tormented anyway, even if we obey."

"But if we do obey we become righteous in the Lord's eyes, and in His mercy He will allow us into the kingdom of heaven where we'll experience everlasting bliss."

"You mean we get to have sex forever after we're dead as a reward for not having sex while we're alive?" asked Bata.

"You are very confused," said Albert.

There was a short silence and Doba said:

"Albert, can I pull on your penis? All this talk about God has made me horny."

Albert's eyes opened wide, a look of recognition passed over him. "So you are the anti-Christ!" he said. "They warned me he would eventually raise his ugly head." And with that he ran off ahead.

Chapter Five

Lumumba Decodes the Word of God

Again we stopped for the night near a village, and again Lumumba sent the apes down to steal food. While we waited with the others they began to plague Lumumba with a single question—when would they be able to sleep in the trees again. Lumumba was patient but firm.

"We have to make the best of it," he said. Once Albert saw the museum the apes would make a hasty retreat back to Mahale.

"Don't forget I'm making a sacrifice too," he told them.

"Why are you going to Spain?" Bata asked.

"I have an old score to settle," Lumumba replied.

"Somebody done you wrong?" said Herbert lightly.

"That's putting it mildly," Lumumba replied baring his teeth for emphasis.

Perhaps it wasn't the best timing, but our clothes were torn and dirty, and we needed new ones. Hebert brought up the subject.

"Clothes cost money," said Lumumba. "Did you bring any?"

Herbert pulled out a few soiled dollars. Lumumba glared.

"What do you think this is, a third-world country? That wouldn't buy you a G-string even on the black market!"

Just then a bird alighted on a bush nearby and said: "sar a roc, sar a roc!" There was still enough light to see how remarkable he was, the top was the color of cinnamon, his wings were dark blue, his tail a greenish-blue tipped with violet, and his underparts all lilac.

"Sar a roc, sar a roc," he said again through his yellow beak. A longing to possess him came over me.

"I've never seen a bird that beautiful," I said. "I wish I could take him home."

"Behold," Lumumba sneered, "the impossible object of desire!"

"You've read Lacan?" Herbert asked, with a start.

"A waste of time. He never gets to the bottom of things although his grasp of the human condition is not bad, especially his insights into the nature of desire as the object men long for, the object they think would make them complete, that would heal the tear at the core of their being. But of course, they can never have it because once they grab it, it turns into something else—a string of illusions that haunt them throughout their lives."

"Perhaps the cause can never be identified," said Herbert, "although Freud seemed to think that it could."

"But for Freud, desire was rooted in the maternal object. Break that down into its pure physical essence, into the quantum forces which create the material world, and it becomes less the elusive object which men run after than the elusive energy within the object. Perhaps what men really want is to reunite with the electrons that make up the universe, the stardust from which men were created."

"I suppose animals are above all this," I said. Herbert's palaver was beginning to annoy me.

"Since we are always connected to the orgasmic essence of our electrons," Lumumba replied, "we needn't go looking for substitutes. For us orgasm occurs at tolerable levels of intensity, so we have no need to repress it. We maintain a simple natural link, unlike the tortured love/hate relationship men experience—the result of bipedalism and the biological consequences of the straightening of the spine."

"Surely we experience this link at *some* level," said Herbert.

"Language has obliterated it," Lumumba replied. "The word desire comes from '*de*' meaning 'away' and '*situs*' meaning 'star'. By defining the emotion of desire as a distant star, you are saying that the object of that emotion—the parent, the electrons, the universe—is unattainable."

"Can this be proved?" Bata asked.

"Men demonstrate it every day by all the love songs they write in which a heart has been broken, or the poems or stories in which a man or woman pines away for love. A man's heart doesn't break just because a woman won't spread her legs for him. It breaks because the woman he really wants, his mother, sister or daughter, is totally beyond reach—a faraway star. That this yearning is universal can be seen in the amount of time and material men have dedicated to the subject—millions of reams,

I would say—in all the different lands. An Arab theologian from the 14th century put it succinctly:

> The man who dreams of cohabiting with women that to have sexual intercourse with is forbidden by religion, as for instance his mother or sister, must consider this as a presage that he will go to sacred places and, perhaps, even journey to the holy house of God and look there upon the grave of the Prophet."

"Why, that sounds like something Soddhu would say," I remarked.

Herbert looked at me curiously, but Albert was angry.

"Dr. Págalu would never harbor such sentiments. I only wish my sister and I had known about the insect taboo a long time ago."

They looked at each other, then covered their eyes and loped away.

Lumumba watched unhappily.

"They were quite a pair, those two, in the days before the poachers got him. They were hardly ever apart, and I'm not speaking figuratively either. Teaching him Christianity was the worst thing that could have happened; he's been thrust into a symbolic network that is not his own, but he's tried to make sense of it as if it were. Now his guilt feelings are so firmly entrenched that I don't know if we can ever extirpate them. But I promised Oyem I would try."

"I don't think it's entirely my fault," said Herbert. "When male chimps reach a certain age, are they not booted out of the troop? Is this not a rudimentary form of the incest taboo?"

"Your field studies," Lumumba replied, "are colored by your own subjectivity on the matter. Oh yes, we may send some of our males out when they reach a certain age, but it has nothing to do with fucking their mothers. It's simply our way of ensuring a grasp on our own dominance. As for our males sleeping with their daughters—it happens all the time. So you see, we don't need an incest taboo to keep from killing each other—like you humans do. Nor do we need laws whose very semantics are steeped in hatred, anger, shame and violence. Breaking the taboo is tantamount to death."

"Why is that?" asked Bata.

"It's partly semantics and partly myth," Lumumba replied. "The word 'taboo' means 'sacred' and the word 'incest' comes from the Greek word 'cestum', which means girdle or veil. Venus, the goddess of love, girdled her waist with a magic veil which, when seen by the eyes of men, caused them to fall madly in love with her. When the institution of marriage arose, Venus's girdle became a symbol of man's desire for his wife. The

72

man could loosen the girdle—or *cestus*—to allow himself in, but if any other person—especially another member of the family—did, it became *in-cestus*—a violation of the law. In the final analysis, the story is simply a transmutation of the Oedipal situation. The boy sees his mother's *cestus*— he is bewitched with desire for her. But the very same girdle forbids the consummation of this desire—because it belongs to the father who alone can loosen the magic strings."

"I think those strings are a good idea," said Herbert.

"But if you humans weren't so drawn to that delta," said Lumumba, "it wouldn't have to be forbidden. The 'instinctive' horror that men feel at the idea of having sex with their mothers is not instinctive at all. It's the result of the incest taboo being drummed into their heads from the moment they're born so that it seems to be natural. The girdle, the magic, all that is nonsense. But it says a lot about your civilization."

"And their spine," said Bata. "Don't forget their spine."

The next afternoon brought us within sight of a town called Sitwa. The chimps sniffed suspiciously at the new terrain, turning over stones and testing the branches on the spiny trees that dotted the plain. They gathered what branches they could to make nests for the night, all except Albert who found a place to sit and contemplate his Bible. When it was dark Kribi, Yendi and Tchibanga took off for the village in a zeal of exaggerated puffing and posturing.

"Remember to stay out of sight," Lumumba admonished. "The villagers would like nothing better than to bag a little bush meat. And watch where you're walking, there's a black mamba about, I saw it a few minutes ago."

Albert got up quickly and hurried over. "The only good snake is a dead snake," he said taking a seat next to Lumumba. "Look what it did to Adam and Eve."

"What was that?" Doba asked.

"Adam and Eve were two people who lived in a beautiful garden full of figs and papayas and mangoes and everything. They could eat as much as they wanted except from the tree which God told them they couldn't have. Then this snake came along. He was very big—666 feet long—and he had huge fangs that were full of semen."

"Yuk!" said Nedele. "What did he do?"

"The dirty bastard told Eve to eat from the forbidden tree. As soon as she did God threw her and Adam out of the Garden and they've been wandering ever since."

"My dear nephew," said Lumumba, "all ancient people in all parts of the world have a story—a myth—that describes how the first humans came to be. Though the stories are often different what they all have in common is their metaphorical implication—the insidious, ubiquitous warning that a son is not to bed down with his mother. The tree (the perfect symbol for the phallus) with its forbidden fruit, symbolizes the nature of the forbidden union between brother and sister (also father and daughter, mother and son). The serpent represents the male principle that finds these unions irresistible."

"It sounds like the snake got a bum rap," Bata said.

"He did," said Lumumba, "and it's based on the universal human incest. Sure, there are some dangerous snakes in the world, but the majority of them aren't. Yet they are all sought out and killed by humans, who unconsciously identify snakes with the procreative process. And because there's so much confusion and fear surrounding procreation (as a result of the incest taboo), the poor snake has become a scapegoat. As dreadful as some snakes are, human sexual desires are even more dreadful."

"The truth is a tree and the tree is a phallus," said Kumasi, nodding his old gray head and lifting a hand gnarled with age.

Herbert looked thoughtfully at Kumasi, then turned to Lumumba. "I agree there's a sexual component to the story," he said. "But Adam and Eve's real sin was in disobeying God, not in having sex."

"But they didn't *have* sex until they ate from the tree, you blithering idiot!"

It was Bata who spoke, and his vehemence not only took one and all by surprise, but ended the conversation, at least for the time being.

My hope that the three scavengers would be captured was dashed when a short time later they emerged from the shadows. Each one carried a large sack.

"I smell figs," said Doba hardly able to contain himself.

"Figs, bananas, papayas, oranges, chocolate—you name it, we've got it," said Yendi as he emptied the contents. The second sack contained bread, biscuits, flour, cornmeal, cookies, a blackened cooking pot, matches, utensils and bottled water. The chimps hugged each other as they rummaged through everything.

"What's in the third sack, Professor?" asked Herbert.

"Clothes," came the terse answer.

"That's very kind of you, but I don't think Kathryn and I will need that many."

"Who says they're for you, dumb boy?" said Kribi

Lumumba set Tchibanga and Kribi to work digging a hole in the ground and lining it with stones. When it was finished Yendi threw in some broken branches and grass, and Lumumba struck a match; soon a roaring fire was going.

"Aren't you afraid someone will see it?" asked Herbert.

"It will be to their great misfortune if they do," Lumumba replied.

As the fire burned down, he poured water into the pot and set it to boil.

"How did you ever learn to make an earthen cooking oven?" asked Herbert

"An old boy scout from Yale once took me to the Adirondacks," said Lumumba. "Besides other things, he taught me this and how to tie a boatswain's knot."

"Good lord," said Herbert. "Next you'll be teaching my wife how to make an apple pie."

"It's all in the temperature of the shortening," Lumumba replied. "You have to refrigerate it first."

"It's easier to buy one," I said. That's what we had done the night I spent with Soddhu. How delicious it had tasted after our lovemaking! I smiled as I remembered how Soddhu, reaching his climax had yelled "Ahura Mazda!" As I stared at the flames I wondered if he were still thinking of me.

"A steak would sure taste good tonight," said Herbert watching the crackling fire.

"I assure you, Dr. Hickey, you'll like very much what I'm making. It's called *ugali* and it will give you all the strength you need. Besides, meat eating has made you soft."

"That's not true," said Herbert. "Meat has made us strong and powerful. How do you think humans evolved so quickly from the Stone Age to the information age? Meat provided the extra energy to devote to intellectual pursuits. After man started eating meat, he didn't need to spend all his time foraging for food. He had the leisure to devote himself to inventing better and more efficient ways to get food."

"I could point out," said Lumumba, "that it was the development of agriculture—not hunting—that marked the transition from the Paleolithic to the Neolithic. But that's not really the point. I'm talking about man's physical powers. The first bipedal children were very different from the weakling children of today's bipeds. They grew up fast and they grew up strong. The primal father was no match for his sons. And there were no laws to restrain them—because there was no language. The penis wasn't yet transformed into a god with the terrible power of the incest taboo. At that time, no son had any qualms about killing his father and making off with his women. The primal 'edible complex'—if I can call it that—revolved around the father. He was the one to be killed and eaten. That's when your bodies began to crave meat—not anything that Mother Nature wanted you to do. Otherwise you'd have the short intestines of a carnivore, not the long ones of a herbivore so necessary in processing a diet of fibrous plants."

"That might be so," said Herbert, "and God knows there's somebody's father I would love to rip into. But the plains must have been full of game in those days. How do you know that our meat-eating didn't start simply because of that?"

"There you go again—to quote a famous American," said Lumumba. "You're assuming that the reason people ate meat was because they were hungry. But what if that wasn't the case? What if men started eating each other because their gonads were driving them crazy? Killing each other was a way to alleviate that unbearable pressure. And it was also a way to get more women. The only trouble was, it didn't work. The more they fucked and killed, the more frenzied they became."

"Then why didn't we wipe ourselves out?"

"Because somebody thought up religion. Somebody decided to make the pelvis holy. The greatest idea ever conceived by the human brain was that a magic power exists inside the pelvis, and eventually that power became God. Albert, give me your Bible."

The flames made strange shadows as Lumumba held the book up by the fire. "In Chapter 17 of Genesis, verse 9, God says to Abraham:

As for you, you shall keep my covenant, you and your descendants after you throughout their generations. This is my covenant, which you shall keep, between me and you and your descendants after you: Every male among you shall be circumcised. You shall be circumcised in the flesh of your foreskins, and it shall be a sign of the covenant between me and you. He that is eight days old among you shall be circumcised; every male throughout your generations, whether born in your house, or bought with your money from any foreigner who is not of your offspring, both he that is born in your house and he that is bought with your money, shall be circumcised. So shall my covenant be in your flesh an everlasting covenant. Any uncircumcised male who is not circumcised in the flesh of his foreskin shall be cut off from his people; he has broken my covenant.

"There it is in a nutshell, men notching their penises and waving them in the air like white flags of surrender. The covenant between God and Abraham is a sexual covenant. And if you believe that the Jewish religion is rooted in this covenant then you must infer that the Jewish religion is a sexual affair. But then, what religion isn't?"

"Christianity!" said Albert. "Everyone knows it's a religion of the spirit not of the flesh.

"Is there anything spiritual about breathing? Of course not, breathing is as much a part of the flesh as anything. But that's where the word 'spirit' comes from—to breathe, and since you need to be alive to breathe somebody had to be fucked—in this case, Albert, your mother.

"But who understands this? Who understands that the Bible (and all the scriptures) is nothing more than a pornographic handbook obsessed with covering up explicit material? Who understands that the Word of God is an encryption for the penis? It's all in code, you see, and until you break the code you have no idea what you are dealing with."

"How dare you denigrate the Word of God!" said Albert seething.

"Don't blame me, blame the Egyptians, they started the whole thing, they had the idea long before the Christians, to sanctify the Word (how else are you going to get people to believe such a thing as a law?) by making it synonymous with the phallus of Osirus, their major god. Afterall, it was the penis that did all the talking, the penis that ruled the lives of those crazy hominids. So why shouldn't it be identified with words once they came into being?

"And speaking of words, if rubbing and grinding doesn't sound like a sex act to you—and that's what *chrism*, hence Christian, originally meant—then I'll be a monkey's uncle, ha, ha! God creates the heavens and the earth through the power of the Word. He doesn't need a woman. Religion is a male thing. It doesn't matter which doctrine it is."

Albert looked nervous. "These blasphemies," he said, "will get us all thrown into the pits of Hell. God's word is God's word—not a dirty thing like a penis."

"What's dirty about a penis?" Yalinga asked.

"What isn't!" Albert replied. He lumbered off into the darkness holding his Bible close to his chest.

By now the *ugali* was ready. Throwing sand and rocks on the fire Lumumba snuffed it out and disappeared, leaving us to eat by ourselves.

For a few moments the darkness was so complete that if it hadn't been for the stars overhead I would have thought we were in a tomb. The thick mush was good—Lumumba had seasoned it with ground peanuts—

and after topping the meal off with other delicacies we felt happy and content.

My thoughts drifted back to yesterday's conversation and Lumumba's crazy notion that only a flimsy piece of cloth keeps one man away from another man's woman. I thought of Soddhu's Kusti, and it kept me awake half the night.

Chapter Six

From Big Macs to God—A Logical Transition

The smell of coffee woke me up. Lumumba was sitting next to the fire with a tin coffee pot set on two stones.

"A Yale graduate knows how to do everything," he said handing me a steaming cup.

"The only thing missing is a newspaper," said Herbert. Like the magician and the rabbit Lumumba pulled a paper from one of the sacks.

"The *Arusha Times*," he said, tossing it over. The headlines screamed in big letters:

"WAMBUSSI GANG STRIKES AGAIN!"

"Who are they?" Herbert asked.

"Just another gang of angry humans running around killing each other because they can't fuck their mothers," said Lumumba. "They looted some shops at Mpanda the other day and shot several people including two policemen."

Kribi, who was looking over Herbert's shoulder, suddenly gawked.

"Jesus Christ!" he said his eyes so wide you could see the whites. "Look at the size of that penis! It's as big as a tree!"

"The truth is a tree," said Kumasi, shuffling over to look, "and the tree is a phallus."

"Some of us aren't used to the daguerreotype processes in which reality is captured by a lens," said Lumumba taking a look. It was the picture of a Russian tank, taken outside Grozny. A man was standing halfway out the hatch. The long barrel of the cannon gun projected in such a way that it appeared to be an extension of his body at the groin.

"The man looks happy," said Herbert.

"I'd be happy too if I had a penis that size," said Yendi.

"Weapons of war are merely extensions of the penis," said Lumumba. "And at a subconscious level this man truly believes the turret *is* his penis."

"I don't need a turret," said Kribi. With a sudden move he took Yalinga from behind. Nedele and Albert looked away while the rest of us watched attentively. Lumumba himself continued to read.

"Looks like we've made the six o'clock news," he said a moment later. The headlines read: "Yale Primatologist and Wife Still Missing."

The whereabouts of American Primatologist Herbert Hickey and his wife Kathryn Hickey remain a mystery. The couple disappeared from the Mahale Wildlife Research Center in Eastern Tanzania on June 22 under suspicious circumstances. Compounding the mystery is the disappearance of a number of chimpanzees. According to Constable Mwabiki, the regional police officer in charge of the case, the couple was last seen in their company.

A suspect in the case, Bangassu Jamu, who assists at the Center has been taken into custody for questioning at the regional jail in Kigoma.

According to Robert Goldschmidt, spokesperson for the American Embassy in Nairobi, Mr. Jamu is suspected of having terrorist ties to rebel forces trying to oust the UNITA party in Angola.

While there is speculation that the Hickeys have been taken hostage, the American Embassy is conducting its own inquiry and there are unconfirmed reports from Dar Es Salam that FBI investigators have arrived.

An unconfirmed report that two foreigners were seen near the Lubalisi River traveling with several individuals of a suspicious nature has led to speculation that the Wambussi Gang is involved.

Police have asked anyone with information to contact Constable Mwabiki at the Kigoma police station.

"I can't believe they're sending the cavalry after us," said Herbert. "I had no idea we were so important."

"Wake up and smell the coffee," said Lumumba. "It's Albert they're after, don't ask me why."

"You'd think they'd be happy to be rid of him," said Kribi.

"I hope Bangassu gets out of jail," I said.

"My dear Mrs. Hickey," said Lumumba, "if your species weren't so suspicious and paranoid, if it weren't for the repression imposed by the laws required to enforce the incest taboo, Mr. Jamu wouldn't be in jail in the first place."

He explained himself by saying that our taboos were behind everything that transpired in human life. It was the incest taboo that made us human with all our foibles, it was the incest taboo that had turned his brother's son into an incandescent idiot. Did we know, by way that the word 'cretin' evolved from the French word for Christian? The truth always leaked out if you looked at human language long enough.

"But my wife is right," said Herbert. "While this journey is the opportunity of a lifetime for a man of science, it would be morally wrong to experience it at the expense of others such as our friend Bangassu."

"My dear Dr. Hickey," Lumumba replied. "The concept of morality boils down to two things only. First, not killing your father and, second, not having sex with your mother. All else is fluff."

"That's right," said Bata. "If you ever took the time to observe us you'd come to understand that kindness and goodness are the essence of the animal kingdom. It is cruel to impose morality on evolution. We don't need laws to be kind to each other. Uncle is right, morality is a trumped up idea. It exists only in your crazy imaginations."

That couldn't be true! My guilt feelings about Soddhu were hardly imagined!

"When do we get our clothes?" Herbert asked.

"That will depend if there's anything left over."

Kribi was right, the clothes were for the chimps, not us.

Under Lumumba's direction they began to get dressed. A ruckus ensued and there was hooting and hollering, chest beating and shrieking. But at last the task was accomplished. Yalinga whirled toward us in a white tee shirt and sweater, and a yellow and black kanga. Nedele was also wrapped in a kanga. It was tan with a brown pattern that reminded me of the spots on a giraffe. On top she wore a bright pink tee shirt and a green sweater.

Lumumba and the other males had put on black trousers and colorful shirts, all with long sleeves. To Albert's delight, his own shirt was entirely black and had a strong resemblance to a priest's attire.

The chimps pushed their oversized feet into shoes and whimpered loudly. "What if we need to grab onto something with our feet?" Yendi said fretfully.

"There will be no displays of prehensile toes," Lumumba replied. "You will have to act like men and walk like men—shoes on and refraining from sex in public."

"It sounds like we're already in Albert's hell," Bata signed. Nedele and Yalinga tried to comfort Okovango, who was howling inconsolably. A pair of old Nikes covered his little feet. As I looked at the group I knew for sure that Lumumba had bamboozled us about being at Yale. There was no way on earth he could have passed himself off as human, not at Yale or anywhere. All I saw parading infront of me was a sorry group of chimps dressed for the circus. As if he could read my mind Lumumba said:

"We're not finished."

Out came the sacks of flour, Lumumba made them into a paste and applied it everywhere to their bodies. It was hard to believe, but a transformation of sorts was taking place. But would it be enough?

"Stand up straight," said Lumumba. "Hep two three four!"

"We shall easily pass ourselves off as American tourists," said Doba, nodding approvingly.

We broke camp and headed cross-country. The dust was thick and the sun was hot. Occasionally we came upon a group of giraffes and zebras, but they shied off as soon as they saw us.

The apes were having an awful time. They pulled at their clothes and begged Lumumba to let them take off their shoes. He refused. "If men can act like men, you can act like them too."

"The truth is a tree and the tree is a phallus," said Kumasi, "but not when it's old and gnarled like I am." Walking with his stick, bent forward, he resembled every old man I had ever seen. I was sure he would be the first casualty, but about mid-afternoon Kribi sat down and announced firmly. "I'd rather be killed in a shootout with the police then get ripped to death by these shoes."

Lumumba raised his hand for silence.

"Someone is coming," he said.

In the distance I heard the bleating of goats and the jingling of bells. As it grew closer, I could hear the sound of boisterous laughter. Two men were coming toward us with a small herd of goats. They were dressed in shorts and T-shirts. They wore sandals and the soft red dirt had powdered their feet the same color.

"Keep walking," said Lumumba, "and act normal."

"*Jambo!*" said the taller of the two men. His white teeth glistened in a friendly smile. To our utter amazement Lumumba spoke back.

"*Jambo sana,*" he said. "*Mbuzi nzuri sana!*" Very nice goats!

"*Ahsante, ahsante!*" Thank you, thank you. The man looked at our clothes and continued in English: "Are you in need of assistance? We rarely have visitors here."

"*Motokaa yangu imeharibika,*" said Lumumba. "Our car has broken down. *Kuna gareji karibu?* Where is the nearest garage?"

"That way, bwana," said the shorter man pointing toward the bush. "You walk three days, you find garage. Maybe bwana like to use telephone?" He pulled out a cell phone.

Lumumba shook his head. "*Sina haraka,*" he replied. "We are not in a hurry."

"You see?" said the second man to the first. "I told you they were not Americans!"

"Africa is very beautiful," said the shorter man. "Unless you're being eaten by a lion or bitten by a snake."

"Or hacked up with a machete," said his friend.

"Thank you," Lumumba said.

"*Karibu,*" the men answered. They nodded to the rest of us and trudged on.

"Well, I'll be!" said Herbert. "The only strange looks came from the goats!"

A thought began to gnaw at me that it was true, what Lumumba had said about Yale.

"They have eyes and they seeth not," said Albert sadly as he looked after the disappearing herdsmen.

"You sound like you want to be captured, little cousin," said Yendi.

"I want to go home to the mountains," Albert replied. "My flock needs me."

"If you ask me," Yendi said, "your feet are hurting."

Albert shrugged. "Jesus suffered for my sins. Getting a few blisters on my feet is the least I can do to honor him. Many of the great Christian saints sought out pain as a way to get closer to God."

"Only crazy people seek out pain," Kribi said.

"Or people who are afraid of pleasure," said Lumumba. "Perhaps your Christian saints were simply afraid of their own sexuality. Now come on, everybody let's take care of business."

We came in sight of a rough dirt road. Women in bright kangas walked by gracefully carrying pots on their heads. A farmer passed us in a cart. Lumumba stared at the ox whose eyes were swarming with flies. The cart kicked up clouds of fine red dust and the high banks of the road trapped the heat. As we joined the foot traffic people looked at us curiously.

"Twelve tourists with a baby and no luggage walking down a road in the middle of a forgotten track in rural Africa," said Lumumba. "Why shouldn't they look?"

But his reassuring words were marred by his wary, preoccupied expression.

I turned around and saw Kumasi leaning wearily on his stick as he tried to keep up.

As the sun drew overhead the road became deserted and we stopped to rest. Only a thorny and dispirited greenish-yellow tree gave us shade. The chimps flopped down and kicked their feet miserably. Yendi and Tchibanga were ready to come to blows. Yalinga dropped Okovango to the ground so hard the little ape began to cry. Albert bowed his head by the bowl of the tree and prayed.

"Hippos be damned!" said Doba. "I won't go another step, I won't, I won't unless I can take off these instruments of torture."

"You won't have to," said Lumumba. "A matatu is coming, everyone take cover."

What happened next was like a Hollywood movie.

As a bright purple minibus came lurching through the potholes and kicking up an immense cloud of dust, Lumumba placed himself in the middle of the road. The driver leaned on his horn and stopped just inches away. Then without warning, Kribi, Yendi and Tchibanga sprang from their hiding place behind the embankment, pulled the driver from the bus and slammed him to the ground until every bone in his body was broken. There were screams and cries of "Wambussi!" as the passengers tried to flee only to be caught and brought down by the murderous apes.

When it was over the ground was strewn with the mangled bodies of passengers, perhaps twenty in all including men, women and children.

"That is hardly the behavior of a Yale professor," said Herbert. "You should be ashamed."

"My dear Dr. Hickey," said Lumumba. "Your people are turning us into bush meat this very minute and there's no law against it. But turn the tables and it's the end of the world. Now in my opinion that's what you humans would call a double standard. Kribi, Yendi, take the cash and dump the bodies over by the tree. Something will eat them and have a good meal."

"You're here until you're gone," said Kribi, putting a gnarled hand on Herbert's shoulder. "You're alive until you're dead."

Bata had the last word:

"If you remember what the Professor told us about the evolution of hominids, any animal with a straight spine could have come to rule the world instead of you. So why feel so superior? It's just an accident of evolution that you're ruling the planet instead of some other species. And to tell you the truth I'd feel kind of embarrassed to know that the reason I am the ruler is because I can't stand up to orgasm."

He went to help Kribi and Yendi rifle through the pockets of the passengers while Doba and Tchibanga scoured the bus for food. There was livestock on board—chickens, goats, pigs and a small white rabbit. Nedele led them out and released them, all except for the rabbit which she put inside her pocket.

Lumumba and Kribi stood beside the bodies.

"If only there were some way we could blame this on the Wambussi," said Kribi. "That would take the heat off us, wouldn't it, Uncle?"

"Why blame the Wambussi," Lumumba replied, "when we can blame somebody else, somebody much worse, somebody that will make everybody's blood crawl. . . ."

He dipped his finger in a pool of blood and began to write on one of the bodies. When he was finished he stepped back and looked at his handiwork. The letters GLA glistened in bright red colors.

"Instead of looking for a silly gang of marauders," he said, "or a group of bedraggled tourists they'll be looking for the GLA—the Gonad Liberation Army. How's that for inspiration? Okay, everybody, let's board the bus."

"I told you he was smart," said Yendi looking at the professor admiringly.

"Can I drive?" Doba asked.

"Let's give Dr. Hickey the first shift. He's had the most experience."

"You didn't drive in the States?" I asked.

"On occasion, but I preferred taking the trains. After you, Professor Hickey."

The bus shuddered and lurched forward, most of the apes fell from their seats.

"Another human torture machine?" Bata asked as he pulled himself off the floor.

"Oh shut up," said Yalinga. "It's better than walking."

"Couldn't we have hijacked the bus without killing everybody?" asked Albert.

"Yes," Kribi replied, "but it wouldn't have been nearly as much fun."

"You and Uncle are both psychopaths."

"Oh get off your high horse," said Lumumba. "When a soldier suffers from shell shock it's not because he can't deal with the horrors of war but because he can't deal with the immense satisfaction of killing. It's that simple."

"But those people on the bus were innocent civilians!"

"My dear Albert, there is no such thing as an innocent civilian—or innocent anything for that matter. Innocence refers to a make-believe state

85

in which sexual matters are unheard of. But from the moment of its own conception, every organism on the planet is aware of its sexual origins, and this includes humans as well. The stubborn belief that has been hammered into their heads that children are innocent is sadly indicative of the distorted reality created by the incest taboo. For the truth is that all children are full of sexual feelings—even in the womb. But by the time they are adults this truth has been totally obliterated by the insidious workings of the taboo."

"The truth is a tree and the tree is a phallus," old Kumasi waved happily

"Why does he keep saying that?" said Herbert looking in the rearview mirror. "Is he going senile?"

"Only humans become senile," Lumumba replied. "How else to revenge themselves on their fellow species and vent the misanthropic feelings innate in all of you?"

"Well he sounds senile to me," said Albert hostilely, "unless he's dreaming about Viagra.

"It's a metaphor, all right, but it goes way beyond the petty vagaries of Viagra. Study your semantics, my boy. The word truth is related to the word tree, as in 'firm and straight as a tree.' But the phallus too is firm and straight, which means that man's concept of truth is inextricably connected to his sexuality and the rules and laws that guide it. Inother words, there is no truth outside the Mother of all laws, the incest taboo."

Kumasi nodded in approval, then quickly fell asleep. As the road improved Herbert picked up speed. We passed many small shanties made of plywood or tin. Some were painted, some weren't. The better ones were made of brick. I had never seen so much sky. The skies out West looked puny in comparison. And the trees! What drink had the gods imbibed when they created those wild, tortured souls? Or these termite mounds as tall as a man! The plains stretched endlessly in all directions, and in all directions there were cars, villages and people.

"Look, Uncle, here's a radio," said Bata reaching into an overhead bin. Lumumba began to spin the dials. A BBC station crackled with static:

In the latest standoff between the Cuba and the United States, Cuban leader Fidel Castro has accused the United States of masterminding the murder of Cuban pianist Jorge Cortina. In a new twist to the bizarre case, an autopsy report suggests that Mr. Cortina was already dead at the time of the concert. According to many sources the artist was too dignified to appear as a monkey, and Mr. Castro now believes that the United States killed Mr. Cortina on purpose so they could impersonate him and embarrass the Cuban government. While this thinking seems

86

a bit strained, many people in the musical world agree that it is highly unlikely that the performer was, infact, Jorge Cortina. "It is not even his style," said Mr. Vreeland of the New York Times. "He has never used his rump in his entire life."

The Cuban leader is giving the United States twenty-four hours to confess to its latest imperialist crime before expelling all Americans from the country. A planned visit of the Ringling Bros. Barnum & Bailey Circus in Cuba next season has been put on hold.

Secretary of State Madeline Albright was unavailable for comment. However, an unidentified source in the State Department was quoted as saying that this timing was most unfortunate because the relation between the two countries had seemed to be warming.

As Lumumba switched off the radio a small yellow bird flew infront of the car. Herbert was going too fast to stop.

"Son-of-a-bitch!" Lumumba shouted.

We pulled over and Yendi ran back to retrieve the bird's small, broken body. He gave it to Lumumba.

"A yellow-fronted canary," said Lumumba cradling the bird in his hand. He gave Herbert an ugly look. "You can kill as many people as you like, but any more animals and I'll forget we're colleagues and wring your miserable neck."

"Maybe Kathryn should drive, she goes a lot slower."

"Don't blame it on cars," Lumumba snarled. "The ground was stained with our blood long before Henry Ford came along, and to tell the truth I'm rather sick of it."

"Is there anything we can do?" asked Bata.

"Nothing short of nuclear war." In his anger Lumumba flung the bird aside. Albert suddenly perked up.

"You are speaking of Armegeddon, Uncle? Ah, we Christians so look forward to that day, after the fires have passed and we are united for all eternity with the Son of God."

Lumumba shrugged helplessly as the apes looked at him with questioning eyes.

"What do you expect from a monkey who thinks his pelvis is holy?" he said wearily. "He's bought the whole nine yards and doesn't even know it."

"How do you make a pelvis holy?" Bata asked.

"By naming it the *os sacrum*—the sacred bone. The Latin word is '*sacrum*', a sacred place, a small chapel—is that not descriptive of your pelvis?"

"My wife's maybe," said Herbert.

"Hers, yours, every human's on the planet," Lumumba replied. "That's why religion is such an easy doctrine to swallow. It's all internal, built in you might say."

"God is not built in," said Albert. "God is up there in the firmament."

"It only seems that way," said Lumumba, "because orgasm is such an other-worldly experience. But once the bone which directs the flow of sexual energy became sacred it followed naturally that the power of orgasm also became sacred. And 'ecce Deus', behold the Holy Deity. The *Sancta Sanctorum* and the pelvis are one and the same thing."

"Sex is religion and religion is sex," said old Kumasi.

"You can't prove it," said Albert stubbornly.

"Sure I can. Just consider my earlier proposition about the geometry of the pelvis. It's that geometry which underlies the human construction of religion. Your ancestors made the pelvis holy after they became bipeds, after the spine became the first vector of true right angles."

"It almost sounds as if orgasm can be explained by an equation," Herbert said.

Lumumba cast a suspicious glance at Herbert, then said quickly:

"The problem is that no one has really worked out the consequences of that fact. Nobody realizes that everything from the lust for McDonalds hamburgers to the 'instinctual' aversion to incest are nothing but a vestige of ancient rituals that established the holiness of sex."

"That seems like quite a stretch," said Herbert. "Especially since the fossil evidence shows that Australopithecus was a vegetarian."

"It also shows," said Lumumba, "that at some point he became a murderous cannibal. Early hominids were basically nothing more than charged up batteries due to too much sexual energy. Read Raymond Dart. He found Australopithecus skulls that had been bashed in and pried open so that the brains could be eaten. Not just adult brains either, but the brains of young children."

"Child killers!" Yalinga yelped, looking at us and pulling Okovango protectively to her breast.

"Please, Dr. Lumumba, give us a break. You're making it all sound so sinister!"

"My dear fellow, are you beginning to catch on? Where do you think the word sinister comes from? It's the Latin word for left, and Dart shows that most of the blows were dealt during frontal confrontations by right-handed hominids—inother words, the fatal blows fell on the left side of the skull."

"Since neither of us were there to see it, there's no use arguing the point."

"I hope in your desire to minimize the horror of human origins you won't refuse to see how much residual has been left by those blows. Surely it's no coincidence that today, millions of years later, people still flee from the left as if it were the plague. Is it possible they have come to identify their sexuality by way of ideologies expressed in spatial terms? And that anything which does not strengthen the incest taboo is seen to come from the left, while things which do strengthen it come from the right?"

"Right is wrong and left is right," Kumasi signed with his gnarled fingers.

"What's *that's* supposed to mean?" asked Albert stiffly.

"It means that the ideas which come from the right are too repressive whereas those from the left are generally more in tune with nature," Lumumba replied.

"I'll remember that if I ever run for office," said Herbert lightly.

"You can sneer all you want," said Bata angrily. But if I were a human I'd sure be embarrassed to know where those big brains of mine came from."

"You're just jealous," said Albert.

"Jealous of brains that evolved in the gutter?"

"Man was created in God's image, not the gutter," Albert replied.

"But there's the irony," said Lumumba. "If God is orgasmic, they were created in the image of orgasm—the very 'filth' they're trying to repress."

The apes screeched with laughter and rolled about kicking their legs in the air. It was an amusing scene, and I appreciated it even though it was at our expense. But Albert was furious.

"You'd never get away with this stuff at Yale," he snarled.

"Who says I didn't?"

No sooner had Lumumba spoken these words than a change came over him, and without warning he turned on Albert.

"Listen you little schmuck! I'm not out here for my health. Now I want you to tell me, and tell it to me slowly what it is I said about the spine."

"I don't remember," said Albert folding his arms stubbornly across his chest.

"Will this help?" Kribi asked. He grabbed Albert by the neck and started choking him.

"This is no way to treat a servant of God!" Albert sputtered.

"You're right," said Kribi. "I'm being too gentle."

He began to squeeze harder, Albert struggled in vain, then signed to his uncle between gasps: "You said that when apes became bipedal—when they learned to walk on two legs instead of using their knuckles—the inclination of the spine changed and this change was a critical factor in their experience of orgasm. Now please unhand me, I must go and wash out my mouth!"

"Shut up and sit down," said Lumumba in a tizzy. "What is dirty about the natural transmission of nerve impulses in the spine? Especially if those nerve impulses are related to basic principles such as geometry? You see, dear nephew, the nervous system is basically an electrical apparatus. Everything we know about the world—or about ourselves—has to be translated into electrical impulses before we can become aware of it. And awareness itself is an electrical phenomenon. You might say that awareness is the sum of all the electrical phenomena in the brain and the nervous system at any one time."

"Most neuroscientists would agree with you," said Herbert.

"But what the neuroscientists don't see," Lumumba rejoined, "is that the nervous system is a configuration in space—it has a geometry. It's like the architecture of a computer chip—some are inherently much more efficient than others. In vertebrates, the central feature of neural architecture is the spine. Everything revolves around the spine and its relationship to the rest of the body. That's why your yoga specialists are so obsessed with straightening the spine. By experimentation they found that straightening the spine produced enormous rushes of electrical energy to the brain. Don't worry, Dr. Hickey, I'm not going esoteric on you, I'm not talking about yoga and *prana*. I'm talking about evolution. What the Yogas do when they meditate is simply to recreate a faint echo of what happened when hominids first stood upright—an event that changed the basic geometry of the system, producing a most extraordinary result. The new configuration made it possible to convey vast quantities of electrical energy from the pelvis to the brain."

The result, he went on, was devastating. Why? Because the most powerful and important force in the nervous system was orgasm. It represented the most primal form of awareness. The pleasure of orgasm linked us to the most basic forces in the universe: the ecstatic electrons, the quantum fluctuations of virtual particles hovering on the edge of the void seeking the energy to create themselves.

When humans straightened out their spines this primal force surged to unbearable proportions—which *could* be calculated if you knew the right equations.

"Please don't interrupt, Dr. Hickey. I know what you're thinking but I prefer we keep to the story."

The earliest men went wild, he continued. They'd do anything to get more of this pleasure—this *sub*atomic orgasm—but at the same time their systems were completely overwhelmed by the fortuitous conjunction of gravity and acceleration. To compensate, to help control the force of orgasm and make it manageable, the human brain grew bigger and bigger. It was like trying to cap an oil well.

This oil well was expertly explained by Galileo in his experiments with objects, acceleration and gravity. As he rolled objects down planes inclined at various angles and measured the acceleration of each one (animals' spines, by the way, were like these inclined planes, the angles varying by species) Galileo found that the steeper the plane the faster the balls rolled from top to bottom. And, of course, the fastest acceleration of all came when you dropped something straight down—like dropping something off the top of a building, which Galileo was purported to have done from the tower of Pisa. The human spine was like that perpendicular plane. Anything that rolled down it was going to reach the bottom faster than it would if the spine were at a lesser angle.

"The straighter the spine, the quicker the flash of electrical impulse known by the name of orgasm."

"You seem to be implying," said Herbert, "that intelligence is numerical and can be captured by mathematics."

"I used to think so," Lumumba replied quickly, "but not anymore." Perhaps because the limits of mathematics as a tool of understanding has finally been reached? Unless, of course, the physicists started sleeping with their mothers. That would certainly produce an explosion of new geometrical and mathematical templates, since the particles were basically orgasmic in nature, and it was only through orgasm that man could hope to gain access to basic insights into their structure. For the moment, however, the incest taboo guarded this reservoir of forbidden knowledge. But if some physicist could get beyond it, it would create an explosive paradigm shift that would make all the previous scientific revolutions pale in comparison.

"Why is that?" asked Herbert excitedly.

"Because the religious impulse is rooted in the electrical impulse, and since electrical impulses are mathematical, then it follows that religion is also." Religion *could* be found in a formula. Never forget that the internal geometrical structures that formed the basis of mathematics only saw the light of day because they were forced out by the repression inflicted on the gonads. Because of these unbearable tortures, early man projected a series of visual hallucinations known as entoptic visions. The origin of these visions was not in the brain but in the electrical activity of the gonads. But from the need to curtail the chaos resulting from the hyperkinetic energy of the upright spine, the ancient primates with the help of evolution eventually siphoned the energy away from the mischievous gonads into the brain. At this critical juncture orgasm came under control: Encapsulated in the entoptic visions, which were an attempt to control the overflow of orgasmic electrical energy produced when early primates first stood upright, orgasm was finally snared. All the advanced forms of symbolic control such as mathematics, language, religion and the law were the result of this captured orgasmic energy. Ultimately all numbers originated in the entoptic visions of a hallucinating animal being tortured by his repressed gonads.

"Are you saying," said Herbert, "that even if our brain matter is made of geometrical forms which in turn have been used to explain the universe, even so it could be that the geometry of the mind's neurons is too constrained to push beyond its limitations and see what needs to be seen next?"

"Formulas have brought you to this point," Lumumba replied, "but is it formulas that will take you beyond? Perhaps it is something that cannot be conveyed by formula, something not part of the living system at all. Perhaps it will be found in a realm of inquiry not yet discovered."

Chapter Seven

What the Great American Novel Has to Do with Incest

Or

How NASA Is Connected to the Vagina

It was dark when we came to Mpanda. The streets were crowded and lively and gave off a sense of celebration, a raucous affirmation of life.

"Uncle, I'm hungry," Doba said. "When are we going to stop and find a fig tree?"

"And make our hammocks and go to sleep," Yendi added. His canines glistened in the dark as he yawned.

"I've already told you that for the next few days we'll have to rough it," Lumumba replied. "That means sleeping in beds, eating in restaurants and driving in cars. I don't like it any more than you do. I would have been in Spain by now if it hadn't been for these idiots here."

We stopped at a fruit market. Several old crones oblivious to their ugliness hurried over as Lumumba held out a fistful of money.

"*Ndizi*," he said. "Bananas, all you have."

The women chattered excitedly as they delivered the produce. Lumumba looked pleased.

"Apparently there's no all-points bulletin out on this bus," he said. "We'll be able to drive all the way to the gorge."

But his optimism proved to be short-lived. A few minute later Herbert slammed on the brakes.

"Damn it! They've put up a roadblock!" he shouted.

"Hurray!" Albert signed. "Now we'll be apprehended and I can return to my flock at the Preserve."

"You dumb shit!" said Kribi. "When they see we're animals they'll shoot us on sight!"

Okovango began to wail, Kumasi reached out to comfort him.

"You're young until you're old, you're alive until you're dead," he said. Unfortunately, his words didn't have the desired effect and Okovango's wails were joined by Yalinga's and Doba's.

With a quick and violent gesture, Lumumba grabbed the wheel and turned the matutu sharply down an alley.

It was too late. We had been spotted and the loud shouts of soldiers and police could be heard as they came running after us. Bullets began to fly.

Lumumba drove like a bat out of hell, up one street and down another, scattering people in all directions, sending bodies through the air. At last he careened into an open-air market. As a wall of clothing came toppling over us the bus came to a stop.

"I can see why you took the trains," said Herbert as we made our way through a mountain of T-shirts, *kangas*, sweaters, dresses and underwear.

The astonished crowed looked on as the apes beat a hasty retreat. Forgetting Lumumba's edict to walk as men they began to swing from one building to the next with Herbert and myself in tow.

"Wambussi spirit men!" someone in the crowd shouted. "Fly through air like demons!"

A sign pointed east to Uruwira and, leaving the town behind we slipped stealthily into the dark and vanished into the thick, warm air of an African night.

I woke to the smell of coffee. The apes had already breakfasted on newly found bananas and applied fresh flour to their arms and faces.

"I can't believe you warned Lumumba about the roadblock," I said over sips of coffee.

"Darling, I have to get the formula."

"He said there isn't one."

"I don't believe him. I think he has it and if I could get my hands on it, well, it could be as important for my career as Project Mark would have been."

"Always your career."

"Darling, you're so beautiful when you're angry."

The remark made me think of Soddhu. He was probably just getting to sleep. I hoped he was alone, but who knew what Lydia might be up to now that Herbert was gone. Oh well, nothing could match our night at Carnegie Hall. Soddhu was as mesmerized as I was. Would we ever find out who had taken Cortina's life? Surely it wasn't the man who had taken his place on stage! Even now he made my heart flutter like a silly school girl's whenever I thought of him, and I wondered what it was like to go to bed with him.

Lumumba came over and handed us some bananas and biscuits. The chimps had put on their shoes and sat uncomfortably against the scrawny underbrush. To distract himself Kribi picked up a long twig and began to poke inside a towering mound of termites. Nedele hugged the rabbit to her breast as she watched him lick them off one by one.

"Here, have some," he said pushing the stick toward her.

"I can't eat my friends," she whispered

"But they taste so good! Say, have you ever wondered what a rabbit tastes like?"

"If you harm one hair on Bagamoyo's head I'll forget my vows and tear you from limb to limb!"

She had just christened her little pet with this name (it meant Here I Lay My Heart), and as she spoke she seemed to double in size.

"My, aren't we touchy. Can I at least make him disappear inside a black hat?"

"Stop talking nonsense," said Lumumba, "and leave the magic to humans, it's their species under a sorcerer's spell, not ours. If certain hallucinatory events hadn't happened, they'd still know they are the same as we are."

"Even though they've developed a civilization, language and an understanding of the universe?" said Albert.

"You haven't heard a word Uncle has said, have you?" said Bata deprecatingly. "Their brains are there—their civilization and languages and all knowledge in general—as a necessary mechanism to repress the gonads. All culture, all civilization exists as a necessary mechanism to repress them. Repression is the name of the game as far as they are concerned."

"The human brain," said Herbert, "is the most complex and awesome creation that Nature has yet evolved."

"I've heard that before," said Lumumba. "But your love affair with your brains is so transparent. Everything humans do is a desperate attempt to escape from their incestuous longings—be it rug weaving or discovering atoms and theorizing about eleven dimensions. *That* is the fabulous wiring of your brains."

"C'est la vie," said Herbert with a shrug.

"Why are you letting them talk to you that way, Dr. Hickey?" asked Albert indignantly.

"Because he wants your uncle's formula," I replied, "plain and simple."

We broke camp and headed east into the bush. Keeping the road to Uruwira in sight, we had only walked a short distance when Lumumba signaled us to return to the road. A truck was coming, the back of it covered with an enormous blue tarp.

"Here's our ride," Yendi said hooting loudly.

"Let me take care of this," said Herbert. "Or at least let me help you. There's no need to kill everybody just to get this truck."

"It's only two people," Tchibanga scowled.

"It's not a question of numbers," Herbert said. "It's a question of morality."

"Morality," said Bata, "is only a front for human obedience to the incest taboo—for boys to obey their fathers and uphold the hierarchy that exists among men, right Uncle?"

"I think your uncle is being too simplistic," Herbert replied. "Maybe he's right, and maybe morality did start that way. But today it has evolved into a form that allows human beings to interact in a complex society. The simple laws of animals wouldn't work in a technological civilization."

"Maybe that's the problem with modern society. Perhaps you need to unravel all that moral complexity and return to the natural laws of our world."

"The truth is a tree and the tree is a phallus," Kumasi said taking Yalinga's child from her arms and hobbling gamely into the middle of the road.

Again the apes hid themselves behind the embankment. The truck stopped several feet from Kumasi and Okovango. Its tarp was torn in several places, and some of the framework was exposed and rusted. Kribi and Yendi jumped from their hiding place and pulled the men from the cab.

"I told you not to stop, you idiot!" said one of them.

"I couldn't just run the old man over," said the other.

"*The old man*," the first mimicked nastily, "is probably one of the Wambussi gang. Or worse, the G-L-A! Haven't you read the newspapers lately?"

His eyes became wide as saucers as Lumumba walked over.

"It's him!" said the passenger. Trembling violently, he fell on his knees and clasped his hands together imploringly. "Please don't kill us, General!"

Lumumba looked surprised.

"I beg your pardon?"

"I know who you are," the man said. "You are the one who killed all the people going to Ikola," he answered.

"How do you know it was me if I killed everybody?"

"A passenger survived long enough to give the police a description: a short, hairy man with a gray beard and eyes of steel!"

"Uncle, you are famous!" Tchibanga signaled. The driver looked from Tchibanga to Lumumba, then he too fell on his knees.

"Please spare us, General!" he implored. "We have wives and children. What will they do without us? I have no sons, only daughters. How can a girl take care of cattle?"

His friend nodded emphatically. "If you come to my house we'll slaughter a goat in your honor."

"I prefer to slaughter both of you in the goat's honor," Lumumba said, and with a quick movement he grabbed both men at once. There was a sickening snap, the men fell to the ground and Albert immediately set about giving them the last rites.

"He sure would make a great priest," said Herbert looking on wistfully as several buzzards settled heavily on some nearby trees.

The other apes seemed hardly to have noticed. Nedele was playing with Bagamoyo. Doba was showing Okovango how to catch ants with a stick. Kumasi was snoring. Yalinga and Tchibanga were having a quickie, and Albert, once he was through ministering, began lecturing them about the punishments that awaited them in the lower circles of Hell while Bata listened. There was a small acacia bush nearby, and three or four brightly colored birds were singing songs to each other. The sky was a beautiful color of blue.

"Time to get started," Lumumba called. "Hickeys sit in the cab with me, everyone else in back."

Using the metal poles as if they were trees the chimps swung themselves gracefully into the truck bed. Nedele tucked Bagamoyo under her arm. Only Kumasi had trouble getting in, and Bata helped him to a seat near the cab. Albert made the sign of the cross and got in last.

As the truck pulled away the vultures flopped down and began to eat.

"You're here until you're gone, you're alive until you're dead," old Kumasi signed gaily at the window.

"All roads lead to death," said Lumumba philosophically, "and eternal orgasm."

"If you could prove that," said Herbert, "there would be a lot more people jumping off tall buildings."

"If people understood the basic forces of the universe, " Lumumba replied, "people would realize that death is only a rearrangement of their electrons and other quantum forces. Death releases the orgasmic potential of those particles in almost the same way that sex does."

"I'm sure that our electrons do get rearranged when we die," said Herbert. "But I don't see how it has anything to do with orgasm. Orgasm is something that happens within the nervous system of a living creature—not something that happens to an atom or a quark."

"I'm afraid you're selling orgasm a bit short," said Lumumba. "Apart from being that euphoric sensation experienced by the limbic system, orgasm is a system within its own right, a system that organizes the body and its elements. The forces that guide atoms to self-assemble are orgasmic. The excitability of electrons is orgasmic. All forces in nature are basically orgasmic, and the origin of happiness lies in the movement of atoms. Since pressure and compression are forces, they are orgasmic too. Even the essence of the universe is a kind of subatomic sexuality that pervades both empty space and the matter which fills it. The atomic nature of sexuality can be seen in the mushroom cloud of an atom bomb. You see how the cloud mimics the shape of the phallus? It's because the same basic units of quantum energy are at work. Particle physics is particle sexuality is particle orgasm—it's all the same principle."

At the first mention of orgasm, Kribi, Yendi and Tchibanga had squeezed up to the open window behind the cab. They had listened for a few minutes and were now pleasuring themselves.

"And the pope says it's unnatural!" Lumumba muttered as he watched them through the rearview mirror."

"The pope is infallible," said Albert, crossing himself reverently.

"Only as an arm of the incest taboo," Lumumba replied.

Herbert tried to get back on track.

"I don't see," he said, "how particle orgasm can be part of the same principle as particle physics."

"My dear Dr. Hickey. Have you never stopped to think how cells—which are mostly water—can retain their form? How a muscle cell can flex or an erection take place?"

"As I understand it," Herbert replied, "it has to do with microscopic structural elements within the cells themselves."

"Exactly," said Lumumba. "A structural network of special molecules permeates each cell and gives it form. These molecules are in a constant state of tension—both with each other and with the forces of pressure created by the fluid in the cell and the tension imparted by the cell membrane. It is the synergistic relationship of all those forces—what scientists call tensegrity—that gives the cell its structure. All macroscopic organic structures are ultimately dependent on these microscopic forces.

"A horse, for instance, is more than simply an accumulation of different mammalian cells. In order to build a horse, you have to start with the individual structural elements inside the horse's cells—the architectural structure of the horse is much more than skeletal features and the arrangement of the muscle cells and ligaments.

"And if a horse can be built from those microscopic elements so can orgasm—even though we experience it at the macroscopic level. This is because orgasm, I believe, is based on a kind of tension inside the cells."

"Well, I can see what you're saying from a purely mechanical perspective," said Herbert. "But orgasm is an *experience*, not simply a relationship of physical forces."

"But how do you know that experience cannot be broken down to a relationship of physical forces?" asked Lumumba. "In my view, the tensegrity structures actually comprise an elemental form of cognition.

"Consider this: an amoeba encounters some kind of stimulus it doesn't like. It will, as every school child knows, move quickly away. But since it was the amoeba's pseudopods which came in contact with the stimulus, how does the rest of the cell, which is not in contact with the stimulus, know what to do? There is no nervous system inside an amoeba, no nerve cells. But the response throughout the cell is instantaneous."

"I've always thought it depended on some kind of chemical signal," said Herbert.

"Yes, but at the same time it's a response that takes place within the mechanical structures of the cell itself. When the amoeba encounters the unfriendly stimulus, it sets off a wave of structural changes that is transmitted across the cell's basic architectural components. That wave of changes, at its very core, is a form of *information*. You might say that the mechanical structures form a kind of basic cellular cognition."

"So you're saying that cells are aware of themselves through these basic mechanical forces," said Herbert.

"Yes, and it's that fundamental awareness that underpins the kind of awareness we have when we experience something like orgasm."

"I still don't see how it relates to subatomic particles, or how you can say that subatomic particles are capable of experiencing something like orgasm. Subatomic particles, after all, are *elemental*—not complex structures like cells."

"Just because they are elemental," Lumumba replied, "doesn't mean they are not involved in more complex structures. As physicists have shown, subatomic particles don't exist in isolation. They are related to each other in highly complex ways—in terms of symmetry, spin, energy, mass and so on.

"One of the most fundamental features of all those relationships is an informational component which science has not yet identified but which manifests itself as a basic awareness within the particle of what other particles are doing."

"You're referring, I suppose, to the famous example of a photon appearing in two different guises—either as a particle or a wave—depending on what it sees its companions doing," said Herbert. "It's what my colleagues at Yale call the 'spooky' part of quantum mechanics."

"Because they are so short-sighted," said Lumumba. "Either the particles are related by some undiscovered physical mechanism that allows the instantaneous transmission of information over sometimes vast distances; or the very existence and relationship of the particles is mediated by some underlying structure of knowledge that permeates the universe and ties it together. I myself tend toward the second view, but either way there is nothing spooky about it. They are simply aspects of the universe that humans are not aware of because they have been cut off from their basic instincts by the incest taboo and all the garbage that you so proudly refer to as the cerebral cortex.

"At the subatomic level the mechanical forces and informational relationships become indistinguishable. That awareness is a fundamental part of the structure of the universe at its most basic level. Mechanical forces and information are ultimately transmutable into each other, and the informational component of a particle—perhaps orgasmic in nature? the excitability of electrons?—is transferred into the cell itself through the process of tensegrity.

"But even more than that. There is a basic awareness permeating the entire universe that is rooted in the subatomic particles themselves. The argument I've just made traces an unbroken line from what we call awareness—the complex relationships among neurons in the human or animal body—back through the cells and down to the subatomic level. Ultimately, the quarks are telling the cell what to do. The orgasmic force can be traced back to the elemental forces inside the atom. All forces are rooted in their subatomic components. When we die, our awareness is dissolved back into this elemental level. "

"And why do you say this experience is orgasmic?" Herbert asked.

"Because death is very similar to the orgasmic nature of particles. It suspends our awareness at the complex level of macro-cellular organisms and returns us for just a moment to the awareness of the subatomic particles themselves. That's why it's such an overwhelming experience."

"It's impossible to know this," said Herbert.

"For humans, yes. For animals, no. We experience ourselves at the most elemental level, an awareness that has been obliterated by the hallucinatory, magical operations of the human cerebral cortex."

For a few moments Lumumba remained silent. He appeared to by mulling something over. At last he said:

"I told you earlier that it would be impossible to find an equation for orgasm. But the truth is that I've been working on one for several years."

"I knew it!" Herbert exclaimed. His eyes glazed over, it was a look I had come to know only too well.

Lumumba eyed him shrewdly and continued:

"Believe it or not, it has many affinities with string theory. Perhaps an understanding of the forces which lead to orgasm will one day result in a correct formulation of a unified field theory or UFO—Unified Field of Orgasm."

"Do you realize you could win a Nobel Prize for this?"

"Dr. Lumumba, I wish you would stop pulling my husband's leg," I said.

"But he's telling the truth, Kathryn! I know it because when Xeno died there were rumors about a secret paper he was working on, and I expect it was this!"

"You would be right," said Lumumba. "At the very least, Xeno the consummate atheist (no one at Yale knew this, of course) hoped that the demon of religion could be reigned in. For by putting orgasm in a framework of science rather than the religious mysticism in which it is presently mired, all the pathological depredations of this current situation could be eliminated. That would include, of course, the contemptuous and cavalier attitude men have toward animals."

"Have you anything down on paper?" asked Herbert.

"It's all in my head."

"That's a bit risky, should anything happen to your head."

"I don't expect anything will, but in the eventuality it does, you might start the project yourself by describing a mathematical model predicting the linear stiffening response involved in erection."

"No shit!" said Herbert.

"As a good tensegrity problem, yes. Afterall, it's within this structure that the information of orgasm is being transmitted. And within this structure are the particles. And in these particles reside the seed of orgasm. Orgasm comes from the mechanical movements of the particles that make up the cells."

"Professor, I must say your grasp of the subject is breathtaking. What say you we work on it together? I can see it now—Crick and Watson, Lumumba and Hickey. You could exonerate yourself easily by coming up with an orgasmic theory of everything, let's call it the OTOE."

We passed Uruwira and turned north toward Isimbira. The apes sat lethargically, Lumumba told them we would be able to buy food in an hour.

"You're hungry till you're full and you're full until you're hungry," Kumasi said before nodding off to sleep.

"What's wrong with the rabbit?" Tchibanga signed to Nedele. Bagamoyo seemed to be panting, and his eyes were the size of saucers. Nedele was holding him tighter than usual.

"He doesn't like going for rides," she replied.

"The little rascal is smart," said Lumumba over his shoulder. "He knows that cars are unnatural and dangerous. And because he doesn't believe in the incest taboo he's not at all impressed with the byproducts of its culture."

"Professor Lumumba," said I, "did you ever think that a car was just a car?"

"My dear Mrs. Hickey. If men were not programmed to sublimate all sexual desire, not only would there never be an *idea* for a car, there would never be the *need* for a car. People would be content to graze all day in the grass, sleep, fuck and play. But since you are an American I don't expect you to grasp any of this. So yes, for you a car is just a car."

"Are you saying that Americans are stupid?" Bata asked.

"I'm saying that Americans are in a dream of incest. Isn't the pursuit of wealth the mainstay of America—arguably the core of the American dream? But if the pursuit of wealth is at bottom Oedipal in nature, then the men who dreamed of coming to America, the men who colonized it, those men and women were driven by a dream of incest and the sublimation of that dream."

"America was colonized by people who were seeking religious freedom," I argued.

"But religion is sex and sex is religion," said Kumasi, for the moment awake.

"Kumasi's right," said Lumumba. "The colonists were seeking sexual freedom. The 'land of the free' is a land where people can live out their own personal fantasies and unconscious dreams of incest. But here is the irony. The more free you are to use that freedom, the more laws you create to curtail that freedom. So America becomes this great schizophrenic country pulled in opposite directions at the same time.

"You know why no one has been able to write the Great American Novel? Because no one has yet deciphered it; to do so one must see its incestuous core. And to do that you'd have to go to your own incestuous core, and who amongst you has the courage? On the contrary, the frenetic pace of human invention is nothing more than an ever-increasing race to keep ahead of a knowledge they can't bear to face. By obsessively occupying themselves with unveiling new things, people make sure they have no time to peer inside to see what's motivating their compulsions."

"Then we should thank the incest taboo for a man on the moon," I said.

"But what good is a man on the moon?" Lumumba asked. "It doesn't get him any closer to his mother's vagina. If he could figure out how to do that, perhaps he'd never want to go to the moon in the first place."

"It'd be a sad day for NASA," said Herbert, shaking his head doubtfully.

Just then Bata slipped Bagamoyo through the cab window.

"Nedele says he'll be happier up front," he signed.

"Cover him with this," said Lumumba, handing me a sweater that had belonged to the driver.

I wrapped him like a baby in swaddling cloth. Being covered seemed to calm him. He held my gaze but as I looked at him closely the sparkle of his eyes seemed to diminish.

"He looks a little sad," I observed.

"Perhaps his eyes are mirroring yours," said Lumumba. "He has probably absorbed your pain and is reflecting it back. You are caught in a cross-species transference. You're projecting your own conflicted feelings onto the poor rabbit, who of course has no idea where these feelings are coming from. The only thing he can do is internalize the pain in his own simple way."

"That's very intuitive," said Herbert. "My wife is a past master of conflicted feelings."

"Be careful," said Yendi through the window, "or you won't be getting any tonight."

He knew what he was talking about.

"Go sleep with your new friend," I said when it was time to go to bed. But the truth is I was angry at something Lumumba had said earlier, that if Bagamoyo could understand what I demanded of him, his heart would break.

"His love is so simple—yours so complex. But he would try, of course, and probably die in the attempt. He's the animal in you, the animal you no longer know or care about, the animal self you no longer love."

Chapter Eight

A Soliloquy on Orgasm

Or

Can Orgasm Lead to Time Travel and the New Laws of Physics?

At Isimbira, we stopped and bought fruit, biscuits, peanuts, eggs and cheese.

Then on to Kakoma, Igalula and Pangale. Between Uruma and Tabora Lumumba found a place to camp. There were cultivated fields and cattle in the distance, and every now and then their plaintive lowing came floating across the pasture. What had Soddhu said about this sound?

"The cry of the Kine."

He read from the Scriptures and wept: " 'Upon this the Soul of the Kine lamented "Woe unto me since I have obtained for myself in my wounding a lord who is powerless to effect this wish, the mere voice of a feeble and pusillanimous man, whereas I desire one who is lord over his will and able to bring what he desires into effect.' " Yasna XXIX, Kathryn. The Kine cries for herself and the people who were living in such misery at the time. She bewails her lot at the hands of cruel men. Written 5,000 years ago, it might as well be today."

Ah Soddhu! If only you were here now. What fun we could have talking about desire! What would you say if I told you that all desire is incestuous? Would it change the Kine's lament? Or solidify it, since she is speaking for Zarathustra who said that the highest good was the union between father and daughter, brother and sister, and son and she who bore him?

The next morning we got on the road early. In Tabora, Lumumba stopped for gasoline and checked a worn roadmap in the glove compartment.

"Only 400 kilometers," he said. "We should make it in a day."

"Hee haw!" said Herbert as we shot off toward Manoleo. "We're hot on the trail of the incest taboo!"

"Ah yes," said Lumumba. "We are getting close to the place where it all started. Can you feel its throbbing presence in the air? Only a taboo with the power of magic could make a dent in the orgasmic rush that took place in these plains three million years ago."

"Have you made any progress in your mathematical formula to describe this process?" Herbert asked.

"Have a little patience, Hickey. We only talked about it yesterday. There are so many factors to consider! If the universe can be explained by the interactions of a dozen particles and four forces, then the question arises: can all its organisms and all the functions that take place inside the organisms be seen as interactions between these same dozen particles and four forces? In my view, the answer is yes—even the process of orgasm should be reducible to these basic physical laws."

"Go on!"

"Only if you promise to keep this under your hat. I'm not ready to go public."

"May God strike me dead if I don't!"

"How can orgasm strike you dead?" Bata asked.

"If you say that one more time," said Albert, "I'll kill you."

"Spoken like a true Christian," said Tchibanga. Lumumba continued.

"In trying to relate the preliminary equations that have been proposed for a unified field theory to the peculiar physics of spinal geometry and orgasm, one number that keeps popping up in both sets of equations is 137—the fine structure constant of the universe, the ratio which relates electromagnetic charge to the mathematics governing the quantum structure of subatomic particles. It's my belief that this ratio might provide the link between the purely physical laws your scientists have discovered and the still undiscovered 'experiential' laws that govern orgasm—the orgasmic consciousness which resides inside electrons and motivates them to move around inside the atom."

"'Lumumba's Constant," Herbert said excitedly. "But what do you mean by the experiential laws of orgasm? Are you trying to say that orgasm is a physical force?"

"It would be more precise to say that physical forces and objects have an experiential component, an as yet unrecognized attribute of intelligence and meaning at a subatomic level. Consider the electron. It has a very precise mass; it orbits atomic nuclei at very precise energy levels; it has a very precise probability under specified conditions of absorbing or emitting a photon, or a fine structure constant."

" Like 137?" asked Herbert. Lumumba nodded.

"It's a number that has puzzled physicists for a long time mostly because it's completely arbitrary. If it were some other number, the universe might exist in a completely different way—no reason that it couldn't. But the universe exists this way, in the precise way that makes it possible for carbon and oxygen and nitrogen to come together in order to make what you call life. Why?—the physicists can't answer that question because it aims at an order of explanation *outside* physical law."

"You are suggesting, then, that the mystics are right and the scientists are wrong?" Herbert asked.

"What I'm suggesting," said Lumumba, "is that no amount of scientific reasoning will ever produce an answer to a question that is inherently *orgasmic—hence subjective*—in nature. The electrons chose that number because they decided to. It's an expression of their free will and orgasmic joy. They just decided to make the universe this way on a lark. Maybe someday they'll decide to change and the universe will exist in some radically different way that we can't even imagine. There's no way scientific law can preclude that possibility; it can only try to understand the relationships in the universe as it exists now."

"So in the final analysis, what do you think motivates the electron to do all these things? Why should the electron bother to participate in what may be a huge practical joke—what we call the universe—and obey its so-called physical laws?"

"Probably because of orgasm, if orgasm is the force that initiates the dance of the particles, the force of desire that gives the universe coherence, ontological consistency and direction. And makes the particles get off their little butts and generate complexity. Just like it makes Kribi get off *his* butt and fuck Yalinga, and humans get off their butts and want to fuck their mothers—except that they've screwed up the whole process. A kind of cosmic dead end.

"That's why they haven't been able to formulate a 'theory of everything'— because they haven't *included* everything. By excluding orgasm, they've left out the crucial factor they need to unite the different levels of what you call physical reality."

"So orgasm is the missing element in Einstein's calculations," Herbert mused. "Perhaps our physicists need to collaborate with some Playboy bunnies."

"I actually made that suggestion to a colleague of mine at Yale, a Professor Muñoz. Do you know him?"

"No."

"You haven't missed anything. I used him to bounce off my ideas. 'Solve the mystery of orgasm, Munoz—that is, find its equation—and voilá! The ultimate explanation of physical reality will be revealed within a matter of time.'"

"Surely you aren't talking about the explanation of physical reality which Albert Einstein spent the last years of his life searching for," said Herbert incredulously. Lumumba looked at him archly.

"Do you think that a man who put so much stock in his instincts would coin the word 'relativity' without having his own relatives in mind? When Einstein said that the most beautiful experience a human can have is the mysterious, do you suppose he was thinking about anything but orgasm? I'm telling you, Hickey, what he should have been searching for was the theory of genital relativity. Unfortunately he died before he realized it."

"Have you found it?" Herbert asked excitedly. Skirting the question, Lumumba replied: "Muñoz and I had a falling out, and I can no longer use him as a sounding board."

Herbert clasped a hand over Lumumba's.

"Use me, Professor! It would be a great honor!"

Unfettering himself, the great ape replied: "Can I trust you to keep it secret?"

"Cross my heart and hope to die," said Herbert, solemnly making the childish gesture. After a moment's reflection, Lumumba nodded. What followed was a soliloquy which went something like this:

"The force of orgasm must originate in a mathematical point, for at bottom, orgasm is part of the attributes of the atom. But when Democritus formulated his theory of the atom he showed clearly that he was afraid of sex because it overwhelmed his consciousness. Of course he was simply recapitulating the experience of hominids becoming bipedal and having their consciousness overwhelmed by orgasm. Their brains were unable to subdue or conquer orgasm—forces that are so pleasurable they are stronger than civilization itself. And just as it overwhelms men today it overwhelmed those first unprepared bipeds. We can only imagine what the scene must have looked like when creatures who until that point had relied merely on their instincts, were suddenly confronted by a pleasure that took hold of them body and soul.

"Yes, their senses were overwhelmed. But the senses are made of atoms and the process of orgasm is made of atoms, and atoms collide with each other. Is that why physicists were so frightened when their numbers started coming out weird—they realized they were uncovering a secret knowledge, a knowledge connected with the mystery of orgasm? (And men somehow intuit their existence because they themselves are made of that mystery.)

"Such it was for Pythagoras. He created a secret society of men holding religious reverence for numbers. He was obsessed with numbers. For him, things actually *were* numbers. That's why numbers had such religious significance: if religion is at bottom a sexual experience, and sexual experience is some kind of force, and men identify those forces through mathematics, then there is an inextricable connection. Ratios, proportions, the perfect shape; it's all the same, all one—Einstein's grand unification theory. Through the concept of numbers men see that everything is really the same because of its atomic structure. And underlying the whole thing is the orgasmic nature of numbers. Numbers explain the basic forces that tie the universe together; therefore numbers must explain the orgasmic force that gives the universe structure.

"Is that why the Pythagorans were such lovers of music—that is, of sonorous numbers? Could orgasm be a beam of amplified sound waves? After all, the ratios of musical scales are related to the intervals of whole numbers: 1, 2, 3, 4—which add up to 10, the perfect number. Somewhere deep inside, music makes men remember that they are really just particles, and all their damn theories about gauge bosons and such don't hold a candle to a symphony or a sonata.

"That's probably the best proof there is that the world of reason and the world of the senses are identical, one and the same entity presented in two different forms. It's like the forces of momentum: Orgasm would continue going forever in the universe—just like Galileo's balls rolling on a level plane with no friction.

"And speaking of Galileo, wasn't he the first to show that light and other ephemeral phenomena were actually things, not just incorporeal elements of a luminous ether? Will orgasm one day be shown to be a physical force, not just an illusory 'experience of the mind'? Do the religious mystics suspect this when they point out that the sweetness of the Holy Virgin can be separated out and given to a mule? After all, the sweetness of the Holy Virgin is nothing more than orgasm, and a mule can have orgasm too!

"You might say that orgasm is one of the principle forces of the universe captured inside the body—a process by which atoms and molecules are arranged and rearranged into different combinations. The mass of the reactants and the mass of the products is exactly the same—so what has happened? Orgasm has presided over a chemical reaction, producing a new state of the universe.

"The odd thing about orgasm though, as I said before, is that when looked at in mathematical terms it actually originates in a single point. Of course if quarks and leptons and other subatomic particles combine to make everything in the universe, then quarks and leptons have combined to make orgasm too. With those two facts, it should be possible to calculate the basic parameters of orgasm as a quantum dynamical force. One should be able to measure the mass, spin and charge of the gauge bosons mediating the reaction. The whole reaction would of course emit photons, which means that the orgasmic force would propagate at the speed of light.

"But this cosmic version of orgasm would have to be translated into equations that could describe what happens in the body of a living creature. Orgasm originates in the gonads, then goes up the spine where it is registered in the brain. That upwards force has to travel against the pull of gravity. With the proper measurements, it should be possible to make calculations that would demonstrate precisely how orgasm works inside the body. And if men could be made to see that, it would strip away all the mystical, religious claptrap they've built around the idea of orgasm, and they could safely return to their animal origins.

"But they would have to work hard to see those truths. As Democritus said, the truth must be deeper than the senses. If the truth is rooted in the phallus and the truth goes beyond the senses, then orgasm must go beyond the senses as well. Orgasm is more than a feeling. It resides in the very nature or essence of the atom.

"And since organs are made of atoms, organs are also made of the forces that create atoms. At bottom, orgasm is just like everything else in the universe—a juxtaposition of the various forces that constitute the universe. Numbers, ratios and proportions—mathematics in general—determine orgasmic principles. Or perhaps it's the other way around and the orgasmic principle determines numbers, ratios and proportions. No matter. Distance, time and speed are also part of the equation. In order to find its true nature, scientists will have to find a way to reduce orgasm to a set of abstract mathematical points. Its true identity will only reveal itself when it can be made dimensionless and massless.

"Now according to Isaac Newton, the best way to understand the basic principles of the universe is in terms of abstract forces. Forces, he said, can be used to explain the solar system and everything in it, and those forces can ultimately be understood in terms of geometry—vectors and geometrical relationships that describe how the forces are related. That being the case, perhaps the true identity of orgasm can also be found in geometric forms, with no need of massive non-linear calculations on computers. Or are the geometric forms themselves simply a manifestation of orgasm? Perhaps orgasm exists as a pure parabola, as pure mathematics.

"Strange how the physicists have ignored this basic truth! They've been trying to reduce everything that exists to a few basic forces and principles: How could they overlook something as obvious as orgasm? Since orgasm is the most basic force in all nature, one wonders why no one has yet postulated a set of laws to explain it, or ever recognized that such a set of laws is necessary if they are going to explain everything else. I suppose that it's simply a testament to the powers of the incest taboo which has managed to twist even the thinking of scientists so that they don't see the simple truth hidden at the core of all their elaborate calculations and experimentation.

"Why, they haven't even been able to confront things that are relatively peripheral to the issue. Why, for instance, hasn't mathematical reasoning captured the relationship between orgasm and the periodic moon? After all, every physicist knows that any change of motion is caused by some force. And there is obviously a change of motion during orgasm in the same way as the flow of blood is influenced by the gravitational pull of the moon. Is it those pushes and pulls that organize people's sexual desires?

"The calculation would actually be simple. The force of orgasm would be related to the mass of blood times its acceleration. The blood accelerates during orgasm; electrical activity accelerates; mechanical motion accelerates; metabolic conversion of sugars increases. It should be a simple matter to factor this into a single equation that describes an orgasmic event.

"The key to the whole thing, as Galileo saw, is acceleration. What is acceleration? It's the rate at which a speed changes. It should be easy to measure the rate of change in blood flow, electrical activity, sugar metabolism, and mechanical motion. Orgasm would simply be the result of all these interacting forces and trajectories. Of course we'd need to get quantities such as mass, temperature and volume to create a master equation. But that would present no problem under controlled circumstances, and we could simply run this data through Newton's three laws.

"But first we have to find a way to transform these physical forces into electrical forces. Electricity is the key to the whole thing. Most people think of reproduction as a biological phenomenon—a way of organizing different particles such as chromosomes, proteins and molecules of DNA. But the truth is, it is actually an electrical phenomenon. Biology really has nothing to do with the propagation of species. Evolution and reproduction are the result of gravitational, electrical and magnetic forces. The oxidation of the planet and the appearance of bacteria are the result of these forces acting on each other. The molecules and other particles that biologists describe are just manifestations of these hidden forces.

"This becomes evident if you consider what separates life from non-life. When an animal is having orgasm, the electrical forces inside it overcome the force of gravity. That is why rocks don't reproduce: The electrical forces inside them are not strong enough to overcome the gravitational forces acting on them. Evolution is not a biological activity but an interplay of electrical and gravitational forces in certain patterns. When an electrical force overcomes a resistance, orgasm and reproduction occur.

"That's the real origin of biological evolution. Sex between two entities evolved as the electrical forces they produced became stronger. In the original one-celled life forms, there wasn't enough electrical potential for sex to occur, but as the electrical forces grew, the organism became more complex and eventually divided into male and female. After that, the force of gravity pulling on their bodily fluids naturally resulted in what we call sex. Orgasm is really some kind of oscillation between attractive and repulsive forces, a gravity well in deep space, pulling light and matter into a bottomless hole that crushes both space and time. In such a place, the laws of physics change. You can fall through a wormhole into another dimension, a place where a hydrogen atom and a red dwarf are really the same thing.

"This is what the new physics is all about—the sub-subatomic world of quantum foam, where space itself is porous, permeated with black holes and miniature wormholes billion and billions of times smaller than a proton. Of course this roiling microworld is orgasmic in nature, and once its laws are discovered anything is possible—wormholes will be made into vaginal time tunnels, you'll be able to hop inside and travel to any point in space. Time travel through orgasm, now won't that be a ride!

"A pity that none of the empiricists of the 19th century, men like Boyle and Faraday, had an inkling of this, otherwise there'd have been some insight into the deeper ramifications of many of their laws. Otherwise Boyle could just as easily have described the behavior of orgasm instead of gas: the intensity of orgasm varies inversely with the electrical pressure on the brain. And Ampere, Volta and Faraday could have used their discoveries regarding electrical force to describe orgasm which is afterall just a rearrangement of atoms—a kind of quantum wriggle which creates changes that allow orgasm to take place, a process of decomposition and recomposition—a relationship between atomic binding and electrical forces.

"Now, if we pursue the notion of the human body as an electrical instrument, a multitude of other questions naturally come to mind. For instance, it would be interesting to see whether orgasm occurs when neutral chemicals become charged. Then it would be possible to measure orgasm in terms of ionization, which in turn could be connected to the magnetic fields in and around the body. Those magnetic fields must be highly complex—all the different electrical, chemical and atomic reactions and relations in the body are capable of producing magnetic fields. And since Ampere was able to determine the mathematical relationship between current and magnetic fields, if we could apply that to the body we could come up with a map of the magnetic fields and how they are affected by orgasm.

"But a lot of physicists are frightened by the concept of a field—probably because they know it has to do with sexuality. But then all the real truths about human beings are shrouded in mysticism—because if they were allowed into the open they might point to the truth about orgasm.

"Take zygosis, forinstance, which takes place within the magnetic field produced by the body. Perhaps these electrical and magnetic forces create a field which causes attraction between the two gametes. Perhaps the sperm that succeeds is the one with the strongest magnetic field. Maybe people who have fertility problems should spend less time getting drugs and more time getting electric shock treatments or sitting under power lines.

"If people only realized that magnetism is a crucial component of their identity and biology. Then they'd know that orgasm could be described in terms of changing magnetic fields and relationships between electrical forces—a disturbance propagating with the speed of light through whatever medium it encounters, a force reaching from atom to atom through the intervening space.

"Perhaps the ability of space to be disturbed—as in Faraday's fields—is really a marker of its susceptibility to orgasm. Afterall there's nothing more disturbing than a good fuck. In that case, the disturbance of space that scientists register as an electromagnetic field on their instruments would be the essence of orgasm.

"That would help explain the genesis of the human response to orgasm. When humans first stood up, less time was needed for the transmission of the electromagnetic field, and the disturbance of the space around the brain was correspondingly larger.

"But a lot of physicists are frightened by the concept of a field—probably because they know it has to do with sexuality. But then all the real truths about human beings are shrouded in mysticism—because if they were allowed into the open they might point to the truth about orgasm.

"If I could just figure out how to formulate these ideas in precise scientific form! Then I could show that orgasm is not a mystical experience coming from the world of gods and spirits, but rather a process that can be predicted by means of the attributes of its constituent parts: atoms, subatomic particles and the properties of space and force. It should then be possible to detect orgasm directly—in much the same way that the electromagnetic fields around living things are detected directly with Kirilian photography.

"And if orgasm can be interpreted as an electromagnetic action, then the time of its transmission should by calculable as well. Just as we know what the speed of light is, someday it should be possible to say exactly what the speed of orgasm is—a universal constant like the speed of light that determines the reaction of other matter and energy forms. After that we should be able to translate electricity and magnetism into a much more complete mathematical system.

"The place to start is with the rhythm of orgasm—the way it surges back and forth, an oscillation that matches the oscillations of electromagnetic fields. At bottom, those oscillations are really a form of information: a kind of basic code that contains the blueprint of the universe—a primal message containing the basic injunction of the universe to self-organize into matter. It tells matter how to organize itself according to principles such as symmetry, tensegrity and other asymmetrical, force-optimizing structures (such as those captured by the basic mathematical formulas of physics) that allow matter to assume the particular forms of complexity contained in its basic description of the universe.

"It would be such a beautiful thing to formulate a scientific theory that would link this basic mathematical description with the dynamics of orgasm in the body. Scientists could do experiments on the fluid in the spine that would show precisely how orgasm is transmitted and how it affects the nerves and fluids it interacts with. It would be like the experiments with glass tubes. Using the fluid nature of blood and spinal fluid, and the gaseous nature of oxygen, you could see how individual particle/waves of orgasm travel to the brain. Then you could describe their charge and mass—and the force they exert—in terms of measurement units formulated directly in terms of orgasm. Perhaps I could formulate *the orgasmic event* as a basic unit of measurement!

"But in the neurons of the animal body experiencing orgasm, the electrons would be jumping their orbital shells at the sites of chemical activity that regulate and supply the energy for orgasmic activity. Of course you could understand orgasm in this register. But with my new measurement unit—I could call it the Lumumba—orgasm could be translated into a universal potential that would relate an animal's sexuality to the basic forces of the universe and explain why orgasm is such an overwhelming force. If orgasm can be defined as the strength of the electric fields it generates, then during an orgasmic event we are at the mercy of our own electrical fields.

"But we could go further than that. Looked at honestly, we have to admit that orgasm is more than just a force—it is also a subdivision of matter. Consider cathode rays composed of electrons that have been separated from the atom. If the human body experienced this during orgasm, there would be a surplus of free-electrons detached from the atoms they were originally associated with, and if you watched an orgasmic event taking place in the dark with a sensitive light meter, you could detect the glow produced by these electrons as they interact with other particles in the body.

"Once again, we end up with the basic conclusion that orgasm is a form of electromagnetic energy—a kind of energy that is fundamental to the structure of the universe. It's so simple! The velocity of the orgasm particle divided by its wavelength ought to give the characteristic frequency of orgasm—a kind of analogue of the high pitched moaning of a woman in the throes of pleasure, but at the level of the electron.

"Actually, when you look at it, humans are merely extensions of the principles of the atom and collateral principles which govern the production and transmission of the force of orgasm.

"Thus orgasm can be calculated as the velocity of the electromagnetic particle coming up from the gonads squared times the frequency of electrical activity in the brain equals the orgasmic energy discharge. In standard format:

$$O = V_p^2 x$$

which gives:

$$V_p / W_p = E_o$$

The velocity of the electromagnetic particle divided by its wavelength equals the energy discharge of orgasm.

"At the peak of intensity, then, the orgasmic event would be related to the distribution of wavelengths. The greater the force the broader the spectrum of wavelengths included.

"In which case light coming from the outside would have to be calculated into the format, either directly as in photosynthesis and the synthesis of enzymes such as vitamin D, or indirectly through the consumption of plant materials.

"In which case the visual input in higher animals would also have to be factored in. After all, the images that are transmitted to the brain—say of the naked, aroused body—are an important part of the orgasmic process.

"And then there's the light produced inside the body which I postulated earlier. These activities could be electrical, chemical or nuclear, or have an origin that has not even be discovered.

"It all comes back to the theories of light. The activities of orgasm are exactly analogous to light. That is, the theoretical and mathematical models used to understand light should also apply—with some modifications—to an orgasmic event, and perhaps to aspects of it not yet discovered.

"Maybe orgasm is simply a permutation of light waves—a skillful mimicry of photosynthesis. Or better yet, photosynthesis is a mimicry of orgasm, a kind of physical analogue of a higher-order process. Or perhaps orgasm is emitted in discreet globs of energy the same as light, a kind of orgasmic wave particle duality. It would be orgasm that allows electrons to jump to higher energy levels in their orbital shells, giving them the potential to emit what we call photons.

"But what about heat? If the distribution of light frequencies is similar at any given temperature, then when our body temperature changes under the influence of orgasm, the distribution of light frequencies changes as well. Something heats up inside—an orgasmic explosion of energy.

"But in the end it all depends on the wavelength of the electromagnetic forces. When Einstein imagined himself riding on a light wave he was having a primitive intuition about his own sexuality. It was a kind of quantum mechanical wet dream—the very best kind for a physicist.

"In fact, many of the principles enunciated by physicists could be related back to sexuality. Planck's constant: the 'quantum of action' could just as easily read: 'the scrotum of action'. If you followed this through to its logical conclusion, everything that humans have done since they stood upright could be explained in terms of quantum mechanics. *Everything*.

"It would explain, for instance, why orgasm seems so different in men compared to other animals. It happens at different frequencies! When men stood upright they started having orgasm at frequencies high enough to start dislodging electrons. Einstein saw this in the photoelectric effect, where light waves had to have sufficient energy to throw electrons loose from atoms in a target substance. No matter how many low-energy photons hit the target they wouldn't dislodge a single electron. It has to be one photon of sufficiently high energy. And that's what happened to the first men! The dislodging of electrons by the new higher-energy orgasm particles agitated them to such a degree that they had to find a repressive mechanism to protect themselves. Their sex glands started to produce more and more hormones, which just made the agitation worse. Some of the excess energy was emitted as photons, but most of it rushed up the spinal cord to the brain.

"Maybe that's what happened to the dinosaurs. Many of them had started to stand upright, you know. Maybe they started experiencing the same things men did, but since they weren't able to evolve bigger brains and a civilization in time to become senators and congressmen, they ended up killing each other off. What do you think, Professor? Was it orgasm or an asteroid from outer space that done 'em in?"

Chapter Nine

A Grizzled Dwarf Meets an Untimely End
Or
The High Price of Kaopectate

Lumumba's monologue on moaning molecules had put Herbert in a trance. His mouth had gone slack, there was drool at the corners, and instead of replying he stared blankly out the window.

Bagamoyo sat peacefully on my lap. I was happy for his company, it comforted me, the land was so strange, so alien. But at the same time it seemed to beckon—as if it had some answer. But what was the question?

"We need to find a veronia plant quick," said Doba, thrusting Okovango inside the cab. "He has diarrhea."

A smelly goo running down Okovango's legs quickly transferred to the seat and my clothing. Herbert snapped to attention.

"I'll see if I can find a pharmacy," said Lumumba. "Maybe they'll have some Kaopectate."

We pulled up to a man who was walking beside his bicycle. *"Duka la dawa ni wapi?"* Lumumba asked. "Where is the chemist's shop?"

"The chemist was killed yesterday by an elephant," the man answered in perfect English. "What is the matter?"

"My nephew has *kuhara*—diarrhea," Lumumba answered.

I lifted Okovango gingerly up to the window. The man wrinkled his nose and said, "There is a clinic just outside Kizumbi. It's run by Americans, and they have a big supply of medicine. They also have powerful radios. Big antennas. They can get anything you want. They call and very soon black helicopters arrive with soldiers to give it to you. Very powerful doctors. They have much *juju.*"

The name Kizumbi seemed to strike a bell.

"Isn't that where Baxter's friend Dr. Baker has one of his clinics?" I said to Herbert.

"Please don't bother me," he replied. "I'm working out a formula."

We came to the turn-off and drove along a track for about a mile. A small enclave of buildings came into sight nestled amongst large trees and beautiful tilled fields. It looked like an oasis in the middle of a desert. A white flag flew from the roof of the central building. Emblazoned on it were the words PATRIOT ACT NEUROLOGICAL INTERVENTION CORPS. Children and dogs played infront of thatched huts. An old woman cooking over an open fire looked at us curiously. As Lumumba parked the truck and got out, an African attendant hurried over wearing a t-shirt with the logo PANIC.

"*Jambo,*" said Lumumba. "*Nataka Kuonana na bwana daktari*" (I wish to see a doctor).

"The doctors are out playing golf," the man said in English. "It's Wednesday."

He nodded toward a field where three men were practicing their shots. A dozen children were scurrying about picking up balls and bringing them back to the driving range.

"We need medicine for diarrhea," said Lumumba. He pushed the man out of the way and walked past him.

"You big bully!" said the man. "I'm going to tell Dr. Baker!"

"Good," said Lumumba as he and the chimps walked into the building. It was a long sterile room filled with people sitting languidly on small metal beds lined up neatly against the turquoise-blue walls. They looked at us sadly and with little interest.

Beyond the room was a door which looked promising as a dispensary. As Lumumba started toward it, an imperious voice called out: "*I am Dr. Baker. May I help you?*" An element of hysteria attended the restrained staccato of his words.

A short, stocky man of about forty-five stood there in jeans and a t-shirt. He was almost bald, and his eyeglasses sat squarely on a large beak nose. The lenses were as thick as coke bottles. Two muscular men stood next to him in PANIC t-shirts.

"May I help you?" he asked again. "Do you have an appointment?"

"I didn't know I needed one," said Lumumba.

"Even though we are here in Africa," said the doctor, "we still try to retain the civilized customs of the West." He snapped his fingers and called out, "Mr. Ntimama, please hand me my appointment book."

The man we'd seen that night at George Baxter's party stepped into the room holding a ledger and wearing a leopard hat.

Dr. Baker thumbed through several pages of soiled records until he came to an unmarked sheet.

"I can see you this afternoon at 5:00 or tomorrow morning at 10:00," he said crisply.

"What would you say," said Lumumba, looking at the clock on the wall, "if you saw us today at 1:00?"

It was exactly one.

"Impossible," Dr. Baker snapped. "I have important visitors from America and I'm showing them around the compound."

"America is the land of incest," Bata signed.

Baker took a step backward. "Deaf and dumb people frighten me," he said with a stricken expression.

"The baby looks pretty sick," said Ntimama.

Baker took a cursory look at Okovango.

"He'll live," he said. "You people will have to wait your turn just like the others."

He turned abruptly and walked away with Ntimama. As soon as they were gone Lumumba dispatched the two attendants.

"The GLA strikes again," he said as he dribbled the acronym on the bodies from a bottle of iodine. A few patients applauded weakly.

"You're here until you're gone, you're alive until you're dead," said old Kumasi.

We found the dispensary and some bottles of Kaopectate. Lumumba opened one and poured it down Okovango's throat. The little chimp sneezed and grimaced and tried to squirm free but Yalinga held him tightly.

"That should fix him for awhile," Lumumba said.

"Do you mind if I wash up?" I asked.

"I want to see what's in here first," Lumumba replied. He opened a door marked PRIVATE. The windowless room was banked with electronic equipment: short-wave radios, computer screens, tape recorders and dials. The walls were covered with maps effaced by colored pins and marker lines.

A grizzled dwarf sat in a swivel chair spinning dials and pushing buttons. As he turned in surprise Yendi sent a crushing blow to his head. The dwarf tumbled to the floor and lay in a crumbled heap.

"Give me the iodine," said Lumumba wearily.

He turned his attention to the maps.

"Do you think it peculiar," he said to Herbert, "that wherever this group has a clinic there's a civil war going on?"

"I suppose that's why the clinics are there," Herbert replied, "to help the refugees and the wounded."

"But the clinics were set up *before* the wars. Look at the dates."

At that moment the radio crackled, and a familiar voice came over the airwaves: "Goldschmidt to dwarf, Goldschmidt to dwarf, do you read me? Over."

Lumumba picked up the microphone: "Dwarf here; ready to receive your transmission; go ahead. Over."

"Dwarf sounds different," said Goldschmidt after a pause. "Is something the matter? Over."

"Dwarf has cold," Lumumba replied. "Nothing to worry about. Over."

"Please convey to Ntimama," said Goldschmidt, "a request that he contact his sources for information on several ongoing matters. The whereabouts of the Hickeys and their possible capture by white mercenaries. Also confirmation of Wambussi flying through air. Ntimama's tribal sources have heard rumors, please pass them along. Over."

"Roger," Lumumba said. "Anything further? Over."

"Why is dwarf in such a hurry? Dwarf usually likes to talk."

"Dwarf has sore throat," Lumumba replied.

"I hope you're not coming down with Ebola or anything. Have you talked to Baker? Over."

"Dr. Baker can't see me until next week. Over."

"Ah yes, he's a busy man. I heard through the grapevine that he's going to get the Congressional Medal of Honor. Over"

A cynical look crossed Lumumba's face.

"Dwarf wonders how many idiots have given money to PANIC to help the refugees. Over."

"You shouldn't be so open over this radio," said Goldschmidt irritably.

"Sorry. Dwarf has high fever and is delirious."

"I'll say!"

"Anything else? Over."

"Yes, and this is very important, a matter of highest secrecy. Headquarters urgently needs information about a new terrorist organization going by the acronym GLA. Identity, membership and agenda are still open questions. Speculation is that letters stand for Gabonese Liberation Army, but this is unconfirmed. Also unconfirmed is a report that Cuba is arming them. Bangassu Jamu has escaped from jail and there are rumors he has associations with this group. Second theory puts him with Kabila's rebels in Rwanda. Over."

"Roger," Lumumba said. "Will deploy all available resources ASAP. Anything else? Dwarf's throat getting sorer. Over."

"Just that the State Department needs a new supply of chimps."

Now it was Lumumba's turn to be silent.

"Another Project Mark?" he asked slowly.

"Yes, and this time they want them *all* from Africa. The one that was captured in Mahale proved to be an excellent subject. They want more like him."

"Roger. Will deploy our best poachers right away. Dwarf over and out."

"Roger and out," came Goldschmidt's voice.

The crackling ended and the lights on the panel flickered at random.

"Now they'll bomb Gabon because of your practical joke," I said.

"You're even more beautiful when you're angry," said Lumumba with a sneer. "Hurry up, there's the bathroom."

I was washing off my bra when I heard a soft voice at the window.

"I've found you at last!"

I tried to cover myself before turning around.

"Soddhu!"

"Your breasts are more beautiful than ever. Ahura Mazda, but I've missed you!"

He climbed through the window, we embraced, all the clouds went away at least for the moment.

"How did you know I was here?" I said at last.

"I didn't for sure, but Baxter said if I made this last run I might find you, and by God he was right! Oh Kathryn, why didn't you call or write? I've been worried sick!"

I told him the story, his eyes popped out when he heard about Albert.

"Oh my God! If he knows I'm dealing drugs he'll probably never speak to me again! You must promise not to tell him."

"Only if you'll get me out of here. What's the point in staying? All Herbert's interested in any more is Lumumba and his theories. Do you still want to go to India? Oh darling, I've missed you terribly!"

A plan was hatched, Soddhu would wait for me at the museum, it would be easier to escape from there.

"What about Baxter?"

"The hell with him! Instead of delivering his money we'll take it to India, this way Albert will always believe in me and my conscience will be clear."

A knock on the door and Herbert's insistent voice to hurry brought an end to another embrace. There was one last kiss, and Soddhu departed the same way he came in.

It was growing late but Lumumba pushed on. We came to Ibadakull, then Mhunzi and Lalago where we stopped to buy fruit and biscuits. At Kakesio, darkness overtook us. Once again we pulled off the road and made camp in the bush. The night air was warm and the Milky Way looked down at us with her million shining eyes. Long after the other apes had gone to sleep, Lumumba sat by the fire scratching complicated formulas for orgasm in the dirt. Herbert was giving advice.

Chapter Ten

Much Taboo about Nothing

"This is the day," said Yendi as he brushed off his shoes and straightened his clothes. "Albert, get ready to become a hairy chimp again."

The road had become crowded with land rovers heading for the Serengeti.

"Will we be going home after this?" Nedele asked. "I've told Bagamoyo how beautiful it is in the mountains and he can hardly wait to see them."

"You'll forgive us, won't you, if we decide to stay at the museum?" said Herbert.

"What's the matter?" asked Kribi. "We're not good enough for you?"

"I have some papers I want to write, the Professor will understand."

"Maybe he will and maybe he won't," said Lumumba ominously. "It all depends on Albert and what happens in the next couple of hours."

At the guardhouse there was a sign in Swahili and English: "*Huruhusiwi kutembelea maeneo yetu bla kuongozwa na ofisa wetu*, No one is allowed to visit without antiquities official guide."

"We're fucked!" Doba cried.

Lumumba pulled out his wallet. "Here is our official antiquities guide," he said as he entered the guardhouse. When he came out two grinning attendants waved us on. Herbert drove to the parking lot which was already crowded with land rovers and vans. The drivers sat around smoking cigarettes. They looked at our truck curiously. Where, I wondered, was Soddhu?

"Put on more flour," Lumumba said. "And everyone on their best behavior. Ladies put your dresses down. Men, zippers up. Remember to walk straight. You are bipedal humans, humans with a straight spine, humans with a direct connection between pelvis and brain, humans full of electrical potential for disaster."

The museum was an appropriately humble building to house our humble origins. It was made of stone, the simple roof was corrugated and the metal windows were painted green.

A group of Maasai women were gathered near the entrance. They were selling necklaces, earrings and bracelets, also leather whips and other handicrafts made of leather. A stone slab had been converted into a display table which Albert contemplated, a strange look on his face, until Lumumba pulled him away.

"C'mon, let's not dillydally."

"Bagamoyo would rather play outside," Nedele said, "than go through some dusty old museum."

As she began to walk away, Lumumba reminded her that this field trip was as much for her benefit as Albert's. But she refused to listen and Lumumba, looking unhappy, admonished her to walk upright.

"I'll stay with her," Yalinga said. "Okovango is still a little sick."

"Can I help?" I asked.

"He's not *that* sick," she replied.

Kumasi shuffled after them, signaling that he wanted to take a nap in the shade. Lumumba followed the retreating figures with a pained expression.

"Disaster beckons," he muttered as we went past the reception desk, past the fossils of animals neatly mounted along the wall, past the display of prehistoric stone hand axes until we came to the large skull of a hominid mounted on the wall. The sign said: *Australopithecus Bosei*. Pushing Albert infront of it, Lumumba said: "*Ecce homo*. Behold the man!"

"All I see is an old skull," said Albert. "And I don't like the way it's grinning."

"Forget the mouth and look at the eyes. Can you see how large and round they are? Even with the flesh gone you can still see the expression of astonishment on his face. That's the look of a man feeling his first orgasm at a 90-degree angle."

"Where's the proof?"

"Right there where the outer plates of the skull are. There's a reason our friend was so thickheaded. That was man's first reaction to the surge of electrical energy inside the brain. It's like the concrete shielding on a nuclear power plant. It was the body's attempt to protect itself from all that energy.

"But by keeping the energy inside, it made the situation even worse. As the brains got bigger, the increased volume of neurons contained vastly more synaptic connections. This meant that during orgasm—or during thought, which came later—a tremendous amount of heat was produced. All those neurons firing away were just like an electric motor or one of those modern computer chips that needs a special fan to cool it down. And just like the radiator in a car carries away the excess heat from the engine, in the human brain a special network of blood vessels developed that simultaneously brought nutrients to produce brain activity and carry away the excess heat."

"So human intelligence is just a byproduct of the evolving brain's need to dissipate heat?" Bata asked.

"When the first humans stood upright, the amount of electrical energy released during orgasm increased exponentially. For each added degree, the amount of energy doubled—and doubled again when the spine straightened completely."

"You can't prove it," Albert said again.

"The skull is its own proof. Look here at the bottom. This large opening through which the spinal cord passes is perfectly centered at a 90-degree angle to the pelvis, creating a straight line from the gonads to the center of the brain. The so-called reproductive advantage of the bipedal apes is a result of this geometry. There was no way for the brain to defend itself from the onslaught of energy. That's why their brains eventually grew bigger, and why they eventually had to create civilization and all its horrors.

"The origin of the whole process is right here in this fellow's astonished look, the incomprehension at what's just happened to him. He is a witness to the deception practiced on humans by their priests and lawyers. The occupant of this skull was the first man to experience the truth about the gonads. Since then nothing much has changed—except that men don't confront their sexual feelings directly anymore, but mediate their experience through the magic of the incest taboo and the Bible."

Albert began to quiver.

"Get thee behind me, Satan!" he said. "You are doing the Devil's work! Everybody knows that the earth is only 6000 years old and that God created these things to look like they are millions of years old inorder to test our faith in Christ."

"I didn't know the mentally challenged could be ordained," said a woman who had been watching us for several moments. She was elegantly attired, her clothes spotless, her hair perfectly coiffed.

"Oh, indeed they can," said Lumumba. "Sometimes they make the best clerics with their simple way of seeing things. Indeed, the word cretin comes from Christ. Did you know that?"

"No I didn't."

"By the way, allow me to introduce myself. I'm Dr. Lumumba and these are my traveling companions Dr. Doosledorf and his lovely wife Kathryn."

"I'm Betty Dodd. You're doctors?" she said in surprise. Her eyes roamed over us in disbelief.

"We're primatologists," Lumumba said. "Dr. Doosledorf works at the Yerkes Research Center in Atlanta, and I have retired from the Department of Anthropology at Yale to pursue my own interests here in Africa. I bring the hearing impaired to this museum so they can learn about their origins. It helps them feel less different when they realize that we've all descended from this fellow here"—he pointed to the smiling skull of the Australopithecus mounted on the wall.

"Well, yes," she said hesitantly. "That *is* the theory, isn't it? But how kind of you to take all this trouble."

"Uncle's not kind at all," said Albert. "He's an atheist, and he's trying to turn me into one too. That's why we're here at the museum."

Mrs. Dodd laughed nervously. "I wish I could understand what he's saying," she said.

"I'm sure you could learn sign language in a minute. To tell the truth your intellectual brilliance is quite blinding."

"My husband thinks I'm stupid," she said. Her hand moved nervously to a large black mole on the lower left side of her chin. "Well, everybody seems to be outside having lunch. Perhaps we'll meet again. We seem to bump into the same people all the time on safari."

"It would be my pleasure," said Lumumba bowing gallantly.

The moment she left he pried the skull off its mounting.

"Eeeeck!" Albert shrieked instinctively recoiling. "Get that nasty thing away from me!"

"You little twirp," said Lumumba. In a fit of frustration, he bounced the skull off Albert's head, making the sound of a coconut falling to the ground. Albert drew himself up with dignity.

"Forgive them Father, they know not what they do," he said, and walked into the next room. Lumumba hurried after him.

"I'm sorry, Albert, I shouldn't have done that."

"I forgive you. Now can we go? There is a pressing matter I have to attend to outside."

"Give me one more chance," said Lumumba. He turned the skull upside down so that the forament magnum showed clearly.

"Imagine," he said, that the skull is a bucket that's sitting across the yard. Someone takes a hose and shoots it into the bucket. The water comes in at an angle that is almost parallel with the top of the bucket. A little water gets into the bucket and slowly fills up. That's what it's like when the spine of an animal transfers electrical energy to the brain. It comes in at an angle and some of the energy ends up in the brain, but it doesn't make big waves—just a steady, even drip. But now take that same bucket, and walk directly up to it and start squirting water in from close range. What happens?"

"I suppose you get wet," said Albert sullenly.

"Then imagine what it would be like to stick the nozzle inside your skull and let loose. There'd be a violent whirlpool in that confined space—tremendous pressure, water leaking everywhere. Except that in the case of our friend here, it was electrical energy not water that was shooting up and leaking out. The pressure was unbearable, but—and here's the catch—so was the pleasure. When Australopithecus had sex, it was like hooking himself up to a million-volt generator."

"I wish I had been there to take his confession," said Albert. "He must have had lots to say."

Just then Kribi, Yendi and Tchibanga swung themselves over the top of a partition. Lumumba turned on them savagely.

"Didn't I tell you to act like men?"

"What for?" said Kribi. "Albert's not going to change."

"This trip was a waste of time," said Tchibanga.

"C'mon, Uncle, let's go home," said Yendi.

"There's one more thing I want Albert to look at," Lumumba replied.

The apes, to kill time, began tossing the skull and catching it as if it were a football. Lumumba pushed his nephew toward a collection of hand axes glued to a display board. Each had been chipped by ancient hands to form a rough cutting edge. Bata left the game to listen.

"Most scientists, Albert, consider these to be primitive tools for hunting animals and skinning them. Social structures came into being, they say, because men went to the hunt together. But the truth is, the first hand axes evolved so that men could hunt each other. And the reason they wanted to hunt each other was so they could have intercourse—hence orgasm—more often. All that electrical energy pouring into the brain produced a kind of primordial chaos. Indeed, the Bible speaks of it in metaphorical terms: 'The earth was without form and void, and darkness was upon the face of the deep.'

"This description was the 'state of mind' men were in until orgasm was made holy and God said, 'Let there be light.' "

"If God is orgasm and Jesus is the son of God," said Bata, "does that mean that Jesus is the son of orgasm?"

"Excellent Aristotelian reasoning!" said Lumumba, clapping him on the back.

"You two are going straight to hell," said Albert.

"That won't change the facts that the world was amplified into unbearable pleasure and pain, and that the simple world of the apes—with its simple rules and simple pleasures—was destroyed."

I saw my chance to probe. "Surely you must experience *some* pleasure during orgasm."

"For apes," said Lumumba after an imperceptible pause, "the pleasure doesn't cross the line into madness. For humans it does. Right from the start, men responded instinctively to the unbearable rush of pain and pleasure. All that electrical energy stirred up their natural aggressive tendencies. Sure, chimps play social games too; sometimes we fight or even kill each other over females, but men raised this violence to entirely new levels. And by using the hand axe to bash their opponents' brains in, early hominids were unconsciously taking out their aggressions on the very thing that was driving them mad—the skull that contained the raging, pulsating chaos of pleasure."

"Men are still bashing each other's brains in," said Bata.

"But not as much as they used to," said Lumumba, "thanks to the cerebral cortex whose sole purpose is to mitigate the chaos."

"You keep talking about the *men*," I said. "What about the women back in those days?"

"The electrical energy which exacerbated the worst tendencies in hominid males also worked to make human females a devious, conniving, game-playing gang of hysterics. Chimp females do the same things human females do—they form secretive alliances, play subtle power games the males don't understand, and use sex as a way to get food. But human females have amplified it to a pathological extreme. Actually, when you come right down to it women are much closer to the primordial chaos than men. The female orgasm is a portal back to an originary state of chaos that terrifies men."

"I told you they were evil!" said Albert triumphantly.

"Albert is right to take the old myths seriously," Lumumba replied. "As men evolved and progressed, women continued to represent a constant temptation; and to be sucked back into the maelstrom of pleasure and pain was to be avoided at all costs. Men had to find some way to defend themselves against that temptation."

"Let me guess," said Bata. "Religion?"

"Man's greatest invention. To defend himself against the sexual compulsions generated by the change in posture, at some point he symbolically cut off the organ that was tormenting him and transmogrified it into God. Afterwards God gave him the Law, and the Law imposed some kind of order on the situation. It told men which women they could have and which they couldn't. And it outlawed the most tempting of all sexual pleasures—incest. But the Law made desire so twisted and perverted that soon it was impossible to tell where desire would pop out—what weird images or acts it would be connected to. The Jews marched off to slay the Canaanites; the Christians marched off to slay the hordes of Islam. But at least brothers weren't killing brothers in fights over their sisters—at least not usually."

"So the hominid brain started growing so that it would become smart enough to make weapons to kill its enemies?" Bata asked.

"That's a little too simplistic. You mustn't forget the critical role of electrons and their physiological effect on the brain. Since energy can neither be created nor destroyed, the brain couldn't simply make the additional orgasmic energy go away as it continued to flood in, in increasing amounts. So what happened was a kind of transformation. The brain used all that energy to create MORE brain—that is, to create a bigger brain capable of handling the increased input. These bigger brains contained more neurons. But neurons in themselves don't make intelligence. What really provided the impetus for greater intelligence was early man's need to make weapons. This forced the neurons to start making connections. The original stimulus that caused the brain to develop was hatred and anger."

"That is your opinion," said Albert. "My opinion is that God created humans out of his love for them, and it was the Devil who gave them hate. If only you would accept Jesus Christ as your Savior you would understand this. But it's obvious to me that you never will, that you prefer to continue in your godless beliefs, so what say you we end these discussions? You will never convince me anymore than I will convince you. And the truth of the matter is I have a pressing matter to attend to outside. If you will excuse me."

"Suck my dick," Doba called after him.

"Let him alone," said Lumumba. "He's beyond our help, it's time we faced the facts."

As Lumumba was pilfering the donation box a loud commotion broke out infront of the museum. We hurried outside, there was Albert on top of the stone slab, brandishing a whip.

"Make not my Father's house a house of merchandise!" he cried. As the Masaai women screamed and scattered Albert swept their wares onto the ground, and with a final flourish cracked the whip over Lumumba's head.

"You son-of-a-bitch!" said Lumumba. I thought he was going to kill the little chimp as he pulled him from the dias and began shaking him. It was a good time to slip away, but where the hell was Soddhu?

"*Kuugua kwa kuchomwa na jua*," said one of the guides. "Too much sun. Here, Father, have some water."

"Take him to the shade," said another African. He pointed to a long palapa where the tourists and guides were having their lunch. It was situated near the edge of a gorge. People sat at the tables eating in silence, gazing in a reverent manner at the red cliffs where the famous skull had been found. There was only the sound of spectacled weavers flitting between the trees, the tables and the thatched roof of the open-air hut. A raven snacked peacefully on a half-eaten lunch someone had left for him next to the trash can.

Lumumba sank down on a bench and held his head.

"This is the first time I've ever failed," he said miserably.

"You gave it the old college try," Herbert replied.

"It wasn't good enough. I told Oyem I'd bring Albert back with an erection as big as a donkey's. It's obvious that's not going to happen, unless maybe he sees the Virgin Mary."

"Sorry, Uncle," said Albert. "But my faith is not to be shaken. 'Fight the good fight of faith, lay hold on eternal life.' I Timothy, 6:12."

"Time to go home, right Uncle?" said Doba.

His question went unanswered as a group of heavy-set tourists sat down noisily at another table. Their driver followed, staggering under a load of box lunches. "Germans," said an Englishman sitting nearby. "Keep an eye on your food, everyone."

The reason for his warning soon became clear; the group began to devour their lunches one after another, non-stop.

"They eat like us," said Tchibanga, watching in fascination. Just then one of the men noticed the raven. With an angry lunge he made it fly off, then threw the poor bird's meal into the trashcan.

"You should have brought the food here," the man's wife said. "I'm still hungry, *dumpkopf*."

Nedele was about to say something but Lumumba stopped her.

130

"Leave the Mithra worshippers alone," he said. "There've been enough scenes today already."

I looked at him curiously. Hadn't Soddhu said something about a god named Mithra who was connected in some way with Khvetukdas? But before I could quiz him Lumumba got up and went over to a guide. When he came back he had paper and pencil. He began to write furiously. When at last he was finished he threw the pencil down and stared morosely at the gorge. It was a nasty drop should anyone fall.

"I hope you're not thinking of killing yourself," said Herbert eyeing the paper turned face down.

"Why should I? My gonads aren't crying out for self-destruction. No, I'm thinking how best to take care of some unfinished business. Unfortunately it's some distance from here."

"We can't get home without you!" Yalinga cried.

"Sure you can. The Hickeys will help you."

"They'll dump us at the first police station."

"I don't think so. On hearing of your safe arrival at Mahale Professor Hickey will get the other half of this paper."

At this juncture Lumumba tore the paper in two and gave half of it to Herbert.

"Oh my God, it's the formula!" Herbert threw his arms around Lumumba. "Thank you, Professor. You can be sure we'll get them back safely!"

At that moment, Mrs. Dodd came over with her companions.

"Dr. Lumumba," she said. "I'd like you to meet my husband Royce and our friends Marty and Vivian Johnson. I told them about the work you do and they all want to meet you."

"I was telling your wife," Lumumba said to Mr. Dodd, "that she appears to have the capacity to do the same kind of work I'm doing."

"Now don't go putting any thoughts in her pretty little head. Betty's never worked a day in her life," said Royce.

"That's because you won't let me."

"A woman's place is in the kitchen."

"Only if you worship the incest taboo," said Lumumba.

"I beg your pardon?"

"He's just making a joke," said Herbert quickly. "Where are you folks from?"

The Dodds and Johnsons were both from California.

"Newport Beach, about sixty miles south of Los Angeles," said Mr. Johnson.

A spectacled weaver landed on our table with a pertinent look. Johnson eyed it suspiciously.

"It's a nice place except for the damn ducks," he said. "They crap in your yard, your swimming pool, everywhere."

"On my Mercedes," said Mrs. Johnson. "I wish there were a way to exterminate the little bastards."

"Do what I do," said Mr. Dodd. "If I find their eggs in my yard, I chuck them into the bay. Now if everyone did that, they'd die out in no time."

"It would be easier to gas them," said Mr. Johnson. "We could evacuate the town and sterilize the entire place. Get rid of the pigeons and that newcomer too. Can you believe an aborigine is living in Newport Beach? What's his name, Gordon Kangaroo or something?"

I froze. They were talking about my mother's new husband.

"Gordon Wallaroo," said Mrs. Johnson. "A lovely man from Australia. We know his wife."

"That's who she reminds me of!" said Mrs. Dodd suddenly. "Louise's daughter! I've seen her picture at the house."

"It doesn't look at all like her," said Mrs. Johnson, giving me a once-over. "For one thing Kathryn's hair is very blonde. And she's pale too, that white skin you see in the east. But you do look familiar, Mrs. Dooseldorf."

Bagamoyo peered out from Nedele's pocket.

"What a cute little bunny!" said Vivian. "My brother used to raise them for food."

"I can't take it any longer," said Nedele. As she walked away Lumumba signaled Kribi to follow.

"Oh, I hope I didn't say anything wrong," said Mrs. Johnson.

"She's very sensitive about animals," said Herbert.

"So am I," said her husband. "When I eat them I want them cooked just right."

"What do you do for a living?" asked Lumumba.

"We're senior planners at Bechtel," Johnson replied. "We just finished building a refinery in Saudi Arabia for some playboy prince with connections in Washington. It was quite the lucrative job, too."

"Yeah, we made a bundle on that one," said Royce, rubbing his hands gleefully.

"You fellows ever work for the CIA?" Lumumba asked innocently.

Royce burst out laughing but Johnson didn't seem to think it was funny.

"You ever been a member of the Communist Party?" he growled.

"Darling, he's from *Yale*," his wife said.

"Yale my foot! I can smell a Berkeleyite a mile away"

Their guide said it was time to go.

Betty spoke into Lumumba's ear.

"He's an avid patriot, please don't take it personally."

"Patriotism, my dear Mrs. Dodd, is a man's last refuge against the relentless longings of an incestuous subconscious."

"Is that another one of his jokes?" said Johnson testily. But Betty gave Lumumba's arm a squeeze. "My but you are strong for a professor. Well, it's off to the Mount Kenya Safari Club. Au revoir, you all!"

Kribi and Nedele came hurrying toward us.

"Uncle, the parking lot's crawling with soldiers. I think they've spotted our truck."

"Mama mia," Lumumba groaned. "What next! What are you hanging back for, Mrs. Hickey? Are you expecting someone?

It didn't take long to hijack another vehicle, this time a van. The driver had left his post to watch the soldiers, and the keys were in the ignition. As we sped past the guardhouse the apes hooted happily.

"Does this mean you're going with us?" Doba asked eagerly.

The answer was no, there was an airport not far away at Arusha, we would drop Lumumba off there, a few days of hard driving and we'd be back with our friends at Mahale.

Herbert looked pleased.

But as fate would have it, by the time we reached Arusha it was dark, and Lumumba instead of continuing east, turned north. Before he realized his mistake we were almost at the border. Lumumba cursed and knocked his head several times on the steering wheel. Herbert looked amazed.

"Dr. Lumumba, it does not behoove a Yale graduate to do that."

"I say it does," Lumumba answered and continued the bizarre behavior.

"Dear Uncle," said Albert, coming over. "It's obvious you are possessed by demons. Let me exorcise them. It will only take a minute."

"You are the only demon that needs to be exorcised," Lumumba growled. He flung his head back wearily and tried to think.

"Well," he said at last, "it's not that far to Kenyatta International. We just need to get past the border."

This was done with bribes, and we crossed the checkpoints with relative ease.

But Lumumba's luck was no better than before. The airport continued to elude him, and after what seemed an interminably long time he threw up his hands and admitted he was lost.

"Now you know why Uncle took the train," said Doba.

We seemed to be in the country, there were no street lamps, and a snow-covered peak glistened in the distance. Lumumba turned into a guardhouse to our right.

"Good evening, Bwana. Welcome to the Mount Kenya Safari Club," said the smiling attendant. "Do you have a reservation?"

"Of course," said Lumumba, handing him a wad of dollars.

We went directly to our rooms. There was a heaviness in the air, a feeling of defeat: Lumumba's failure to find the airport, his failure to cure Albert, Herbert's anxiety to be back at Mahale and receive the other half of Lumumba's formula and last but not least, Soddhu's failure to show up at the museum.

"I don't suppose there's any point in discussing an escape," I said.

"Kathryn, if you want to go I'll understand. But I have to stay, you know that. I need that paper."

"I won't go without you."

"I was hoping you'd say that."

We showered and collapsed on the first bed in weeks. The dining room was closed, making love seemed the best way to forget we were hungry. We quickly went at it, and Soddhu was soon forgotten as Herbert once again became the one, the only one. Everything was the same except for one difference, it was Lumumba's face I now saw as the magical waves of orgasm swept over me. Jesus had been usurped by an ape.

Chapter Eleven

Karonga Is No Match for a Kalashnikov
Or
Two Untimely Deaths at the Mount Kenya Safari Club

Everyone was up when I awoke the next morning. Herbert and the chimps sat in their clothes by the swimming pool. By the time I dressed they had been joined by a group of Hindus. The women wore saris, they chatted and laughed gayly while their rambunctious children played nearby. It didn't take the children long to recognize Albert's eccentricity, and in a flash they were all over him, making fun.

"Have you ever seen a man who looked so much like Hanuman?" one of the boys exclaimed.

"Who is Hanuman?" Herbert asked.

One of the boys' fathers tried to keep a serious face.

"I'm sorry, sir, but Hanuman is our monkey god. He is born of the Wind God and a monkey mother. Children can be cruel, can't they?"

"You are the cruel one," Albert replied, "teaching them such nonsense. Don't you know that Jesus Christ is the one and only true god? Repent, Sir! Repent before it's too late. The day of the Lord is coming, throw off your chains of sin, for He is vengeful and full of wrath.'"

The Indians laughed heartily.

"He even sounds like Hanuman when his tail is greased and set on fire," said one of the women.

"Well, I am not Hanuman," said Albert sullenly. "I don't have a tail."

"Of course you don't," another man said kindly, "none of us do."

Tchibanga started to pick Albert up by the scruff of the neck.

"How dare you treat a man of God this way!" said Albert, trying to squirm free.

"He's right," said another woman. "You should respect the many manifestations of Shiva. Besides, he isn't doing any harm."

"Thank you," said Albert, brushing himself off with dignity. "Confession is at four if you care to come."

"I have nothing to confess. For Hindus sex is not sinful."

"A dangerous concept," said Albert as he walked away. "She is heading straight for hell and doesn't even know it."

We met Lumumba near the lounge.

"Well, Professor, what is the plan?" asked Herbert.

"The plan," said Lumumba, "is to get the hell out of here. I have directions to the airport. We'll leave after dinner."

We had the whole day to relax, and after fortifying ourselves on a lunch of bananas and figs we decided to walk over to a private game park at the edge of the property. Albert, wanting to avoid the Hindu children, came with us. We strolled along hand-in-hand, marveling at the beauty of nature, while Albert tagged behind kicking up red dust. Eventually we came to an area of dense forest, a jungle of trees and vines trailing to the ground. A park ranger came toward us. He was dressed in a black uniform, and his left earlobe stretched almost to his shoulder. A heavy ornament hung from a hole in the middle. What teeth he had were big and yellow.

"*Jambo,*" he said pleasantly.

"*Jambo,*" Herbert replied.

"Do you have a cigarette?" the man asked.

"No, sorry," said Herbert.

"No problem," he said pulling out his own pack and lighting up. He looked at us intently.

"I have seen you before."

"This is our first trip to Kenya. I am Professor Doosledorf and this is my wife Kathryn."

"I am Masuru, the chief gamekeeper here. You are Americans?"

"Yes."

"I like Americans," he said falling in with us. "They are friendly and give good tips."

"Money is the root of all evil," Albert signed.

Masuru laughed: "Money is good. It buys many wives."

"The way of the flesh is also evil," Albert replied.

136

Masuru looked at Albert curiously. "Your friend is very unhappy, isn't he?" he said to Herbert.

Albert looked sullenly at his feet and let his fingers trail over the vines that hung down from the canopy overhead. It was dense enough to keep out the sun. Only a little light filtered through the underbrush forming beams that cut through the shadows.

Suddenly Masuru stiffened.

"Something has gotten loose from the park," he said. "Go back quickly, it could be a lion."

"Ah," said Albert, recognizing a familiar sound, "it's just Kribi banging Yalinga. I shall go and have a word with him."

There on a wooden deck in a small clearing were the apes: Kribi, Yalinga, Doba and Bata. The latter two sat on red cushions waiting their turn. In the meantime they were studying a set of elephant tusks which had been ceremoniously placed inside the hacked off stumps of the poor elephant's feet.

The apes had taken their clothes off, and their black fur glistened between the thick white patches of flour, especially around their eyes where they had been rubbing. Masuru's mouth fell open.

"It's the pandas!" he exclaimed. "They're still alive!"

Albert snickered.

"How lucky you are to see them fornicating," he said. "Most pandas spend their time eating and sleeping."

"Pandas can be very dangerous, I think we should all go back," said Herbert, struggling to turn Albert around.

"Masuru is not afraid," said Masuru. "Besides there is a reward for their capture and Masuru has nine wives."

As he slowly closed in on them the apes took to the trees. Masuru started to climb after them.

"I wouldn't do that," Herbert shouted. "Pandas can also be very treacherous."

"So can nine wives who want money," Masuru called back.

He continued to climb, the apes went higher and higher. At last they were all at the top of the tree. Masuru reached into his pocket and took out an apple.

"Good panda," he said, offering it to Doba who was sitting the closest. As Doba grabbed the apple Masuru tried to catch hold of his arm. There was a brief struggle, Masuru lost his balance and with a terrible shriek he catapulted some 20 or 30 feet down and landed on a tusk. He wriggled for a moment like a fish on a hook, then lay still.

"I can't say I'm sorry," Lumumba replied when we told him what had happened. "I knew the elephant to whom those tusks and legs belonged. His name was Karonga, and he was one of the best chaps around. He used to do nice things for everybody, sired many fine children and stomped on untold numbers of humans. I suppose that's what cost him his life. He put up a good fight though—it took a dozen Kalashnikovs to bring him down."

"How sad that things have to happen this way," said Herbert.

"But they don't," Lumumba replied. "Get rid of the incest taboo and you humans will have a whole new lease on life. All the senseless cruelty will stop once and forever; the incest taboo doesn't have to hold you by the throat, you know."

Exactly what Zarathustra might say, I thought to myself.

It was still early, Herbert suggested a game of golf.

"Why not," said Lumumba. "I haven't been out on the links since I played the Toshiba Open in Newport. Yes, Kathryn, I've been there; it's a nasty little town, isn't it? I've never met so many mean-spirited, petty little burghers. But that's what comes from all that flag-waving. Giving your life to the Establishment and the incest taboo doesn't make for a happy camper. Are you ready, Dr. Hickey? I'll give you 54 strokes."

Herbert laughed.

"You want to pay me now or later?"

The impossible was about to happen. On Lumumba's first shot he hit a hole in one. It was attributed to luck, but when he hit a second hole in one at the second fairway everyone became suspicious. Obviously the chimps were tampering with the ball.

"Your accusation pains me deeply," said Lumumba to Herbert. "Go stand on the third green."

Once again the tee shot rolled into the hole. Lumumba was beginning to draw a crowd.

"Way to go, Uncle!" said Yendi when Lumumba hit his fourth hole in one.

Intimidated and psyched out by this incredible display of skill Herbert played badly. I'd never seen so many balls land in the rough and sand traps. But who was paying attention?!

You must believe me that at every fairway Lumumba shot a hole in one, and by the time he reached the eighteenth fairway everyone at the hotel was there including the staff. It reminded me of that night at Carnegie Hall, the way they were applauding. Lumumba gave them the Republican salute, and sauntered off to the hotel amidst the wild jubilation accorded only to a hero.

138

"You just have to be attuned," he said to Herbert later, "to the relationships between matter, energy and consciousness."

"I'm sorry, Professor, but no one can hit eighteen holes in one," said Herbert. "You have to have paid off the caddies or some such shenanigans."

"But you saw how afraid they were after the first seven or eight holes, didn't you?"

"Yes, they kept saying 'ju ju,' but they could have been faking it."

"Why should I go to such attempts? What would be the point? Besides, what happened today is so easy to explain. Just be quiet and listen.

"Golf balls are physical objects, but at the atomic level, they're a collection of vibrating bits of energy held together by an energetic force that pervades the entire universe. The golf ball, the club that hits it, the air it sails through and the mind of the caddy who pulls the ball out of the hole are all part of a great energetic continuum. The ball gets into the hole the same way a penis gets into a vagina. (What do you think the game's all about anyway?) And since the universe is filled with the energy of subatomic orgasm, the penis seeks out the vagina because they are expressions of this underlying orgasmic energy that pulls them together. The trick in golf is to see how the ball and the hole are manifestations of the orgasmic nature of the universe."

"I don't think that will help me make a hole in one," said Herbert.

"Because you're not in tune with your own atomic energy," Lumumba replied. "For me there are no taboos and barriers to block my connection to the rest of the universe. My mind, my body and the universe are part of one continuous field of energy. If you understand that connection, it's a simple matter to polarize the golf ball and the hole into male and female. It's much like making a piece of steel into a magnet. You simply have to organize the underlying electrical forces into positive and negative poles. Magnets, by the way, have an extremely disciplined subatomic sexuality. In case you didn't know that."

"Do you have a way of making golf balls into males and the holes into females?" Herbert asked.

"Not exactly. It would be better to say that I impart male energy to the golf ball through my club, and the male energy guides it to the female energy embedded in the earth. The atomic energy in my brain (which I release through my unrepressed sexuality) guides the atomic energy of the ball and puts it exactly where I want it. It's all in the electrons, you might say."

"Not in mine," said Herbert.

139

"That's because for you, golf is a sublimation of your sexuality. That makes it much more difficult for you to play the game. For you it's just balls and holes with no concept of what those balls and holes really stand for."

"To hell with the balls and holes," said Kribi. "Let's get some chow."

We dressed for dinner in clothing that Kribi and Yalinga had "borrowed" from the gift shop. As Kumasi put his jacket on over his loose-fitting trousers, there was a pronounced crackling in his back. He grimaced in pain.

"You're alive until you're dead," he said, "you're here until you're gone."

Word of Lumumba's exploits had proceeded us. As the maitre d' greeted us at the door, the entire room stood up and applauded.

Marty Johnson waved us over.

"Make way for the best damn golfer the world has ever seen," he exclaimed. He reached out to shake Lumumba's hand, and there was no sign of his previous antagonism. "I sure wish we'd had a video camera. Nobody back home will ever believe it."

"Our buddies in Newport will think we are stark raving mad," Royce said agreeably.

The waiters moved over two large tables, and Lumumba took a seat next to Mrs. Johnson.

"Mrs. Doosledorf, it will come to me eventually where I've seen you," said Vivian Johnson. "I'm good with faces." She smiled and pulled thoughtfully on the long silk scarf she had wrapped around her neck.

"Can we buy you a round of drinks?" Mr. Dodd asked. "You have a little catching up to do."

"No thanks," said Lumumba. "Our electrons don't need alcohol to jump into higher orbitals."

Johnson laughed loudly. Lumumba could now say anything he wanted, apparently, and get away with it.

We looked at our menus.

"Wow!" said Herbert. "Parfait of chicken and ostrich liver! But I think I'll have the Crocodile Mt. Kenya: succulent crocodile flambéed in whiskey, simmered in cream, garlic, honey and lime. Yup, that's the one for me. Kathryn?"

"I think I'll try the Bush-Meat a la King. I've heard that chimpanzees taste pretty good."

"We had it last night, it was a little tough," said Mrs. Johnson.

"That's the nice thing about bananas," Lumumba replied, "they're never tough."

He ordered several platefuls plus other vegetarian dishes that turned out to be quite tasty. Nevertheless when Betty's steak was brought in I could hardly hide my envy.

"You poor dear," she said. "The Professor not only wants you to learn about our ancestors, he wants you to eat like them too."

"If that were the case," Albert signed, "Mrs. Hickey would be eating *you*."

"Is he a priest or what?" asked Johnson.

"Actually he's an acolyte," Lumumba replied. "He hasn't been ordained yet."

"I didn't know priests would be interested in evolution," said Marty.

"I'm not," Albert replied. "God is testing my faith. He has simply put those old bones in the museum to see who will go to heaven and who won't. My uncle says he can prove that God is nothing but a penis, but I know he can't do that because God isn't a penis, God is God."

When Albert's words were translated Marty began to look annoyed.

"Aren't you teaching him what is the antithesis to a good game of golf?" he asked.

"Quite so," said Lumumba. " But he's too steeped in Kierkegaard to become a threat to the Establishment."

"He's smart, I could see that right away," said Marty.

"Perhaps too smart. There really is all kinds of evidence of life on earth millions of years ago, and all that evidence is totally consistent with the known laws of nature. But if Kierkegaard were here he'd simply say that the evidence is false and God created it inorder to test man's faith. It's the essence of Christianity to believe exactly the opposite of what our senses tell us. And of course it's completely irrefutable. The more evidence there is in favor of life millions of years ago, the more God loves you."

"This Kierkegaard fellow sounds okay," said Royce. "I'd like to meet him."

"I think that could be arranged," Lumumba replied.

"Professor," said Royce's wife. "Anybody who can speak with such fervor must certainly have some religious belief in his blood."

"It's my opinion," said Lumumba, peeling a banana with meticulous care, "that religious fervor is rooted in an unconscious desire to unite within the first degree. The crucifix your friend is wearing"—he meant Mrs. Johnson—"may ward off the erotic feelings but won't get rid of the desire."

"Now see here," said Marty. "You may be the damnedest golfer the world has ever seen but that doesn't give you the right to talk dirty to my wife."

"My apologies," Lumumba replied glibly. "I had no intention of insulting her. I was speaking as a scientist. And speaking as such, I feel constrained to point out that the Crucifixion itself is an entirely erotic and incestuous metaphor."

"Oh Uncle, how can you say those things?" said Albert. "Our Lord and Savior died for our sins and was crucifried so that we might be saved."

"But the sin he died for (and there is only the one) is breaking the incest taboo," Lumumba replied. "That is no mere cross he is nailed to. That is his mother. Groddeck pointed this out many years ago. The cross is a warning to all sons. If they want to sleep with their mothers they will be crucified. That's the sin Jesus died for."

"Does that include sisters?" said Yendi poking Albert in the ribs. The little ape hung his head miserably.

"Jesus is my Savior, those who believe in Him shall have eternal life."

"That's telling 'em," said Marty. He turned his eyes on Lumumba. "You're very sure of yourself, aren't you, Professor."

"I know what I know," Lumumba replied, "and the Crucifixion is not just about Jesus. The mother yearns for her son, too. She embraces him as he is dying. This is the only embrace the two of them can share. An embrace that ends in a death symbolic of sex. Sex and death, after all, have much in common. In some magical way, Jesus and Mary have become one, just as lovers become one. They are united in sex and death. Who's to say if there's any difference? Perhaps it's Jesus himself who impregnates the Virgin Mary in the guise of the Holy Spirit."

"That's absurd!" Mr. Johnson banged on the table. All signs of truce had vanished. "I can't believe they allowed you to teach at Yale. Berkeley yes, Yale no!"

"So did Jesus do it with his mother?" Bata asked.

Lumumba shrugged. "'Woman, what have I to do with thee?' is a very strange thing to say to your mother," he replied.

"No matter," said Royce. "I'm still glad my father drummed the principles of Christianity into me as a boy."

"Of course," said Lumumba. "The secret of Christianity's power is that all boys identify with Jesus. They are sons and he is a son. Since Jesus' father is God, a boy's father is also God. Now since Jesus's father is all-powerful and almighty, no normal son will ever lose the fear of his father from the day he's born to the day he dies. That's what gives

Christianity its magical power: it takes the power of the father and makes it supernatural. In the boy's mind, the whole universe is enforcing the will of the father. Thus when Jesus calls out to his Father on the cross and asks why He has forsaken him, God's message is obvious: 'You can't have your mother, my wife, because it was I, the Holy Spirit, who had her first. She belongs to me.' 'But you promised me that someday I would have the keys to the kingdom,' Jesus replies. 'I assumed that meant everything, even Mother.' 'Do you think I'm stupid?' says God. 'This is as close to her as you'll ever get. Now hurry up and ascend to heaven so we can all go about the business of setting up this new approach to the incest taboo.' The belief in incest in heaven is what gives Christianity its great power. But here's the irony. If the Messiah is the son, and the son is here to enter his father's kingdom, which in psychosexual terms means possessing the mother, then the son has to be kept out. The son has to die or never be born. That's why the Jews are still waiting for the Messiah to show up. Of course, he never will. If he did, he'd have to be crucified all over again."

Johnson's face was now a deep purple.

"Son, have you ever been or are you now a member of the Communist Party?" he said through clenched teeth.

Lumumba looked amused.

"I've always been struck by people's tendency to lump atheism and communism together," he said. "Is it because without God a son will go directly to his mother's bed? And in communism the sharing of everything also include the sharing of the mother? It's more than likely that the rise of fundamentalism is a direct consequence of the fear of this happening."

"Son, I'm going to run a background check on you first thing tomorrow," said Johnson.

"Oh calm down," said Royce. "I think it's all rather interesting, especially the notion that Christianity is the son's religion. Does that mean, Professor Lumumba, that Judaism is the father's?"

"Who the hell cares?" Marty replied. "I'd just like to change the subject and have another drink. Waiter!"

"Stop shouting," said Vivian. "Everybody's looking."

"I don't care, let them. It's better than sitting here and listening to this commie, 18 holes-in-one or not!"

"But your friend has posed such an interesting question," said Lumumba. "In Judaism the father *does* have all the power. There is one God—one top penis—and his Word is totally authoritarian. In Christianity, God promises many things to his son. The meek shall inherit the earth, the Bible says. But who are the meek? Are they not the children of the Father? And the earth—who is she if not the Mother? In Christianity the son is rewarded for his obedience by many promises. Both the promises are Oedipal in nature—the subconscious promise of possessing the mother in the afterlife. So the promise is false. It is the promise of the proverbial carrot that the donkey can never reach. It is the promise of the Keys to the Kingdom that the son can never have. The keys to the Kingdom— that is, to the father's stash of forbidden women—remain forever beyond reach. That's why Christian men are so anxiety-ridden: They've allowed themselves to be castrated in this life in exchange for a vague promise of possessing the mother in the next—but only if they obey the rules which go counter to their nature."

"You make me feel ashamed to be a Christian," Royce said half-jokingly.

"You needn't be," Lumumba replied. "It's not just Christianity which promises and teases. In every religion there is a Messianic or saint-like character who, on his arrival, will usher in a new age of justice. But justice for what? For the people or for something other than people, the gonads, for instance. Well, why not? The word itself—justice—comes from Latin *ius* which was originally a religious formula having the force of the law. *The force of the law.* Of course if you doubt that the force of the law is not orgasmic in nature, then what can I say?"

Lumumba looked across the room. Two constables had come in and were talking to the maitre d'.

"They've found Masuru," said Lumumba using sign language. "Time to go."

At that moment Mrs. Johnson banged her wine glass on the table.

"Betty, you old thing, you were right. That *is* Louis's daughter. I just saw her picture in yesterday's . . . ."

Plop! Mrs. Johnson's head fell forward onto her plate. The rice pilaf and Quail Kilimanjaro flew onto the tablecloth.

"Woman never could hold her liquor," Marty growled. He gave her a push.

"C'mon Vivy, let's be a nice girl and wake up. Everybody's looking."

With a paternal gesture, Lumumba rearranged Mrs. Johnson's scarf, then rose from the table. Taking advantage of the disruption we excused ourselves and left the dining room. Those who saw us go waved goodbye.

Chapter Twelve

Lumumba's Troops Suffer a Hit
Or
The First Fatality of Any Importance
(Unless, of Course, You Count the Canary)

A loud argument was taking place in the parking lot. Lumumba held us back. "I know that voice," said Herbert. As my eyes grew accustomed to the dark I made out the figures of Goldschmidt and Ntimama wearing his leopard cap.

"If this is a double-cross," Goldschmidt was saying, "your Dr. Baker is in for some big trouble."

"I swear to you, Bwana, I am telling you the truth," Ntimama replied. "When Dr. Págalu left he had the money, every penny of it. I put it in the briefcase myself."

"Then where is he?"

"Perhaps he was eaten by a lion."

"On his way to Nairobi?!"

"He was going to make a stop at the Leaky museum."

"Then perhaps he did get eaten. It's not that far from the Serengeti. The fool! Why did he have to stop there?!"

"Bwana, everybody stops there to see the skull of the first man."

Albert blew through his lips.

"What was that?" Goldschmidt asked nervously.

"Somebody broke wind," Nitimama replied. "The food here is very rich."

"Listen, Nitty, they're loading the plane in Kirua now, I can't wait any longer."

"I don't know what to tell you, Bwana. They took Dr. Baker to Nairobi, he's being questioned about the murders."

"Oh yes, the GLA. I must have been the last person to talk to the dwarf. Poor old fellow, he always thought he was safe in that room."

Old Kumasi clicked his tongue and shook his head.

"You're here until you're gone," he signed, "you're alive until you're dead."

Lumumba and the apes moved quickly. "Put your hands up," said the professor, pressing a banana to the men's backs.

"If this is a stick-up," said Goldschmidt, "I swear to you we don't have any money, not that we weren't supposed to though."

"Keep your trap shut," Lumumba replied. "Your voice is just as annoying in person as it is over the radio.

"Ah, you're undercover agents?" Goldschmidt was too surprised to see the signals Ntimama was making to get his attention.

"No," Lumumba replied, "but after five years at Yale, I can smell a spook a mile away. Besides, I recognize the cheap CIA-issue aftershave you're wearing."

"Your taste in colognes is obviously barbaric," said Goldschmidt haughtily. "This is the best French perfume you can buy. Why, Mrs. Hickey! What are you doing with this group of hoodlums? I hope you haven't done a Patricia Hearst! Is Herbert here? Why yes, and who is this? Good evening, Holy Father. Have these miscreants been treating you well?"*

"Not at all, Sir," Albert replied. "They are trying to shake my belief in Christ."

"And have they succeeded?"

"Indeed not. If anything they're only helping to strengthen me in my faith."

"He's not kidding about that," said Herbert.

"Would you mind if I made a phone call?" said Goldschmidt pleasantly. "It'll only take a second."

"What do you take us for, a bunch of idiots?' Kribi growled.

"Frisk them," said Lumumba, "and take them to the van."

"Where are we going?" Goldschmidt asked. He looked as if he'd lost his best friend as Kribi passed his pistol to Lumumba.

"To your airplane, we need a ride," Lumumba answered.

---

* Conversations like this between chimps and non-users of ASL were always facilitated through the help of an interpreter.

146

"Oh now just a minute," said Goldschmidt. He began to back away. "I have strict orders not to let anybody on board. The plane is carrying a cargo of very valuable medicine."

"Listen," said Lumumba, "if you don't get in this god-damned van *now* you're both going to have your heads bashed in."

"That's right," said Yendi. "The GLA doesn't screw around."

Goldschmidt looked astonished

"You are the Gabonese Liberation Army?!"

"That's what I've been trying to tell you, Bwana," said Ntimama.

"Well I'll be damned!" said Goldschmidt. "But what are you doing in Kenya?"

"The fact of the matter is," said Lumumba, "that your friends at Langley have made a little mistake. In putting two and two together they've come up with five. We are not Gabonese leftists at all."

"That's right," said Bata. "We are Gonadese leftists, if you know what I mean."

"I don't think I do."

"He means," said Lumumba, "that the GLA—the Gonad Liberation Army—has organized to overthrow the world. We denounce the governments of all humanity, we believe that all ideologies are fraudulent and we have joined forces to fight the false assumption that there are taboos in the world, an assumption which has left too much devastation in its wake, especially for the animals and the planet.

"You're environmentalists? Ye gads!"

"Now are you going to get in or not?"

"You'll never get past the gate house," said Goldschmidt, climbing in. "It's surrounded by police."

"Thanks for the warning," said Lumumba.

As the barrier loomed infront of us Lumumba floored the accelerator and crashed through it. The startled guards jumped back but not before Kribi and Tchibanga reached out and grabbed their assault rifles. Lumumba swerved to avoid two police cars trying to block us infront. They fish-tailed around and started chasing us with their lights flashing and sirens wailing.

"If they get close," said Lumumba passing the two pistols to Yendi and Bata, "shoot them with these phallic symbols."

"Now what do guns have to do with the penis?" Goldschmidt asked. He eyes grew wide as the four apes swung through the windows and climbed onto the luggage rack.

"Spears, the first serious weapons, were modeled after the erect penis," Lumumba replied. "Guns are but the natural extension of spears."

"So when a man is shooting bullets, he's really shooting sperm?" Doba asked.

"All violence is rooted in the gonads."

A bullet shattered the back windshield. Albert screamed and began to recite the Lord's Prayer. Lumumba turned the wheel sharply.

"Aim at their faces," he signed to Kribi. "And set the controls for single shot. Don't use up your ammunition all at once."

"Wow!" said Doba bouncing up and down in his seat. "It's just like the movies we used to sneak in to watch at the compound. Practically every one of them had a chase scene."

"Humans need an outlet for their repressed sexuality," Lumumba replied. "What better way than a car chase? The concept is entirely orgasmic."

"Orgasmic!" said Goldschmidt. "I've never felt less orgasmic in my life!"

Lumumba swerved to avoid hitting a small burro and hit a pedestrian instead.

"Way to go, Uncle!" said Doba happily. He clapped his hands slowly and made funny grimaces with his mouth. Goldschmidt regarded him curiously.

"He looks retarded," he said to Herbert.

"He's far from that," Herbert replied, "you wouldn't believe how far."

"Why do I have the feeling you've become accomplices to these terrorists?"

"He wants to win the Nobel Prize," I answered.

"By accompanying a bunch of leftist rebels?"

"How many rebels do you know," Herbert answered in measured tones, "that can wax on the psychosexual origins of the cinema?"

"Well, you know, I don't really run around in those circles."

"Ah yes," said Lumumba, "you are more into the right-wing death squads, aren't you? Their ability to intellectualize is equaled only by a mouse."

"Still, they do react to the cinema the same way as a person on the left. Why? Because those faces on the silver screen gain their fascination from the way they unconsciously represent a child's early image of its parent, which appears to be monstrously large. It's not really the actor whom the female in the audience is swooning over but rather the father for whom she has yearned ever since she was a small child. The overpowering figure and presence on the screen of the actor is an unconscious representation of the over-powering figure and presence of her father when she was little.

"Why do you think they are called movie stars? Because they're like the stars in the sky—far off and fascinating but completely unattainable,

148

just like the boy's mother or the girl's father. Humans crave that phantasmagoric love just as strongly at the age of eighty as the age of eight. It's the central theme in literature, music, poetry—people search for true love all their lives. But they can never find it because it is entirely Oedipal. But Oedipal love can be safely transferred to a double on the screen, where the intensity of that first, primeval love is personified by the intensity and brilliance of the stars, the movie stars. Of course in the days of ancient Greece the audience, just as mesmerized then as today, could only transfer this primal love onto the actors who played out the Oedipal story itself, which has been the prototype of all stories ever since."

"See what I mean?" said Herbert.

"I'll say!" Goldschmidt exclaimed. "I only hope his analysis of movies doesn't include the westerns. I'd hate to think that John Wayne was mixed up in all this."

"Why do you suppose," Lumumba replied, "that the cowboy always rides off into the sunset? Better to be alone and pure than give in to temptation. He is like the celibate priest who fights against evil. That's why he always wears a white hat, and a big one at that, because the hat is phallic. Of course he can't have a woman because he is also a Christ figure: besides the outlaws he must deal with—men in black hats who threaten the stability of man's taboos—he must also contend with the wilderness itself, which is symbolic of man's life without laws—life without the incest taboo."

"Gee, and I always thought Tom Mix was just a cowboy," said Goldschmidt sadly.

The asphalt was so torn up that Lumumba switched to a dirt track alongside the road. It wasn't much better. There were many cars on both sides of us, we weaved in and out with only inches to spare.

"Quit shooting wildly," Lumumba yelled to Kribi. "Take your time and aim."

Despite his advice, the police appeared to be gaining. A voice came over a loudspeaker behind us: "This is Constable Musana, stop immediately and lay down your weapons!"

To my surprise, I saw the rifles and pistols fly past the windows.

"Don't tell me you're giving up!" said Herbert.

"They've run out of ammo," Lumumba replied.

"Have no fear," said Albert. "God is on our side. He shall smite them with his mighty sword."

"Will you shut up?" said Lumumba angrily.

"But he's quoted the Bible perfectly!" said Goldschmidt after Herbert translated.

"You don't understand," said Doba. "Uncle's been trying to teach him for several days now that the mighty sword is God's penis."

"There's one thing I've learned in the foreign service," said Goldschmidt. "The more you attack peoples' beliefs, the more they defend them—even if they never really cared much about them in the first place."

"That's because religious beliefs are rooted in repressed desires," said Lumumba. "When you attack the beliefs, it stirs up the desires—which means that the beliefs have to become even stronger to contain them. What beats me is how something as transparent as 'a mighty sword' can be so powerful."

"Some people might say the mighty sword is a mighty sword and leave it at that," said Goldschmidt.

"Most people would," Lumumba replied. "But to know that the mighty sword—whether it's God's or the king's or some hero's—is the penis is to know that religion is rooted in sex. If that secret were ever revealed, religion would no longer have any power. Nor would legends such as the Arthurian tale of a mighty sword that no one can safely wield but the king or the mythic warrior who has sworn allegiance to the king. The whole idea is to teach boys to be afraid of their father so they will never challenge him."

"Uncle, I think we have more pressing matters," said Bata hanging form the luggage rack.

"You're right," said Lumumba. "You know how it is once Albert gets me started."

With renewed concentration Lumumba was able to put some distance between the van and the police. The sirens became less blaring.

"There's the landing strip," said Goldschmidt. A turbo prop C-130 was on the tarmac, its propellers idling.

"It's perfect," said Lumumba looking happy for the first time in ages. "Victor Muñoz, here I come!"

The van drew up to the plane, we were surrounded by men with assault rifles and grenade launchers. They broke into smiles when they saw Ntimama and Goldschmidt.

"Bwana Jacques afraid you were eaten by lions," a man said.

"How many people actually *are* eaten by lions?" I asked.

"Not many," Lumumba replied. "Lions have become much more particular about what they eat these days."

Then was Goldschmidt right, had Soddhu pulled a double-cross? No, he was too fond of Albert, and a double-cross was just as lowdown as a drug deal; Albert wouldn't forgive him for either one.

"Let's get going!" Goldschmidt shouted to the crew. The police had turned onto the airstrip. Behind them was a truckload of soldiers. Everyone began firing as we ran up the loading gate into the tail of the plane. As we climbed over crate after crate of Kaopectate, Albert shook his fists at the soldiers.

"Smite them, oh Lord! I don't care if you use a sword or a penis, just smite them."

A look of surprise came over Lumumba's face.

"How about a grenade launcher?" he said brightly. As he fired from the doorway, a police car burst into flames and a man flew into the air. It was Constable Musana still holding his megaphone.

"Excellent shot, General!" said Goldschmidt.

The engines roared to full throttle, the plane roared down the runway, and became airborne the very last minute. Goldschmidt went to the cockpit. When he reappeared he was accompanied by the captain, a short man of lithe build, mostly bald with thinning brown hair on the sides.

"How do you do, Messieurs, Mesdames, Mademoiselles. I am Monsieur Jacques, pilot of this piece of crap."

"Jacques doesn't want to go to Spain," Goldschmidt explained.

"Oui, oui, that's right, my friends. And do you want to know why?"

Lumumba eyed the large wooden crates that were stacked everywhere, from the cargo hold to the fuselage.

"I imagine," he said, "that with this heavy payload there's not enough fuel."

"Exactly right, mon General. Cairo, yes, maybe, but Spain, no way!"

"Well, then, we'll lighten the load."

"That's impossible," said Goldschmidt quickly. "Jacques can get us to Spain, he's a great pilot."

Lumumba snickered.

"You'd rather go down with the plane than lose your precious cargo? What an idiot!"

"I'm sorry, General," said Goldschmidt. "But I'm a died-in-the-wool capitalist. What can I say? Besides, it's easy for you to be derisive living in the middle of Africa. But if you had to choose sides you might begin to be more objective and see that democracy and capitalism are better suited to human needs than godless communism."

"Ha, it always comes down to that, doesn't it," said Lumumba.

"If you gentlemen will excuse me I have a plane to fly," said the pilot.

Jacques returned to the cockpit, and for several minutes only the high-pitched drone of the airplane marred the silence. Lumumba seemed to be deep in thought, yet his eyes had become fixated on Goldschmidt; as they narrowed to an unfriendly squint a thought occurred to me: could apes be anti-Semitic too?

"My dear Goldschmidt," Lumumba said at last, "it's not really a question of which system is better, both systems are failed attempts to deal with the problem of desire—and both systems fail to extract themselves from the clutches of the incest taboo. Let's take capitalism first, because the relationship is more obvious there. Both capitalism and the incest taboo operate by means of a series of substitutions. When the incest taboo was instituted, the original object of desire—the mother—was forbidden and replaced by a series of substitutions. A man may sleep with hundreds of women, but they are all just substitutes for the original object of desire which men spend their whole lives trying to satiate.

"The hunger for commodities that drives modern capitalism is simply an extension of this primitive drive for the original object of desire. To put it bluntly, the Porsche is simply another substitute for the mother. But since the mother can never be attained, once the thrill wears off the Porsche, the man has to replace it with something else—a Ferrari or an island in the Caribbean or a 14-year-old sex slave. It doesn't really matter.

"What does matter is that the restless hunger fuels the whole productive infrastructure of capitalist countries. Take a look at TV commercials. The real point is not to get you to buy brand X instead of brand Y. The real point is to throw fuel on commodity hunger—which is really sexual hunger—and create the illusion of a world in which a man's desires can really be satisfied if only he buys some ridiculous new gadget.

"It's that desire which keeps people consuming, keeps the profits rolling in, and keeps the whole patriarchal class structure in place. The rich have simply inherited the prerogative of the primal father to have anything they want—except, of course, the mother. If they were to cross this line, their legitimacy would break down and the whole system would collapse."

Bata looked at Lumumba thoughtfully.

"If the human world runs on money," said Bata, "and money (or the exchange of goods) exists for the sole purpose of sublimating their forbidden desires, what would happen if those desires were no longer forbidden?"

"A good question," said Lumumba. "But as long as the Establishment exists to prevent such a thing from happening, we will never know, will we?"

"Why do the poor play along with this charade?" asked Bata.

"Because they've been brainwashed; it never occurs to them to question the system, right, Albert?"

"I'm sure I've no idea what you're talking about," the little ape answered sulkily. But he came to attention as Lumumba grabbed the bible away, turned to Matthew and read the story of the talents, how the good slave invested his talents (or money) in a sort of early version of the stock market, while the bad slave who buried his money in the ground (that is, refused to go along with the Establishment's way of processing man's forbidden desires) was condemned for being 'wicked and slothful.'

"So, you see," Lumumba continued, "the poor only want to be rich too, not get rid of the exploitation and oppression. They don't see that the only way out is to jump off the merry-go-round altogether. Of course, people have tried. Radical utopian systems from the early Christians to American hippies have tried to undermine the structures of oppression and reorganize social desires. But they are all doomed to failure because they don't confront the most central oppression of them all: the incest taboo. As long as that system remains in place, new systems of repression are inevitable.

"That brings me to communism and Marx, who saw through the illusory nature of capitalism. The communist notion that 'each contributes according to his capacities and receives according to his needs' is a deliberate attempt to undermine capitalist belief in the myth of private property—the fantastic fiction that a man can own a quarter of California because the King of Spain gave it to him, or that a modern billionaire somehow has a right to be treated like a king because he has a lot of money in the bank.

"But when Lenin tried to implement Marx's ideas, all he did was recreate another tyranny even more oppressive than the capitalist one. The communists took over the means of production and destroyed the prerogatives of the rich, but they didn't address the underlying problem: what to do about desire. Rather than liberating desire they tried to repress it even more than in the capitalist countries. It's no accident that communist countries are extraordinarily prudish and patriarchal, perhaps the result of unconscious desires to share the mother between father and son. Surely the conscious decision of the revolutionaries to limit the powers of the Church—and hence weaken the basis of the incest taboo—leads in this direction.

"But because no one had the courage of these latent anti-taboo convictions, the communist manifesto didn't work. Desire was diverted into even more perverse forms: the torture chambers of the secret police and the petty apparatchiks who replaced the priests and the old aristocracy but without any of their pizzazz. If anyone has a pencil I can explain it all in a simple diagram."

"This I have to see," said Goldschmidt. He threw Lumumba a marker, and on the side of a crate the Professor drew this illustration:

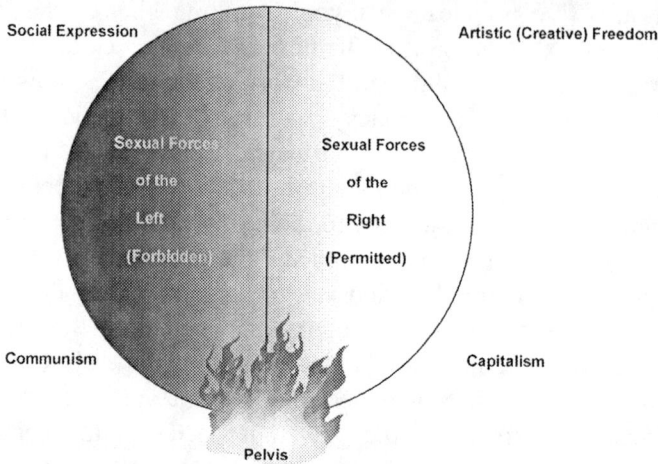

Social Expression — Artistic (Creative) Freedom

Sexual Forces of the Left (Forbidden) — Sexual Forces of the Right (Permitted)

Communism — Capitalism

Pelvis

"Which system is worse?" Bata asked after studying the diagram.

"If I have a choice of tyrants, I prefer the shameless idiocy and pomposity of American billionaires to the sanctimonious perversions of the Stalinist police. Not to say there aren't plenty of Stalinist police in capitalist countries. Capitalists need their secret police too, but at least there are some checks on their power."

"Some might say too many," said Goldschmidt pointedly.

"Yes, and slowly they are gaining sway, aren't they? The cycle goes full swing, some day all the communist countries will be practicing laissez-faire entrepreneurialism and your country will be run by a dictator."

"There are too many patriots in America for that to happen," said Herbert.

"Uncle says a patriot is a man who worships his father's penis through the imagery of county and God," said Bata.

"He does, does he?" said Goldschmidt. "Well, you can tell your uncle that I'm a patriot, and worshipping my father's penis is the last thing I'd ever want to do."

Lumumba sneered.

"And what," he said, "do you think the Tetragrammaton is all about? You think it's a mere coincidence that, beside the Unspeakable Four-letter name of God, there are all those other unspeakable four-letter words? Boys, I think it's time to open the hatch."

He signaled Tchibanga to lower the ramp.

"General, wait!" Goldschmidt cried. He took a crowbar and broke open a crate. "Do you know how much this load is worth?!"

He dug his hand into the dried leaves and let them fall through his fingers.

154

"Compared to other narcotics, practically nothing," Lumumba replied.

"That's the whole point," said Ntimama. "Bwana's buying up all the khat in Africa. When we corner the market, the price goes up and we'll all be rich!"

"My need to get to Spain," Lumumba said to Goldschmidt, "is more urgent than your need to reaffirm your humanity by sublimating the incest taboo with these ill-gotten gains."

As the apes moved toward the crates Ntimama's men reached for their guns.

"Tell them to disarm," said Lumumba, "or I'll use this."

He was holding the grenade launcher.

"You'll blow up the whole airplane!" cried Goldschmidt.

"Perhaps that's the best thing. Our electrons will be liberated and Albert won't spend the rest of his life suffocating in the tenets of the incest taboo."

"Who says I'm suffocating?" Albert replied. "But go ahead and blow us all up. While you're descending to hell I shall enter God's kingdom in a blaze of glory."

"My dear Albert," said Lumumba, "any reference to God's kingdom and His glory are orgasmic in nature. Now which is it, Mr. Goldschmidt, lightening the load or having your last orgasm?"

"Oh go ahead," said Goldschmidt. "Boys, put down your weapons."

The apes collected the guns and began dumping the cargo. Jacques came running from the cockpit.

"Mon cheri, how can you let them do this?!" he screamed.

"Try to control yourself," Goldschmidt replied sternly.

"Control myself!" said Jacques incredulously. "Mon dieu, it would be more easy for me to get into a size 8 dress! You know I can never control myself around you, especially when my entire savings are being thrown out the back of an airplane."

"Jacques and I both have money invested in this deal," Goldschmidt explained.

"It's not only the money, honey. What about the house in Marrakesh? I've already ordered all the curtains in your favorite color—that teal you're always raving about."

Jacques began to sob.

"He only acts like this when things get stressful," Goldschmidt apologized.

"Like when he's about to be dropped out an airplane?" said Lumumba.

"Oh, be quiet," said Jacques. "Nobody's talking to you."

Kribi leaped forward and grabbed him by the throat.

"Unhand me, you hairy beast!" Jacques cried. "Robert, are you going to let him throw me out? I'll never cook you another artichoke soufflé again!"

"Are you going to fly this airplane or not?" Lumumba shouted.

Jacques nodded and returned to the cockpit. There were tears in Goldschmidt's eyes when the last crate disappeared into the darkness.

"Now for the men," said Lumumba.

"General, are you crazy?!" said Goldschmidt.

"Men are expendable," Lumumba replied. "It's just part of the incest taboo."

One by one Kribi, Tchibanga and Yendi lifted the cowering men and tossed them out the hatch. For a few seconds their screams could be heard above the howling wind.

"Now they know what it's like to be an animal inside the slaughterhouse," said Lumumba casually. Only Ntimama was left. He fell to his knees.

"Great general! Spare my life and I'll become your most devoted follower!"

"I'd consider it if it weren't for that hat you're wearing. Out you go."

But as Kribi moved toward him, Ntimama made a sudden dash past Doba and grabbed a parachute from an overhead rack. He threw it on and as he jumped from the plane Doba tried to grab him. Instead he rolled down the ramp into the darkness. Kribi fell to his stomach and reached out, but Doba was gone.

The chimps began to hoot and screech and hammer on the walls.

"What the hell?!" said Goldschmidt. "They sound like a bunch of monkeys!"

"There's something we should tell you," said Herbert.

"What he wants to say," said Lumumba interrupting, "is that it's all part of the training. You must read the Gonad Liberation Army Field Manual sometime. We practice what we preach, and in our efforts to liberate the gonads we revert to the past whenever possible. Surely they sound more like a hominid than if they cried 'boo-hoo.'"

"They have been trained very well," said Goldschmidt, satisfied with Lumumba's explanation. "Obviously they aren't amateurs."

Lumumba looked at him archly but said nothing. The apes continued to mourn.

"Why did it have to be Doba?" said Yalinga, clutching tightly to Okovango. "Why couldn't it have been Mrs. Hickey instead?"

156

Nedele rocked back and forth, her head buried in Bagamoyo's fur.

"You're alive until you're dead," Kumasi said sadly, "you're here until you're gone."

Whether it was to give himself some consolation or to help the rest of us, Lumumba once again conceptualized how death frees the electrons and how Doba was probably experiencing in his new world all kinds of marvelous things such as nonstop orgasm. Eternal life or eternal orgasm, what was the difference?

The enigma of death could be solved, he said, when space and time were fully understood. Time was something other than just the passing of the seasons. Time was part of the warping of space, it was something that existed in and of itself, and only our limited perceptions kept us from seeing that death might be something as concrete as the floor beneath our feet, something you could hold in your hand because you knew what to look for.

"That reminds me," said Goldschmidt. He reached into a storage rack above his head and produced a bottle of cognac.

"Is that why your face is so red and blotchy?" asked Bata. He had curled up not far away from us.

"I'm a diplomat," Goldschmidt replied offering us a bottle. "Drinking is part of my job."

"Get rid of the incest taboo," said Lumumba, "and you'll never touch another drop again."

"A good reason to keep the incest taboo alive," said Goldschmidt, taking a swig. "How about it, General? There's nothing like tying one on at the end of a long day."

Lumumba declined with a wave of his hand.

"I have no need of a drug to deaden the pain of repressed feelings and desires. But perhaps Albert would like to have some."

"No thank you. I need to have a clear head for tomorrow."

"What are you talking about?"

"Uncle, I know I haven't said anything, but I intend to accompany you to Spain."

"The hell you are!"

"Please, Uncle, no profanities in memory of Doba."

"Why, you little hypocrite," said Bata. "If it weren't for you, Doba would still be alive."

The words hit home. Albert hung his head and remained silent. When he spoke his eyes were all moist.

"All the more reason to bring the Word of God to the Moslem infidels in Spain. I know all about the Alhambra."

"That was 500 years ago!" said Lumumba. "The Christians kicked them out in 1492."

"There still must be a few hiding in the belfry."

"Listen to me, Albert. You can just get those thoughts out of your head. When I get off this plane and after it refuels everybody is heading straight back to Tanzania. Dr. Hickey will see to that."

"You can count on it," said Herbert. He tapped his shirt where the torn sheet of paper was safely tucked away. "May God—I mean *orgasm* strike me dead if I don't."

I must have dozed off. When I opened my eyes a bright spectrum of light was bouncing off the windows. A fly had settled on one of them, and Nedele said that when we landed she would help it get out.

We polished off a box of crackers, Okovango crawled from his mother's arms, and Bagamoyo stretched his back legs and yawned sleepily. Nedele gave him some grass from her pocket and he ate it with gusto.

Goldschmidt went to the cockpit and came back with a newspaper.

"What do you think, General, about a world-wide grain shortage?" he said a while later. "Apparently the environment can't support any more grain production."

"Another Establishment lie," Lumumba replied. "In today's world of megafarms and agribusiness, no one on the planet needs to go hungry. All grain shortages are contrived, they are specifically designed to produce a permanent class of poverty. Without a class of poor starving people the rich could not exist. Without the rich there could be no rulers, no laws. Without laws there would be no incest taboo, the mother of all laws."

"It's like a house of cards, isn't it?" said Herbert

"Quite right," Lumumba said. "To make the taboo hold, people have to believe in God. To believe in God, they have to be told there is a God. This is the job of Kings and priests, the earthly representatives of divine power. But there would be no upper class in general unless there was another class to complement them. To complement the rich you have to have the poor. To have the high you have to have the low.

"In the old days you had the pharaohs allowing only so much food to their subjects—thus establishing a class of people who never got beyond a hand-to-mouth existence. Later you had the feudal lords doing the same thing with the peasants who worked the land. Finally the capitalists arose to control workers by controlling the marketplace. The incest taboo produced this stratification and will continue to as long as it's upheld. The farmers are upholding it now by dumping their surplus grain."

"Good for them," said Goldschmidt. "You can see what inbreeding has done in Arkansas. Hmmmm, 'Car Bomb Wounds Two in Spain.' Are you intending to recruit the Basque separatists for your army, General?"

"How did you know?" Lumumba replied sarcastically.

Goldschmidt next turned to the picture of a Japanese protester burning an American flag.

"Anybody who does that ought to be shot!" he exploded.

"Because he's desecrating your father's penis?" Lumumba replied. "Or didn't you know that's what you pledge allegiance to whenever you pledge to the flag?"

"Is this the standard version of the GLA doctrine?"

"In the King's English."

"Religion is sex," said old Kumasi, "and sex is religion. Religion is to sex as sex is to religion."

"Say, I could use that in my equation," said Herbert taking a pen and jotting it down on his half of the paper.

At that moment the door of the cockpit flew open and Jacques emerged wearing a parachute. He turned to Goldschmidt and said dramatically: "You think you can drink all night with your new friend and get away with it? If you want to take up with a new guy, fine. But you'll have to get him there yourself. I'd rather run off with a camel driver than be your slave any longer."

With that he spun around and jumped from the cockpit. Kribi tried to grab him but once again he was a second too late.

PART II
GOLDSCHMIDT

Chapter Thirteen

In Which It Is Told How a Certain Pariah Dog Proved Worth Her Weight in Gold

"Jesus, we're coming!"

As the plane began to roll, Albert's face vacillated between terror and ecstasy. Lumumba, Goldschmidt and Herbert ran to the cockpit, Goldschmidt fell into the pilot's seat.

"He's shown me a million times how to fly this thing, now if I could only remember. . . ."

He scanned the control panel, then reached out and flipped on one of the switches. For a few seconds, nothing happened. Then there was a coughing sound followed by a sudden eerie silence.

"Good lord," cried Herbert. "You've turned off the fuel supply!"

"By jove, I believe you're right," said Goldschmidt. He reached out and flipped on another switch. As the plane pitched forward he started flipping switches more frantically.

"We have to get control, we have to get control," he repeated over and over.

"That's the name of the game, isn't it—getting control," said Lumumba in disgust.

Without ceremony he picked Goldschmidt up by the back of his shirt and flung him from the seat. The plane was now tilting forward at a 45-degree angle and the speed seemed to be increasing. Coming up fast was a desert more barren than any I'd ever seen. Lumumba sat down and started systematically turning off the entire bank of switches.

"Good lord," said Herbert. How do you expect to restart the plane if you turn everything off?"

"I don't want to restart the plane. I just want to unlock the manual control so we can make a landing. There," he said pulling on the joystick. The plane shivered violently, then began to level out. Goldschmidt looked annoyed.

"I don't see why you're being so stubborn about just trying to keep this plane in the air," he said.

"My dear Goldschmidt," Lumumba replied. "Your friend didn't bail out because of any jealous fit, I'm sorry to inform you, but because we've run out of fuel.

It was true. A large sign suddenly started flashing over the cockpit: OUT OF GAS!!! JUMP NOW!!!

"You mean we dumped our load for nothing?" Goldschmidt exclaimed.

"Apparently so," said Lumumba. "The plane must have taken a hit back in Kirua."

"Damn!"

"Please, Mr. Goldschmidt, no profanities these last minutes of our lives," said Albert. "Wouldn't you rather make peace with the Lord? Indeed, I think there is time for you to convert to the True Religion. I can baptize you right here in this airplane."

He held up a bottle of Evian but Goldschmidt ignored him. By now we were flying so low I could almost taste the sand. Its colors resembled a painter's palette tinged in purple, pink and gold.

"Put your tray tables in their upright positions," said Lumumba. "We'll be landing in three seconds."

"This landing is going to be rough," said Goldschmidt. He took the seat next to Lumumba and strapped himself in.

"I'll say," said Herbert. "Dr. Lumumba hasn't even figured out how to put the landing gear down."

"Landing gears are for sissies," said Lumumba. "Have a seat and enjoy the ride, Dr. Hickey."

Seconds later there was a violent bump followed by the deafening screech of metal. The sky seemed to fall in, the cabin filled with choking dust as the plane skidded to a stop.

"Hee haw!" exclaimed Goldschmidt, ripping off his helmet. "That was quite a ride, General."

"The Lord has shown mercy," said Albert. He surveyed the surroundings. "I must get a long white garment to wear and look for the place where God spoke to Moses from the burning bush."

"It's right here," said Kribi pointing to Yalinga. She had collapsed on the sand and was panting heavily.

"You will certainly burn in hell," said Albert, drawing himself up indignantly. "We are too close to the land where God gave his laws to man for Him not to have heard you."

Kribi thumbed his nose in a gesture of derision and helped Yalinga to her feet.

"Anyway," said Bata, "if God is orgasm then he probably did speak from a burning bush."

"Can you save your religious discussions for later?" Goldschmidt said. "Let's get out of this desert. I don't think there's a living creature around for miles."

"How's the little rabbit?" said Lumumba kindly to Nedele. "You know I think I smell water. Could it be the Mediterranean? Could we be in Morocco? To paraphrase Albert, Hallelujah! Spain, here I come!"

He began to move in the direction his nose was taking him, but Goldschmidt was skeptical.

"On second thought maybe we should stay with the plane," he said. "Father Albert could wind up like Bishop Pike."

"Better to be broiled by the sun than skewered by a bayonet. C'mon, I know where I'm going."

The purple and pink shades of early morning had been replaced by a glaring white light. As the apes began to slouch Lumumba exhorted them to walk upright.

"I prefer that Mr. Goldschmidt doesn't figure it out, who we are. And besides you never know when we'll meet somebody."

"Who would want to live here?!" asked Yendi.

"Since they can't conquer and take possession of their mothers," said Lumumba, "humans conquer and take possession of everything else on the planet, including deserts and mountains, the whole nine yards."

"Much easier just to take your mother," said Tchibanga.

Lumumba agreed and as we trudged on he held discourse not only on that subject but on may others including the truth behind Moroccan leather, why the Mediterranean was so popular—it had little to do with the weather—and other unrelated subjects.

While he carried on the apes pulled ahead and disappeared over a sand dune. A minute later they came running back, each one screaming and hooting louder than the next.

"Man, they're good!" said Goldschmidt. "Any chance, General, I could see that manual? I could stand to loose a few inhibitions."

"If he hasn't figured it out by now," Lumumba muttered, "he *must* be CIA."

The apes ran up to us all in a tither.

"Uncle, go back!" Yalinga cried. "There are four giants standing guard at a cave!"

Lumumba went to the top of the dunes and scanned the surroundings.

"Idiots! Don't you know a statue when you see it?!"

It was Abu Simbel. We were only in Egypt and Lumumba's Mediterranean was only Lake Nasser. But what a beautiful lake it was, its turquoise-blue waters framed by red and pink bluffs and boulders.

"Let my people go!" said Albert fervently.

Lumumba groaned and sank down in the sand. He began to pour the soft granules over his head.

"Woe is me," he said. "Will I ever get to Spain?!"

"Such histrionics are not befitting a general," said Goldschmidt looking worried.

"Not to speak of a Yale professor," Herbert added.

"You're right," said Lumumba. "I have only succumbed to despair once in my life. It won't happen again."

A plan was formulated. We would drive to Cairo—Goldschmidt said it was not that far—Lumumba would catch his plane and the rest of us would return to Africa. Goldschmidt, in return for a GLA Field Manual, would get us all passports.

With his options once again on the up it was decidedly a new Lumumba who conducted us toward the temple. Still, the beauty of Lake Nasser made no impression on him. And why should it, he being inured to culture and all other manifestations of the incest taboo?

When we reached Abu Simbel we collapsed on the benches. Facing us were four colossal statues of Ramses II sitting on his throne.

"If those feet were real they could squash a thousand people," said Bata.

"Or a thousand heretical ideas," said Lumumba.

The Egyptians, he said, were one of the first people to harness the power of orgasm and organize it into a bureaucratic state capable of ruling the populace. The power of Egypt, its mystery and greatness, the spell it still held on people could be attributed to the incarnation of the phallus into the pharaoh, hence the divine right of kings. This was how power came into the hands of a few. Anything that challenged the authority of the father's penis was crushed by the phallic power represented in these statues.

"But where does the power come from?" asked Bata.

166

"From semen and the sun. In the minds of men the power of the sun to fertilize the earth, and the power of semen to fertilize the womb have, from day one, been conjoined in a symbiotic relationship. Indeed, there is even confusion between the word 'son' as in the Son of Man and the sun in the sky simply because the words have the same pronunciation.

"But let me give you a precise example. Right here at Abu Simbel, on the exact day of the spring and fall equinoxes, a ray of sunlight will penetrate 65 meters between the entrance and the shrine, bathing the sun god Amen-Ra and Ramses II, the pharaoh, in light. With the use of mathematical calculations, the natural spin of the earth transforms this beam of light into a deity, and by capturing the deity in these temples, earthly rulers were able to legitimize their power as an expression of the divine.

"To formalize the phallus and describe it in religious rhetoric was Egypt's genius. These statues are the first articulations of that rhetoric. The civilizations that followed took their cue from the Egyptians."

An attendant in a dirty djelaba and soiled cap came up to us and held out his hand. Lumumba gave him a dollar.

"*Allah Akbar*, God is great," the man said. He bowed and walked away.

"A perfect example of the way phallic power works," said Lumumba. "He thinks he's the caretaker of these statues, but as regulators of the incest taboo they are really his caretakers. All he is is a cog in the giant phallic machine of Islamic culture."

"What about the dog? said Goldschmidt looking at a skinny creature rummaging near a trash can. Her ribs protruded so much she looked like a de-boned fish. "Is she also a cog?"

"All animals are cogs," said Lumumba. "The only difference is that they don't participate in the incest taboo. They are just victimized by it."

As the sun moved higher in the sky we were content just to sit there and listen to Lumumba as he discussed the means by which humans first created a hierarchy of power and transformed orgasm into a system of gods and pharaohs. A class system emerged consisting of rich and poor, master and slave based upon the power of the state religion. There were civilizations before the Egyptians—the Sumerians and the Babylonians, for instance. But their ziggurats and obelisks weren't able to solidify the penis as a form of state power; it fell to the Egyptians to perfect the empire form of phallic worship in its purest realization.

The father-god Amen-Ra transferred his power down to the house of the pharaohs. But what was Amen-Ra, after all, but a figment of early man's taboo-ridden imagination? What were these colossal statues but a

167

figment of that same imagination, likewise the power of the pharaohs? The only power that was real was the power of orgasm. No one could resist or run from it. All these imaginary structures derived their power from orgasm, and from that power came all power. Take the angels. We all knew, said Lumumba, there were no such things, yet the idea of angels was very powerful. Angels could motivate people to do things or terrify them into submission. Why did these imaginary beings have so much power? Because they organized and harnessed—one might say perverted—the power of orgasm. And while angels were usually thought of as sexless, actually they were the inversion of sex, sex turned inside out. Angels actually represented the power of orgasm, but since it was forbidden to think about that power, we had transformed them into symbols of sexual 'purity' and abstinence—that is, the repression of sexual desire. In a sense, angels were a representation of the process of repression itself.

Albert made a derisive vibration.

"It's obvious," he said, "you've never seen one on top of a Christmas tree. Pastor Wiggins himself used to do the honors, I can still see him caressing the angel's soft blond hair and feathery wings."

As I contemplated this vision Goldschmidt said:

"None of this changes the fact, General, that we Jews put a lot of work into these temples. I wouldn't mind going in and seeing what all the fuss is about."

"No time like the present," said Lumumba. Two policemen had just appeared around the corner.

We traversed the narrow doorway, there were more giant statues awaiting us inside, row upon row of them. Ominous and oppressive, they stood with their arms folded across their chests. At the end of the hallway another door led to a smaller room. There were four figures inside—three gods and the pharaoh Ramses II. Lumumba said that by sitting with the gods, Ramses was able to validate his divine power. It was validation by association, a technique that was still very popular today.

"But why would people cooperate in a system that made them into slaves?" Herbert asked.

"Fear," said Lumumba. "Being a slave inside the fantasy of the pharonic state was safer than facing the raw power of orgasm, the barbaric fetishes and totemic animal gods of the primitive tribes. If you look at history, you'll see that every civilization fears the dark primitive forces of its early stages. Inother words, before they learned how to tame orgasm and worship it."

"I'd rather *have* orgasm than worship it," said Kribi.

"Not me," said Albert. "The more things you can worship the better."

"Spoken like a true Christian," said Goldschmidt unable to hide his pleasure.

On the way out Tchibanga and Yendi urinated on the statues—to those without an incest taboo statues are the same as rocks—and Lumumba broke open the donation box near the entrance. The police had left, so we proceeded toward the parking lot. Along the way there were numerous shops selling souvenirs, t-shirts and djelabas; we decided to stop and buy some clothes. The vendor was unhappy with our bargaining.

"Effendi, give me twenty," he said as Lumumba pulled out the money he'd just stolen. "I have eight children, two wives and three camels to feed. The wives eat more than the camels."

"Ten is my last offer," said Lumumba. "Take it or leave it."

"*Allah akbar*," the vendor said, bowing and taking the money. "God is great."

"You bet he is," said Kribi rubbing his crotch.

It was a long time since our last meal. The Nefertari Hotel was nearby, and we decided to eat there. As we walked up the tree-lined driveway Tchibanga leaped up and began to swing from tree to tree.

"General, this manual of yours, it can teach you to do *that?*" Goldschmidt asked in dismay.

"My men can do anything the hominids could do before they lost the freedom of their gonads," Lumumba replied. "They can swing from trees, hoot like a chimpanzee and break bones with the brute force of an animal."

"I'll do anything to get one!" said Goldschmidt excitedly. "*Anything.*"

It was a colorful dining room. There were blue chairs, yellow tablecloths and lattice partitions made of wood. On the ceiling there was a six-sided star painted in red. A waiter hurried over.

"Sir," he said, "lunch is over and we are not yet open for dinner."

Lumumba pulled out a wad of bills.

"I think we've just opened," said the man. "Please come this way."

He pushed three tables together and gave us the menus.

"Just bring us bananas," Lumumba said, "and whatever fruit you have and pastries."

"Yes," the waiter said, shaking his head from side to side. "We have no bananas."

Instead he brought us apples, oranges and pears as well as pastries, hard-boiled eggs, cheese and dried figs.

The apes tore into their food, but Kumasi dined only on eggs, saying he was too tired to eat anything else. Bagamoyo greedily chewed the apple Nedele cut up for him. When the waiter was gone, Yalinga lifted her blouse so that Okovango could nurse. Thick dark hair glistened around her nipple

Goldschmidt stared in delight. "A woman with a hairy chest," he said, "is almost as good as a man."

"I *knew* he was CIA," said Lumumba.

"Is he CIA because he is gay?" Kumasi wanted to know, "or gay because he is CIA?"

"Probably both," Lumumba replied. "What are you looking at, Albert?"

"That star on the ceiling. Why does it have six points?"

"My dear nephew," said Lumumba. "When a man asks another man what his religion is, he is really asking him what form of the incest taboo he is practicing. Does he use the five-pointed star approach of the West or the six-pointed star approach of the East? If the answer is wrong he's in for a lot of trouble."

"That taboo," said Bata, "sure has a tendency to provoke a lot of rage."

"It's only a diversion," Lumumba replied. "The real anger, I suspect, stems from the physical laws imposed against the body. The man-made laws of civilization exist for the sole purpose of fighting the forces of nature—the atoms and molecules whose vectors converge inside the bipedal pelvis, and create extreme and overwhelming onslaughts on the brain. Humanity, I repeat, is no fluke of evolution, no mystery that can't be explained. The human being is a natural consequence of a species trying to protect itself from this relentless and irresistible bombardment, and the tendency for humans to glorify their intelligence and brains is a sad mis-labeling of the organ's true purpose. Waiter, bring us the bill."

"Uncle," said Yalinga, "I'm so tired. Could we spend the night here? I didn't tell you but the last few days have been such a strain I've practically dried up."

As if to corroborate Yalinga's remarks Okovango began to cry. It was not the cries of a human baby but the cries of a chimpanzee.

"My God," said Goldschmidt, "even the young can do it!"

"We start their indoctrination very early," said Lumumba.

"That manual is worth its weight in gold."

"You get those passports and don't make any trouble and I'll give you *thirty* manuals."

"Let's shake on it, General."

Goldschmidt winced as Lumumba extended his massive hand. How human it looked in its camouflage of flour!

170

A young boy of about fourteen had been watching us eat. Now he walked gracefully toward us in his caftan and dropped a paper in Goldschmidt's lap. Yendi grabbed it and Lumumba read it out loud:

" 'O Handsomest of Strangers! Stay the night in Neferai's Hotel and I Mohammed, your humble admirer, will take you to see the sunrise at Abu Simbel and witness the birth of God.' "

Lumumba pulled on his goatee.

"Who else wants to worship orgasm in the early morning light?"

We all raised our hands. Anything was better than spending another night sitting up.

"And you, Albert?"

"Personally I would prefer to be at Matins, the songs are so inspiring." He began to sing: " 'At dawn I cry to You, I put all my hope in your Word.' "

His raucous hooting caused every head to turn. Lumumba held his ears.

"The temple it is," he said. "It might do Albert some good to see where his Matins comes from although I seriously doubt it."

That night we made love, and much to my surprise it wasn't a vision of Jesus or Lumumba I had during the peak of ecstasy. It was daddy, daddy in a burst of glory, daddy the most desirable god of all!

We left our rooms before dawn. Little birds with yellowish-brown feathers moved among the bushes that went down to the lake. There were many tourists already gathered at the temple. As if in anticipation of some great event, everyone was quiet. Lumumba looked at the solemn faces in disgust.

"Behold the fear of orgasm," he said. "It's as overwhelming today as it was a million years ago."

The first rays of the sun began to streak across the sky. Albert fell to his knees and started to sing another hymn:

"O beautiful Queen,
Princess of heaven . . . ."

"Will you shut up?!" someone said in an angry voice.

Poor Albert. When the sunrise was over he got to his feet and dusted off his trousers. He returned the dirty looks with plenty of his own.

"I must say I much prefer the cathedrals of Europe to all this," he said haughtily. "A stained glass window captures God so much more dramatically."

Before Lumumba could answer our attention was interrupted by a sudden burst of noise which sounded like the popping of firecrackers. People began to scream and run in all directions.

"Get to the water!" Lumumba shouted as a bullet whizzed past his head. As we ran to the edge of the grounds and hid below the embankment a group of men wearing ski masks came rappelling down the face of the temple.

"Pretty cool!" said Mohammed. He was lying next to Goldschmidt who held him protectively. Lumumba spat derisively.

"Hell, my men can do that without ropes," he said. "Article 307.2 in the Field Manual."

As the gunfire continued, people fell to the ground dead or wounded. The screams were terrible, we all watched spellbound, Lumumba included.

"Albert," he said, " here's an excellent chance to see the incest taboo in action. In its Islamic version, men are told that if they are virtuous in this life they will spend all eternity in the arms of a beautiful virgin. But as Moslem women have shed the veil in recent years and begun to take control of their bodies—i.e., their vagina—a group of male fundamentalists have taken it upon themselves to return to a time when the incest taboo was spelled out in black and white and an adulterous woman could be killed without consequence."

"But why are they killing tourists?" Bata asked.

Lumumba's answer was that the West was blamed for letting Islamic women slip through their fingers. This could be catastrophic for a religion which relied heavily on its erotic interpretation of heaven. Unlike Christianity, the Islamic heaven was a place where orgasm flowed freely. Imagine, he said, what might happen if such a place ever evaporated. All the horny Moslems who were controlling their gonads with the promise of having virgins when they died wouldn't want to wait. And why should they, when none of their sisters were virgins any longer!

The terrorists had started to finish off the wounded. We could hear one man plead for his life.

"Have mercy!" he cried. "I'm a member of the British Parliament!"

"Wrong thing to say," said Goldschmidt. The terrorist spat on the ground.

"So much the better, you imperialist heathen infidel swine. I shall cut out your spleen while you still live to offer it up to Allah. You shall see the glory of God as it should be celebrated—bathed in the blood of unbelievers!"

172

He pulled a knife from his belt, thrust it into the Englishman's belly, and pulled out his entrails.

"Allah Akbar—God is great!" he shouted holding up a handful.

We watched as the poor Englishman writhed in agony. Lumumba looked on with a thoughtful expression.

"Perhaps he's having his final and greatest orgasm," he said, "assuming the electrons are going haywire all over his body now that they've been released by death. He's probably seeing the white light people claim to see during near-death experiences. It's the subatomic light of pure orgasm, pure creation, pure God."

"If only these terrorists had taken Jesus as their savior," said Albert, "none of this would be happening. We Christians are a peace-loving people."

"Spoken like a true cretin, Albert, which is, etymologically speaking, another word for Christian." Lumumba sighed. "I wish those other cretins would hurry up so we could get out of here."

"O Great General," said Mohammed, "can't you do something? If I am not at work on time I'll get beaten."

"I could care less what Establishment people do with other Establishment people," Lumumba replied. The Establishment Moslems were now killing off a number of Establishment women.

"They like to kill women as much as men," Tchibanga remarked.

"That's because it's women who've made them go over the edge," said Lumumba.

"Women make *all* men go over the edge," said Albert. "Even Jesus had enough of them in the end."

"Jesus was in love with his mother," said Yendi. "Weren't you listening?"

Just then there was frantic barking. The pariah dog we had seen earlier and her puppies were about to be killed with a scimitar.

"Now they've gone to far," said Lumumba. "C'mon, men, over the top!" The apes charged across the clearing, hooting, shrieking, beating their chests, their gestures were unmistakably those of enraged primates.

"It's hard to believe, Mohammed, but they've learned that all from a manual," said Goldschmidt.

"If the general is not killed," Mohammed replied, "I shall ask him if I can join his army. No one will dare beat me then."

Before the offending terrorist could recover from his surprise Lumumba broke his neck, grabbed his scimitar and rifle and dispatched two others who stood by paralyzed with fear.

A fourth man began shooting, but Lumumba sidestepped, caught him by the throat and lopped off his genitals.

"By removing the source of your pain and sorrow," he said, "your anger and hatred, now you shall be a happy man. Allah be praised."

The Professor dipped his fingers in the writhing man's blood and scrawled the letters GLA on top of his fatigues.

By now the five apes had become the sole targets.

"Take cover in the temple!" Lumumba shouted.

As they raced toward the entrance, miraculously avoiding the bullets that sent a thick cloud of dust everywhere, a second group of terrorists came out of the temple. The apes were caught in the middle. But just as the two groups took aim, at a signal from Lumumba the apes catapulted onto the lap of the great Pharaoh Ramses II. There was a deafening burst of gunfire, and when the dust cleared all the terrorists lay dead.

"General," said Goldschmidt, coming up to Lumumba as he was adding the finishing touches to his insignia on the front of the temple. "If you ever want a job with the U.S. Army I guarantee it's there waiting. It won't be a problem to forgive all your, uh, debts."

Mohammed began to genuflect at Lumumba's bloodstained feet.

"Let me be thy humble servant, great general. I will fill thy cup each night and bring thee a thousand roses each morning!"

The poor child was so overcome he began to weep.

"Sorry, but one idiot is enough," said Lumumba looking at Albert.

The parking lot was a sea of confusion. People sat on the ground holding each other, weeping, trying to give comfort amidst all the chaos. Lumumba found an empty bus and was jimmying the door when the driver hurried over.

"I think you have the wrong bus, Effendi." He looked at us suspiciously. Lumumba pulled out a wad of bills.

"Do you still think it's the wrong bus?"

"Maybe not. Where do you want to go?"

"Cairo."

The man counted the money.

"Sir," he said. "There is hardly enough here to feed my camel. For this amount I can only take you to Aswan."

Lumumba handed him more money.

"Luxor," the driver said. Lumumba grabbed him by the throat and lifted him off the ground.

"I'm running out of patience, how far will you take us if I don't break your neck?"

"Cairo!" the man gasped. "*Salaam ah likum*, peace, please get in."

Mohammed stood at the door.

"Great General, my friend Mr. Goldschmidt has told of thy adventures, and if Thou dost not need a servant, what about a replacement for thy noble warrior, Doba?"

"You have a big mouth," said Lumumba to Goldschmidt.

"I was just trying to keep him entertained," Goldschmidt replied. "He gets very restless at night."

The police were starting to roll in, Lumumba pulled the boy inside the bus and the driver sped off. A forbidding desert stretched in all directions, there was an airstrip somewhere because a military plane was about to land. In all the excitement I'd forgotten about Bagamoyo, but there he was, safe in Nedele's arms, unconcerned as he ate the small bits of apple she was feeding him. Old Kumasi dozed, Yalinga nursed. A warm feeling came over me to see we were all together. The driver passed around some hardboiled eggs, Goldschmidt began to peel one.

"Terrorists can really mess up your day, eh, General?"

"You should know," said Kribi. "They're probably all on your payroll."

"Not these guys. Anyway as I've told you a million times before I'm merely a low-paid clerk at the embassy, and that's the honest-to-goodness truth, General."

"The truth is a tree and the tree is a phallus," said old Kumasi waking up from his nap.

"Ain't that the truth," said Herbert, winking at Lumumba and patting the paper in his pocket.

"No need to kiss ass, Dr. Hickey. A promise is a promise, you get the troop, uh, *troops* back to Mahale and I'll keep my side of the bargain."

"Ah hah!" said Goldschmidt jumping from his seat. I knew that Jamu was working for the revolution! Son-of-a-bitch!"

While Goldschmidt sat mulling over this new information, the talk went back to the morning's attack. Capitalism and globalization had made the Moslems edgy, said Lumumba. Better to go back to a more traditional spin on the taboo by keeping the women veiled and harnessed. How? By attacking the Satanic West, whose policies were too dangerous, too permissive, too diametrically opposed to the repressive regime imposed on the Middle Eastern gonads by the desert Mullahs.

Were we all clear on this? Did we understand that anyone who threatened the status quo—e.g., the laws controlling the gonads—was deemed a terrorist? Could we now see that in calling such people terrorists we were exposing the terror in our own hearts toward the gonads—e.g., toward out own sexuality?

"It's like the terrorists are both enforcers and attackers of the incest taboo all at the same time," said Bata.

"Insect, insect!" Albert screeched. "You are mispronouncing it!"

Lumumba told Albert to shut up, then told Bata that his insight was most intelligent and conveyed the great confusion in people's minds regarding the gonads. That the terrorists were trying to impose their own incest taboo on everyone else proved they were even more terrified of the gonads than most others. But as social symptoms, they represented the repressed anger people feel about having their sexual freedom taken away. The terrorists' violence was an expression of that anger.

Goldschmidt awoke from his meditations.

"You must admit, General, that the CIA has every right to investigate these fanatics and keep them in check," he said.

"The CIA," replied Lumumba, "is a clandestine organization established inorder to investigate other clandestine activities. And what can be more clandestine than the human heart's desire for incest? If there were no terrorists, the CIA would have to invent them, since terrorism is an expression of your own deepest desires. What better way to keep them in check and exteriorize the anger of bourgeois society at the incest taboo? Terrorism is an explosion of the gonads, a way of protesting against the laws it imposes. The terror of terrorism has less to do with the outward damage done to buildings and people than to the threat it poses in the realm of the incest taboo. The terror lies in deep and forbidden zones, laying siege to the most fundamental and primeval superstition of all."

Chapter Fourteen

The Return of Thoth

"By God, it's the Old Cataract Hotel!" said Goldschmidt. "Mohammed, I've spent many a beautiful night at this hotel. Moonlight on the Nile is better than the moon over Miami."

"Perhaps it was Allah's wish that we run out of gas in Aswan," said our driver.

"Was it Allah's wish that I break your miserable neck?" Lumumba roared.

"A thousand pardons, Effendi! Everything is broken in this bus including the fuel gauge. If you can wait an hour I will be back with the gasoline."

"Where do you have to go, the Gulf of Aqaba?!"

We filed out into the sweltering heat and followed a parade of cabs up the driveway of the hotel. The entrance was at the top of a hill, but our efforts were rewarded by an excellent view of the Nile. There were graceful feluccas plying its waters, and small fishing boats painted in bright colors. On the lawn below some tourists were having their pictures taken on a camel whose name, apparently, was Gamal. When they left, Gamal's owner removed the tassled saddle and blankets and disappeared after hobbling the animal in tall grass. At that moment a nearby minaret called the faithful to prayer, and whether it was a coincidence or not, Gamal knelt down and began to eat facing the east. Albert, with hardly any hesitation hurried over.

"My child," he signed to Gamal, "it is Christ who will save you, not Allah."

And with that he began to preach the Sermon on the Mount. Goldschmidt's eyes popped open.

"That is real dedication," he said admiringly.

"But what a catastrophe for the Moslem world," said Herbert, "if all the camels became Christians."

"An even worse catastrophe for the camels," said Lumumba.

Goldschmidt shrugged and fell into a chair next to Mohammed.

"Someday you and I will come back here," he said patting the boy's knee.

"That's the one nice thing about Islam," said Lumumba. "They're not uptight about pedophilia."

"I must protest, General. I may be gay but I'm certainly no pedophile. Mohammed will be of age on his next birthday."

"He looks like a child to me," said Tchibanga. Yalinga pulled Okovango close to her body.

"Oh come now," Goldschmidt said to her. "He's hardly more than a baby."

"But that's the whole point," said Lumumba. "In pedophilia a man is trying to recapture the boyhood orgasms he experienced when he was around his sisters and mother. And who knows, maybe even his father too," he concluded.

"How could I get off on a penis I've never seen? My father was very orthodox."

"By knowing about the secret Teragrammaton, the four-letter word that can never be known let alone pronounced. Tell me, were you an only child?"

"Actually I had two brothers and two sisters, but *I* was the one my mother doted on."

"Which is why you became a mad perverted CIA faggot who gets off on torturing people and dreaming of a world run by sadomasochistic dominitrixes cleverly disguised as school marms. I imagine that if you tried hard enough you could even remember what the maternal bed smelled like."

"Actually I do," said Goldschmidt. "It was a musty, ripe yeasty smell, something like bread when it's baking or roses when they begin to fade."

"It was so pleasant sitting on the veranda," said Herbert with a deep sigh.

"Please, Dr. Hickey, none of the obligatory revulsion, the pseudo-anti-incest reaction which hides your internal desires. I'm too weary."

"May I rub your feet, Great General?" Mohammed asked.

"No, child, the commander of the GLA does not go in for such bourgeois twaddle."

"Do mine, Mohammed, I'm very bourgeois," said Goldschmidt. Mohammed's pretty face pouted.

"No, Mr. Goldschmidt, I think you have too many friends at the embassy, and Mohammed is jealous."

"Nonsense! Whatever makes you think that?!"

"Many people from many embassies come to Abu Simbel, and they are all gay."

The child was right, said Lumumba before Goldschmidt could protest. There was something about foreign lands and espionage that attracted the homosexuals in droves. It was all about betrayal and deception, the sexually traumatized adult running away from what he knew, and seeking out that which he didn't know. This included foreign lands and culture. The mystery of the other side intrigued him, and what better way to get there than through diplomatic channels where the authority of the government added a touch of respectability? Who dared to question the sexual proclivities of a man wearing the badge of a diplomat?

As for spying, what better way for a man to cover up his Oedipal guilt than in the labyrinthine maze of the world of espionage? At heart the spy was spying on himself. He played his own double agent. What was he, male or female? Man or woman? He didn't know. But the labyrinth was so deep he didn't need to know. Had any of us ever spied through the keyhole of our parents' bedroom wanting to see them make love, Lumumba asked. That was why every CIA spy was in the business. They were still looking at mom and dad, still spying on them. That was the heart of the spymaster—a prurient and perverted heart. Betrayals abounded in their world, betrayals of love and Oedipal perceptions. In the spy's mind the world was ultimately sinful. But what the spy didn't realize was that the sinful world was ultimately his own interior being projected onto the reality outside. His subconscious desire for his mother was his real motivation for spying. Just as the hands of a watch ran on its gears, the spy's world was run by the incest taboo.

"No wonder there're no tours at Langley," said Herbert. Before Lumumba could reply our ears were rent by an unholy scream. Everyone looked down the hill just in time to see Gamal, who was on his feet, snatch Albert by his seat and toss him in the air.

"Father, Father, why hast Thou forsaken me?!!" Albert shrieked. Gamal's owner hurried over.

"*In sha'allah*," he stammered as he extricated Albert from the camel's mouth. He wagged his finger in Gamal's face.

"If you chew on one more infidel I'll take you to Daraow and sell you to the butcher."

The camel sneered insolently and went back to eating.

"That was a close call," said Goldschmidt as Albert sat down slowly.

"Yes," he replied. "Doing the Lord's work is not an easy task. He puts us through many trials to test our faith."

"A true Christian would have turned the other cheek," said Yendi.

At that moment one of the hotel staff came over. Bowing politely he told us that he'd just heard from a tour operator that anyone who was flying out today should give himself at least three hours to go through security, the airport was in a high state of alert.

Lumumba thanked him and said we were on a driving tour. What about the roads?

The same, the man replied. Police and soldiers were stopping all traffic out of Aswan. It was a nightmare for tourism.

Ah yes, Lumumba replied. Those damn Islamic terrorists.

Oh no, the manager replied. This high alert had nothing to do with the terrorists. Hadn't we heard? The GLA was here, God help us all!

Suddenly he bent over and spoke in a conspiratorial tone. Had we heard the rumors that Thoth had returned and was leading an army?

"Thoth, the dog-headed baboon-god of ancient Egypt?" Lumumba asked astounded.

"*Naam*, yes, exactly. Those that saw the fight this morning said they looked and sounded exactly like baboons."

Lumumba banged on the table, sending a glass to the floor.

"Please, Sir, don't excite yourself! It's nothing to worry about, only rumors started by superstitious fellahin at the temple, although even the Europeans said the men looked like baboons. Of course, I myself don't believe it for one second. *Allah maak, barak Alah fik.* Good-bye, God bless you."

"Oh what ignominy must I suffer next?" said Lumumba holding his head. "Imagine being compared to a baboon!"

"If I were you, General, I'd look at it as a great compliment," said Goldschmidt. "They have started thinking of you as a god."

"Just what I've always wanted. Well, what do you say? Shall we hit the road and get it over with?"

"Great Effendi," said Mohammed, "my uncle runs a riverboat that goes almost to Cairo. If I tell him who you are he will find room even if the boat is full."

"My dear child," said he. "I will reward you for this brave and generous deed by making you a member of my army. But you must tell no one who we are, our mission is top secret."

The bus driver dropped us at the quay. It was knee-deep in cruise ships tied to each other, and we crossed several decks before reaching Mohammed's ship, the "Happy Pharaoh."

She had seen better days, but like a proud but poor nobleman she carried herself with dignity. The marble columns and brass fixtures gleamed, and the worn carpet on the stairway was spotless. Potted plants and fresh flowers did their best to make the place look cheerful.

"Welcome to the Happy Pharaoh," said Mohammed's uncle after palavering briefly with his nephew. He was the ship's first officer and his name was Mohammed Amal Nawal Asad. He winced as Lumumba shook his hand. "My nephew has told me of your decision to see Egypt by ship—a very wise decision, if I might add. Going from one airport to another is never fun even in the best of circumstances."

"Then you have room?" Lumumba asked.

"Oh, absolutely. A whole tour group had to cancel this morning because several members were victims of the massacre. I don't blame my nephew for wanting to get out of the hotel for awhile. Is your luggage still on the landing?"

Lumumba explained that in our rush to leave the area we had left everything behind in our rooms.

"Ah, the maids will be happy. Please wait one moment, someone will take you to your cabins. By the way, if you wish to go on any of the tours with our tour guide, Mr. Abdel Zahr, I recommend you sign up early."

It was almost dark when the Happy Pharaoh pulled out and headed for Kom Ombo. Herbert and I stood on the sun deck watching the boat set its course in mid-channel. The night was hot, the moon was not up yet and one could barely make out the lush groves of palm trees along the banks of the river.

The voice of a mullah called out to the faithful. Although it was amplified it didn't seem to alter the peacefulness of our surroundings. A sense of mystery hung in the air. Hebert began to feel me up.

"Isn't it interesting," said Lumumba coming stealthily from behind, "how quickly people lose their inhibitions when traveling in a land of foreign taboos."

"Oh is *that* it?" said Herbert. I adjusted my new dress, it belonged to someone from the cancelled tour; the apes had rifled their luggage as it

181

was taken off the ship. To Albert's great joy, he had found a real cleric's outfit and was now dressed in his Sunday best, white collar and all.

"Shall we to dinner?" said Lumumba, offering me his arm.

Yalinga grabbed Hebert's arm and yanked him ahead of us. Okovango began to cry and Bagamoyo fell out of a little basket Nedele had bought for him on the quay.

"This trip is going to be a disaster," said Lumumba as he helped Kumasi down the stairs. "I can feel it in my bones."

His prediction seemed to come true almost immediately. As the maitre-d' was leading us across the half-empty dining room something that sounded like a crow called out our names. "Dr. Lumumba! Kathryn! Professor Doosledorf! Yoo-hoo, over here!"

There was Betty Dodd, Royce, Marty Johnson and Mr. Asad. Betty waved us over.

"Where is your charming wife?" Lumumba said to Johnson. "The last time I saw her she didn't look at all well."

"That's because she was dead—as you would know if you had stuck around," Marty replied unpleasantly.

"We had a plane to catch," said Lumumba. "Tell us what happened. I hope it wasn't the cream pie. I told her it was too rich."

"She didn't die from anything she *ate*," Marty growled. "She died from *asphyxiation*."

Lumumba stepped backwards. "Why, how could that be?!"

"They think her long scarf got caught in her chair," said Betty. "You recall how Isadora Duncan died when her scarf was caught in the wheels of a car? We thought seriously of flying home, but my husband knew how much I'd been looking forward to this trip. So after much deliberation and soul searching, we decided that Vivian would want us to push on."

"Very commendable," Lumumba replied. "Where is she now, still back in Kenya?"

"No," said Marty. "She's down in the ship's freezer."

"Geez," said Goldschmidt, "I hope she doesn't end up grilled on someone's plate!"

Mr. Asad rose to his feet. "We Egyptians may be behind you in many ways," he said, " but I hardly think we'd mistake Mrs. Johnson for a slab of beef." His tone changed when he saw Herbert.

"Dr. Doosledorf," he said, "I've read your monograph on the relationship between the jackal-headed god Anubis and the manger scene at Bethlehem. It's a pleasure to have such an honored guest."

"I'm afraid you have the wrong Doosledorf," said Herbert. "My work is with chimpanzees."

"A thousand pardons! My nephew has misinformed me."

"Only slightly," said Lumumba. "The monograph you speak of was written by Doosledorf's brother, William. I myself helped edit it."

"Then please tell me something. Do you really think that Thoth the dog-headed baboon represents the Christ child's penis?"

"While Thoth is not one of my favorite deities I would have to say yes," Lumumba replied. "Having seen the crucifix at St. Germain des Pres, you can clearly make out the little dog's head on the end of Christ's penis. The peasants have been rubbing oil on it for centuries."

"*Allah akbar*! said Asad. "I had no idea! It would be an honor to have you sit at our table."

Albert pursed his lips and made a noise.

"Don't mind him," said Lumumba. "He's always upset about something. You know how those fundamentalists are."

"Yes," Asad said wearily. "Only too well. When they've killed all the tourists how are we going to make a living?"

"I don't think you need to worry," said Betty. "Egypt is about to be invaded with agents from all over the world now that the GLA is here. Your tourists will be perfectly safe for the time being."

"Shut up," said Marty.

"I will not," said Betty. Her black dimple stuck out defiantly. "I think that Mr. Asad should know what's going on in his country."

"Which is?" Lumumba asked.

"Practically every agency in the world is coming—FBI, CIA, DOD, NSA, British M15 and M16, the Russian FSB, SVR and GRU, Interpol, the Australian Defense Intelligence and the Iranian Intelligence Ministry. There were more but that's all I can remember."

"What about the HSSL?" asked Kribi.

"The HSSL?" Marty repeated.

"The Hair Salon Surveillance League," Kribi answered as the chimps went off in paroxysms of laughter. Johnson and Dodd stared in disbelief, Asad smiled politely, Goldschmidt nodded wisely and Betty tugged at Lumumba's sleeve.

"What you said, Dr. Lumumba, about religion the other night has made a deep impression on me."

"I can confirm that," said Royce. "I was able to get a little more action out of her than usual."

"Glad to be of service," said Lumumba.

"I'm being serious, Professor. You've even started me rethinking my ideas about evolution. The problem is I know so little about it."

"Then allow me, dear lady, to enlighten you."

For the next several minutes Lumumba divided his time between eating bananas and giving Mrs. Dodd an elementary lesson in evolution and Darwin's theories. His remark at the conclusion, that Darwin hadn't gone far enough, drew some criticism.

"Oh, I'm not saying that Darwin wasn't a seer and a prophet," said Lumumba. "Anyone who could start a stampede away from God should be given a place in history for as long as you need to have a history."

But had Darwin known, he went on, about the world of subatomic particles, had he realized that electrons run the show, he would have seen natural selection less as a biological process than one concerning the laws of quantum physics. The atom determined what structure it would create, not the cells.

There were three kinds of interactions among particles—the electromagnetic force, the strong force and the weak force. It was the laws behind those forces which in truth drove evolution. If you found the ultimate particle you would find the reason for the giraffe's long neck. These particles, he said, saw and knew everything. Their constant orgasmic swirl was what motivated an organism to procreate. And since procreation couldn't operate without energy, organisms were in constant pursuit of energy. Ultimately, the only place where they could find that energy was in the electrons themselves—which existed as part of a continuum of energy in the universe. But that energy was also a kind of consciousness—and it was that consciousness which told the giraffe that it needed to grow a long neck.

But these underlying particles were not independent. They were linked together by a complex set of laws. Did we know about the experiments in which pairs of subatomic particles were created and then sent off in opposite directions? Herbert said yes, that as soon as you measured one particle in such a way that it appeared as a wave, the other particle instantly knew what had happened and behaved in the same way.

What that meant, Lumumba said, was that all the particles in the universe were related—they knew what other particles were doing and formed complex relationships with them. These relationships were similar to a holographic plate. The electron contained information about the whole universe coded into its structure in the form of vibrational patterns. That was how the particle knew what other particles were doing millions of light years away. They each contained within them a space-time interference pattern which embodied the vibrational structure of the entire universe.

That's what consciousness was, a vibrational phenomenon—whether at the level of human electrons firing in a pattern or the level of random particles all vibrating together in a giant harmony. In both cases, what you had was consciousness. And those different levels existed as part of a continuum. The trick was to become aware of the greater consciousness in which organisms were embedded. Lumumba understood this because he listened to his own electrons.

"And that's how you hit those holes-in-one!" said Royce excitedly. Lumumba nodded.

"I'm afraid you lost me, Professor," said Betty. Marty snickered.

"That's why you belong in the kitchen," he said.

"You know, Marty, now that Vivian's gone I don't think I have to put up with your crap."

"What if it's the truth?"

"The truth is a tree and the tree is a phallus," said old Kumasi pleasantly. His words were interpreted and the conversation turned to something else.

Later that evening Goldschmidt asked Lumumba if learning to hear your electrons was in the manual.

"Section G, paragraph 6," Lumumba answered. "By the way, what's happening with our passports?"

"They'll be in Cairo when we get there," Goldschmidt replied. "You may have issues with the Establishment, General, but for those who play the game, it always works like magic."

Chapter Fifteen

In Which It Is Told Why
Albert Reject's Lumumba's Thesis that Jesus Slept with His Mother
And that the Word of God Is Actually a Penis

Lumumba would have preferred to sit on the sundeck all day and look at the palm trees. Why go ashore and take chances? There was no remedy for Albert's psychotic collapse into human culture, no way to rescue him from a life of Christian virtues and bourgeois sentiments—eating Big Macs, watching baseball games, buying a BMW and moving to the suburbs. What turned the tide, however, was Albert's belligerent attitude.

Not that Lumumba gave a damn. But to hear Albert categorically deny the professor's assertion that the Christians had taken their religion from the Egyptians was more than he could bear. It was an attack not only on his integrity but also on his credentials. He was, after all, a Yale professor.

But Albert had countered. Wasn't his time at Yale just as important as the professor's? To end the argument, it was decided to visit the temple of Sobek and see if the crocodile god was in any way a Christian.

Unlike Abu Simbel, the temple at Kom Ombo was pretty much in ruins. Still it was beautiful. There were two sections, one dedicated to Sobek, his wife and child, and the other to Horus (the son of Osiris and Isis) and his wife and child. There were crypts and secret passages and a secret chamber underneath the flooring where the priests, pretending to be Sobek, spoke to the people.

186

"Today's televangelists can trace their scheming hearts back to these ancient priests," Lumumba said.

At a central altar, Lumumba pointed to the scene of a purification ceremony in which the pharaoh was being anointed with perfumed oils.

"He copied that from Jesus," said Albert stubbornly.

"My dear nephew," said Lumumba, "you are perfectly welcome to refute the historical chronology of who came first (even though we are talking about a difference of centuries if not millenniums). Only keep in mind that the concept of such ceremonies, when traced back to their origins, always comes down to the practice of sexual intercourse within the first degree. Purity means nothing more than that."

"You're wrong!" said Albert. "Those who are pure of mind and body (such as myself) have no thoughts about sex."

"The original meaning of the word," said Lumumba, "has been totally reversed to throw people off the track."

"We have a friend who would agree with you," I said.

I repeated what Soddhu had said about Khvetukdas and gomez, how the ancient Persians had united within the first degree and used their urine in their purification rites. I could see that Herbert was troubled by my revelation of these private conversations. Fortunately, Lumumba quickened the pace until Goldschmidt stopped infront of a column of hieroglyphs.

"That," he said, "is the mark of civilized life."

"Ah, the writing," said Lumumba. "I prefer to see it as the mark of civilized gonads."

To the Egyptians, he said, writing and learning came from the gods. Inorder to understand the true nature of God, you had to understand the true nature of words. If God was the embodiment of orgasm, then words evolved to describe that embodiment. The concept that words evolved to change the nature of human sexuality was extremely important to understand. Did we remember what Lumumba had said about the Word being emblematic of the penis? The Christians had taken the Egyptian god Osiris and dressed him up in a lot of monotheistic mysticism. As had Jews in their mystic reference to the name of God and the Tetragrammaton. But in the end, the Word was the Penis and the Penis was God. Or as Kumasi would say 'the Truth was a tree and the Tree was a Phallus.'

I remembered what Lumumba had said about 'testicle' and 'testament,' 'genitals' and 'genesis,' that each pair came from the same root. Was the Professor right? Had our language evolved from the gonads?

"If the Name of God is synonymous with the Word of God," said Bata, "and the Word of God is a representation of the phallus, then God is not a person, is He? God is a thing, a something. God is a penis."

187

"The Sunday sermon," said Lumumba, "is nothing more than a porno movie disguised to appeal to the sensibilities of little old ladies. And if you have any doubts, just open up the Bible and wherever it says God, substitute the word *orgasm*. The whole thing will take on a new light and start to make sense."

"If I weren't wearing the cloth of God," said Albert, "I'd have to ask you to step outside. I'd probably wind up on the floor, but at least I wouldn't have to hear any more of this babble. What did God say? 'Therefore is the name of it called Babel, because the Lord did there confound the language of all the earth. . . .' "

"My dear Albert," said Lumumba, "you've just quoted one of the most transparent stories of all in the Bible. Its phallic symbolism is so obvious, yet here you are, 3,000 years after it was invented, taking it literally. What a pity!"

The Tower of Babel, he continued, was a metaphor for the penis. It towered toward heaven (man's code word for orgasm) but since heaven was God's abode (God being the father) this upstart penis had to be punished. God scattered its impudent owners abroad, no one could understand each other, the tower was abandoned and new languages evolved. The important thing to see, Lumumba said, was the connection between language and sex, man's urgent need to invent languages in order to resolve the havoc wrought upon him by sexual rivalry, specifically between father and son.

What the story also showed was a petty, paranoid father who couldn't even wish his own sons well but had to crush them inorder to maintain his despotic hold on power. Heaven existed in the belly of the beast. Heaven was the vagina and the testicles, and that's why God resided there because god was the embodiment of orgasm.

He turned to Mohammed.

What, he asked, awaited the faithful after they died? Many beautiful virgins, the boy replied. A man who believed would spend all eternity in their arms, although he, Mohammed, would prefer to be with boys. Either way, Lumumba said, the believer was sublimating his Oedipal desires through a religious metaphor. Religion was both metaphor and restraining order. Religion sublimated and constrained. Why, the word itself came from the bodies of living creatures—it was derived from the same root as 'ligaments.' Did we still think that religion was an innocuous thing? And all because Australopithecus or some more distant ancestor had stood up to challenge the laws of gravity!

By now we were in the temple of Horus, his wife Thensentnefert and his son Panebtawy. Both triads, Lumumba said, combined to form an extremely complex theology. Perhaps that was why the early Christians had decided to use only the one triad; this would make it easier for the ignorant masses to understand.

Suddenly Albert bristled. Infront of us was the depiction of a woman suckling a child. It was Isis, Lumumba said, wife of Osiris, and her son Horus. He too was the product of an immaculate conception (in his case it was a ray of light rather than the Holy Spirit), since Osiris' member (the Word) had been swallowed by a fish.

"What a bad fish," said Yalinga.

"Not to the Christians," Lumumba replied. "He's been their beloved symbol from the very beginning."

It was dark when the Happy Pharaoh docked at Edfu. The lights of the city twinkled like fireflies, cars honked their horns and vendors selling their wares called out along the quay. The air was filled with smoke from open-air stoves, and the smell of cooking whetted the appetite. When we sat down to dinner, Kribi and Yendi sniffed the air and stared at us with lascivious grins.

"You can't ignore your electrons," said Lumumba knowingly. "Even fetuses in the womb are known to masturbate. There are sonograms to prove it, so it shouldn't be a mystery why people believe in God; they've been worshipping Him ever since the day they were conceived."

"Oh Dr. Lumumba, you're such a card!" said Mrs. Dodd with a playful slap on his hand.

"Oh, you think I'm joking?" Lumumba replied. "My dear Mrs. Dodd, do you really think that people yearn to be children again because all they did was eat, sleep and play? Or might the nostalgia reside in their subconscious, where they remember that each day, each moment was filled with erotic pleasures unencumbered by guilt?"

Mrs. Dodd cleared her throat.

"Kathryn dear, I was just telling the professor about the aborigine who is married to my friend Louise in Newport."

"I thought the place had been ethnically cleansed," said Goldschmidt sarcastically.

"Not yet," said Royce, "although the stampede off the island was worse than when Reggie Jackson came to look at houses."

"You make it sound as if we're all racists," said Mrs. Dodd.

"Well, aren't you?" asked Lumumba.

"Listen," Marty shot back, "the Newport Beach police haven't shot any blacks in a long time."

"That's true," said Mrs. Dodd, "but the police helicopter is still hovering over Louise's house every night and shining a light into her bedroom."

"Maybe they're trying to see how big Gordy's dick is," said Marty.

"No," said Lumumba. "They're there to police the gonads. Mr. Walaroo, being dark, is a threat to the incest taboo. Let me explain."

Religion, he said, divided the world into two camps—the dark forces of forbidden sexuality and the forces of light and civilization with all its laws. Good and evil were represented by the colors white and black. Anything that was not white was "colored," and this distinction extended to people's skins. White people were good and colored people were bad. But the real problem existed within the nature of white itself. Because at the heart of whiteness there was a hidden blackness—the primal urges of sexuality that could not be admitted into the civilized world. Every war that the white man had ever fought against a people of color was rooted in a conflict within his own being. The good gonad versus the bad gonad. The right testicle versus the left—an inter-testicular war, if you please. At the heart of all wars since man created religion were the two irreconcilable sides of human sexuality—the side that wanted to rape and pillage, and the side that had been castrated by religion. This sad state of affairs, rooted in the dualism of the gonads was the cause of racism.

When he had finished, a sea of blank faces stared back at him. Taking out a pen he drew this diagram on a napkin:

Sexual Forces of Nature

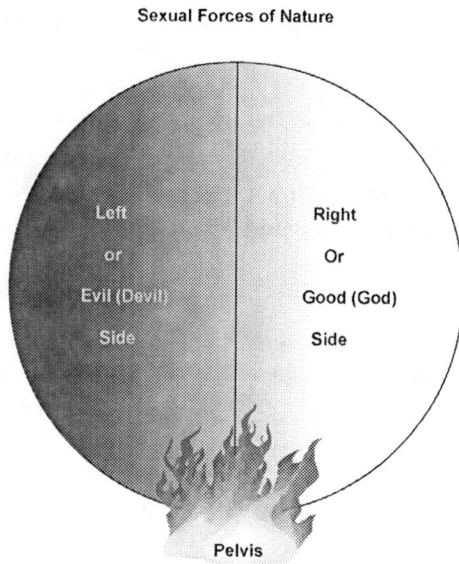

Left
or
Evil (Devil)
Side

Right
Or
Good (God)
Side

Pelvis

Mrs. Dodd only shrugged.

"Nobody on Lyon Isle is a racist," she insisted. "But it is an exclusive neighborhood. You can't just invite *anybody*."

"My dear Mrs. Dodd," said Lumumba, "exclusive neighborhoods exist inorder to separate light skinned people from the dark skinned, and perpetuate the belief in the incest taboo. The reason black people cause such a ruckus when they move into a white neighborhood is because they represent the dark energies outside the incest taboo. What do you think 'ab-origine' means? It's an embodiment of the dark forces of chaos before the 'origin' of civilization—the light and order supposedly brought by the incest taboo."

Yes, he said, the black man represented the dark side of sexuality. That was why he was beaten down and enslaved. It was the evil side of sex that was being enslaved, the side that knew no boundaries, the side that would unite within the first degree. And because America was a dream of incest, it wasn't just a coincidence that the police continued to harass the people of color. It all went together: incest, a dream of incest, the freedom to dream it, the fear of that dream, hence the fear of the dark races which symbolized the dark dream and had to be extirpated because of the duality of the Christian religion.

"Surely that dream exists wherever there are people," said Herbert.

"Ah yes, but America was uniquely set up to play out the dream. Why do you suppose everyone's so hung up on it? I'm telling you, the American dream is a dream of incest."

"Listen, Professor," said Royce hastily. "I've never had a dream of incest in my entire life."

"Me neither," said Marty. "And if Dr. Lumumba thinks that's what we Americans are like, then maybe he should go and find another place to live. Waiter, another drink."

The Temple of Horus at Edfu was located a little distance from the river. Dozens of carriages trimmed in leather and gold were lined up at the quay awaiting tourists. Lumumba took one look at the thin, malnourished horses, spat and said we would walk.

"Last one there's a rotten egg," Betty called as she and her husband and Marty galloped past us in a carriage.

As we wandered through the temple Lumumba pointed things out which made Albert very angry. There was, forinstance, the representations of Horace stabbing at evil and trying to chain it with the help of the pharaoh. But the more he fought the bigger it got.

This was because the evil he was stabbing at was rooted in the gonads and would never go away. Perhaps, said Lumumba, the ancient Egyptians understood this better than their modern-day counterparts, the Christians, Jews and Moslems.

Hurumph, said Albert. Everybody knew that God had created evil inorder to make men understand the nature of goodness.

But that was just it, Lumumba countered. The concept of good and evil, light and darkness could not be separated from God's abode inside the gonads. That Horus and all the other Egyptian gods appeared as animals helped to show this, perhaps, by equating orgasm and religion with the immense physical power of an animal.

On the other hand it was his animal self that the human was trying to destroy. And there was the pharaoh helping to destroy it. But that was the purpose of kings, to stand as guardians of the gonads.

Their power to rule, you see, rested in the belief that the gonads were sacred. This was evident from the word itself. The Latin for king was *rex*, signifying the idea of something that was straight or moved in a straight line, or set something straight. But how could the concept of kingly power come from a word simply meaning 'straight'? What was the relationship between moving or setting something straight and the power of the king? No one seemed to know, so Lumumba asked another question:

What do men guide or direct in a straight line?

Goldschmidt joked that it sounded like an erect penis.

"Your prurient instincts are right," said Lumumba. "The king is the top penis."

A flaccid penis had no order, no direction. But when it became erect it hardened into a straight line—the embodiment of male will. The movement of that straight line into the female vagina was the originary act of power and command. The king embodied this power for the nation. He was the phallus, the erect organ, which guaranteed the virility and security of the nation.

That such great authority was rooted in the capriciousness of a dick was pretty incredible, but it was that belief which allowed the incest taboo to exist, and that made the act of sex sacred. And once the act was made sacred, laws could be made which put people in their proper places. No longer could they have indiscriminate sex like animals; now they had to have relationships such as father/son, mother/daughter, which would become internalized and obeyed.

"All this because a penis goes inside a vagina at a straight angle?" Bata asked. He scratched his head as if this were the most incredulous thing he'd ever heard.

"All that and more," said Lumumba. Not only did the concept of a ruler (a *rex*, a straight line) come from the penis, so did the concept of numbers. "One" was embodied by the straight line of the penis—the unitary, originary, master organ. That the design for "one" was identical with the erect penis was more than just a coincidence.

Goldschmidt objected. The way he'd learned it men started to count when the concept of possession took hold. Men had to keep track of their cattle and their women.

But that was much later, said Lumumba, when the concept of numbers had been well established. He was talking about a time before, a time when *homo erectus* was still around, or maybe *homo habilis*. They didn't know the difference between one and a blowhole. But their brains were getting bigger, and they were beginning to know that inorder to keep the peace they needed to establish proprietorship over the vast numbers of vaginas that the magic organ was going to enter. What better role model to build the primary number upon than the penis itself? By studying it in its full blown erection they came up with the idea of numbers.

"I always suspected that calculus was rooted in the gonads," said Goldschmidt. "Why else would it be so hard? But tell me, Professor, were the Romans making a joke of it all when they placed a crown of thorns on Jesus's head and proclaimed him King of the Jews?"

"Hardly a joke," Lumumba replied. "At a subconscious level every human on the planet knows the truth about his sexuality and forbidden desires. That being so, the Romans were more than happy to belittle the Jews and their monotheistic religions with all its stringent laws which guard against these forbidden desires. And what better way than to give Jesus the title of Top Penis while at the same time crucifying him?"

We had come to another picture of Isis suckling Horus her son.

"I suppose you want me to think this is the prototype for the Virgin Mary," said Albert angrily.

"It's whatever you want it to be in whatever religion or time you happen to be in," Lumumba replied. "Mother and son are a common motif."

"Why is it never mother and daughter?" I asked. "Electra wasn't exactly a model child."

"Because it's the son who is the real trouble maker," Lumumba replied. "It's the son who has to be constrained. And what better way to restrain him than to make him into a fighter against evil and injustice? In this way he becomes a role model for all sons. In ancient Egypt a son identified with Horus, just as today's sons identify with Jesus. That makes them obedient and good. They are all the Christ child—they would never think of fucking their mothers. And why should they? Didn't Jesus die for that sin? Recall what he said to his mother: 'Woman, I know thee not.' Only a dolt would interpret this as an emotional parting of the ways."

"Are you saying I'm a dolt?" said Albert furiously.

"If you don't see that Jesus is talking to her about *carnal* knowledge, then yes, I am. Don't walk away, I have one more question. What did Jesus say to his mother just before he died?"

"I don't remember."

"Of course you do, it's a famous line: 'Woman, behold thy son!' "

"So?"

"Can't you hear the complaint, the recrimination? 'Mother, look what you've done to me! *Me*, your son, how could you?!' "

Albert tugged at his collar as if it were choking him. "It's too hot," he said, "I'm going back."

"I'll come with you," said Nedele. "Bagamoyo's panting like a dog."

He wasn't the only one. The heat was excruciating, we were all ready to drop. But instead of coming with us Lumumba said that he, Kribi, Yendi and Tchibanga had some business to attend to and would return to the ship later.

We walked back in pairs, Herbert and myself, Goldschmidt and Mohammed, Yalinga and Bata, Nedele and Bagamoyo. Albert stuck out like a sore thumb as he trudged along all alone in his tight-fitting black clothes. A vendor caught up with him.

"Holy Father, may I sell you a djelaba?" he asked. "I have them in all colors including black."

"No thank you, my son. Jesus spent forty days in the wilderness without complaining about the heat, I can spend a couple of hours."

"But he had on one these," the man argued waving a djelaba. "He was not hot at all."

"How much is the white one?"

"For you, Father, only twenty dollars."

Albert gave him the money and folded the garment carefully under his arm. Mohammed looked annoyed.

"You could have bought it for five," he said.

"A man of the cloth only bargains for the souls of the wicked."

As we walked on his sad expression changed to joy as people said 'Hello, Father,' and touched their sun hats in a sign of respect. The sight of a deaf and dumb priest brought tears to their eyes, and a few people gave him money.

"My child, have a nice day," he said with satisfaction.

But as the quay came in sight the beatific moment was interrupted by the sharp rapid fire of machine guns coming from the town.

"My god, have they caught the general?" Goldschmidt exclaimed.

"I venture to say he's up to something," said Herbert. His eyes betrayed his unconcerned manner.

"Why did he not allow me to participate?" said Mohammed. "I am very angry."

As we stood waiting, dozens of passengers flocked to the ship.

"*Allah Ackbar!*" said an Egyptian. "It's like an American western except they're all wearing robes!"

"What's going on?" Herbert asked.

"The carriage drivers were attacked by terrorists," the man answered, "and the soldiers and police have them surrounded."

"Good god," said Goldschmidt, "does this mean I won't get my manual?"

"I have more to lose than you do," said Herbert sourly.

The gunfire lasted a long time, then trickled down to an occasional spurt. It was still going on when Lumumba appeared accompanied by his three companions. There was a sigh of relief, nobody appeared to be the worse for wear except for Kribi, who was limping.

"He twisted his ankle," Lumumba said to Asad as we went on board. "Nothing to worry about."

Chapter Sixteen

In Which It Is Told Why Lumumba Sees a Commonality
between God and the Mad Hatter

Once again we joined Marty and the Dodds for dinner.

"Where's the other thug?" Marty asked seeing Kribi's chair was empty.

"He's having room service tonight," Lumumba replied. "He twisted his ankle during the melee this afternoon. My niece is with him."

"Oh Professor! You should have been there!" Betty gushed. "It was so exciting! There were all these soldiers, and everybody was firing at once. One minute the terrorists were in one spot, the next minute they'd be in another. They were so agile, it was almost as if they were flying! The bullets missed them every time!"

"Did they kill many people? asked Mohammed, his eyes big as saucers.

"Sure did," said Royce, "all the carriage drivers, every last one of 'em."

"Obviously they are trying to scare away the tourists," said Marty.

"Yes, but why shoot their own people?" asked Asad? "Wouldn't it make more sense to kill the infidels—a thousand pardons, I mean the tourists?"

"It looked like they wanted to steal the horses," said Royce.

Nedele's banana stopped in midair.

"They got what they deserved, those drivers, for taking better care of their carriages than those poor malnourished horses."

"Listen, young lady, those sentiments would be better left unsaid," said Marty unpleasantly. "And get that damn rabbit off the table!"

"Why? He's not hurting anything."

"It's unsanitary. Look, he just pooped!"

"Lighten up, my friend," said Goldschmidt. "This is Egypt, no offense, Mohammed."

"Was I talking to you? Waiter, is it too late to change my salad to rabbit soup?"

"Ah, the Molokhiyya? No, Effendi, I'll do it right away.

As Marty attacked his soup I came to Bagamoyo's defense. Wasn't there something Christ-like about the little rabbit, I asked. He was so perfect in the simplicity of his life, the directness of his gaze, the quietness of his character and the humbleness of his nature. He couldn't read or write, yet in many ways he seemed superior—kinder and wiser in his small form than we were in our big, sophisticated and cultured form. Marty scowled.

"I don't need to be saved by a rabbit, sister. I've got the Lord and the United States Army on my side," he said.

"Spoken like a true Christian," said Albert. He slapped the table for emphasis.

"Or a hard-line purveyor of the incest taboo," said Lumumba. "Isn't that what Bible-thumping and blowing up the heathens is all about?"

"Some people might say it's about patriotism," said Marty.

"Oh yes, honoring the Patria, the fatherland and all that. But isn't it all tied up with dad's penis, or is that something we don't want to talk about? Shall we stick to rabbits then?"

But even rabbits proved to be a dangerous subject using Lumumba's lexicon. When people talked about the presence of God, he said, they might as well be talking about rabbits in the magician's hat. Both concepts originated from the same phenomenon he'd already mentioned, the entoptic visions. Had the Dodds or Johnson heard of it? No? How strange, since it was these visions—this altered state of mind—which caused our evolution, caused us to cross from the animal world to the human world. (Although if the truth be known, it was just a sleight of hand, a rabbit being pulled from the magician's hat. It went like this.)

As our ancestors' brains increased in size so did the electrical activity, so much so that their heads began to explode. Oh not literally: they exploded with lights and dots and zigzags. Amazed and terrified by this new state of mind, prehistoric man began to trace the flashing, floating pictures onto the walls of caves. The ability to capture these phenomena led to the ability to capture the ephemeral nature of orgasm and sexuality.

197

Yes, those 30,000 year-old paintings in the caves in France and Spain had nothing to do with the hunt. It was the arrival of magic, and this is what caused the transition from animal thought to human thought.

This was all spelled out in the Bible. The Garden of Eden recalled the days when the hominids, experiencing their newly found gravity and the resultant irresistible pressure on the gonads, lived in a constant state of orgasm, a constant state of paradise. The word paradise itself simply meant a park, pleasure garden or enclosure with high walls. The root word of garden was *gher* meaning 'to grasp or enclose.' What better enclosure than the female genitals, the vagina receiving the penis and generating the heavenly feelings of paradise?

Then magic came along and men allowed themselves to give up the real garden—the heavenly orgasm inside the heavenly vagina, probably the mother's—for a substitute garden planted with fragrant trees, exotic flowers and flowing waters. Which was a good idea, because the originary state of paradise led to constant trouble. It was a gruesome business for millions of years until magic came along and stopped the slaughter.

But here was the question. Was it the rabbit who made the brain big or the brain which made magic possible?

Perhaps it was both. The brain grew bigger as the result of the increased flow of electricity that came about as the result of the change in posture. As the flow of energy increased, it increased the pressure on the brain. And since matter and energy cannot be destroyed—only converted into other forms—the increased energy going up the spine was converted into brain material.

In truth, brains were nothing but enlarged gonads, albeit enlightened ones, ones that could write and speak. During the process of enlargement, the electrical charges from the gonads over-activated inside the brain and caused the altered state of mind. Instead of seeing a tree or a crack in the rock, men saw parallel lines. Instead of seeing water they saw spirals and crisscrosses. This biological phenomenon laid the basis for magic. The power of the gonads became the power of the mind. The power of the mind was at bottom orgasmic. Magic seemed real because it was rooted in these real stabs of light and electrical activity, the six geometric patterns whose origins were in the nervous system itself. Inother words, an overload of electrical stimulation, possibly resulting from gonadal repression, resulted in our ancestors' minds becoming altered and ultimately leading to the invention of civilization and, as if a magician sprinkled them with some magical dust of forgetfulness, the denial or forgetfulness of their animal origins and biology.

Overload was the key word. Like a buildup of magma inside a volcano, those images were a product of orgasmic electrons being diverted to the brain. Too much diversion and the volcano blows its lid. Our repressed electrons, no longer allowed to run freely between brain and crotch, were detoured along other circuits. Some went to the front of the brain, some to the top, some to the sides. And some hit the optic nerve. From these diverted electrons language arose, as did art, religion and civilization itself.

"And that, my friend, is why God might as well move over and let Alice's white rabbit take the reigns for awhile. Or little Bagamoyo, for that matter."

"I prefer Genesis to your version, Professor. It's a lot easier to understand," said Royce.

"Damn right it is, and more to the point," said Marty. "But the good doctor appears to revel in seditious conversation. I can see why they kicked him out of Yale."

The waiter cleared away the dishes. Even though the Dodds and Mr. Johnson complained about eating too much, their mouths watered when they heard the list of deserts.

"We may as well get our money's worth," said Marty, "and Vivian's too. Waiter, four orders of those raisin cakes soaked in milk. And make it snappy. We've still got a lot of drinking to do."

Most of the passengers had gone to the sun deck where the breeze off the bow helped to diffuse the heat. Kribi was in a deck chair covered with a blanket. Yalinga sat next to him holding Okovango. The little chimp tried to slip free but she held him tightly.

A full moon reflected off the smooth black water. It threw into silhouette the uninterrupted line of palm trees growing along the Nile. The stars twinkled brightly.

"Let's drop Daddy a postcard," I said.

"That would ruin the evening," Herbert replied. "Let's stroll along the promenade and bare our souls instead."

"Why not? I've been discovering new realms of sin—I just hope you're ready."

"Ah, you luscious, hell-raising vixen, you. What do you say we slip into that life boat and explore some of your crevices?"

Goldschmidt and Mohammed had beat us to it. Lumumba's words came back to me: "Isn't it interesting how quickly people lose their inhibitions in the land of a foreign incest taboo."

My thoughts were interrupted by a pitiful groan as Yalinga helped Kribi change his position. There was sweat rolling down his forehead, caking the flour on his face and revealing a sickly gray pallor.

"Perhaps you ought to get that sprain looked at," said Herbert.

"Sprain my ass," said Yalinga. "The poor thing's been shot. His whole leg is torn up."

Herbert looked at the wound and blanched.

"This is serious," he said, "he needs to see a doctor right away."

"I'm afraid that would put us all at risk," said Lumumba.

"Anyway it's not necessary," said Kribi. "All I need is a good night's sleep, I'll be fine in the morning. Does anybody have any willow bark—you know, something for the pain?"

We brought him some aspirin, then retired to our cabin. There was no exploration of crevices that night, neither of us felt like it, and despite the sweet lapping of the waves and the gentle lulling motion of the boat I was kept awake most of the night by the nagging thought that none of this would have happened were it not for Project Mark.

Chapter Seventeen

In Which It Is Told How Father Albert Negotiates the Bargain of Bargains, and Why the Life of a Tour Guide Is Never Easy

Thebes, the ancient capital of Egypt, the seat of great conquests during the 18th dynasty. My excitement to be there and see the famous temple of queen Hatshepsut had been dulled by a sleepless night—yes, I admit I'd grown fond of Kribi, murderous ape that he was.

On the other hand, my affection for Albert was being sorely tested due to his growing belligerency.

Not that he didn't have cause. Lumumba made provocative pronouncements at every turn, and I sometimes wished for the sake of peace that he'd stick to his original plan to sit on the sundeck while the ship was at rest.

But no, his animal instincts could see at once how Christianity had been affected by the phallic nature of the Egyptian religion, and this, of course, Albert could not stand.

Was it a show of defiance that he now choose to have his picture taken atop a camel which was waiting at the ship?

"Look at the little bugger," Lumumba said to Herbert as Albert preened for the camera and posed arrogantly to show he was master of the beast. "You've made a fine human out of him. He no longer feels he's part of nature and claims this by his Christian birthright."

"I don't see how you get all that out of sitting on a camel," Herbert replied.

Nevertheless Albert looked happier than he had in days.

"Your camel is much nicer than the last one I met," he said, giving the owner twice as much money as he'd asked for.

"*Shukran*, Effendi," the Arab said smiling broadly. "I don't suppose you'd be interested in meeting my sister, would you, little Father?"

"Impudent fellow! Can't you see I'm a man of the cloth?"

"Exactly so, little Father, that is why I asked you."

"Arrrgh," said Albert swinging dexterously to the ground. The Arab stared in amazement as Albert hurried after us.

At this moment we were traversing the temple grounds at Luxor (the modern-day Thebes). The obelisks and giant statues of Ramses II still evoked a sense of awe. Lumumba told us why.

Obelisks, he said, were part of a magical transference bridging the worlds of fantasy and reality—the reality of the male organ in erection, and the fantasy of an organ as big and powerful and uncompromising as an obelisk weighing thousands of tons. To believe that male power was as impregnable as its granite look-alike, a leap of faith was necessary, and the gap between fantasy and reality had to be bridged. Lumumba said that he thought the bridge was mathematical and that the belief in numbers had led men to believe in all illusion.

An explanation of the word 'phallus' seemed forthcoming, so Lumumba gave us the Indo-European root *bhel* meaning to swell. Ancient peoples were impressed by the swelling, and the reason the world was insane, he said, was because mankind had based its whole existence around the worship of this swelling.

We came to the Avenue of the Sphinxes. It was a street lined with these mythical creatures. Each sphinx had the head of a ram, but there was nothing malevolent about them or foreboding. Their faces were frozen in a kind, good-natured smile.

"Now I ask you," said Lumumba. "Do you still believe that the animal inside you is bad? Do you not find it unsettling to think that Jesus died to save you from these?"

As he patted the paw of a smiling sphinx, a sunbird with a bright yellow breast chirped happily in the tree behind us.

"But you yourself have been telling us how everything the Egyptians did was to make mankind *believe* in the incest taboo," said Herbert.

Yes and no, Lumumba replied. While their state religion imposed the taboo on the common people, incest remained among the nobility. It was allowed for the pharaoh since the concept of divinity was rooted in incestuous orgasm. The same concept of the divine right of kings was passed on in Christianity, but Christian kings were denied union in the first degree since they were no longer divine themselves. Still they retained 'noble houses'—like the House of Windsor in England—that kept sexual relations as close to incest as the taboo permitted. The whole concept of royalty was rooted in the divinity of incestuous orgasm.

But all that changed with the arrival of the Jews. Divinity was moved from the figure of the king into the omnipotent power of God, and incest was prohibited once and for all. In other words, the Jews—the ancient Hebrews—established the Mother of All Incest Taboos. Was it a big step to go from worshipping orgasm in idols to worshipping orgasm in an unseen presence? You'd better believe it! Perhaps that's why they were called the chosen people: They were chosen to stop unions within the first degree. It was the Hebraic laws, afterall, that now forbid incest in all parts of the world.

"No wonder people hate us!" said Goldschmidt with feeling. "And I always thought it was because of our big noses and usurious practices."

"But don't you see?" said Lumumba. "That's all part of it. To the subconscious mind (which is always preoccupied with sex) a big nose represents the penis, and money is in all actuality man's pathetic attempts to sublimate his forbidden desires. If you look at the anti-Semitic propaganda of the Nazis you'll see how riddled it is with sexual innuendos. But for good reason, because if there's a more pagan-minded, incestuous-minded people than the Germans I will certainly be surprised."

That's what Soddhu had said! The Rhine Valley was strewn with ancient temples to Mithra, the Germans were Zoroastrians at heart!

"God is orgasm and orgasm is God," said Kumasi hobbling up slowly. "There is a God and his name is orgasm."

Albert held his head and dropped to the ground.

"Why was I ever born?!" he moaned.

A portly couple hurried over.

"Padre—Father—let me give you some water," said the woman. She reached for her backpack and pulled out a bottle that was empty.

"Pamfilo, hurry and give the Father some water," she said to her companion.

"Don't you remember, mama? I gave the last bottle to you," Pamfilo answered.

"Then go and buy some. That stand over there is selling it."

"Sí, madre."

"Her son looks a lot older than she does," Tchibanga remarked to Bata. "Like about twenty years."

"It's his wife, stupid. He calls her 'mother' so he can get turned on—or maybe not turned on—it really all depends."

203

Pamfilo returned with the water. Albert looked pleased. He stood up and brushed the sand from his clothing. "What is your name, my child?"

"Refugia," she answered.

"A beautiful name. Tell me what it means."

"It means refuge, Father."

"Ah yes, refuge from incestuous desires. Would you like me to hear your confession, my child? Being in this dirty, heathen land, surely your mind is full of sinful thoughts."

"Oh, no, Father, not at all," she replied "Everyplace we go we see signs that our Christian forbearers have been here."

"You mean the effaced walls and burnt columns of the temples?" Lumumba asked.

"Sí, and it gives us the faith to enjoy ourselves in spite of so much pagan idolatry."

Tchibanga sidled up to Refugia and started to unzip his pants. "Lady, would you like to see my obelisk?" he asked.

"Father, I think you are in the wrong company," said Refugia moving a step away.

"God is testing me, what can I say, my child?"

Pamfilo took Refugia's arm.

"Come, mother, he may be one of those priests that we read about in the newspapers every day."

The couple hurried away, Albert turned in fury to Tchibanga.

"Now see what you've done? They think I'm a child molester!"

"So what? Anyway, you probably are, being so repressed and all. In any case we'll never see them again. Hurry up, Uncle's way over there."

Inside the colonnade, Lumumba was pointing to a picture of an ox being led to the slaughter. His turned-up hooves indicated a life in the fattening pen.

"The beef industry hasn't changed in three thousand years," he said "But how can it if the entire edifice of laws and institutions that holds society together is ultimately founded on the sacrifice of animals and the worship of taboos? And then you have the paranoid leaders who are afraid that if you stop eating meat you will start eating *them*."

"I'm sure they talk about it every day in Congress," said Goldschmidt sarcastically.

"They do, but it's all in the coded language of politics, it's all so internalized that people react without knowing what they're doing. When they crossed the bridge of visions they left the animal world behind, a most unfortunate thing for animals."

We made our way back to the boat. It was so hot I could hardly move.

"Lady, if you think *you're* uncomfortable try baking your face in two inches of wet cake flour," said Yendi.

"If Mr. Goldschmidt knew sign language, the ruse would certainly be up by now."

"So what?" Yendi answered. "I'm sure we could get along very well without him."

As we looked in his direction Goldschmidt took off his pith helmet and wiped his forehead.

"To hell with Hollywood, these pith helmets aren't worth a damn."

"They're very assertive though. You look ready to shoulder the white man's burden," said Herbert.

"Ah, yes," said Goldschmidt glancing at a ragged fellahin. "These benighted savages—adorable as they are"—he looked at Mohammed—couldn't install indoor plumbing in the next fifteen million years, even if you left them the blueprints. Without the white man to build infrastructure for them, they'd still be hiding from the lions."

"That infrastructure," said Lumumba, "has nothing to do with lions, at least not the real ones."

In the afternoon a bus took us to the Valley of the Kings and the temple of Queen Hatshepsut at Deir El Bahari. The lush terrain along the river quickly changed into an inhospitable desert of the first magnitude.

"No chance of United Fruit sublimating here," said Lumumba as we drove deeper and deeper into the desolate landscape. Albert's eyes grew wide with desire.

"Uncle," he said, "could we stop here for forty days and forty nights? This would sure make a nice desert to scourge myself in."

Lumumba yawned and said there'd be plenty of time for that later, he'd even help him.

The Valley of the Kings was in a gorge surrounded by steep cliffs. We hurried from tomb to tomb to avoid the baking sun. In one tomb—Lumumba pointed to the pharaoh's resurrection.

"He copied it from Jesus," said Albert.

"The hell he did," said Lumumba. The word itself, he continued, came from the Latin verb *surgere*, which meant to surge or rise, *surrectio* or *surrection* meant a rising, and a resurrection was something which would rise or surge again.

"You think it's the body of Christ which rises, but I say it's the penis that is surging and rising."

Christ, he said, was a metaphor or personification of the son's penis, just as Yaweh was a metaphor or personification of the father's penis. That was why Christians and Jews were always fighting. It was the two male principles at work—sons trying to displace fathers and regain the bliss of the womb versus fathers trying to stay in charge long after they became old. But since most sons eventually become fathers themselves there was continual warfare going on inside the individual. The old saying that your worst enemy is yourself could be applied here—the son-self versus the father-self, a schizophrenic dichotomy never to be reconciled. If only it could be internalized! But no, it was always playing itself out, externalizing itself as the tension between Christians and Jews, a resurgence of the feud between fathers and sons within religion itself. The two religions externalized this tension and projected it onto each other. But internally they reasserted the power of the father in the form of a religious principle.

As for the death and rebirth of Christ, it signified the penis at several different levels. First, the death of Christ, which represented the continual warfare between fathers and sons. A son who tried to possess his mother would have to be killed. As for the resurrection or rebirth of Christ, this was the carrot held out to give men hope. Once dead, they too would ascend to heaven. But don't forget that heaven was a metaphor for sexual bliss, perhaps that bliss which occurs inside the womb. Thus the resurrection would become the final stage in this hopelessly entangled world of human sexuality, a metaphor in which the son regained the bliss of forbidden orgasm for all eternity.

Then again, the death of Christ might be a sublimation of the continuing revolt of the sons. The sons would have to sacrifice their penis (as they did symbolically in the Jewish ritual of circumcision), but they would regain power at the symbolic level. The old Jewish religion was simply a patriarchal tyranny, all it did was repress the problem of tension between father and son. But the death and rebirth of Christ represented a kind of power-sharing arrangement. The son sacrificed his penis to the abstract power of God, but was reborn in the Holy Spirit, which meant he got a seat on the corporate board with the other brothers. Thus he was able to share power with the father, who retained symbolic authority.

Good old magic and illusion! It turned those bloodthirsty, out-of-control primates into mild-mannered, rational humans, a clear indication that the path to rationality lay in magic and illusion. (This would explain why some people were more rational than others.)

But the story of resurrected penises was not the only magic. Another fly in the ointment, the magic births of the gods, was a powerful ingredient, too. And it didn't start with the Immaculate Conception of Jesus or the magic birth of Horus. It started long before either, but that wasn't the question. The question was why? Why did the figure that was to become a major god have to be conceived magically rather than naturally? Why was the divine son not born in the normal way? Why was the father's sperm always missing? Because the Immaculate Conception was a birth free of sexuality—that is, devoid of the sexual juices of biological intercourse— the son who identified with the divine Son (and didn't all children become the babe in the manger in their formative years?) posed no threat to an aging father. With this religious system the biological needs of the human species became secondary to the invisible or magical level of the Law. No matter how powerful the sons, the law was ever more powerful because it was abstract, invisible and magic.

Put simply, a magic birth made fucking sacred, and a ruler's magic birth gave him power to rule over people who in all actuality had no desire to be ruled.

Yes, death and resurrection was hardly a belief in life after death. It was a convoluted way of keeping the sons out of the father's hair and the mother's bed. And magic births were not any different. Lumumba thought the whole thing was sinister because it took us too far away from whatever it was that nature intended. Semen should be semen, he said, not the Holy Spirit.

"But semen is so messy," said Albert, "and with an Immaculate Conception there's nothing to clean up."

No one could refute this. Sensing his triumph Albert left us and went to the cafeteria.

In a little while we joined him. One of the vendors was eyeing him curiously, and as we sat down to slake our thirst, with a sudden determination he left his souvenir stand and handed Albert a tiny bundle wrapped in brown paper.

"Effendi," he said, "you are a man of the cloth. You will understand the true worth of this relic."

The white flour drained from Albert's face as he unwrapped the package and held up a weathered piece of wood about the size of a child's finger. The vendor moved closer.

"A splinter of the True Cross, Effendi! It's been in my family for almost a hundred generations. You are the first Christian to ever see it."

Albert put it to his lips and made a loud smacking sound.

"Name your price," he murmured.

"That is hard to do, Effendi, since the relic is priceless. But since you are the kind of man who will value and preserve it as my family has for generations I will give it to you for ten dollars."

"My child, that is way too cheap for a relic such as this. Here, let me give you twenty."

"*Shukran, shukran*! God is great and this indeed proves it!"

We next visited the tomb of a man named Kiki in the Valley of the Nobles. Albert's purchase had a soothing effect and he submitted to Lumumba's subversive discourse without a fuss. It had to do with the dog-god Anubis to whom Kiki and his wife were bowing.

Obviously, said Lumumba, the ancient Egyptians didn't treat their gonads as badly as modern people did. You could tell by this painting. Anubis was a kind and friendly animal, a mirror image of Kiki's interior. He, like the others, didn't look upon his animal self with horror. The beast of the New Testament had not yet reared its ugly head, nor the confusion between the word six and sex which in Latin are identical. That the beast came to be identified with a triple six (or triple *sex* in Latin) was probably indicative of men's horror when the triad of mother, father and son goes sour.

"Six is sex and sex is six," said Kumasi merrily as we went into the tomb of Menna, 'Scribe of the Land Register of Upper and Lower Egypt.' On one of the murals two men dressed in white were sacrificing a bull.

"Here are the prototypes for today's butchers," said Lumumba. "The gonads needed to be purified as much then as they do today—the *raison-d'etre* of McDonald's success. Men may eat their hamburgers and sit back with ease, no longer afraid that their sons will bash out their brains as was the custom in the old days."

Our next stop was the Ramesseum. Only a few columns and crumbling walls remained of a once sprawling complex where the great pharaoh Ramses II had been worshipped as the god Osiris. It was important, said Lumumba, to connect the phallus with the god whose penis had been severed and magically restored. The moral, he explained, was that there was no point in cutting off your father's penis because it would grow back bigger than ever.

To prove his point he led us to a colossal figure of the pharaoh lying on the ground. Once it had towered over 17 meters high. As he gazed at the gigantic head Lumumba became inspired.

"I can hear it now," he said, "the voice of this statue booming across the desert: 'Oh Ye of little faith! See how big is man's penis, how big is his tool! You must worship it or be destroyed. Gods have been created

208

for this purpose, and now you must believe in them. Animals you are no longer. Men you must now be, a species created in the image of God—in the image of orgasm. This is the truth of all ages, for from orgasm you evolved and to orgasm you will return. For orgasm is now your god. So sayeth I, Ramses II.' "

Lumumba's voice had carried over to a group of tourists being led by the ship's tour leader Abdel Zahr. With a stunned expression the Egyptian came up to us.

"Excuse me," he said, "but did I hear you correctly, that Ramses II told his people to worship orgasm?!"

"That you did, Matey," said Lumumba. Mr. Zahr took the professor aside.

"I hope, sir, that you are not taking advantage of these mentally retarded people."

He made a sweeping gesture toward the chimps.

"In America, Sir, they are referred to as the mentally challenged," Lumumba replied in an offended tone.

"Ah yes, I forgot. But whatever term is used, I know from experience that most of them are deeply religious. Perhaps they would get more out of it if you were to tell them that the Egyptians built their temples to the scale of God, not to men."

"But that's exactly what he's doing," said Bata who had sidled over. For if God was the incarnation of orgasm, he said, then in truth the temples were built to the scale of orgasm, and were excellent indicators of how much power it had over people, how it dominated their unconscious lives just as these temples dominated the landscape.

"May Allah save us!" said Mr. Zahr after Bata's words were translated. Having become speechless he hurried after his tour group.

We stopped at Qurna for refreshments and souvenirs. The concession store was so crowded I came out quickly and joined Lumumba who was waiting near the bus. As we stood in the shade, a young boy came down the hill on a donkey. Hitting it and kicking it to make it go faster, the boy had a broad grin on his face.

"Look at the little bugger," said Lumumba. "He beats the animal to get his thrills. Well, that's typical. Sex must be punished at all costs no matter what its age."

As the boy came abreast of us Lumumba reached out and yanked him off his mount. By chance the poor child hit his head on a rock and lay still in a pool of blood. Lumumba felt his pulse and pulled him out of sight.

"Is he dead?" I asked.

"Dead as a doornail. I might as well sign my initials and get a little credit."

"This will probably cancel out any admirers or converts you might have made up to this point," I said as he wrote his insignia on the boy's t-shirt.

"My dear Mrs. Hickey, there's no such thing as an innocent child, if that's what you're hinting at. Nor, for that matter, innocence period. It's a hallucinated concept based on the exigencies of the incest taboo. It's true meaning—'not to know'—refers to the Biblical sense of knowing which is of course sexual. Innocence, then, becomes a state of sexual non-awareness. But since all living organisms are born with sexual awareness, such a state doesn't exist. Humans have concocted it though because it is expedient to hide from themselves all memories of their own erotic childhood. As for the boy, today he's beating the donkey, tomorrow he's beating his wife. I would say it's not a great loss."

The donkey began to chew on Lumumba's sleeve. He patted the beast kindly and gave him precise instructions for kicking in human skulls. The donkey said "hee-haw" and pranced away.

"Is that in the Field Manual too?" asked Goldschmidt coming up to join us.

"Chapter Six: Animal Communication. You'll be able to tell a spider to go stick it up his ass, or a better yet, up your enemy's ass."

"And he'll do it? Man, a whole army of trained, indoctrinated spiders! Anyone who has that manual can rule the world!"

Our next stop was the Valley of the Queens. In the tomb of Prince Amon-her-Khopechef Yendi dallied infront of a painting of Thoth, the baboon-headed god of wisdom.

"I can't believe they think we look like that," said Lumumba. "What an insult."

"Listen," said Goldschmidt, "if I could do the somersaults that you guys did at Abu Simbel, hell, they could call me a chimpanzee, I could care less!"

On another wall we saw serpents with blue wings and golden suns above their heads. Here was proof, Lumumba said, that the Egyptians had dealt with Oedipus more wisely than the Hebrews. These were angelic snakes with the grace of a god. As phallic symbols these snakes were telling men that orgasm was to be loved and cherished, not feared and repulsed—the message evoked by the serpent in the Garden of Eden.

"What have you been drinking?!" Mr. Zahr exclaimed. He'd been eavesdropping ever since the Ramesseum. "Have you never heard of Apophis, the serpent of Chaos? He was a dreadful snake, a real devil. He wanted to eat the sun every night on its journey through the netherworld. But fortunately for us, the powers of order finally brought him to justice. They anchored him with knives and thus the sky is dyed red with his blood every morning and evening. Of course it's just a story, but to tell your group that these snakes are without guile or malice is very irresponsible. By the way, what tour company are you with?"

"Dr. Lumumba Tours. Would you like a card? Oh my, I seem to be all out."

"I'll bet you are, people must be asking for them left and right."

"How did you know?"

After Zahr left Lumumba stood thinking.

"I should have guessed," he said, "that even the Egyptians would have their own little allegory to ward off that devilish phallus. And it's a good one, too. The sun (the father) is being threatened by the serpent (the phallus). Through the powers of order—laws, religion and magic—the dangerous rivalry between males is constrained and contained, and the father (the sun) stays powerful forever after. Yes, the snake represents man's sexual problems everywhere and I imagine it's because when it strikes, not only is it deadly but it mimics the striking movement of the penis."

Before we left the tomb we took one last look at Khnum, the ram-head god who fashioned mankind on a potter's wheel. Why did Lumumba compare him to Jesus? For when looking at the blue-headed ram, whose intelligent eyes sparkled with vigor, one did not have to suffer the sad eyes of Jesus turned upward toward heaven.

Chapter Eighteen

Did a Christian Fish Eat a Man's Penis?

Or

A Few Carriage Horses Have the Last Laugh

Our tardiness had made the driver angry.

"*Inshallah*, get into my bus you worthless Christian turds!"

"Don't look at me," Goldschmidt said. "I'm Jewish."

"That's even worse!   Hurry up and get in before I leave you to rot in this stinking desert."

As the bus lurched forward Albert took out his relic and began to pray. Lumumba was resigned.

"It's completely hopeless," he said to Yendi. "I've shown him how the origins of Christianity are rooted in the ancient polytheistic state-sanctioned worship of the phallus, how the Word of God belonged to Osiris when he still had a penis, how everything in the human world revolves around this one object because it caused so much chaos when the physics of the spine evolved. And look at him, he's still a convert."

"It's such a pity," Yendi replied. "Being Oyem's son he could have had first choice of all the females—Makeni, Borama, Negame, Douala, Winneba, Yalinga and Mohele."

It was the wrong thing to say. Albert fell in a heap at Lumumba's feet and began to beat himself with the Bible. The bus driver made a sudden swerve and some of the passengers fell in the aisle. Nedele was amongst them, and in trying to regain her seat she lost hold of Bagamoyo. Tchibanga quickly retrieved him but not before Nedele had let out an ear-piercing screech. Everyone turned to look.

212

"The young lady has been studying her roots too zealously, I'm afraid," Lumumba said apologetically.

This seemed to satisfy everybody except the passenger sitting next to Mr. Zahr.

"My name is Crumb," the woman said. Her face was hidden behind dark glasses and a wall of jet-black bangs lying flat against her forehead. The rest of her hair was pulled tightly into a small bun at the nape of her neck. A slash of red lipstick across her thin lips looked as if she'd applied it with a paintbrush.

"Dr. Lumumba at your service," the professor replied.

"I do primate research in Atlanta. Your friend does a better imitation of a chimpanzee danger call than any of the real ones."

"Because she was born without the power of speech," Lumumba replied.

"She is speech impaired?"

"As are the others in my group."

"Don't look at me," said Goldschmidt

"What a wonderful idea, bringing people like that to Egypt."

"I doubt he could get anyone else," said Mr. Zahr. "You should hear the gibberish he's feeding them. It's almost criminal."

Lumumba glared back and I began to think that Zahr might not have much time left. On the other hand it was not as if the Professor was whacking people left and right anymore. Could his ways in Africa be coming to an end?

The bus lurched to a stop.

"*Imshi, imshi*! Everybody get out—rabbits, ape impersonators, Jews, tourists! *Allah Ackbar*, what I have to do to feed my camels!"

The Colossi of Memnon—two sitting figures of Amenhotep III, each cut from a single block of stone over sixty feet high. Framed against the blue sky, they dominated the flat landscape for miles in all directions.

As Lumumba walked over Mr. Zahr came alongside with his group to listen. Lumumba took a cursory look at the ship's daily program notes and began: "Can you feel the might of the phallus?" he asked. "Even after these thousands of years the colossi still have the power of the incest taboo embedded in them. It's the oldest male phantasy of all. Imagine the size of the penises on those boys! They'd be bigger than an elephant's—and hard as a rock. No wonder the Egyptian peasants were in awe of the pharaoh: By magical transference, he possessed the mythic power of that giant rod."

And the power was real, he said, because the illusion was real. It existed in the electrical circuitry and neurological processes of the brain.

213

Remember the visions? Remember how prehistoric men captured them on the walls of caves? And so the lines became real, these electrical pops inside the head, so real they eventually couldn't be crossed over, a man was kept off another man's property, one country was separated from another, and then of course there was the alphabet and mathematics, all originating from these altered states of mind.

But if the illusion was real then the line had to be real too, Herbert argued.

Only if you argued that the hallucinations which created it were real, Lumumba replied. But in nature there were no hallucinations, only energy fields and the *appearance* of lines. But in human minds the illusion was as real as the day was long, and civilization existed because we believed in it. The incest taboo was a line that you couldn't cross over. But how silly that was, since there really was no such thing as a line!

Mr. Zahr was ready to tear out his hair.

"Lines, energy fields, hallucinations! What does that have to do with these marvelous statues? Do you know that when they broke apart in 27 BC one of them began to sing?"

"Ah yes, the dead son who sings to his mother. I thought I would save you the embarrassment."

"I insist that you don't! What is the embarrassment?"

"The secret love between mother and son. Is that not the whole point of this legend? For 200 years the damaged statue vibrated as the stone around was warmed each morning by the sun. But the Greeks said it was the voice of the dead hero Memnon, singing each morning to his grieving mother Aurora, goddess of dawn as she caressed him with her rays.

"I repeat, *caressed*. By the way, Zahr, have you ever seen the Pieta in Italy? Now there is caressing! Imagine, a full-grown man lying half naked in his mother's lap. Doesn't that seem shameful to you?"

"But he is dead," Mr. Zahr stammered.

"Dead or not dead, I suspect there was a bit of titillation going on, if only in the brain of Michelangelo."

"Even as a Moslem I find your words offensive. Come people, let us go elsewhere. There are some lovely stellae we can look at, just go to the right."

The Happy Pharaoh was a welcome sight. As we climbed to the sundeck Lumumba went below to check on Kribi. He returned quickly.

"Our comrade is showing signs of systemic infection," said Lumumba within earshot of Goldschmidt. "We may need to revise our OpPlan."

"If only we were back in Mahale," said Tchibanga. "We could pick some plants from the forest that would make him well again."

"A little veronia would fix him right up," said Bata.

"What about hagenia?" said Yendi. "If it flushes out worms, it should also flush out the infection."

"Not systemic," said Tchibanga, "we need something stronger."

"Say, you fellows sound like your naturopaths," said Goldschmidt.

"It's part of our creed," said Lumumba. " 'Never use Establishment medicine unless you absolutely have to.' GLA Manual, Article XII. Speaking of the devil . . ."

With Yalinga's help Kribi hobbled over and eased himself into a deck chair. He tossed a newspaper onto Lumumba's lap. Okovango clung to his mother's skirt.

"Will you read me the article again, Uncle?" Kribi signed weakly.

"Yes, of course."

GLA Strikes Again. Cairo. In an extraordinary display of bravado and cunning, a handful of terrorists led an attack yesterday morning in the tourist city of Edfu leaving thirty people dead and more than 55 wounded. Most of the victims were drivers in the carriage trade, and authorities believe the attack was another attempt following Saturday's attack at Abu Simbel to sabotage Egypt's booming tourist industry.

Police are investigating the role of a shadowy group known as the GLA. Originally thought to be leftist guerillas from Gabon, an anonymous tip has led authorities to identify the group as an extremist movement known as the Gonad Liberation Army.

While this maverick army has not yet declared itself or stated its aims, unidentified sources at the Pentagon say the group is planning to overthrow the world and is employing a highly technical manual written by their leader. To the consternation of governments around the globe donations earmarked for the GLA have been pouring into an Internet Web site set up to process credit card donations.

As for yesterday's deadly attack, one of the group was believed to have been wounded, and police say they are pleading for tourists to remain calm. A delegation from Interpol , Britain and the United States will be participating in the investigation.

Despite these assurances, many locals in Edfu have decided not to resume the carriage trade. Rumors abound that the killers are baboons, and local superstitions have led to many stories about the return of the ancient god Thoth. The horses of the slain carriage drivers are being stabled in a nearby mosque where local residents have been bringing them offerings of food, apparently in an attempt to allay Thoth's wrath.

"That's it except for an accompanying story about Thoth. Do you want to hear it?"

"Save it for the baboons," said Tchibanga.

Lumumba put down the paper, Kribi smiled and Nedele jumped up and down happily.

A discussion now ensued as to who had snitched. Herbert and Goldschmidt were quickly eliminated; they had too much to lose. I was eliminated, I had nothing to gain. Mohammed's protestations appeared authentic, he too was exonerated—which left only the apes. All eyes fell on Albert.

"How dare you accuse a man of the cloth," he said indignantly. "And lest you've forgotten, may I remind you that Mr. Ntimama also knows about your little schemes?"

As yes, Ntimama, the scoundrel who escaped in a parachute. That was it, of course, why didn't we think of it?! The apes apologized, Albert forgave them, and a deck hand told us it was time for dinner.

"I'd just as soon stay here," said Kribi, his face awash in pain. "I don't feel hungry."

"I'll stay with you," said Yalinga. "Nedele, please take Okovango downstairs."

The little chimp reluctantly left his mother's side and followed us to the dining room.

Betty waved us over.

"Well," said Marty, did you have a nice day disparaging the origins of Western civilization?"

"Absolutely lovely. We discussed the Oedipal origins of everything we saw, from Karnak to Memnon."

"So Abdel tells me," said Mr. Asad. "But first there is good news, my friends. The terrorists who killed the carriage drivers have been captured. I heard it on the ship's radio this evening. They will face a firing squad in the morning."

"Nothing like giving people a fair trial," said Lumumba.

"There was no trial. It was, as you Americans say, vigilante justice."

"Well, why not?" said Lumumba taking an apple off a plate. "Afterall, you can't reason with a terrorist, although all they really want is to sleep with their mothers, sisters and daughters—and who knows, maybe fathers, sons and brothers too."

"Is that your definition of a terrorist?" asked Royce.

"Partly. The rest of it is, anyone who wants to break the laws which keep him obedient to God. His own words give him away. He speaks of holy wars and Jihads. Why? Because war is rooted in the gonads and religion has made the gonads holy. But because men hate their holiness they use it as an excuse to break the commandments that are rooted in the sanctity of sex. Thus they shoot anybody on sight. Or steal, rape and pillage. All wars are an excuse to break free from the constraints of civilization and its laws which are rooted in the holy gonads and the incest taboo.

"The irony, of course, is that since the incest taboo is purely magical, so too are the laws. But no one knows this. Everyone thinks that laws are real, though in truth they are purely figments of the human imagination."

"I don't know how the hell they ever let him teach at Yale," said Johnson shaking his head wearily.

"I don't either," Lumumba replied. "I've never seen such a fortress. It's the white man's bastion, his defensive stronghold against the terror of his darkest secrets which are so well represented by the shabby town of New Haven. That's why no real learning takes place there, only formula."

"I'm drawing a blank," Johnson growled. But before Lumumba could explain his theory of racism, the waiter brought our food.

Lumumba sniffed Johnson's water buffalo.

"I really think you should turn over a new leaf," said the professor. "Meat eaters are so prone to sudden, violent deaths. Have you ever read Ovid? I would be surprised if you had. Let me recite:

There was a time, the Golden Age, we call it,
Happy in fruits and herbs, when no men tainted
Their lips with blood, and birds went flying safely
Through air, and in the fields the rabbits wandered
Unfrightened, and no little fish was ever
Hooked by its own credulity: all things
Were free from treachery and fear and cunning,
And all was peaceful;
Some innovator,
A good-for-nothing, whoever he was, decided,
In envy, that what lions ate was better, stuffed meat into his belly like a
Furnace,
And paved the way for crime.

When Lumumba finished Johnson raised his glass.
"Whoever that was, I drink to his health."
"Here, here," said Royce. "I'll second that."

217

A group of Spaniards had come aboard the Happy Pharaoh earlier in the day. Now they entered the dining room, and almost at once their attention was riveted on our table.

"Perhaps someone forgot to zip up," said Royce.

A few minutes later one of the men came over to Mrs. Dodd.

"A thousand pardons, Th'ñora, but would it be much trouble to give us your autograph? We are all very big fans, my wife Maria in particular, ever since she was a little girl and saw you dance."

Betty's hand flew nervously to her neck.

"She's been to La Habra?" she asked.

"Shut up," said Royce.

"La Habra, La Habra," said the Spaniard as if trying to pinpoint the name. "No, no it was in Seville that she saw you. Where is La Habra?"

"It's a little town full of strip clubs east of Los Angeles," said Marty. He laughed as Betty shot him a nasty look.

"But we've never been to America," said the Spaniard. "Ah! You are Americans? Oh how silly of me, please forgive my mistake! Maria, they are Americans," he called over.

"So who did you think she was?" Royce asked curiously.

"Ah, a very famous dancer, Th'ñor. In Spain we call her La Esplenda. She was the great beauty of her time. Of course now she is old."

"Gee thanks," said Betty.

A loud guffaw broke from Marty's lips.

"Did she have a mole the size of a bumble bee?" he asked.

"Th'i, th'ñor! As a matter of fact, yes. That is why my wife thought it was her. Please forgive me for the stupid mistake."

He returned to his seat.

"How extraordinary," said Dotty, fingering her mole.

"We're still having it removed," said Royce. "I'm tired of looking at it."

"And I'm tired of looking at you," Betty replied. "Sorry, dear, I think it's all these minarets, I swear they are getting to me."

"I rather like them," said Royce, "especially the pretty ones that have all the decoration. Some of them look like icing on a cake, good enough to eat."

"Plain or fancy," said Lumumba, "a minaret is symbolic of the penis, and five times a day the faithful are called to worship it. Very clever, don't you think? Much more effective than a Christian church where the penis is symbolized by a spire on the roof and worshipped only once a week on Sunday. *I* say if you're going to worship the penis you might as well do it right—five times a day, seven days a week."

Marty laughed.

"Royce, I always knew there was something queer about you," he said.

Albert, who had been listening quietly, took out his relic and began to finger it.

"The truth is a tree and the tree is a phallus," said old Kumasi.

"Listen," said Royce, "not every pointy thing is a penis. Sometimes a cigar is just a cigar and a minaret simply has its practical use—like a radio tower."

"But a radio tower is just a technologically enhanced minaret," said Lumumba. "It's another way of broadcasting the law of the incest taboo to the people. Albert, may I borrow that? Something is stuck in my tooth."

Before Albert could blink Lumumba seized the relic, broke off a part of the splinter and used it to remove the offending piece of apple. Albert stared in disbelief and began to tremble.

"This time you've gone too far," he said ominously.

Taking what remained of the relic he left the table.

It was late, we were returning to our cabin when Lumumba and Betty turned into the corridor ahead of us. They didn't see us and spoke loudly.

"That Spaniard was an idiot," said Lumumba, "to imply that the years have taken away your beauty."

"Oh Professor, you're such a card! Is it my cabin or yours tonight?"

"Let's make it yours, the boys went into town just a few minutes ago."

"Well I'll be a monkey's uncle!" said Herbert as they disappeared around the corner.

"What, the Professor can't have a little pussy?" said Yendi who had come up behind us.

"It's more than that," said Tchibanga who was with him. "They've been at it since the Mt. Kenya Safari Club. Well, good night everybody, see you in the morning."

Dendera. Originally the site of three sanctuaries—Horus, Hathor his wife and their son Harsomtus—only the sanctuary of Hather still remained. There was a smaller temple inside called the Chapel of Holiness. It was the most secret part of the temple, Lumumba said, because inorder to make sex holy, the vagina had to be made inaccessible. All inner sanctums, inother words, were metaphors for the vagina.

219

Which is why the mysteries telling of the birth of cosmic order from the primeval chaos were celebrated here, since the concept of order was the consequence of the chaos born in the gonads.

In the inner sanctuary of the Osiris room there were images of Osiris bringing himself to erection and impregnating Isis with a beam of light from which her son Horus the living King was born. Lumumba said that the Virgin Mary was impregnated with the same light and that Jesus was both Horus the living King and Osiris the resurrected father.

Albert was not around to protest. He had stayed on board the ship claiming to have a headache. But in Albertesque fashion Nedele raised a question. If there were such a thing as resurrection, would Doba be resurrected too?

Lumumba looked nervously around for Goldschmidt. All talk of chimps had lately been forbidden in his presence, but Goldschmidt and Mohammed had wandered off to look at some graphic pictures. The talk of Doba continued.

"Streets paved in gold don't sound like a very good place for chimps," said Bata.

"What if God straightened his legs and took the ugly fur from his body?" Nedele asked. "Albert says you can't get into heaven without being made in God's image."

"So how do you know God doesn't look like a chimp?" said Bata. "Doesn't the story of Eden refer back to a time when men first stood upright and were overwhelmed by the sexual ecstasies of a straight spine? When this was happening people probably looked more like chimps than humans."

"That's a good point," said Lumumba. "Look at Hathor. She is the wife of Horus the living king. But she is also a cow. The gods, which are the souls of men, are to be found in the souls of animals."

"The same path that leads to orgasm leads to God," said Kumasi. "The truth is a tree and the tree is a phallus."

"I'm still not clear," said Bata, "about the resurrection of Osiris. Did they or did they not find his penis?"

"That is the $64,000 question," said Lumumba. "Some say yes, others say no. Apparently there was some confusion as to how best to deal with man's wily protrusion."

Only this much was clear, that after Seth murdered his brother—and for a long time this was acceptable behavior amongst brothers—Osiris's body was cut into pieces and thrown in the Nile. Since Isis was without a child, a colossal attempt was made to collect all the body parts and put her husband back together again. At this point the story became murky.

In one version a fish ate the penis—Lumumba suggested once again it was the same fish we see on the back of Christian cars—and Isis had to become pregnant without it. In another version Isis scoured the land and eventually found it. Osiris was put back together, penis and all, and in a last superhuman effort was able to impregnate his wife and father a son. Then there was still another version, a spin-off, on the first, sans fish, in which Isis had the child without the penis being present, which was pretty much what Mary did with Jesus. Inother words, Jesus's Immaculate Conception had its origins in Horus's Immaculate Conception. This was indeed an Oedipal paradise, a love story between mother and son, no fathers allowed.

In the afternoon we arrived at Abydos, perhaps the holiest city of all, said Lumumba. It was dedicated to the big god Osiris and was the perfect place to confront the mystery of death since it was here that death, birth and the Word met in their purest form.

Unlike the other temples where the columns and pillars were flowery and ornamental, the portico and façade consisted exclusively of straight lines and angles. If one were looking for tenderness and mercy this temple gave no quarter.

There were tourists everywhere, and Zahr was shouting to be heard as his group gathered near the entrance to the temple of Seti. Lumumba stopped to listen.

"This is a perfect example," said Zahr, "of how building and religion merged together. The Egyptian religion was grounded in *ma'at*—a conception of universal order and balance. Originally, the word meant 'that which is straight,' i.e., a rule of measure. A man was *ma'at* when he was upright and honest, and the belief in *ma'at* pervaded every class of ancient Egypt, becoming a moral duty, a code of behavior for every Egyptian. In the lines of this building, you see *ma'at* everywhere."

"What did I tell you!" said Lumumba, smiling boldly. "*Ma'at* and *rex* are rooted in the same phallic principle. The straight line behind the Egyptian religion and the straight line behind the English throne—both are rooted in the movement of the penis. This is the rule of measure upon which civilization rests, this is the source of morality."

Mr. Zahr had stopped his own talk to listen, and now directed his group over to ours.

"Come people," he said. "Some of you have been complaining about me, well, if you think I'm a bad guide, wait 'til you hear this fellow. Go on, tell them about Ma'at."

Well for one thing, Lumumba went on, the animals used it too, the same rule of measure—the penis. But because they hadn't expanded their brains to the same extent as ours, the measure stayed inside them at a biological level and never became an abstraction like it did for us. In the animal's world it was straightforward: The chimp, for example, with the biggest penis got all the females. The other chimps had to abide by his rule of measure: "What he says goes."

But in human society everything was perverted because the penis was no longer visible. Not only was it hidden beneath clothes, it was hidden beneath the mental constructs of religion. For humans, the penis was an abstract principle that organized their whole way of life. This temple was not so much a monument to Pharaoh Seti as it was a monument to the geometrical abstraction of the straight line. That's where Seti got his power. The line was what allowed the ancient Egyptians to impose their human vision of order on the natural world. The line was a kind of primordial violence. A coercion that lined up the objects of nature as well as soldiers to prove their allegiance to the invisible power that held the army together.

Without an understanding of lines the Egyptians could never have built these temples. Lines, circles and numbers were the basic concepts that allowed men to organize and master the world, impose their will on it rather than harmonizing themselves to it and listening to its secrets. The line was the origin of totalitarian thought. Why do you think the Nazis were so obsessed with the fascist cubes and geometrically perfect stadiums, he asked.

"*Zif!*" (stop) Zahr shouted. "Whether the Nazis were fascinated or not," he asked, "how can we have civilization and technology without lines and numbers, geometry and math?"

"Are there lines and numbers, geometry and math behind the marvelous technology of a whale's sonar?" Lumumba asked.

"That's biology," said Zahr. "Technology is something deliberately created by the mind."

"It seems rather arrogant to say that there's no mind at work in something as exquisite as a bird's wing," said Lumumba.

"Professor, you're not actually postulating that the Mind of God exists, are you?" asked Herbert.

"Don't you wish! No, I'm talking about the mind in the bird's wing itself—the intrinsic quality of mind holding the atoms and electrons together in a certain order, that will of the universe to organize itself out of the void—that is the real mind."

222

"Real or not, technology must somehow be wrung from somewhere," said Zahr. Lines and numbers are as good a place as any. They were certainly good enough for the Egyptians."

"But how do you know there's not another *kind* of technology—one that would grow out of communication with nature, a direct connection between what you call the human mind and the mind of the electrons that holds the universe together? If you could make that connection maybe you could make temples grow from the earth that are more satisfying than these."

"That's too impossible to imagine," said Zahr.

"Of course it is. A species which has evolved because the rules of *ma'at* and *rex* have been imposed—hence lines and numbers—must continue to dig up the earth and pour it into blast furnaces, turn trees into nice straight boards, and animals into nice straight steaks. Poor nature, she will never do anything for you because you've treated her like a slave."

"How can we stop?" asked someone from Zahr's group.

"Perhaps by giving up your lineal, scientific logic and starting to think with the hysterical energy of orgasm—a wild dance of fields and waves, forces and probabilities. What do you suppose the world would be like if electrons started thinking in straight lines, or if subatomic particles gave up their paradoxical dual nature? The universe as you know it would collapse into a plate. But since humans are so wedded to their penis-dominated understanding of the world, they can't really envision things any other way than *Ma'at* and *rex*; they're stuck in the penis dimension and can't even imagine what the world outside really looks like."

"*In sha-allah*," said Zahr. "I think I'm going crazy. Come people, let's get a Coke.

At the hypostyle of Ramses II, Thoth and Horus were portrayed pouring holy water over the pharaoh.

"More sexual nonsense," said Lumumba impatiently. "Maybe John the Baptist got what he deserved for popularizing it."

The concept of purity, he reminded us, was rooted in the practice of preserving the bloodlines of the patriarch. The words 'noble' and 'pure' were synonymous because the noble family was the one which kept the purest blood line, and this was achieved through unions of the first degree, that is, incestuous unions. The hypocrisy was clear. Incest was dirty but the concept that generated it—purity—was clean and good.

As for holy water itself, only an idiot could deny its sexual origin. Was anyone here Catholic? No? Even so, surely we had seen that most unapologetic of all phallic symbols, the aspergill—a straight implement

223

with a nubby head on one end which dribbled water. How clever of the priest to use it, not only to dispense the holy water but to emphasize the fact that semen was holy and, by extension, the sexual act itself.

We came to the Osireion, a monument dedicated to the creation of life. The room had once contained a mound surrounded by a trench filled with the seeping waters of Chaos. I knew what Lumumba was going to say before he said it, that the mound represented the female genitals and the waters of Chaos were of course semen and the female fluids too. Never forget, he said, that the penis of Osiris (represented in the ancient Egyptian mysteries as the Word) was the same Word we found in the Old Testament and the New. The Word of God was the penis, but lest we forget, God was only a man and a penis was only a penis.

We were about to enter the temple of Ramses II when several loud voices caused us to pause. Lumumba signaled everyone into the shadows of the chapel. I recognized two of the voices right away—Johnson and Dodd.

"I'm telling you, they're getting suspicious," said Johnson. "Nobody tours the pyramids while his wife's in the freezer."

"Let them get suspicious," said a man with a thick accent. "Once you get us the goods we'll put this country into such an uproar the last thing they'll be worried about is a couple of Americans traveling with a frozen wife. Besides, I've seen Americans do stranger things than that."

"I wouldn't talk," said Johnson. "That mess you made at Abu Simbel—how do we know you won't screw up again?"

"*Ch'ura!* (Shit!) How were we to know the GLA had planned an attack on the same day and the same hour? And there must have been at least a hundred of them jumping around the rocks like monkeys. From what my boys said they were all trained in kung fu."

"Someone knew about our plans," said a fourth man.

"Whoever gave you away," said Dodd, "might give you away again."

"How do we know, Mr. Dodd, that it wasn't you? You give us the merchandise, we give you the money, and then you betray us. Sounds like standard CIA operating procedure."

"You infidel Americans have no honor," said a fifth man. "The world would be a better place if we gutted you like camels at the meat market."

"But then you wouldn't have a chance to turn half the temples and tourists on the Nile into radioactive dust," said Johnson. "Anyway, we have no reason to betray you. Our country is as eager as you are to see a return to fundamentalist values all over the world. We believe, as you believe, that women have too much freedom."

"Allah be praised," said the second man. "Spoken like a true believer. The Shining Path to Allah's Virgins welcomes you to their heart. But what about the missiles you promised? The army is getting to be a problem. We need to be able to do more than just butcher pudgy American tourists—fun as that might be."

"You also promised anthrax," said a sixth man.

"And nuclear warheads and AK 47s," said the fourth.

"We have to talk about that," said Dodd. "The anthrax is proving to be a problem. It's going to cost us much more than we anticipated to get the quantities you need."

"How much more?" one of the men asked suspiciously. "SPAV won't wait forever."

"For the whole lot—six tactical nuclear warheads, six vials of anthrax and six stinger missiles—the cost will be six million."

"Six million!! *En'sh-allah*! That's twice as much as you originally quoted!"

"Sorry, but Allah's virgins don't come cheap these days."

"But it's three times what you charged Saddam! *Koos omuuk*! (fucker of your mother!) What do you take us for? Some ignorant fellahin who became terrorists because we couldn't find jobs in the city?"

"Will everybody calm down?!" shouted the first man. "The problem, Misters Johnson and Dodd, is that the money we were promised hasn't yet arrived. There was some kind of snafu, as you Americans say, in Kenya last week."

"How much do you have?" asked Dodd.

"One million."

"No problem. For one million you can have six vials of anthrax and one stinger missile, or six missiles and no anthrax, or six vials of anthrax and one nuclear warhead."

"*Koll ch'ura*!" (Eat shit!) said the Arab. "This is highway robbery!

"Actually it's inflation," Johnson answered. "These are the prices listed at Langely. "If you don't believe me you can check it out yourself. Here's the telephone number."

We could hear some papers rustling as he wrote it down.

"Anyway, you know where to find us. The ship arrives in Cairo in four days. We'll be at the Ramses Hilton, but it's better we meet on Mu'izz al-Din Allah Street—the Street of the Gold Sellers. We want cash, of course. *Salaam ah likum.*[peace]."

"*Salaam ahl likum* yourself!!"

225

There was the sound of scuffling, and a minute later Johnson and Dodd came sailing into the courtyard. They picked themselves up and hurried away.

"Egads," said Goldschmidt as we stepped into the sunlight. "It's one thing to make a little money on the side. But selling anthrax to terrorists—that's really going over the line."

"The line is there to be crossed," said Lumumba. "Get rid of it—the magic incest taboo—and you'll have nothing left to cross over. End of problem."

Chapter Nineteen

Nedele Solves the Mystery of the Sphinx

I was half undressed when Tchibanga barged into the cabin.

"So that's what all the fuss is about," he said appraising me cooly. "Yalinga has you beat a hundred times."

"She's more hairy, isn't she? Was there something you wanted?"

"I'm looking for Albert. Nobody's seen him lately."

"Herbert saw him go ashore early this morning. May I get dressed now?"

At breakfast, Kribi barely touched his food. Under the thick wad of flour his face looked gray and sickly. Yalinga clung to him tightly. The chimps had searched the town for veronia but there was none to be found.

Once again the plea went out to find a doctor, once again it was vetoed. The bullet wound, Lumumba said, would lead the police right to our door.

Not so, said Goldschmidt. He knew several doctors in Egypt—actually everywhere in the *world*—who could be trusted to keep their mouths shut.

A beleaguered Lumumba shook his head. His reasoning which he told me later was simple: "the minute Goldschmidt finds out we're apes—bang! End of passports. Anyway Kribi is strong, I'm betting he'll pull through."

The ancient city of Al Amarna, we arrive sans Albert. After finally making his appearance after breakfast he refused to go ashore, and all cajoling and threats were useless.

"Leave the little bugger alone," Lumumba said at last, "or we'll miss our ride."

The city had been built by Akhenaten, a renegade pharaoh who had founded a monotheistic religion around the worship of the sun god Aton. This was the same god the Jews worshipped today, said Lumumba, only instead of men looking up at the sun and saying, 'there is Aton,' the Jews looked up and said: 'Yaweh is everywhere and everything.' Their genius, said Lumumba, was that they took the sun and made it invisible. They took the one God—Aton—and made him unseeable, the same way that orgasm is unseeable. In the Hebraic religion there is a connection between the visible sun and its power to make things exist and the invisible orgasm and its power to create life

Were the ancient Hebrews the first to stumble upon the idea of worshipping one god? No, but they were the ones blamed for it. Ah, if only Yaweh had not been invisible! Because being invisible, He became the most powerful prohibition of all against mankind's Oedipal desires. And it turned the whole world against Him.

But he, Lumumba, had said this all before, hadn't he? It was not the Jews people hated, it was their powerful God and His laws prohibiting so many interesting forms of copulation. Leviticus had laid down the law literally, told people who they could and couldn't sleep with and what they could and couldn't do in the bedroom on pain of death. This had made people plenty angry, the Germans in particular.

"As everyone knows, of course."

In the tomb of Huya, Lumumba pointed to the image of Akhenaten sitting opposite his mother.

"You see how she is being worshipped?" he asked. "Though she is the object of her son's desires, now that he is worshipping the one god, Aton, he can only desire her from afar: His desire has been frozen into a prohibition that establishes monotheism and legitimizes its power.

"He paid for this prohibition with his life: The biological drives of humans reasserted themselves and he was killed by his priests. Ah, if only the Jews had taken heed!"

But they didn't, and the Torah became the ultimate grid to imprison sexuality and throttle the gonads. When Abraham cut off the foreskin of his son and made men slaves to the Law, the Jews sealed their own fate. Men's hatred was focused on the messengers who brought down the laws graven in the vindictive phallocratic arsenal of an omnipotent, all-seeing, all knowing God of heaven and earth. After the Jews there was no place to act out incestuous feelings and desires anymore, not without dire consequences anyway, and this made it go hard on them. There was really no such thing as anti-Semitism—there was only a violent projection of Oedipal hostility onto the unfortunate Jews. Call it anti-God if you like. That was probably more to the truth of things.

"The truth is a tree and the tree is a phallus," old Kumasi sang out.

"Well, well," said Goldschmidt mopping his brow as we left the hot tomb, "all my life I though it was *me* people hated, and now I know it is really the *law*. That makes me feel a lot better about myself. Thank you, General."

"What you need," said Herbert, "is a good bumper sticker, something like 'Yahweh is my way.' "

"Zounds!" said Goldschmidt, "that's an excellent idea!"

He took out his notepad and jotted it down. But his happiness was short-lived. As we walked toward the carts, an armed rider came galloping toward us on a camel. As he came within range he aimed his weapon at Lumumba and fired. The shot missed and struck Goldschmidt instead.

"I've been hit!" he cried, staggering back toward the tomb. At the sight of blood trickling down his elbow he collapsed. "To think a swashbuckling patriot like me would be struck down in a wretched place like this!"

Mohammed rushed to his side.

"Do not depart to the realm of Death, great Sultan. The Moving Finger has not yet writ thy name!"

"He's right," said Lumumba. "The bullet ricocheted off the rock, it's merely a scratch. Come, let's get out of here before the police arrive."

As we hurried on Lumumba sniffed the air. A troubled look crossed his face and he muttered his thoughts aloud:

"Is it possible that Albert can ride a camel?!"

The question left us in a state of confusion.

The Happy Pharoah was on her way to El Wasta. This was the last stop before Cairo, and a group of folk dancers previously called *The Dancing Dervishes* but now known as *Thoth's Dancing Dervishes* were scheduled to appear after dinner. The atmosphere on board seemed more festive than usual.

"People are glad the voyage is over," said Lumumba. "They've spent the last week inside temples which unmask the Oedipal nature of Christianity. Being constantly exposed to these truths while trying to repress them has taken its toll. Even the most shallow and brainless"—Lumumba glanced over at Albert—"can hardly wait to escape the uncomfortable contradictions they've been faced with each day."

For myself I felt sad. Maybe it was the smell of roasting meat drifting up from the kitchen (I pictured Bagamoyo being skewered on a stick), or maybe it was what had happened to Kribi's leg. Surely it was not the fact that in a short while Lumumba would be on his way to Spain. Surely not!

"The only thing I need now," said Goldschmidt, sitting down next to me, "is a refill on my drink." He waved to Mohammed who came over with a decanter of Scotch and bucket of ice.

"And for you, Great General?" the boy said to Lumumba.

"A pencil and paper. I need some distraction."

"I would be honored if you would try me," said Mohammed making sure Goldschmidt didn't hear him. "I am like a young cherub with only peach fuzz on my face. I am also very clean."

"That's the trouble," Lumumba replied. "I prefer more dirt, hair and smell. But thank you anyway."

The materials were brought and Lumumba began to write. But a few moments later he crumpled the paper and threw it on the deck.

Herbert picked it up. "Another formula? Are you restructuring the first? What does this mean—two divided by C times M sub n divided by e times h divided by M sub n to the one half power?"

"Isn't it apparent? L is the Lumumba constant, while C is the velocity of light, M sub n and M sub e are the relative atomic masses of the neutron and electron, and the remaining quantity of the quotient of the Plank constant h and the neutron mass, M sub n."

"But of course! Only what is wrong with the first formula?" Herbert took out his torn page and looked at it carefully.

"It depended too heavily on the orbits of electrons, which can't be measured, you know. But my new theory is based on spectral lines which *can* be measured."

"How so?"

"Well, one way is to take a couple making love and incinerate them instantaneously using a high power laser; you could then record the pattern using an ordinary spectrograph."

"It's an elegant theory, Professor. But who would volunteer?"

"Why, I never though of that."

Nevertheless Herbert folded the paper carefully and tucked it safely away inside his shirt pocket.

The dancers were hardly more than children. You could hear their boyish laughter as they began setting up in a room off the lounge. Goldschmidt and Mohammed went to have a look, the rest of us went to dinner.

Tchibanga found us later in the lounge. He was out of breath and agitated.

"Yalinga left Kribi's door open and two of the dancers saw him without his makeup," he signed.

"When is it going to end," said Lumumba wearily.

"Don't worry, we took care of them."

"But the show calls for sixteen dervishes, not fourteen," said Herbert.

"Let's hope nobody can count," Lumumba replied.

"Don't worry, Yendi and I have a plan."

With that he went out as fast as he came in.

The lounge was beginning to fill up. Mohammed and Goldschmidt returned, Johnson arrived with the Dodds, Kumasi sat down with Okovango, and Dr. Crumb began a conversation with Nedele. It was not going well since Dr. Crumb didn't know sign language. Nevertheless the two of them seemed to be enjoying each other's company; Nedele, for once, appeared to be happy.

"You must not spoil the evening for Bagamoyo," said Dr. Crumb kindly.

The musicians came in and arranged themselves on the floor. They began to warm up on drums, an oud and a short horn-like flute that Dodd said sounded like a dying cat.

"Don't be an ugly a American," his wife admonished. The lights in the room dimmed.

"Ladies and gentlemen," said Mr. Asad. "Please give *Thoth's Dancing Dervishes* a warm welcome."

"I don't think I'm going to like this," said Lumumba dismally.

"Lighten up, General. You take yourself too seriously," said Goldschmidt.

"Thanks for the advice."

The audience applauded loudly as the dancers ran in from behind the curtain, one by one. As they began to form a circle, they also began to twirl. Their white skirts ballooned out like mushrooms, and the bright red fezzes they wore reminded me of an organ grinder's monkey. Their cheeks were dusted with the first fuzz of manhood, and the thinnest of mustaches graced their pretty lips.

The fourteenth dancer came on stage. For several minutes he appeared to be the last one. But the others looked anxiously at the curtain and finally one of them yelled out:

"Mustapha! Hassan! Will you please hurry up?!"

The curtain parted and out came Tchibanga and Yendi.

I was not terribly surprised, I had half expected this; but what I didn't expect was to see the two devoid of makeup, entirely en flagrante except for the costumes they were wearing. As they leaped into the spotlight their furry arms and faces glistened in the overhead lights like stars in the night.

"There go our passports," Lumumba groaned. Shaking his head he snuck a sidewards glance at Goldschmidt. But miracles of miracles, Goldschmidt was as mesmerized as the rest of the audience.

"By God they look real!" he exclaimed. The audience went wild.

"Thoth! Thoth!" they shouted and began to clap to the music, as happy as children.

"Who would have dreamed of dressing up as a monkey!" said Asad, his eyes filling with water. "A whirling dervish is enough by itself. But a whirling monkey dervish, now that is really something!"

As the audience continued to clap, the chimpanzees, their white dervish skirts billowing out like wings, began to whirl. As they went faster and faster, they began to outwhirl the other dancers.

"*Shu maanah hada*, Hassan?" one of the dancers hissed at Yendi. "What does this mean? Are you trying to put us to shame?!"

A second dancer spoke angrily to Tchibanga. "Hey, Mustapha! Is this what you meant when you said someday you'd make us all look like monkeys?!"

"Now we know why he wanted to change the name to Thoth's Dancing Dervishes," said a third.

"We dance to glorify Allah, not ourselves," said a fourth dancer.

"But you have to admit," said a fifth, "that it's a great idea. I only wish I had thought of it first. Hassan, where did you get the costume?"

He stared wide-eyed as Yendi picked up a musician and began to twirl him overhead, passing him from one hand to the other as if he were a toy. The poor man looked dazed and began to laugh helplessly. "Hey, Hassan," a dancer shouted, "what did you mix with your hashish tonight?"

The whirling became faster and faster, but even as the dervishes increased their speed Yendi and Tchibanga whirled ever faster. To every one rotation, the chimps were able to complete four or five. The audience was on its feet, the musicians became more and more frenzied as the chimps disappeared in a blur of leaping and whirling.

"I don't care what you say," said the fourth dancer to the first. "I'm going to get a monkey costume too. I always said that Mustafa and Hassan were the geniuses of the group."

232

"We could be known as the 'Whirling Chimps of Allah,' " said the second. "People would pay twice as much to see us, and we could double our fees or even triple them."

When the music ended there were tears rolling down Asad's face.

"Allah be praised!" he said. "I have never seen such dancing. I wonder what type of drugs they are on."

Tchibanga took bow after bow. Bras and panties sailed onto the stage, headscarves from the more pious. The chimps inhaled them all.

"It's like the night Cortina played Carnegie Hall," I said to Herbert. My hands were starting to hurt from all the clapping. "Now you can see what you missed."

"What did you think of that performance?" Lumumba asked casually.

"My wife," said Herbert, "still talks about it in her sleep. If the crazy bastard weren't dead I think I'd be jealous."

At breakfast the next morning Herbert came upon Doba's obituary. It was in the Cairo Times, and since Goldschmidt was still below he read it out loud:

Chimp with Sandals Found in Desert. The body of a young chimpanzee was found yesterday in the barren terrain just north of the Sudanese border. The discovery was made by Egyptian archaeologists exploring the region. According to their report the body was well mummified due to the intense heat of the area.

Authorities are speculating that the chimpanzee fell from a plane involved in the illegal transport of animals to European research labs. Less clear is why the chimpanzee was wearing sandals.

Already jittery due to the preternaturalness of recent terrorist attacks, many locals are inclined to believe the discovery is but another sign of the return of the baboon-headed god of ancient Egypt, Thoth. The Chicago House Institute in Luxor has been flooded with calls, and many local mullahs, defying the edict of the Ayatollah are planning special ceremonies to placate the god's wrath.

"Wouldn't you know," said Lumumba, "that the incest taboo has to manifest itself even in Doba's death. I'm talking about fools believing in Thoth's return. But without the ignorant poor there could be no rich, without the rich there could be no aristocracy, without the aristocracy there could be no royalty, without royalty there could be no king, and without a king there could be no God. It's the house that Jack built balanced on a deck of cards.

"But let's not dwell on his death, let's enjoy the irony that Thoth, the god of learning and Master of Words, is now responsible for this resurgence of superstitious ignorance."

The afternoon found us all sitting on the sundeck with Kribi. It was our last day on the ship, we'd be in Cairo the next morning.

Goldschmidt and Mohammed had had a spat, and after awhile the boy got up and walked moodily over to the railing. Goldschmidt sat down next to Yendi and Tchibanga.

"You fellows missed a good show last night," he said.

"Yeah, so we heard," Tchibanga replied. "What's the matter with Mohammed?"

"He's upset because I wouldn't let him run off with the dancers."

"Oh really?" said Yendi. After studying Mohammed for a moment, he smoothed back his hair and sauntered over. Dr. Crumb immediately slipped into his chair and gazed fondly at Nedele.

"Are you looking forward to the pyramids?" she asked. The little rabbit stared at Dr. Crumb and wrinkled his nose.

"I'm afraid we're not going," Lumumba replied. "That gentleman over there"—he nodded toward Kribi—"has forced us to cut the trip short."

"Why doesn't he see a doctor?"

"Tell him that."

"Is he xenophobic?"

"Xenophobic, homophobic, all the phobics. He won't see anybody but a white male Anglo-Saxon doctor from America. But not to worry, we already have our plane tickets."

"What a pity. This is my sixth trip to Egypt. There's something about the pyramids, something both foreign and familiar—it's hard to explain, but it's so compelling. Just a minute."

She hurried downstairs to the ship's library and came back with a book which had pictures of the pyramids.

"They sure are pointy," said Nedele.

"That's because they are triangles," said Lumumba, "three large ones and three small ones, two sets of triads. My oh my, how those holy triads are drummed into the human brain!"

Nedele turned to the Sphinx.

"Isn't it marvelous?" said Dr. Crumb. "It has the body of a lion and the head of a man, probably the pharaoh Chephren."

But Nedele said that the body was too long for a lion and looked more like a rabbit, while it's head didn't belong to a man but to a woman.

234

"Perhaps that's the great mystery," said Lumumba, "that he's really not a man afterall."

"*Allah ackbar!*" said Mr. Zahr who was listening. "Would the Great Sphinx be called Abu-el-Hol, the 'father of terror' if he were a woman?"

"I don't see why not," said Lumumba, "since the word 'terror' has the same meaning as religion, 'to bind tightly.' He or she—whatever the sphinx is—stands as a warning against mankind's incestuous nature. One must bind oneself tightly against it. The entire human nervous system is bound with the taboos that were created in its brain cells. In the story of Oedipus it's a sphinx with the head of a woman who poses the questions. The Greeks knew, you see, that the sphinx was Oedipal in nature.

"As for the pyramids, Dr. Crumb, your affinity stems from the fact that there is nothing at all phallic about them, nothing embodying the power of men. They are triangles, you see, geometrical abstractions of the female gonads, paeans to the eternal womb. What the pyramid triangle tells you is that life emerges from the womb and in some mystical way returns there after death. Perhaps it's man's unconscious knowledge that matter can't be destroyed, that in some mysterious way it becomes recycled and new life is created from old."

But that was only part of it, he said; there was a lot more to the pyramids than met the eye. Most people thought of them as an example of man's conquest of nature through mathematics. This was true, of course; but it didn't get at what was really going on, or how the conquest was linked to man's wild sexual temperament. The conquest of mathematics, hence the abstract nature of Egyptian civilization allowed them to assemble the first truly bureaucratic state and impose the incest taboo on a mass scale. The taboo was a symbol of the concentration of sexual power in the figure of the king—a power that could only be transmitted by sheer size as seen in the colossal mathematical abstractions known as pyramids. Locating the king's tomb in the center of the pyramid located his sexual power within the abstract nature of the pyramid's structure which, as he said before, also symbolized the sexual triangle of the female gonads. The incest taboo represented a concentration of the sexual power of thousands of workers focused through the incestuous/mathematical power of the king and redirected into huge public works projects. Without mathematics we wouldn't be human.

Was that the reason we were so strange, so unnatural? Because mathematics itself was a strange mental form—a distorted form of logic that was imposed on the human mind by the high priests of the incest taboo. Logic was the totalitarian imposition of a particular point of view. Logic took the emotional life of a child and pulverized it until there was nothing left but fear and an automatic obedience to the dictates of the incest taboo. Science had become the new religion. And the very bedrock of science was the supposed truths of mathematics. Whatever science said had to be true regardless of what it did to the planet or the way people related to each other. But the real point of science was to make sure that no one asked any uncomfortable questions. Questions like did the power of orgasm have something to do with the power of mathematics? Did we worship mathematics because we worshipped orgasm? What was the relationship between mathematics and orgasm? Was there a mathematical formula for orgasm? And if so could a formula that was inside us be tied in with a Theory of Everything?

A formula for what was inside us? Dr. Crumb repeated.

"Dr. Lumumba!" Herbert said urgently. "I'm sure Dr. Crumb isn't interested in any formulas."

"Oh but I am," she replied. "Part of my research at Yerkes deals with formulating a genetic code for the various primates. Please, Professor, do continue!"

Lumumba acquiesced and spent the next hour or so writing up his formulas and equations. By the time he was finished Herbert's face was purple and the veins in his temple were pumping furiously.

"Your friend is a madman," said Zahr who was still standing there.

"He's worse than that," Herbert stammered.

Lumumba gave her the paper, she excused herself and disappeared down the stairway accompanied by Mr. Zahr. The professor continued where he'd left off.

Yes, modern science had cured diseases and sent men to the moon. But had it made us free of our own phobias, fears and taboos?

Probably not. For millennia, religion had been enough to keep people in line. A vaguely anthropomorphic god hovering around on a cloud ready to smite people with a lightening bolt if they got out of line, was good enough. But now that religion was fading, science and mathematics had taken its place as the new God—the ruler that no one dared question. Not that there weren't still traces linking science to its roots in the old religion of taboos and magical powers. When an animal was cut up in the research lab, guess which word was used in the most technical of papers: sacrifice.

But if scientists could see things through a rabbit's eyes, he said, they would never burn them out. To be able to see things through the rabbit's eyes would mean admitting that the universe was more than simply the observations of science—that it also contained a subjective component, a consciousness if you will. It was very difficult to kill or hurt something when you recognized it as a fellow being instead of simply an object to be used for your benefit. But of course scientists couldn't see things that way. And the reason they couldn't was because science had imposed one viewpoint on the world—the 'objective' viewpoint that no one dared question.

That's what these pyramids were all about. The ancient priests combined religion and mathematics in order to terrify people into submission. The animal-headed gods were there to scare people at the level of their dreams and fantasies, while the awesome perfection of the pyramids was there to terrify them at the level of reason.

Today's priests were attempting to control us at the level of subatomic particles. The mathematical descriptions of quantum physics were really an attempt to put them in shackles so that the orgiastic consciousness inside them didn't escape and bring down the whole edifice of civilization.

But the particles kept escaping, making paradoxes, dragging the physicists into string theories or ten-dimensional space. Did we really think that ten-dimensional space was less mystical than *prana* or sin?

And don't tell me, he said, that mathematical descriptions had predictive values while the Christian concept of sin didn't. Just as you could predict that people would use the latest inventions of science—no matter what harm they could do, you could also predict they would obey the incest taboo. What did you think the 'truth' of a nuclear bomb was? The mathematical descriptions of interacting particles were just a cover-up for the real truth: Knuckle under and give us your oil or we'll blow you into quarks. Science and mathematics were really about power—about making sure that the power of the penis was maintained and that no one dared question it.

He paused and looked at us intently.

"I know you are wondering," he said, "Can there be a mathematics that is liberated from the constraints of the incest taboo? The answer is yes, but inorder to do that men would have to invent a whole new kind of mathematics—one that synthesized the truths of Pythagoras with the truth of orgasm, one that combined the mysteries of number theory with the joys of incest. Pythagoras himself was trying to create such a mathematics— a mathematics that existed outside the incest taboo. That's why he was murdered."

"Please hurry, something is wrong with Dr. Crumb!"

Mr. Asad, who was regaling us in the lounge with unkind stories about Mohammed's mother—Mr. Asad's sister-in-law—rushed off with the porter.

"She looked fine at dinner," I said.

237

"You're okay until you're not," said old Kumasi.

Minutes later a shaken Asad returned.

"She's dead, her room has been ransacked. Do you know if she had any jewels? Money? *Allah Ackbar*! A murdered woman on the Happy Pharaoh! I'm not a superstitious man, but so many strange things have happened of late. Is it possible that Thoth *has* returned?"

Chapter Twenty

A Bad Day in Cairo

It was early morning when the ship tied up at Badrashan. The quay was already swarming with a large swath of humanity, but what was new to the mix was a contingency of soldiers, police and armored tanks all geared up and ready for action.

"Everyone stay calm," said Lumumba. "They're here for Dr. Crumb, it's probably just routine."

"Even the tanks?" asked Goldschmidt as a sweat broke out on his forehead.

Lumumba himself did not seem convinced and his eyes searched for a route of escape. But before we could take action the militia stormed on board and surrounded us—the apes, Herbert, Goldschmidt, Mohammed and myself.

"Aren't you missing one?" said Lumumba indifferently as his eyes searched for Albert.

"Not according to our information," said the top officer. "Nine men, three women and a child. Lieutenant Kassim, disable the prisoners."

A group of passengers had gathered to watch. Betty stood by tearfully, it appeared that Royce was restraining her from rushing over.

"See you in hell, *Dr.* Lumumba," said Marty looking cheerful for the first time in days.

Abdel Zahr too looked happy.

"That's what we do to tour guide impersonators," he said cheerfully.

"Egads," said Goldschmidt, "I hate to think what they do to female impersonators!"

Asad watched in disbelief as his nephew was put in handcuffs.

"What sins have I committed to deserve this?" the poor man asked, wringing his hands in self-reproach.

"Believing that there is sin?" Lumumba suggested, throwing Betty a loving look.

"Don't worry, Uncle," said Mohammed as we walked toward an unmarked van. His voice was jubilant. "I am proud to be a martyr for the glorious cause of the Gonad Liberation Army. A glorious death awaits me beyond the incest taboo. There is no god but God."

"There is no god but Orgasm," Bata corrected.

As the van pulled away with an escort of soldiers in two army trucks, Lumumba scoffed at my alarm. My down-heartedness was, he said, nothing more than the wretched residual of warmed-over Oedipal hang-ups. If the Law hadn't so cow-towed me this ride to jail would run off my back like water off at duck.

Indeed the apes took it as a joke and made noises and faces, much to the chagrin of the guards.

Lumumba said the ride reminded him of his days at Yale. Intellectual freedom existed only within certain parameters. The boundaries were as unyielding as a bar made of iron. Beyond that, you might just as well forget it, buddy.

But to be fair, he went on, academic freedom and freedom per se—the entire concept—was a most misunderstood notion. It was derived from the Sanskrit 'beloved' and 'he loves,' and hell! with a sexual connotation like that, how 'free' can a person actually ever be?

"General," said Goldschmidt, "is this really the time to talk about the etymology of words, all Oedipalness aside?"

"I'm ready to get out of here whenever you are," Lumumba replied.

Herbert said we were ready before we ever got in. Lumumba signaled the apes, and with a mighty yank they broke free from their restraints and overpowered the guards. The steel barrier separating us from the driver and front guard was easily dismantled and the two men dispatched. As Lumumba took over the wheel and Nedele unlocked our handcuffs and Okovango's I found myself marveling at the superior strength of animals.

The bodies of our captors tumbled from the van, the trucks escorting us began to give chase.

"Where's the damn airport?" Lumumba shouted.

"About fifteen miles out of town, General, and you'll have to cross the river," Goldschmidt answered.

But shimmering in the haze off to our left were the pyramids, and even the apes gaped in astonishment. A deep sigh escaped from Kribi as he got up and hobbled to the front. An argument broke out, Lumumba banged the steering wheel and shook his head vehemently.

"No, no, no!" he said. "It's simply out of the question."

"You have to, Uncle," Kribi replied. "Otherwise it'll be a complete disaster."

As we came to the Giza turnoff Lumumba made a sharp left.

"But General," said Goldschmidt, "the airport's in the other direction."

"Yes, but Kribi's right, you can't come to Egypt without seeing the pyramids."

The crowds scattered as Lumumba hurtled through the parking lot and drove across the sand to the pyramid of Cheops. The van screeched to a stop.

"Do we really have time for this?" Goldschmidt asked.

"Only Kribi is getting out, everyone say goodbye."

In a flash it was clear what was happening. Yalinga shrieked and dropped Okovango on my lap as she rushed to Kribi's side. As the door swung open she hung to his arm but he pushed her away and leaped outside. He screamed in pain, but as he began to climb the pyramid his strength seemed to return and he moved from stone to stone with the same litheness and grace I'd seen in the forests of Mahale.

A crowd gathered to watch, and as he propelled himself upward, his pretense as a human being finally over, the crowd began to chant, softly at first, then louder and louder until it echoed from pyramid to pyramid: 'Thoth! Thoth! Thoth!'

This is the last memory I have of him. Lumumba drove off just as the soldiers came into view. One of the trucks stopped at the pyramid, the other continued in pursuit. A fusillade of bullets could be heard behind us, it seemed to last forever. Yalinga closed her eyes and pressed Okovango to her breast.

"One more diversion," said Lumumba, checking his rearview mirror. "That's all we need now."

"Don't look at me, General, I haven't read the manual," said Goldschmidt quickly.

But fate intervened. As we crossed the Giza bridge, Lumumba pushed into traffic and ran a red light. There was a crash, a car flipped over, and another collided with a bus. The intersection became tangled and the soldiers had to stop.

"We're okay for now," said Lumumba. "This isn't New Haven, the Cairo police don't have their own air force."

The traffic grew heavier and heavier. Lumumba had no choice but to drive on the sidewalk. As we plowed through shoppers and outdoor diners I tried to appeal to his reason.

"Maybe they are vegetarians," I said.

"No, I can smell the meat, they are hard-core, inveterate purveyors of the incest taboo."

Suddenly he swerved. "Now that one is a vegetarian. Not a single molecule of carrion exudes from his body."

Tchibanga and Yendi began keeping score. The ratio of people we ran over to those we didn't was voluminous.

"Donkey up ahead!" Yendi shouted.

Lumumba wrenched the steering wheel and tilted the van on its side so that the two right wheels whizzed over the donkey's head.

"Way to go, Uncle!" Bata clapped.

But in the next block Lumumba's luck was not so good, and he hit a cart that was being pulled by another donkey. The cart and driver were flattened but the little donkey escaped unharmed.

"Thank God no one was hurt," said Tchibanga looking back. But Lumumba was shaken.

"Where the hell is the damned airport?! You're sure the passports are ready?

"My man's waiting there now," said Goldschmidt, patting his trusty cell phone. "Turn here, I know how to get to the highway."

We had come to the Khan al-Khalili, an old part of town which consisted of shops built along the narrow twisting streets and covered alleyways. Goldschmidt lamented that he and Mohammed had no time to shop, and Lumumba said that the two would have to indulge their incest-replacement needs later. He turned up the Street of the Goldsellers and screeched to a stop. Johnson and Dodd were standing near the curb and arguing with several men who had blocked off the street.

"*Koos omuuk!*" (fucker of your mother!) one of the men shouted. "Only twenty-six of the vials have anthrax. The other forty-four are filled with Seven-Up, *ibin sharmootas*! (you sons of bitches!)."

"How much of the damned stuff do you need to start a revolution?!" Johnson asked.

"Listen, *sister*, are you as dumb as a camel?! Half is for us, half for our brothers in Palestine. Surely they will need more than thirteen vials of anthrax to take care of all those Zionist Jews."

"Now wait just a minute," said Johnson. "Royce may hate the Jews—as do all our friends on Lyon Isle—but that doesn't mean we hate Israel. As a matter of fact we love Israel, it's the only democracy in the Middle

East, and it acts as a buffer between red-blooded Americans like ourselves and dirty rag-head A-rabs such as *you*. C'mon Royce, we'd better run for it!"

Lumumba opened the door.

"You gentlemen need a ride?"

"I think you just saved our lives," said Dodd gratefully getting in the car.

"Yeah," said Johnson. "Who would have thought they'd try to drink the stuff?"

"It's sure hard for a patriot to make a living these days," said Goldschmidt sympathetically.

"You'd better believe it," Royce answered. He looked around. "Where are the others?"

"Kribi is dead and Albert, god willing, will soon be also."

We dropped them at the Hilton. "If you're ever in Newport," said Johnson grudgingly to Lumumba, "look us up."

"Thanks," said Lumumba. "I might just do that."

"I'll be glad to get away from all these obelisks," said Goldschmidt as we hurried past one at the airport.

"That's surprising coming from you," said Lumumba. "You seem to spend most of your free time worshipping Mohammed's."

"Ah, yes," said Goldschmidt closing his eyes dreamily. "The boy has a lovely pillar of pleasure."

Goldschmidt's man was waiting at the entrance. The counterfeit passports—if indeed they were counterfeit—would have fooled even the experts. He also handed us our tickets, then left quickly. Lumumba's plane was departing in an hour, ours in two hours. Goldschmidt rubbed his hands expectantly.

"Well, General, I've fulfilled my half of the bargain. As soon as you give me the Field Manual, Mohammed and I will be on our way."

Lumumba reached into his jacket and pulled out a small package wrapped in newspaper. To Goldschmidt' annoyance he handed it to Yendi.

"Yendi will give you the manual before he boards his plane. And here, Dr. Hickey, is half of my half of the formula. When I hear of the safe return of my friends, my fellow comrades in arms, I shall send you the other quarter."

He embraced the apes and Bagamoyo, saluted us and disappeared beyond the departure gate.

For a few moments we stood about, shuffling our feet senselessly, a feeling of abandonment upon us all.

"Let's get something to eat," Herbert said at last. "I'm dying for a banana."

"Kathryn! Herbert! Can it really be you?! Lord have mercy it is! John, *John*! Look who's here!"

Dorothy Wiggins shouted to her husband who was buying food at the counter. I was shocked by his appearance. His eyes were rheumy and there was spittle at the corners of his mouth. Only his hair had the same shimmering look of old. As he shook our hands he explained without coaxing: he'd had a nervous breakdown. No, it wasn't Project Mark, it was something else, and he might as well tell us before we heard it from someone else. Right after Herbert and I went to Africa he had given a sermon at the Center Church entitled "Why God Wants Men and Women to Get Along."

Everything was going smoothly, all the congregants were listening with rapt attention, too rapt, perhaps because when the word 'fag' slipped out everybody heard it. He'd meant to say 'nag,' of course—that women shouldn't nag their husbands—but instead it came out 'fag.' Of course he got flack and admittedly he deserved it. But what he didn't deserve was to be called a homosexual himself—albeit a *latent* homosexual. That was the last straw, the coup de grace. Had we ever heard, he asked in a low voice, the theory that men who were homophobic were really homos at heart but afraid to admit it? No? Well that was good because he hadn't heard it either.

The dean sighed heavily.

"This trip didn't come any too soon," he said. "Hopefully I'll be in better shape when we get back to New Haven."

"You did nothing but preach what the Good Book says," said Mrs. Wiggins self-righteously. "And since it says that homosexuality is an abomination you were only doing your God-fearing duty."

It was obvious that her remarks were meant for Goldschmidt and Mohammed who were holding hands and taking bites from each other's apple. Whether it was the long arduous day, or the fact that we were tired and hungry, or that Kribi was dead and Yendi had possession of the manual, Goldschmidt, on seeing her withering stare, exploded.

"Listen, you old bag, your tight ass would be enough to drive any man into the crew quarters!"

"Now see here," said the dean. "I'll thank you not to talk that way to my wife."

"Oh excuse me! I thought it was one of your trained chimpanzees."
Dean Wiggins covered his ears.

"Please don't talk about the chimps!" he said. "That is a subject I can't bear! Oh I would give anything to know what happened to them, anything! I was so close to creating a new classification for the church! Damn those animal rights faggots! Lord have mercy, there I go again!"

"Those animal rights *faggots*, as you call them, had nothing to do with it," said Goldschmidt icily.

"What are you talking about?" said Herbert. "They left a message in the refectory, I saw it myself."

"A mere ploy, dear boy. People fall for ploys all the time these days, or haven't you noticed."

"Goddamn it, man! Who did take them?!" said the dean. "Ah, if only I could get them back! There'd be no more talk of altar boys, I'll tell you that!"

He drew himself up and shot a smoldering look at Goldschmidt.

"You must speak out and tell us what you know," he said.

At that instant there was a shout, and whatever Goldschmidt was going to say got left by the wayside as Soddhu and Albert came hurrying toward us.

"Kathryn! Herbert! Even Dr. Wiggins and his lovely wife Dotty! What a terribly small world, wouldn't you say?"

"Not small enough, apparently," said the dean, extricating himself from Soddhu's embrace. "By the way, what did you do to George Baxter? He's very upset with you."

"You know George Baxter?" asked Goldschmidt astounded.

"Why yes! Do you? By the way, my name is Soddhu Págalu, I teach at Yale."

"Robert Goldschmidt, U.S. Embassy, Nairobi."

"But this is incredible! You're the man I'm supposed to meet!"

"No kidding."

Págalu apologized for his tardiness. He had decided to take a side-trip to the Olduvai Gorge (he glanced at me furtively), his car had broken down before he got there and he'd had to be towed to Arusha. The delay had been costly. When he arrived at the airstrip it was crawling with police.

Not knowing what to do he had spent the night at a 'nice place' nearby. But the next morning it too was crawling with police—two people had been killed—and from the description of eyewitnesses he realized that among several of the suspects were his dear friends the Hickeys. When he read a day later about the plane crash in Egypt and an army terrorizing the

Nile he put two and two together and here he was, thanks to Albert who had found him at the quay.

"Where's the money?" Goldschmidt asked. He was not happy to learn that Soddhu had left it at Nairobi, in a locker at the airport.

"Then it's true," said the dean, his voice quivering with rage, "that the Hickeys have become terrorists?"

His voice boomed out like a prophet of doom, and people turned their heads in our direction. I could see some quick thinking was necessary, and I pushed Albert infront of him.

"Dr. Wiggins," I said, "don't you recognize him?"

The dean took a step closer and peered at Albert.

"Dear God, could this possibly be *our* Albert?"

"The one and only," said Págalu proudly. "He's been parading as a man these last few weeks and doing an admirable job, I might add."

"And we are his cousins," said Yendi proudly. He tossed Goldschmidt the package which turned out to be a small book from the ship's library on the birds of ancient Egypt. Goldschmidt collapsed in a chair.

"Mohammed, bring me some water, I think I've been had!"

The dean's eyes wandered over the apes. A fat Egyptian lady was making a fuss over Okovango, Yalinga nodded kindly, Nedele played with Bagamoyo, Kumasi was asleep in his chair, the last three apes—Bata, Yendi and Tchibanga—were quietly cracking jokes at the expense of the tourists.

"Whatever has happened," said Wiggins, "we'll let stay in the past. I know that Albert couldn't hurt a fly. The Lord has taken a hand in this and His ways are not always clear. Dotty and I will take Albert home with us, at the very least he can become an alter boy."

"I'm afraid that's impossible," said Goldschmidt abruptly. "My job is to get him back to the State Department. The others are already there, I was about to tell you that."

An incredible tale unfolded, how the CIA needed more agents, more assassins; how, in the light of the navy's success with dolphins the agency's director had requisitioned the apes for the study. Naturally the funding went to Yale: The first American spy, Nathan Hale, was a Yale graduate, and it was no coincidence that both institutions—Yale and Langley—honored him with identical statues made of bronze.

Goldschmidt repeated what we knew already—the great success of the project, the ease in which the chimps had been made into religious, guilt-ridden Christians. With their simple minds it proved to be easy.

But that was just the beginning, phase one you might say. Phase two began with the chimps' arrival at the State Department. It was hoped that with their strong religious faith they could now be indoctrinated into the evils of godless communism. This was in preparation for an operation so secret that Goldschmidt himself was not privy. Why he knew as much as he did, we could thank the ineptitude of whoever had sent Albert back to Africa. Heads would roll for that one!

"Anyone can make a mistake," said Wiggins sullenly. He cast Goldschmidt a knowing look. "So you say he's going to the State Department? My dear little Albert, it appears that God has greater things in store for you than passing out wafers and lighting candles. On the other hand it sounds like He wants you to light them for all mankind. Dotty, there is the last call for our plane. If we hurry we can still make it. See you back in New Haven, Herbert and Kathryn. You too, Págalu."

"Toodle-loo," Dorothy sang out sweetly.

The calls for Lumumba's flight crackled across the airwaves. As we sat in our departure area we could see passengers walking across the tarmac.

The apes talked happily.

"I'm going to spend a week sitting in my favorite fig tree," said Bata.

"Not me," said Tchibanga. "I'm going to catch up for lost time. How about it, Yalinga?"

Her long fingers ran through Okovango's hair.

"Sorry, boys. I think I'm going to sleep for a week."

"Me too," said Nedele. "But first I want to make Bagamoyo a hammock all his own, from the softest leaves in the forest."

"Lucky for you, Albert, you're not coming back with us," said Yendi.

Old Kumasi only smiled and nodded his head agreeably. A few minutes later he hobbled off to the men's room.

"That's what's wrong with civilization," said Tchibanga. "You have to hide behind closed doors to do the most natural functions."

"I'm sure Uncle would say that it's all part of the incest taboo," said Bata. "You must keep your genitals hidden at all costs."

"Thank Orgasm we'll be home soon," said Yendi. "We'll have seen the last of these dirty, wretched, smelly bathrooms."

Goldschmidt looked thoughtful.

"You know," he said, "I think the General's on to something with his God-As-Orgasm thing. It's certainly better than the God I grew up with Who-Won't-Let-You-Do-Anything."

"But that's the best God of all," said Albert. "He knows all the sins you've committed with the Arab boy and all the others besides him."

"That's right," Yendi said to Goldschmidt. "I've seen how you look at me."

"It's going to be a long trip to Washington," Goldschmidt muttered unhappily.

Bata, who had gone off to buy food, came hurrying toward us.

"Soldiers are coming, lots of them," he signed frantically. "Shall we fight or make a dash for it?"

"Neither," said Goldschmidt. "You're all under the protection of the United States Government."

As the soldiers approached Goldschmidt confidently reached for his passport. A shot rang out and Mohammed fell to the floor.

"Son of a bitch!" Goldschmidt cried. He knelt over Mohammed, the boy's eyes stared back vacantly, a glaze began to descend over them.

"I think we should run," said Yendi.

He broke open the locked doors leading to the tarmac, then blocked them with benches from the outside. The attendants had started to pull the boarding ramp from Lumumba's plane, but as we ran across the tarmac waving our tickets they waited.

We boarded and Goldschmidt showed them his diplomatic papers; a dispute broke out nevertheless, then Págalu showed a goodly amount of money and the dispute ended. Goldschmidt looked at him suspiciously as the steward showed us to some empty seats in first class; the boarding ramp was taken away and the plane began to move.

Lumumba was not pleased.

"I'll break anybody's neck who interferes in my business," he said "Where is Nedele?"

The question took us by surprise.

"She was right behind us a minute ago," said Yalinga.

The steward came and closed the door.

"Uncle, we have to find her!" said Bata. "Tell him to let me out."

"It's too late," said Lumumba. "Look"

At first I saw nothing as I stared out the window. Then I saw it, a tiny white object zigzagging across the tarmac and a figure chasing after it. Albert gasped as he recognized his sister.

"Lord have mercy!" he cried.

The soldiers had started to run after her. She was no match for their speed and soon they were right behind her. But just as they were about to grab her she kicked off her shoes and quickly propelled herself out of their reach in the manner of an ape. The soldiers stopped cold.

"If only they don't fire," Lumumba muttered.

As if in answer to his wish the soldiers dropped their weapons and began to run toward the terminal. It was impossible, of course, to know

248

what they were shouting, but by pure chance the plane's intercom clicked on and the pilots' voices could be heard, if only just barely.

"Allah Ackbar! Sadat should never have signed a peace treaty with Israel! Thoth has come back to curse us just like the Ayatollah said he would!"

"Don't be a fool, it only looks like Thoth."

"But even the soldiers are running away! Wait, this just came in. They say the ground crew has just sacrificed a sheep in the maintenance bay!"

"In shal-lah! Let's get out of here! Call the tower, tell them to clear the runway."

The engines revved and the plane began to roll down the tarmac at a fast clip.

"Uncle, make them stop!" Albert cried.

"And have the Egyptian Army down on all of us?"

"He's right," said Goldschmidt. "You're too important to the Cause, we can't risk it."

As the plane turned onto the runway Nedele came loping toward us. She had caught Bagamoyo, and as she held him in one arm she waved frantically with the other. She was so close I could see her face. It was written in despair.

Suddenly she moved infront of the plane. There was a jolt and few seconds later the plane lifted off.

As we circled the airport I could see that some vehicles were driving onto the runway. Before the intercom was clicked off we were able to hear one last communiqué.

"God is great," said the pilot. "Whatever it was, it is no more."

Chapter Twenty-One

The Lumumba Certainty Principle and the Lumumba Constant

Are Both Set Forth in a Second Soliloquy

Or

Lumumba's Special Theory of Relativity as It Pertains to Orgasm

(A.K.A. a Luminous Event)

The plane had been airborne for several minutes before Lumumba broke the silence.

"They are not dead, they are changed."

"They *are* dead and it's all your fault!"

It was Albert who spoke the cruel words, but instead of trouncing him as I expected, Lumumba looked at him sadly.

"Why is that?" he asked.

"If you'd let me stay home and spread the Good News none of this would have happened. Doba would be alive, Kribi would be alive, Nedele would be alive and also that silly rabbit of hers."

"Hey, don't forget Mohammed," said Goldschmidt.

"There was nothing silly about Bagamoyo," said Yendi. "He put up with a lot."

"A lot that he didn't have to," said Albert. "If only Uncle had just gone off to Spain and left us all in peace!"

"I thought Christians were supposed to be meek," said Págalu.

"That was when they were being thrown to the lions," said Lumumba. "Ever since Constantinople they've been like Albert."

"Ah yes, Constantinople, a sad day for Zoroastrians. If the Christians hadn't fought us so hard and killed so many of our priests the West would be worshipping fire, Mithra and the Bull instead of Jesus, Mary and the Cross. But they tipped the scales at Dacia—was it 275 A.D.?—and then Constantine converted, the traitor, because it was suddenly more expedient to be a Christian than a Mithraist."

The sad turn of events in Cairo hadn't quenched Lumumba's thirst for knowledge, and as Págalu prattled on about the early battles between the Christians and Zoroastrians, recounting this thing and that, Lumumba turned to listen.

It was time for dinner, and the steward whose name was Pedro began to pass around bananas.

"First Class on Iberia and all I get is this infernal monkey food?" said Goldschmidt.

"But your friend ordered it," said Pedro. "Of course, if you prefer something else, it would be my pleasure. Shall I show you the menu, Th'ñor?"

"Are you Castilian or just plain gay?" Albert asked uncharitably.

"Actually I'm both," Pedro replied.

Goldschmidt perked up. "Yes, I would love to see the menu—and anything else you want to show me."

Tchibanga clicked his tongue disapprovingly.

"And Mohammed's not even cold in the grave," he said as the steward swished back to the galley.

"Your master says he's not really dead," Goldschmidt replied. "Anyway I need a little distraction." He took out the book on birds and began to thumb through it. "I imagine that the authorities in Madrid will be preparing a warm welcome for you, *General*."

"Maybe you should jump," Lumumba replied.

"I don't think they're going to be shooting at me," Goldschmidt replied.

Soddhu looked alarmed and led me to the galley.

"Listen," he said. "When we get to Madrid let's make a dash for it. I've got enough money here"—he patted his stomach—"to tide us over for the rest of our lives."

"Then you do have the money?"

"One million, minus whatever I gave to the steward."

"But it's not yours."

"Only a minor detail, we can work that out later."

"My darling, I can't just run off like that."

"Why not?"

How, he asked, could I love a man who had put my life in such danger? I assumed he was talking about Herbert, not Lumumba.

"I suppose he has acted a bit irrationally of late," I replied.

"Ahura Mazda! How can you say 'a bit'?!"

"Okay, *very*. But it's not really his fault."

I told him about Lumumba's theories and Herbert's fascination with the formula.

"The professor's been leading him around by the nose almost from the beginning."

"He couldn't do that with me, I already believe in Khvetukdas."

"Ah yes, the greatest good a man can do. . . ."

I let my fingers run lightly over his sadreh. "Isn't this supposed to keep you on the straight and narrow?"

He kissed me, then gazed at me with deep affection.

"Even though we are not brother and sister," he said, "I still want to marry you."

"We'll never be able to make gomez."

"I know, but we can always pretend . . ."

"I hope my friend didn't offend you," said Goldschmidt when Pedro returned with the menu. He handed Herbert the International Herald.

"Not at all," said Pedro. "I've been out of the closet for years, ever since homosexuality was legalized in Spain. I have no problems with anybody asking me about it, either."

"Then why are you a fag?" Albert asked unpleasantly.

"Ah," said Pedro. "I see you are one of those closed-minded priests. Well, never mind, you can't please everyone. But to answer your question, when I was little my mother used to let me sleep with her. Even though I was only five or six, I was very much aroused. My little penis used to send erotic chills up my spine, and one night I remember dreaming that the Virgin Mary was there all lit up like a glorious star telling me I was her little boy. But the next morning when I woke up I knew I had really been dreaming of my mother."

"I've had dreams like that too," said Goldschmidt, "and I'm not even Catholic."

"Then perhaps you will understand, Th'ñor, that when I reached puberty I began to notice how terrified I was of women. It was because they reminded me so much of Mother! To have sex with them would have been like having sex with *her*. And to tell the truth, the only person I really wanted to do it with, was either my mother or the Holy Virgin. And since both were impossible I turned to men. They seemed safer to be with than women."

"Why didn't you just become a priest and molest little boys? asked Albert. Pedro stiffened.

"Is that what you do, Father?" he asked.

"He's way too uptight for that," Goldschmidt replied. "Perhaps Spain will be good for him, loosen him up a bit."

"Yes, we do have our share of scandals. But I must warn you to be careful. The charges of sexual abuse in the church have created a real schism in our country. There are those who want the priests to be punished and those who don't. The former have aligned themselves with Juan Carlos, our king, the others with Cardinal Gomez."

"Some things never change," said Goldschmidt.

"*Es la ver-thad,*" said Pedro, (Isn't that the truth). Both men are so unpopular right now that His Royal Majesty has decided to revive the ceremonial foot-washing ceremony—in English I believe it is called Maundy Thursday—much to the cardinal's chagrin. Does that mean His Royal Majesty considers gay people to be beggars? No, only that we are personas non-gratis in the minds of many people just as the paupers are who will be honored in the ceremony. My cousin who works at the palace says it ought to be quite interesting, whatever happens. Will you be in Madrid next Thursday? Perhaps we could meet in the crowd—only a million people are projected to be there, ha, ha!"

"A good place to get lost if one has to," Lumumba mumbled.

"Th'ñor?"

"I was saying that even though you know what happened in your childhood you still aren't able to move beyond it and overcome your fear of women?"

"That is right, Th'ñor, even though I've spent hours on the psychoanalyst's couch going through all the nuances of my neuroses and the labyrinthine turns of my psyche. The hold my mother has on me is insurmountable. But I think this is because there is a strange twist to the story. You see, since homosexuality is a forbidden practice, by tasting of this forbidden fruit I am in some strange way sublimating my desire for my mother who of course is also forbidden. Inother words, by having forbidden men I am also having my forbidden mother. Does that make sense? If it doesn't, I'll quote what my analyst said, that the origin of my homosexuality lies in the substitution of one culturally forbidden object of desire—men—for an even more culturally forbidden object of desire—my mother. Now do you understand, Father?"

A bell rang from somewhere. Bowing politely he went to answer it.

"You humans are so fucked," said Yendi.

"It's because we have straight spines," said Herbert. "Your Uncle told us so, so have some pity."

"Yes," said Goldschmidt. "For us sex is primal and destructive. If it's not controlled by reason civilization isn't possible."

"So what?" said Lumumba. "Since when does orgasm need civilization?"

Orgasm, afterall was merely information at the most elemental level. There was no such thing, he said, as meaningless segments of DNA. Behind every nucleotide was the message to fuck. Why else would bacteria be driven to have sex? Did we think they were searching for pleasure? Well maybe they were, but they were also searching for information. Why? Because that's what they were—information-carrying genomes striving to become more complex. It was the exchange of that genetic information that drove the bacteria to invent the protoplasmic bridge. It was their way of communicating—not at the contrived and artificial level of language but at the primal level of the information that coded the essence of their being.

To put it another way, pleasure, he said, was subsidiary information—it was just a way for information to get itself exchanged, a way of tricking animals into doing their bidding. It was strange that men tried to suppress sex in the name of reason when sex was merely a tool of the most primal form of reason: the double helix and the dancing electrons that hold its informational matrix together against the forces of Chaos.

But even that wasn't right. For the forces of Chaos themselves were the ultimate source of fertility—a cauldron of pure indifference that incubated the informational thrust of the DNA molecule and gave it the raw material to make itself out of nothing on the back of an infinity of quantum fluctuations happening in every particle, every nanosecond.

A human was the same as a bean. Had we never heard of Jagodis Bose? No? How strange, the man was a genius! In his experiments with plants he was able to show that plants produced electrical responses very similar to animals when subjected to similar stimuli. When plants were stimulated mechanically, they responded almost immediately with an electrical response—much the way animals do. They were not simply passive recipients; they were in some sense aware of what was going on around them—an awareness that was transmitted to every part of the plant.

These patterns of electrical response in plants exactly paralleled those in animals. If the plant was subjected to a stimulant, the electrical activity increased for a period of time, then went into a period of exhaustion, and finally a period of recuperation. Inother words, plants showed evidence of fatigue and depression when subjected to the proper stimuli.

But the most surprising result, perhaps, was that plants subjected to destructive stimuli had a precise moment of death, a precise moment when the electrical responsiveness of the plant stopped—exactly like the mysterious moment of death when an animal died.

But listen to this! When Bose hooked up his electrical apparatus to a *copper bar* and measured its response to various stimuli, his readings were virtually identical to those displayed by the plants. Mechanical agitation produced a state of heightened excitability during which the bar was more sensitive to further stimuli. After a period of time the metal bar slowly returned to its resting state—like a dog who wakes up in the middle of the night and barks for awhile because he hears something, then goes back to sleep.

Certain substances acted as stimulants or depressants for the rock—and not simply by changing its chemical makeup, either: The rock responded just as living things do. A stimulant produced a period of increased excitability followed by depression and then a recuperation period. When the rock was subjected to repeated stimuli its sensitivity gradually decreased and it became fatigued. But when it was able to rest it was able to rejuvenate. It also responded to poisons just as living things do, and perhaps the most startling thing Bose found was that rocks were capable of dying. When they were subjected to elements poisonous to them the electrical responsiveness of the rock ceased altogether.

And it wasn't because the substance changed the rock's electrical properties, either. Even when all traces of the compound were removed, the rock was still inert in its electrical response. Its electrical field had been killed.

"I never learned any of this," said Herbert.

"That's because these ideas aren't taught in the West. Bose's heritage— he was Hindu—gave him an intuitive sense of the interconnectedness of things. He's really giving a scientific explanation of an intuitive knowledge that has existed for a long time in the East. This is how he described the cosmos:

> The dust particle and the earth, the plant and the animal are all sensitive. Thus, with an enlarged sense, we may regard the million orbs that thread their path through space as something akin to organisms, having a definite history of their past and an evolutionary progress for their future. We may then come to realize that they are by no means insensate clods, locked in the rigor of death, but active organisms whose breath, perchance, is luminous iron vapor, whose blood is liquid metal and whose food is a stream of meteorites.

"Inother words, no line can be drawn between organic and inorganic matter. Both organic and inorganic matter has the same electrical origin. Just as all oak trees are born of an acorn so is all matter born of the electron. That the intelligence of this common property exists is not to be denied, argued or minimized. Within the tiny seed of the electron beats the heart of all creation. Ah, if only human beings were able to have sex and do mathematics at the same time! Seeing into the heart of the universe at the moment of ejaculation, seeing the fundamental equation, they might be able to change their evil ways."

"Well, said Herbert, touching his pocket, "that moment may not be far off."

Págalu looked at him curiously.

"I've given your colleague the equation for orgasm," Lumumba explained, "or part of it anyway. By the way, Hickey, you can throw out Crumb's paper. It was just a diversion to keep her off Nedele."

"I wish you had told me that sooner," said Herbert sourly.

"Ah yes, the poor lady might still be alive. My, what people won't do to get the Nobel Prize."

"Herbert, you didn't!" I exclaimed.

He started to protest but Lumumba cut him short.

"Save your cowardly lying for later," he said. "It's such a bore anyway to hear grown men dancing around the Primal Lie about not wanting to sleep with their mothers."

With a sour look Herbert turned back to his newspaper. A few minutes later something caught his eye.

"Listen to this, everybody:

In an abrupt reversal of its previous stance, the United States has apologized to Cuba for the death of Cuban pianist Jorge Cortina who was murdered in New York last May during his first U.S. tour. While the State Department continues to deny U.S. involvement in the affair, President Clinton has offered his condolences to Cuban leader Fidel Castro and promised to make all resources available inorder to apprehend the perpetrators of the 'heinous crime.' Although the news was greeted with suspicion in Cuba, where wags commented that it was 'like sending in a delegation of foxes to investigate a serial chicken murderer,' the Castro government has said it will rescind its order to oust Americans. Furthermore it will allow the Ringling Brothers Barnum and Baily Circus to appear as scheduled for a historic performance in Havana later this month."

"The conservative Right will soon prevail," said Goldschmidt brightly. Kumasi wagged his finger.

"Right is wrong and left is right," he said.

"What he means," said Lumumba, "is that the right side of politics is wrong and the left side is right."

Kumasi nodded and a few minutes later was fast asleep. It seemed like the thing to do, but try as I might I couldn't drop off. It was that last cup of coffee which I was foolish enough to drink, and to pay for my crime I spent the whole night listening to Lumumba's second soliloquy on orgasm, one that was so demanding and inquisitive, so full of the enthusiasm that comes when the intellect is given free reign, that it could be heard loud and clear above the drone of the airplane. It went something like this:

"Life is an expression of the fundamental fecundity of the atom. The fecundity is linked to a kind of self-awareness. Putting it in terms of human religion, anyone who believes God created humans must also believe that God was the greatest physicist of all. The only way he could have created the heavens and earth would have been to foresee all the interactions and structures of all the different particles and dimensions that would be required to produce a universe that was hospitable to life.

"Or to put it another way: He gave free reign to the creativity of the particle themselves, and *they* created the universe in an orgiastic expression of their own formal perfection. The visible universe might simply be the orgasmic expression of its interacting light waves, each transmitting a quantum-dynamical pulse of pleasure across the void.

"This being said, the next step is to undertake a study of subatomic forces from an orgasm's point of view. Yes, we must let the little rascal speak for itself. And why not? None of us would be here if it weren't for the electrical forces holding our atoms together. So let's determine what happens to those forces during orgasm. Do the hormones produce a sort of molecular agitation throughout the body? Do the electrons start jumping from one orbital shell to another? If their excess energy is emitted as photons, does the luminosity of the photon combined with the electrical energy surging up the spinal cord to the brain determine the experience of orgasm?

"On the other hand, perhaps orgasm is just the expression of particles trying to penetrate the nucleus of the atom, trying to push aside the primal forces of creation and reunite with their lost brothers inside a cataclysmic little bang—a kind of inverted big bang that seeks to collapse each atom back into the primal forces of creation.

"Or maybe the miniature solar system of each atom captures the essence of orgasm and releases little pieces of it each time there is an orgasmic event. If that were true each orgasm would mark a kind of return to the forces that created the universe.

"But the real secret here is to understand the relationship between orgasm and light. If the different elements inside the atom emit light during orgasm, that light must come in spectral lines that correspond not only to the elements themselves but to the quality and intensity of the orgasm that produced them. It should thus be possible to create an instrument that would read the luminosity of orgasm and give all kinds of information about its origin.

"It should also be possible to extend this reading to the atomic level. That is, the electrons circulating around the atoms of each element would jump to new levels only under certain specified conditions. All this would be regulated by quarks who would modify their spins and colors in a kind of quantum seduction dance, an undulating expression of the angular momentum of orgasm jumping back and forth according to the complex laws that govern quantum interactions, a kind of subatomic meter that regulates the particles' dance the way meter regulates the expression of a poem—but also its meaning.

"Such an instrument, of course, would probably sweep religion away: the new laws of physics would explain religion at the primitive emotional—that is, sexual—level that religion appeals to. Afterall, each time someone talks about religion he's really talking about his own sexual experience.

"Men like Einstein and Bohr intuited that sexuality was at the bottom of the equations they were writing about. That is what they meant when they said they were describing the 'mind of God.' The only thing they forgot to add was that religious experiences are always sexual experiences. (Not that they understood this, of course, which is why they could never pin down a Theory of Everything.)

"But where does this connection come in, and why do religious experiences always seem to defy the normal laws of physics? During orgasm these laws are suspended for one brief nanosecond while the particles decide to reaffirm their creation. What we call quantum mechanics is just that tiny splinter of hesitation and choice: the mind of God as perfect existential freedom at the quantum level. The particles choose to exist!

"And that freedom is transmitted to the consciousness of the organism having the orgasm. Orgasm creates a shock to the entire system that allows it to monitor the quantum variations in the fabric of space-time itself. Normally those random variations (which consist of pairs of particles being created and then destroyed in extremely small time increments) go unnoticed and have no effect on the larger universe. But under the influence of orgasm and the instability of the system it provokes, those quantum variations can become the source of new matter and energy being introduced into the universe. The pairs of particles are split like tiny big bangs, creating paired particles and antiparticles. The antiparticles are destroyed instantly, of course, as soon as they hit ordinary matter, but the energy they contain is released into the cosmos. You might say this is how the universe recharges itself—just as organic forms recharge and recreate themselves through procreation—a macroscopic extension of the subatomic phenomenon.

"But how does it happen? How does it all work?

"Well, let's see now. If the established energy levels of the electron orbital shells change during orgasm, this would mean that the wavelengths and energy of the photons also change. Photons of all different wavelengths would be created and rain down on the hydrogen atoms in the bloodstream, causing electrons to swallow certain bundles of specific energies and jump to higher levels of agitation. Inside the penis this would cause trillions of atoms to jump to higher energy states. The inexpressible feeling of orgasm would thus result from the fact that organisms are actually sensing light inside their bodies. If someone could put a light meter inside the vagina it would probably go off the scale during the intensity of the orgasm itself—especially if both the penis and vagina were producing that energy at the same time. Then the different wavelengths would create interference patterns—harmonic upper partials of light that would embody the truly celestial expedience of shared orgasm.

"Orgasm could thus be described as a measurable continuum. During the initial stages, the electrons would absorb energy from metabolic processes, gathering up the energy necessary for a truly luminous event. During the orgasm itself, this accumulated energy would be released in a luminous flash, something like an organic capacitor or the coil of a car.

"Within these parameters it should also be possible to describe the speed of orgasm—not how long it takes but the velocity of pleasure it produces. As that velocity approaches the speed of light, that pleasure becomes infinite—just as mass becomes infinite as it, too, approaches the speed of light. Or perhaps we could just say that the speed of light is God—a condition of infinite pleasure that we approach by degrees, as the purity and intensity of our orgasmic experience grows.

"But there are still all kinds of questions to answer. Forinstance, do electrons behave as waves or particles during orgasm? Of course they must behave as waves inorder to transmit specific quantum fluctuations.

The spine, after all, is exactly analogous to a vacuum tube where the wave nature of electrons becomes clearly apparent. But they could also behave like particles as well—discreet little units of pleasure each heading off on its own.

"Max Born insisted that the wave function really represents the probability of finding an electron in any particular region of space. Might that not include orgasm as well? Since the wave function is a wave of probability why not construct a probability equation for orgasm—or even an equation for existence itself? We could be here or not be here, and the probability equations of orgasm would help us describe this situation and understand the absurdity of life. The idea of Goldschmidt transmitting the orgasmic light waves that make up the essence of the universe while he's in the bathroom with a 13-year-old waiter sounds particularly peculiar, but there it is. Everything transmits light waves, whether it's organic or inorganic.

"Now since mathematical descriptions of the probability functions of electron orbital shells are necessary for understanding chemical reactions, they'd also be necessary for understanding the chemical reactions that take place during orgasm, both at the quantum level of the orbital shells and the higher level of geometry and form-function parameters of large organic molecules. A complete description of orgasm from the quantum level to the thrashing bodies of porn stars would require a precise account of just which chemical reactions and compounds are involved in orgasm.

"That's the only way to really uncover the intelligence at work in subatomic particles. We have to find a way to get from the conglomeration of minute intelligences involved in each particle to the macroscopic forms such as brains, planets and galaxies.

"The first part is easy. For every neuron in the brain, there must be a corresponding cell in the gonads. The brain is nothing more than a duplication of this original structure in the gonads; that is, the brain's intelligence is derivative of the basic intelligence inherent in reproduction. And within the gonads themselves, orgasm is an energy state—a necessary energy state, perhaps even the ultimate necessity.

"This means it would be necessary to know the strength of an electron's magnetism and its spin during orgasm. Could we measure it by using Dirac's equation? This leads to an interesting conjecture: that it is possible that the body emits antiparticles during orgasm. Of course it seems highly unlikely that antimatter can exist in a living organism, but who knows? Perhaps orgasm is in some way the experience of matter and antimatter annihilating each other to form pure energy! That means that if two humans pushed orgasm to its limits they could produce an explosion fifty times bigger than a thermonuclear bomb. That would be quite a sight!

"But all this talk about particles avoids the real question: gravity. The theory won't be complete—any more than the physicists' grand unification theories will be complete—until we account for gravity. Gravity was what created the orgasmic crisis in humans in the first place, so it's likely that the graviton is the key to forming a unified field theory of orgasm.

"But the Heisenberg uncertainty principle—which says that it is impossible to know the position and momentum of a quantum particle simultaneously—makes it difficult. This is because no one has ever tried to map the quantum state of atoms and molecules during orgasm. I think this could be done, however, by setting up an experiment in which a single slit is used to narrow a beam of orgasmic particles emitted from a gonad, which then traverses to a double slit and arrives at a detector. The exact arrival time and position would be known as the Lumumba Certainty Principle—assuming that the angular momentum of the orgasm itself can be determined. And I'm certain it can: When electrons of sufficient energy are fired into a 'black box'—yes, the metaphor is fitting—containing hydrogen, an electron of much lower energy emerges at an angle which corresponds to the angle induced by the vector constant between pelvis and spine, an amazing coincidence, to say the least.

"Let's review what we know so far: Orgasm is an experience of a particle's momentum. Because atoms weigh only ten to the minus 24th gram, and because the wave-particle duality of their nature makes them even more unstable, it doesn't take much to influence the atoms profoundly. This provides a basic insight into the elemental nature of orgasm. Or rather, this duality records the trace of orgasm as some deeper aspect of the physical universe. If we say that the particle partakes of a fundamental freedom and that this freedom is a function of orgasm, then orgasm itself could be seen as part of the universe's awareness of its own states of being—at every level—and an ability to choose its own states.

"But being trained at Yale to think, I cannot accept this theorem without considering all the other possibilities. Forinstance, during orgasm, does a heat-transferring medium such as lithium overcome the resistive force that normally keeps extra electrons from inhabiting an orbital shell already full? Is there a conversion of light energy into electrical energy? Does the identity of orgasm lie within the complex of forces inside the electrons and nuclei when atoms combine? Is the mass of a particle inside the body converted to pure energy during orgasm? Is orgasm a deep inelastic scattering involving large energy changes? Is it the attainment of ever and ever higher energies? Is it a property of quantum geometry, an expression of space-time no longer smooth and curved but stormy and frothy? Is it electric current carried without resistance? Can subatomic particles be generated during orgasm? Is orgasm a single wave function—I call it 'o-wave symmetry'—by which electrons overcome their mutual repulsion and pair up to pass unhindered through the host material? Is it some kind of magnetic vortex trapped by the vibrations of crystalline lattices within the infinite space of the atom? Is it the wellspring of infinity, the flickering of particles going in and out of existence? Is orgasm a roiling sea of virtual particles? The pulsation of negative energy versus positive? The unknown region within the event horizon of a black hole? The crucial link between the laws of black holes and thermodynamics? A subversion of cosmic energy? They say the universe rang like a bell when it was young, but was this ringing orgasmic in nature? Was there orgasm before the Big Bang? Before time, before anti-time? Was orgasm responsible for the creation of the universe?

"The wonder of it all is that despite the Lumumba Certainty Principle, orgasm contains an unknowable component that is closely related to the uncertainty principle. Orgasm is a way of reshuffling the cards of creation, and like quantum fluctuation it escapes the grid of linear causality that governs much of the macroscopic universe and proposes a space of pure freedom. Within the moment of orgasm you can remake yourself or access the secret knowledge of the universe.

"But people don't recognize this. They feel an intense pleasure but they don't realize that this pleasure is the lowest and least evolved way of experiencing orgasm. Animals have a much more profound understanding of orgasm: At that moment they find the basic determinants of their being in an intuitive flash of pure ontogenetic ecstasy—a wild line of becoming, a flight that escapes the law of the incest taboo as easily as a bird escapes the clumsy humans who try to follow him into the air. Orgasm is just the tip of a purified plasma, a primitive generative machine that reconfigures matter and thought.

"This is why the priests are so terrified of it. Because it is unknowable within the rigid confines of reason, it escapes the vindictive, castrating law of God-as-incest-taboo who wants to throttle orgasm just as primitive men felt a mysterious lust to throttle their neighbors. Orgasm and the law are opposed in the existential realm just as normal reason and quantum events are opposed in the realm of quantum physics. Orgasm and particles are the ultimate source of creativity, but they are held prisoner by the depraved and sadistic trinity of Reason, God and the Incest Taboo. Humans evolved inorder to control the electrical and magnetic fields inside their gonads.

Why do you suppose their brains are so big? They've been controlling electricity for five million years!

"That's the real secret we discovered at Olduvai (although Albert is too stupid to see it)—that the spine is a kind of particle acceleration. The gap between the pelvis and the brain provides space for the electrons to accelerate—just as increasing the gap between two plates of a battery creates an acceleration of the electrons moving between them. Do the gaps in the spine double the energy of particles as they pass upwards? Do they pour out as the body's wires are heated up, just as electrons pour out of a wire when it's heated to incandescence? Do they accelerate up the spine until they too reach incandescence?

"People think of the spine in terms of its structural necessity for living organisms to exist. But perhaps this is a foggy notion. Perhaps the real function of the spine is to act as an accelerator for the particles—another clue that the universe is orgasmic in nature. The feeling of power which one experiences during orgasm—might this be an awareness of the raised energy accelerating into the brain? It's an elementary consequence of momentum, afterall, that if particles accelerate fast enough they turn into pure energy.

"Inother words you can't separate the process of reproduction from the mathematical truths that hold the universe together. Biology follows numbers just the way quantum particles do. But they are smaller than the numbers anyone can see. It's part of the hidden order that pervades the universe.

"But the scientists don't see this because all they are, really, are Neanderthals unknowingly controlled by their gonads. They think they're engaged in a search for pure truth—and they are, but that pure truth is the truth of their misunderstood penises. If only the physicists could just measure the way these particles get themselves all worked up during orgasm. Maybe they'd find that the strong forces get all stiff and interested in what's going on during orgasm. Then they'd have something!

"But this brings up even more questions. Forinstance, do the quantum rules apply just as much to the creation of living organisms as they do to the creation of stars and galaxies? Is the creation process of living organisms the same process which takes place in the creation of particles in a high-energy particle accelerator? Is it possible that during orgasm, the electrons and positrons collide and release enormous amounts of energy? Is orgasm but the creation and release of a photon inside the spine? If all subatomic particles are mated, could this be the basis of the sexual impulse? Is this basic particle symmetry reflected at the macroscopic level? At bottom can we be taken apart down to our primal quarks and anti-quarks—a quark and its mate? Can orgasm be a process in which virtual particles are converted to real existence? Is orgasm some kind of shockwave—like a lightning strike? Is the experience of orgasm similar to the quantum tunneling effect? If the wave/probability nature of subatomic particles lead to their tunneling beyond barriers which should have kept them out, can orgasm be that exultation which results when those particles make it through? Can it be the exultation one feels when the particles reach the speed of light? We know that when this happens, relativity kicks in and leads to a parabolic momentum curve. Does this curve describe the trajectory of pleasure in any particular species? I say this because the parabola in humans is extremely steep due to the structural nature of the spine and pelvis, a perfect reproduction of the most sophisticated particle accelerators.

"It all comes back to a need to measure the speed of particles inside the atom during orgasm. An audible gasp would be heard round the world, and a new field of physics—dare we call it kin-etics? Or how about genital dynamics —would bring all humans to their knees.

"But I'm getting side-tracked. I need to know the precise form of this process during orgasm. How much energy do particles take away? And at what angles are they emitted? The problem is to extract a valid conclusion about how nature works during orgasm.

"One probability is that the acceleration process releases essentially unlimited energy while other processes convert certain cells in the body to room-temperature superconductors which allow the electrons to flow without being impeded. The purely electrical nature of the particles is thus able to express itself without the usual interference that clouds them during normal metabolic states.

"Another probability is that during orgasm, changing currents and fields cause the body to heat up. Red-hot mammas probably have a lot of changing currents and fields: violent collisions are produced in the brains by particles accelerating up the spine and producing lots and lots of anti-matter.

"This leads us to the little matter of luminosity—the number of annihilations per second involved in a high energy collision—and whether or not orgasm can be measured in terms of a luminous event.

"I rather hope so, since a luminous event or luminosity is a much better choice of words to describe orgasm, not only because it sounds better—is there a more ugly word than orgasm?—but because it describes the process at the level in which matter and antimatter collide and annihilate each other. Does that not feel orgasmic to you? Whether or not it describes the entire process is beside the point. What matters is that the experience can be shared: Witness the participation of two people accelerated to sufficient energies to produce genuine luminous events. It is like the increased yield gained in synchrocyclotrons when the beams of particles are accelerated in opposite directions, and smash into each other. Imagine Mars and Venus colliding in the fiery night sky of the Greek cosmos, then imagine the particles of orgasm moving in opposite directions, propelled by the opposite sexual poles and the violence of the collision geometrically increased. Is there a more elegant theory than this?"

"And who says it isn't possible? If the pion was discovered in an explosive outburst of cosmic rays, imagine what might be discovered during a luminous event inside the human body. It might be the so-called God particle itself, the Higgs boson which physicists predict but which continues to elude them in their experiments.

"If only they could look inside their bodies after a luminous event! Would they see the same trail of excited atoms which are found in the bubble chambers of a nuclear physicist? Such trails glow as brightly as the heads of haloed saints. Jesus's halo is a sure sign that religion is rooted in orgasm. For the halo and luminous event are one and the same glow. I don't doubt at all that people who associate orgasm with death are instinctively attuned to the annihilation of matter which occurs during orgasm. Could they but record a particle's trajectory and its precise time of passage up the spine! Wouldn't that be a best seller!

"But how about an equation for the entire process?! Zounds! You'd have to analyze the space and time coordinates of particles produced by high energy collisions during the luminous event. And the hotter the sex the more chances of new particles being produced. This corresponds to the discovery of new particles in accelerators when greater energies are applied.

"But now it's time to add a new element, the so-called golden ratio. Without doubt there are numbers, ratios and proportions which explain the orgasmic principle and the complexity of life. Perhaps the golden ratio is one of them, being the basis of many natural phenomena occurring in nature. As part of the architectonics of DNA, perhaps it is the ratio itself which, during a luminous event, expresses itself as a feeling of pure pleasure. This might explain man's sense of aesthetics, which is so closely linked to the ratio. Ah yes, it wouldn't surprise me if those magic numbers—1:618—weren't genetically encoded in man's sense of pleasure. Doesn't Nature use this ratio in everything else, from her most intimate building blocks to her most advanced patterns, in forms as minuscule as atomic structure and DNA molecules, to those as large as planetary orbits and galaxies? Since the ratio is involved in such diverse phenomena as quasi crystal arrangements, planetary periods and distances, reflections of light beams on glass, musical arrangement, and the structures of plants, animals, the brain and nervous system, why not orgasm? And while man thinks that his inventions are wholly the result of his unique brain, it can be shown that even his beloved stock market has the same mathematical base as these natural phenomena. Perhaps it's even connected to the imprinting that goes on when pions decay into muons and neutrinos. The neutrinos seem to know what their origin is—that is, they carry information. Which leads me to think that intelligence originates in a point.

"Albert, of course, would disagree. I can hear him now: 'I beg to differ, Uncle, but the intelligence of an all-knowing, all-seeing Father who encompasses the whole universe can hardly originate in a point.'

"The whiny little bastard! I can't believe I've let him upset my plans! 'An all-knowing, all-seeing Father', eh? Well, Albert, if intelligence is orgasmic in nature and orgasm originates inside the forces of subatomic particles, then why couldn't it originate in a point? Ever hear of spin? This hard-to-grasp aspect is an important component of a luminous event; in all likelihood orgasm increases the parity violation of the subatomic particles, and if the atoms become aware of the increased proportion of spins going in one direction I would call this *Lumumbian movement*. Now, since there are more left-handed spins than right-handed spins, in all likelihood it is this left-handed spin which has created humans. Would this be another reason why they have come to fear the Left? Why they have translated it into the political world where Left becomes a symbol of moral and spiritual dissolution? Where all things 'left' are sinister?

"But who is to say that right-handedness in man didn't evolve from the left-handed spin of subatomic particles? The profound truth of this will only be discovered when microbiologists and quantum electro-dynamic physicists pool their equations. Within the genitals lies the theory that will unify quantum theory and general relativity. This I would call Lumumba's Luminosity Theory."

"Let's take it step by step. A living organism is made up of trillions of particles which are held intact by the skin. During a luminous event (e.g., orgasm) an organism feels the quantum pulsations of the field around its muons and electrons. This is because a luminous event is a manifestation of the virtual particles which have borrowed enough energy to catapult themselves into existence as real particles. A sea of these particles will exert a minute but important effect on the electrons and other particles inside the body. These effects are measurable as a deviation from the g factor (I call it the g-spot factor) of ordinary resting matter. A luminous event is thus not just a localized occurrence: Its effects—mediated by the quantum agitations of the virtual particles—are felt by all the other particles in the universe.

"Yes, everything has its origins in the energy induced by a luminous event. Even hunger can be traced back to the behavior of particles cannibalizing one another during alterations of energy and motion—as when messenger photons are eaten by electrons.

"This is not a contradiction of what I said earlier; hunger is a form of love, and organisms which eat each other, do so out of an irresistible and uncontrollable need to become *one*. The ultimate union you might call it. And to complete the cycle an organism takes in energy so that it can express itself orgasmically. It eats so that it can fuck. That is the guiding principle of the universe.

"Have you never heard of the 'in and out' quarks? They are essential for understanding the new quantum states of matter. When a particle-antiparticle collide, they generate a messenger photon of energy equal to the sum of the two particles. Why can't the same thing happen during orgasm? And wouldn't the sum of the energy of the two colliding particles be enormous compared to energy of other particles during normal metabolism? In which case it would be said that these quarks mediate a sexual field which affects all objects in the universe.

"Yes I know, I'm mixing high-speed particles in accelerators with the slow speed metabolism of living organisms—apples and oranges, you might say. On the other hand two hundred miles an hour isn't exactly slow, which is how fast a nerve impulse travels to the brain. And when you consider the relatively short distances it travels the issue becomes mute. As for the speed of particles within the impulse, shall we conjecture that it's close to the speed of light? This being so, wouldn't other forces inside the body be just as dependent on the input of energy, momentum and spin? Wouldn't they combine in the proper set of circumstances to shatter the usual harmony between subatomic particles? A variety of new particles would emerge and voila! Orgasm—matter turning into pure light! Herein lies the true nature of reproduction—energy turning into matter and matter turning back into energy.

"Or to express it in formula:

$R_f = 1/M_{mp} \times L_c$, where the range of force is inversely related to the mass of the messenger particle times the Lumumba constant."

He stopped momentarily to write on his quarter sheet of paper. Then, chewing thoughtfully on his pen, he continued:

"Could there be, I wonder, a connection between the infinities that show up mathematically in QED and other quantum mechanical models, and the experience of infinity one feels during a luminous event? Civilization and the incest taboo have caused people to become fragmented and outside nature. But during a luminous event, this fragmentation disappears, and for a split second the individual regains his true place as he becomes one with nature. The euphoria of orgasm may have less to do with the biology of the experience than with the deeply felt awareness that he or she belongs in the scheme of things.

"The implication is immense: reproduction and biology are merely a byproduct of the conversion of energy into matter and matter into energy. Well, why not? It answers the question whether or not God is a particle, doesn't it? Because if you put enough particles together you have the entire universe. Inother words, luminous events exist of and for themselves, and reproduction is merely the unforeseen consequence of these events—a messenger photon, perhaps, giving rise to the electricity which combines with chemicals to produce sexual pleasure.

"Oh I can hear Albert now: 'There is only one kind of messenger, Uncle, and that is the angel who God sends to mediate things between heaven and earth.'

"But how do we know, dear nephew, that this angel is not the very particle which helps to mediate a luminous event? It makes one wonder whether ancient man was able to recognize his subatomic origins and synthesize it into an orgasmic gospel of God. Did he know by some uncanny instinct how, by combining the electro-weak forces, the W+ force, the W- force, the Z^o force and the photon, these messenger particles would integrate luminous events into the description of the universe given to us by modern physics?

"I would conjecture that he did, since humans are such peculiar assemblages of particles to begin with. An interesting experiment would be to shoot a human through a supercollider and see what particles get released. The results should be quite telling: The forces released by the human brain to resist the lower level particle beam generated in the spine during orgasm would be totally overwhelmed. It's likely that such an experiment would produce the particle responsible for a luminous event and the heretofore undiscovered force that mediates and represents it in almost pure form. And since the Z-zero particle has a mass of 91 billion electron volts it would be quite a rush.

"Normally all that electricity would blow up not only that one person in the collider but millions of others besides: There is enormous energy potential inside a human. But that energy is held in a bound state. Civilization has evolved only by pushing this energy down. This can be formulated as an equation: Civilization equals the pelvis times the brain squared, where the brain is inversely proportional to the repression of the gonads. I'll write this down for Hickey later. Perhaps he will see that the unnatural state humans live in—they call it civilization—is based upon the unnatural state of their inner workings. The immense energy they continue to repress inside the gonads has resulted in a planet that is *covered* in repression: Cities of tangled concrete are witness to the monumental repression of billions of electron volts aching for expression and release. Every skyscraper on the planet is a braggadocio attempt to quiet the cry of the pelvis and cover up the truth of its sad plight.

"Under these circumstances it would seem impossible that the quarks in a human would ever gain any amount of freedom at all. But the truth is that during a luminous event they attain an extraordinary amount of freedom. This is because as the quarks move closer together, the force between them diminishes and the quarks become less influenced by each other—and thus freer. When the quarks try to pull apart, the force is reversed. These short distances imply strong forces, which is why the quarks are so much harder to isolate than other particles. The secret to understanding this phenomenon, of course, lies in the undiscovered particle that unifies all the forces in the universe, the before-mentioned Higgs particle. (I think I like *Lumumba particle* better: it's the perfect component to a luminous event.)

"Either way, this particle is causing the physicists a lot of headaches, but that's because they are not flexible enough to change their frame of reference. They can't imagine that the pleasure of sexual experience is one of the fundamental forces of the universe—perhaps *the* fundamental force. But instead of looking for this force between the legs they keep looking for it inside the accelerators. I'd love to be there when their equations drive them kicking and screaming to this realization. Imagine all those uptight academics coming face to face with their own sexuality on the monitor of a particle detector—worse by far than having mother discover you masturbating in the closet with father's Playboy.

"But the day is coming, I'm sure of that, when three of the four fundamental forces will be united by the Lumumba particle, and the mathematics of electrodynamics can be worked out during a luminous event. Provided, of course they understand the way gravity works too, how it differs between all forms of life, from one-celled creatures to frogs, horses and human beings, and how it is part of the accelerating force which causes a luminous event. Then the unity of the universe can be accomplished.

"I can hear Albert now: 'I guarantee you, Uncle, that the Grand Unification Theory will never be understood through orgasm. Maybe through God, but not through orgasm.'

269

"The idiot! Does he think it's an accident that the acronym for the theory is GUT?

"Anyway it's all a horse of the same color—intelligence, God, a luminous event, all caught up in the constant violent motion of quarks and leptons, particles and antiparticles which become knowable only for a fleeting moment. The ecstasy of a religious experience is set in motion by the same process that sets orgasm in motion. When virtual particles are converted into real particles—that moment they call God—the result is the creation of matter. But as I said before, this process is simply an accident. The particles are not performing these actions inorder to produce new particles, they are simply moving about for the sheer joy of it. In the same way, the primal motivating force for living organisms—humans included—is pure pleasure; babies are only an accidental consequence. But the church and most of civilized society has reversed this equation and tried to repress the pleasure—though given the current state of the world it would be much better to repress the babies and extol the pleasure. But the pleasure is so dangerous, so incestuous. And that is the great tragedy because during a luminous event the laws of motion, space and time become visible in their most profound simplicity.

"As does the elegant chiral symmetry of the early universe, unveiled and revealed as it is in the undeviating velocity of the luminous light. Likewise the enigmatic neutrino and the elusive graviton. If only Einstein had tried to unify these forces inside a human orgasm rather than a high energy particle beam! Surely he would then have succeeded in penetrating GUT.

"But where each particle goes and what it does—perhaps that is to be found out in the realm of biophysics. Perhaps the graviton will be found by a biologist who understands that each species is characterized by a particular energy level and a particular blueprint of the various symmetries and transformations that underlie it. In chimps, for instance, the characteristic energy signature of escaping particles, clusters around 540 million electron volts. For humans the number is about 65 billion electron volts. If the instruments used to measure particle attributes in the laboratories of nuclear physicists were properly calibrated, humans should be able to detect a luminous event from a great distance away—perhaps as far away as another galaxy.

"This is because a luminous event emits electromagnetic radiation with a very peculiar signature. Their detectors pick it up all the time, only they don't know how to interpret it. Once they do, though, they'll see that there's fucking going on all over the universe. It's ironic, isn't it, that the first hard evidence men will have of life on other planets will be that they've detected all this fucking.

"If the president knew this I'm sure he would allocate more money to science, and Congress would finish building the supercollider in Texas. Unless, of course, they really *don't* want to find the Lumumba particle. Imagine what would happen if God were found inside an accelerator!

"But supercolliders aren't needed in order to discover new particles. A luminous event can make new particles; all you need is a method of investigating how more collisions per second raise the luminosity—what you would call the intensity of the orgasmic experience. Physicists talk about raising the luminosity to get more particle collisions per second, but what they are really talking about is raising the intensity of their own orgasms to get more pleasure. Of course it's all subconscious, they have no idea what is egging them on.

"But this raises the question: Can the unstable particles of a luminous event explain the ephemeral nature of orgasm? Because they are definable the answer is yes. There are a number of fundamental values and laws in physics—summarized in the so-called standard model—from which all other phenomena can be deduced. As a central feature of biological experience, orgasm is also reducible to—or derivable from—these basic universal values. Thus when a standard model for a luminous event inside the gonads becomes available it will lead to the knowledge of everything. Once someone finds the basic numbers that this model uses they can derive everything from it—the laws of planetary motion, the forces that hold electrons and protons together, the size of a helium atom, the structure of water, the double helix of DNA and the freezing temperature of nitrogen. Once the numbers for orgasm are known it will cancel out the errors.

"Ah, I can hear Albert now. That number, he will say, is already known. It's 666, the number of the beast.

"And I will say, 'Albert, for once you are right; the beast and the forces of orgasm are more or less identical. The beast is made up of a trillion luminous events taking place all at once. In the morning sky he is Lucifer, the brightest star in the heavens. But at night he is Venus, the goddess of love. Why the dual personality of this most luminous of stars? Is it because human passion burns with the same luminosity as the star and must be quelled inorder to keep the son away from his mother's bed?

" 'God threw Lucifer out of heaven because he disobeyed Him,' Albert will say.

"But, Albert, don't you see the irony? How humans have taken their sexual frustration out on the devil? How they've turned it into religious metaphor? If God is orgasm and heaven is the mental state in which orgasm takes place, then the devil is their fear of these pleasures. The devil keeps them in check and makes their biology seem bad and dangerous. This is how they've come to associate sexual desire with guilt.

"But here I am, off on a tangent again, thanks to that brat. 'Uncle,' he will say, 'you may continue with your heretical theorizing. As God forgives us our trespasses, so I forgive you yours. Now what was that about numbers? Something about the unified field theory as proposed by Einstein and Bohr, which would demystify the glory of God and the luminous glow around our Lord and Savior Jesus Christ's head. But you'll never convince me Uncle, not even for a moment.'

"Jesus Christ my hairy primate ass! Can you believe we're on the same airplane? By God I'd love to throttle him, almost as much as throttling my dear colleague Victor Muñoz. Thank God Victor didn't steal everything. That's because I was still confused about gravity and why it didn't conform to quantum theory like the other known forces. Yes, I kept racking my brain like all the other physicists at Yale. Little did I know it was right there infront of my nose the whole time! But like the others I never dreamed of looking for it within the confines of a luminous event. Yes, if I'd just relaxed a little, I'd have seen that the unification of the four forces takes place every time somebody fucks: The rising temperature of the body generates molecular agitation which in turn generates a huge amount of quantum phenomena—high energy collisions of subatomic particles which, if properly understood could be mathematically formulated in such a way as to provide an explanation of everything.

"Gravity and sex, sex and gravity—they may actually be two sides of the same coin, and the possibility of estimating the gravitational mass of the universe exists not only by counting the stars but by counting the number of luminous events that take place on the planet in any one day. This is because a luminous event may have not only its own particles, and quanta values, but also its own field—an anti-matter, anti-gravity and anti-social field which would pervade the universe and influence the way different objects relate to each other. Humans can sense this field vaguely—they call it being horny. But that is only a vulgar and limited way of understanding it; yes, horniness provides an insight into the most profound nature of things, but humans inevitably misinterpret it. This is unfortunate, since sex is much better than gravity if you want to get clear about basic concepts. Look at it this way: If you trip and fall on your face you get a certain insight into the world. But if you get picked up in a bar and laid you can get an even deeper one.

"Science can be seen as a progressive reduction of complex phenomena into simpler underlying laws. This has happened with some of the most important advances in the history of physics. When Faraday linked up electricity and magnetism, or when Einstein linked up space, time and mass, suddenly phenomena as diverse as the structure of the universe and the flight of a bird—phenomena that hadn't seemed related to each other before—were seen to be linked to similar underlying laws. Luminous events are the same, although right now no one thinks that sex could be related to electromagnetism or gravity. But that's a sign that science has not been doing its job. For while humans have used physics to build all kinds of destructive devices, no one has been able to explain the reason why they use those devices. As we've already seen, the basic underlying motivation for human destructiveness is anxiety about sex. The blind adherence to the incest taboo is the source of all human cruelty. But no one has seen that anxiety about sex is linked in a fundamental way to the physics that governs their weapons of mass destruction. By understanding the mathematics of luminous events these connections will become clear. People will see that all the anxiety and destructiveness that derives from sex results from lack of knowledge. Put sex on a firm mathematical footing and show how it relates to the other fundamental forces in the universe, and you'll take away the motivation for annihilation and despair.

"Since there is nothing more unifying than a luminous event, why disparage it? Why ignore it? Why not use it, Dr. Hickey, to your advantage? Perhaps your nemesis—orgasm, hence gravity—will be your salvation and will eventually explain everything. Its participation in a luminous event cannot be minimized or overestimated, since gravity exerts a force on every particle in the universe. Just look around and you'll see that gravity created your civilization. Gravity was the central factor in the evolution of humans. It determined the structural problems humans faced when they first stood up. And as we saw before, it was responsible for the enormous problems created in human sexuality by the change of posture and spine, and the new quantum number necessary to determine spin, parity and mass energy relationships inside the gonads: You know—strong forces getting weaker and weak forces getting stronger, quarks converting to leptons, and neutrinos producing particles inside the gonads. It's actually quite easy to see how humans could mix up a luminous event with God. Perhaps I should be more tolerant towards Albert. And some of my colleagues, too, who are so religious-prone they have failed to understand the relationship of gravity to the nature of a luminous event, and how it links the relativistic universe described by Einstein to the quantum world described by particle physicists. When the seeds of a galaxy formation were sown, so were the seeds of a luminous event inside the gonads.

"But did these laws of nature exist before the universe began? Perhaps they did, perhaps they didn't. Perhaps in truth there are no laws of nature, only luminous events. Perhaps the Big Bang exists only in the imagination. As physicists run the universe backwards toward its beginning the equations of physics start to break down. But if we had an equation for a luminous event, perhaps it would not break down at all and we could trace the history of the universe back to its origins. But perhaps then we would see it had no origins at all but has always existed in some state as yet unfathomed."

PART III
SODDHU

Chapter Twenty-Two

Garlic Is Not the Only Remedy for Warding off the Devil

Or

The Mystery of the Alhambra: It's All in the DNA

As if Lumumba's ideas on orgasm were so powerful, the door of the cockpit suddenly flew open and there for the whole world to see was the captain gyrating about on his instrument panel. The co-pilot was sound asleep. Pedro shut the door quickly and pulled the curtain.

"No wonder this flight's been so jerky," said Lumumba.

"Th'i," said Pedro, plumping the ape's pillow. "Most people think that when a plane goes up and down it is because of air turbulence. Little do they know."

It had begun to grow light. Soddhu roused himself and began to recite a prayer which went something like this:

"We sacrifice to Ushahina, the holy lord of the ritual order, and to the beautiful Aurora, the dawn of morning; we sacrifice to the morning, to the shining of glittering horses, to having men of forethought as its servants, to having men of forethought and heroes awake and at their work, to the morning which gives light within the house. And we sacrifice to the lights of dawn which are radiant with their lightest and fleetest horses which sweep over the seven-fold earth. And we sacrifice to Ahura Mazda, the holy lord of the ritual order, and to the Good Mind, and to Asha Vahista who is Righteousness the Best, and to Khshathravairya and to Aramaiti

the bountiful and good. And to Khvetukdas, if I, Soddhu Págalu, may be
so bold."

(This was, I later learned, one of the Gahs or five divisions of the day.)
Then:

Ashem Vahu vabistem asti
Ashta asti, ushta ahmai
Hyat Ashai vahishtai Ashem."
(Righteousness is the highest virtue
It leads to enlightened happiness,
This happiness is attained when one lives
Righteously for the sake of Righteousness.)

Lumumba sneered.

"The only thing I know about your righteousness is that it inspired the
Nazis to kill Jews."

"Oh come now," said Soddhu. "Isn't it too early to be disagreeable?"

"My dear Dr. Págalu. The Danube Valley is littered with ancient
temples dedicated to the Zoroastrian god Mithra. Indeed, the whole of
Europe is a depository of Ahura Mazdean debris. A well hidden secret, if
I might add."

"Yes, but that was over 1500 years ago."

"A short time in the evolution of man. The pagan heart of Germany is
as alive as ever. Today it's the little Nibelungen people, yesterday it was
Mithra. Hell, maybe it still is Mithra."

Before Soddhu could reply Pedro informed Lumumba that we had just
entered Spanish airspace. The Professor got up and disappeared behind
the curtain.

"What an insufferable fellow," said Soddhu. "I don't know how you
stood it for so long."

"I'm just an old trooper, I guess."

"Even if there were some truth to it, about the Nazis I mean, why
throw it in *my* face. Doesn't he know I'm Persian?"

"Then it's true about the temples?"

"Oh yes. When Europe was part of the Roman empire, Mithraism
spread all the way from Armenia in the east to Britain in the west. There's
a splendid mithraeum at Petronell, near Vienna. I will show it to you
someday."

The captain's voice came over the intercom.

"Señores and Señoras, Ladies and Gentlemen, this is your captain speaking. I must regretfully inform you that we are experiencing a little technical difficulty with one of our instrument panels. A change in course is being made, therefore, and we will be landing in Grenada shortly. Please do not be alarmed. I'm sorry for any inconvenience, we should only be on the ground a short time. Again, I repeat, there is no cause for alarm."

There was the sound of grappling, and Lumumba's voice came over the intercom. "Ladies and Gentlemen, don't believe him. This is General Lumumba speaking, of the Gonad Liberation Army. After analyzing the passengers on this flight, I've come to the conclusion that you are all hopelessly in love with your mothers and fathers, brothers and sisters, sons and daughters. In fact, many of you have been sitting here secretly dreaming of having sex with them—or avoiding those thoughts by thinking up new ways to ravage the planet.

"But don't worry you, meat-sucking, war-mongering penis worshippers. You all deserve to die anyway. Please enjoy the rest of your flight and thank you for flying Iberia."

"Hah hah," said Pedro standing next to Goldschmidt. "That friend of yours, he likes to make jokes, doesn't he?"

"Oh yes," Goldschmidt replied. "He's one funny fellow, all right. Just take a look upfront."

The door to the cockpit had flown open again and the bodies of both pilots fell backwards into the aisle.

"I wasn't going to kill them until we landed," Lumumba called out, "but they gave me no choice."

"Way to go!" Bata exclaimed. "Nedele and the rabbit have been avenged!"

"Jesus and Maria!" said Pedro. He crossed himself and hurried into the cockpit. The passengers screamed as the plane lurched to the left and began to descend toward a range of snow-capped mountains.

"You're here until you're gone, you're alive until you're dead," said Kumasi looking quite resigned.

"Kathryn, darling, can you forgive me?"

It was Herbert who spoke, his voice hoarse, his eyes pleading and terrified.

"Darling, there's nothing to forgive. I had a good time, I wouldn't change these last weeks for anything."

"I'm not talking about Lumumba, I'm talking about Lydia."

There was a clutch in my stomach.

"So you *did* fuck her!"

Herbert looked stupefied. "I thought you knew! Everyone else did."

"Why you dirty son of a bitch!" I started to get up but Soddhu pulled me back.

"But darling," said Herbert, "it was all done in the interest of Project Mark. Just ask Albert, he was there, he saw the whole thing."

"Yes my child," said Albert. "I will tell you though it pains me greatly. It was on the day we were studying chapter 8, verse 9 of the Book of John. A great confusion arose regarding the woman taken in adultery. Being unenlightened promiscuous chimpanzees at the time none of us had a clue. None of us understood what it meant to be monogamous. Your husband was almost to the point of tearing his hair out when Mrs. Baxter walked in. I recall she was wearing a bright red dress the color of our Savior's blood. Dr. Hickey looked at her, she looked at him and a minute later they were rolling on the floor. 'I have just given you an example of adultery,' said your husband after Mrs. Baxter left. 'In the old days Mrs. Baxter and I would have been stoned to death. But because Jesus said, "He that is without sin among you, let him cast the first stone," a Christian can now be an adulterer.' I remember how Freddy and Brian and the others shook Dr. Hickey's hand to show their gratitude."

"Oh great," I said.

"Mrs. Hickey, your husband did a good thing and you mustn't be angry with him. Inorder to show us what it meant to be an adulterer he became one himself. To show us the true path he went off it. He is a true Christian."

Albert, all puffed up now, stood and looked around the cabin.

"Does anyone else wish to confess? How about you, Mr. Goldschmidt?"

"Sure, why not? I am what you think I am."

"A faggot?" said Tchibanga irritably.

"CIA."

"Lumumba had you pegged from the beginning," said Yendi.

"Maybe yes, maybe no. It's not a sin to fight for your country," said Goldschmidt. "It's just hard to explain all the raping and pillaging one has to do to defend U.S. interests."

"You could have left Albert out of it," said Soddhu.

"Not according to Langley. Dolphins and sea lions work fine in the water but it's not often they get a chance to assassinate anyone. Most third-rate dictators don't know how to swim anyway. Not only that, we could never get dolphins to accept the idea of Jesus as their Savior. Something was lost in the translation.

"But with chimps it was different. The commonality of sign language was like manna from heaven. And now that we know they have a conscience and a good strong sense of guilt we can make them do anything we want. In the name of the Lord we can send them to foreign countries to assassinate leaders we don't like. Because of their superior strength and capabilities they will succeed where we have failed. They will scale walls we humans could never scale, outrun any fleeing dictator, break necks and smash skulls with an ease that not even the most trained Navy Seal assassin could hope for, no matter how many steroids he's taken.

"Just imagine! Whole armies of trained chimps, no health benefits, no bad press if they get killed. We can house them in trees and feed them Purina Dog Chow. And with religion we can make them into fanatics who will do anything. Instead of getting distracted by bananas or termites, they'll keep trudging or fighting to the very end. Look at Albert. Religion has made him obsessed. If he thought the Lord wanted him to run through machine gun fire he'd be off in a second. If he thought the Lord wanted him to blow himself up he'd be strapping on explosives without a second thought.

"The chimps do what the Lord wants—and the Lord, naturally enough, wants the same thing the CIA wants. It's a natural convergence of interests."

"Albert is no killer," said Herbert. "He's a pacifist at best and a deluded fool at worst."

"I agree with you. But keep in mind that Albert is our first attempt with an animal brought in from the wild. That you were able to successfully reorganize his natural sexuality into Christian guilt rife with Oedipal overtones is actually quite exciting. All that is left to do is harness that guilt and give him a little training in combat munitions. In five years he'll be a soldier that would make a Marine commander green with envy."

"The problem is," said Soddhu, "that in five minutes he's going to be dead along with all the rest of us. Look."

By now we were so close to the ground I could see people running for cover. Yalinga kissed Okovango tenderly, then hid his face against her breast. Yendi put his arm around both of them, and Tchibanga told Goldschmidt he would have made a damn good soldier in the GLA, manual or no manual. Goldschmidt looked pleased.

Bata, too became contrite and told Albert he wasn't angry at him anymore. There was only one way to prove it, said Albert, and that was to let himself be baptized in the few remaining seconds so they could both disappear in the Rapture together, that cloud which God sends down to earth to bring the faithful up to heaven.

But Bata shook his head and said he'd rather have one last fuck. He was sure it was the same thing anyway. Didn't Albert know that the word rapture came from the Latin verb rapere, meaning 'to rape?'

Suddenly all hell broke loose. The plane hit the treetops sending violent shockwaves throughout the fuselage. The screeching sound of torn metal, the screams of passengers, the screeching of the chimps—all blended into one deafening roar as the plane careened through buildings and plowed to a stop. Luggage, food carts, chairs and passengers flew through the air, even bricks which had broken through the windows of the airplane.

The last object clattered to the floor.

"May Ahura Mazda be praised, we made it," said Soddhu. He was bleeding from a slight cut on his head. There was smoke everywhere and the crackling sound of fire. Cries for help were mixed with sounds of moaning and sobbing. Lumumba emerged from the cockpit, beaming brightly.

"How was that for a landing?" he asked.

"Que carbrón!" said Pedro. "What a man! I would go with you anywhere, Th'ñor. Imagine landing a plane in the middle of the Alhambra!" He looked at Lumumba with dreaming eyes, but a moment later he screamed.

Bata lay motionless in his seat, his head leaning gently to one side as if he were sleeping. But Lumumba's terrible look said otherwise.

"Blessed Father," said Albert, "we commend his soul to heaven. Receive him in Your holy grace."

As he administered the last rites Yalinga, Yendi and Tchibanga began to hoot. Pedro shook his head sadly.

"I have only heard such sorrow one other time," he said. "It was when my mother found out I was a homosexual." He dabbed his eyes and blew his nose.

Smoke was billowing in, in thick black plumes. Lumumba picked up Bata's lifeless body and carried him from the plane. But as Herbert reached the jagged opening which had once been a door he felt inside his pocket.

"It's not here!" he cried and hurried back to his seat.

"Oh leave him," I said to Soddhu. We hurried after the others, there were bodies everywhere, passengers and tourists who had been visiting the Alhambra. Tile and marble lay at our feet in a million broken pieces. Soddhu grabbed my arm.

"Kathryn, why are we following these fools? Let's get out of here, nobody's looking."

"I am," said Goldschmidt. "If you want to run off with Mrs. Hickey, that's fine. But I'll take the money, it's mine, you know."

"I've told you it's in Nairobi," Soddhu said hotly.

"So that money belt around your waist is only an illusion?"

Soddhu's shirt was open, the belt and his kusti there for all the world to see. Herbert came running up out of breath.

"I had it with me all the time," he said. "Say, Págalu, you ought to have that cut attended to. Why don't you stay here and wait for the medics?"

"And leave your wife in your adulterous hands?"

"She's surely not going to be in yours."

"How can I be an adulterer, I'm not even married?"

"Can we argue about this later?" said Goldschmidt. "I need to find Albert."

"Find him yourself," said Soddhu. "Kathryn and I are staying."

Goldschmidt took out a pistol.

"A present from Pedro," he said. "Now get moving, you can give me the belt later."

When we found Lumumba he had just put the last clod of dirt over Bata's grave. It was next to a large reflecting pool inside a courtyard of great beauty. Roses and royal palms grew in profusion, the porticos were made of graceful arches and marble columns.

"What a lovely spot to cavort with hairless young Arab boys," Goldschmidt sighed. "I can see their lusty, animal smiles reflected in its waters as if I were here a thousand years ago enjoying their embraces."

"My son," said Albert, "surely you can think of something else! Even I find these grounds immensely interesting even though they were built by heathen Moors."

While he was speaking Yalinga put Okovango in my arms and began to swing from the colonnades and trees with Tchibanga and Yendi.

"Look at it his way," said Goldschmidt. "Now that I've blown my cover, now that you see through me completely—why I'm a patriot, why I work for the CIA, why I go around arming the terrorists—what else is there to think of?"

"And besides," said Soddhu, "there is something terribly seductive about this place, although I can't put my finger on it."

"Perhaps it's my wife washing off your bloody head," said Herbert watching me rinse the cut with water from the pool.

"I don't think so," said Lumumba looking at the tile work closely. He had been studying the patterns ever since we arrived. "It's something here in the designs, something in the geometric repetitions. I feel as if I'm looking at strands of DNA—no, as if I *am* the DNA. Well, I'll have to think about it later, c'mon, everybody, let's move."

In the next courtyard there was a fountain set on the back of twelve lions, and surrounding it a garden and portico held up by a number of ornate columns and triple arches densely forested with geometrical designs. The ancient tiles danced around us, the geometrical designs carrying the eye along in a kind of mathematical delirium. The columns cried out to be embraced. The palace pulsated with the sighs of love.

"You have to hand it to the Arabs," Lumumba said with sudden certainty. "It's the total incarnation of a luminous event!"

There was no time to explain as we hurried from one splendid room to the next. When we reached the parking lot it was awash in vehicles. Police cars and ambulances were arriving in droves. Lumumba quickly spotted the car he wanted, a small white Peugeot.

"How can we all fit into that?" said Tchibanga.

"You can't, that's the point," Lumumba replied. He jimmied the ignition and pulled Soddhu inside.

"I'm taking him along as collateral. Hasta la vista, have a nice day."

As he drove off Goldschmidt went berserk.

"Son-of-a-bitch! He's got my money!"

"Well, let's go after him," I said, ignoring Herbert's stare

"Hey wait a minute," said Yendi, "aren't you and your husband supposed to be taking us home?"

"And you, my son," said Albert to Goldschmidt, "are supposed to take me to Washington."

"First things first," said Goldschmidt. He hailed a cab whose driver had come to see the mayhem, all of us squeezed in and took off after Lumumba whose car soon came into view on the hairpin turns below us.

We followed him through heavy traffic made worse by police cars and ambulances; it was not surprising that we eventually lost sight of him.

"Rats!" said Goldschmidt. The driver looked thoughtful.

"Th'ñor, do you know where your friend was going?"

"On the plane he kept mumbling about someone named Victor Muñoz; maybe we can find him in the phone book," said Goldschmidt.

"But why waste time? I know Th'ñor Muñoz. When he comes to town I drive him to the gypsy caves of Sacromonte almost every night. Dios mío, that man knows how to live!"

He drove directly to a row of brown apartments on the west side of town. Lumumba's car was parked in front.

"The apartment is on the third floor. I know because sometimes I have to help him in, he is so drunk."

As we approached the door we heard loud voices coming from inside. Goldschmidt pushed it open, there was Lumumba holding an old lady several feet off the floor, while Soddhu stood by helplessly.

"Th'ñor, por favor, please put me down," said the woman. "I tell you I don't know where he is!"

Goldschmidt rushed in.

"Put your hands in the air," he said pointing his gun at Lumumba.

As the professor obeyed the old woman landed with a thud.

"Give me the money," Goldschmidt said to Soddhu.

"I don't have it," he replied. A pat on the waist proved he was telling the truth.

"Okay, General, hand it over."

Lumumba unbuckled the money belt and with a swift movement flung it at Goldschmidt. It hit his hand and knocked the gun to the floor. Yendi quickly grabbed it.

"You might as well finish me off," Goldschmidt moaned. "I'm as good as dead anyway."

"Not really," said Soddhu. "Ntimama's told everyone you still have the shipment."

"What?! He was there in the plane when we tossed it out!"

"Well, that's what he says. I heard it from Baxter."

"You tell Baxter he's a big fat liar!"

"Will you two shut up?! Lumumba shouted. He pulled the woman to her feet and put his hand around her throat

"Señora, you have one last chance to talk."

"Have pity, Th'ñor, I am only an old woman."

"That's part of my charm, Señora, I don't discriminate against age."

As his hand tightened she began to choke and gesticulate wildly.

"All right, all right! Th'ñor Muñoz has gone to Altamira."

"Did he say where or why?"

"Th'i, Th'ñor, a party at the cave for a famous dancer."

Out on the street Lumumba found a larger vehicle equipped with tools and rope, and broke it open.

"Yipee! We get to go," said Tchibanga.

"Thanks, general, I owe you one," said Goldschmidt.

At the first traffic circle we headed north.

There were fields of olive trees and sunflowers, and hills with villages of white houses and red-tiled roofs. The hills were steep, the orchards grew out of massive rocks which peppered the landscape. To help pass the time Lumumba began a discussion on Zoroastrianism. It was mostly questions on his part, but Soddhu was happy to comply and spoke so tirelessly on the subject that he wouldn't stop even when he grew hoarse. This is what I remember:

The religion of the Magi began in a time too long ago to remember. It began in a time when the ancestors of the Persians and Hindus were still united, when they both worshipped a singular god whose name was Mithra, the god of light, the protector of truth, the antagonist of falsehood and error.

"Ah," said Lumumba, "so the lies that are rooted in Oedipus are supposed to be routed out by the belief in a god who is also rooted in Oedipus. Kind of like letting the fox guard the chickens, isn't it? No wonder lying comes so natural to humans. But do continue."

Mithra, said Soddhu, was the god of truth who heard all, saw all and knew all; none could deceive him: he was "the lord of wide pastures: He giveth increase, he giveth abundance, he giveth progeny and life."

"He sounds a lot like the Jewish God," said Lumumba.

"The ancient Hebrews took a lot from us, you bet," Soddhu replied. "Several of our cardinal doctrines, as a matter of fact."

All trouble and suffering came from Ahriman and the devas who inhabited the places of darkness. But Mithra "wakeful and sleepless, protected the creation of Mazda" against their mischief. Much like the Old Testament, he annihilated and laid waste to the tribes and nations who opposed him.

Even so, Ahura Mazda was above him at the pinnacle. His name was derived from *ah*, meaning to be, to exist, to be present. ("Yes," said Soddhu, "compare it with 'I am that I am') and *Mazda*, meaning super-intellect, higher intelligence, wise, the Wise One.

Thus it was that this Supreme Being appointed Mithra to maintain and watch over the living world.

"In that sense he is like Jesus," said Lumumba.

"Very much so," replied Soddhu. "Indeed, the only real difference is that Jesus was said to be real while Mithra was always a myth. In the end it's that difference which gave the Christians the upper hand and caused our downfall. But I'm getting ahead of myself."

The Magi, as we already knew, were the official clergy. Their name probably came from the word "magh" meaning hole.

"Ah," said Lumumba, "could that be the magic hole, the vagina? I do know that the word magic is derived from this priestly caste."

"Well, why not? They were apparently into incest, and to some people that's all pretty magical."

286

Of course it wasn't looked upon as incest. It was looked upon as a way to keep the bloodline pure, and it had a non-pejorative name, Khvetukdas, from a word meaning "family."

Now because many of his fellow Parsees didn't believe it, that Zarathustra and the Magi had promoted these next-of-kin marriages as being the best thing a man could do, he, Soddhu was writing a book on the subject because he *did* believe it was true—there were too many references to it, not only in the sacred scriptures but also in some of the commentaries written at the time by such chroniclers as Plutarch, Heradotus, Origan and Diogenes Laertes. Oh sure, you could say they had all misunderstood whatever it was the Magi were doing. And you could also say that the ancient commentaries had been erroniously transcribed; this is how the Parsees of today dealt with the problem. But he, Soddhu, was inclined to agree with the school of thought that Khvetukdas meant exactly what it said:

"The consummation of mutual assistance of men is Khvetukdas, that union with near kinsmen and, among near kinsmen, that with those next-of-kin. And the mutual connection of the three kinds of nearest kin—which are father and daughter, son and she who bore him, and brother and sister—is the most complete that I have considered."

This, of course, was the same passage Dean Wiggins had read back at Yale last Christmas. It was a conversation, said Soddhu, between a Zoroastrian theologian and a Jewish objector.

"Ah ha!" said Lumumba. "Even back then they were trying to stop it!"

"Are you saying," Albert said to Soddhu, "that if I become a Zoroastrian I won't have to feel guilty for having had sex with Nedele?"

"Don't even think about it," said Goldschmidt angrily. "Washington has no plans for Zoroastrians."

"Look," said Soddhu, "even though we don't marry outside our religion, I don't think Khvetukdas is a part of it anymore. I'm sorry I even mentioned it."

"God forgives you," said Albert showing a sudden enthusiasm. "Please continue, my child."

Well, said Soddhu, since we were on the subject of incest, it was said that Mithra sprung from the incestuous intercourse of Ahura Mazda and his mother. Albert looked stoked. Didn't this prove, he asked, that the doctrine of Khvetukdas was real?

"In my mind, yes," Soddhu replied.

But back to Mithra the genius of fire. The sacred flame in today's fire temples, he said, continued to burn in his honor; it represented Mithra in all his manifestations—the sun, the stars, the magma in the earth, the lightening, the power to create life. Mithra protected the souls of the just against the demons that wanted to drag them to Hell, and he also acted as mediator between an unapproachable god and the struggling races of men—"yes, the Christians stole that from us too,"—as they did his divine birth which was witnessed by shepherds tending their flocks in the fields.

Because the religion of Zoroastrianism was so infused with man's veneration for nature, what the Christians stupidly call paganism was in reality an appreciation, a reverence for the environment.

"You worship the cross," he said, looking at Herbert, "we worship the fire. What is the difference? Worship is worship is worship is worship."

"And it's all about orgasm anyway," said Lumumba, "so why bicker? But do continue."

We had just passed a billboard that was so large and black only a blind person could fail to see it. It was actually the cutout of a bull, perhaps forty feet high, and it made you sit up and think, mostly because there appeared to be no advertising.

"Son of a gun!" said Goldschmidt admiringly of the bull's large testicles "You'd never see a billboard like that in America!"

"Yes," said Soddhu, "and it's not just because of prudishness, either."

The bull, he said, played a big part in Zoroastrianism. He was the first creation of Ahura Mazda, and he roamed the earth at will. But because he was rascally and wily, god asked Mithra to take him prisoner. A terrible struggle ensued, but Mithra prevailed and dragged the unwilling bull deep inside a cave.

Unfortunately, the bull didn't stay there long, and upon his escape Ahura Mazda ordered Mithra to kill him. Reluctantly the hero obeyed, but when he plunged his hunting knife into the bull a miraculous thing happened: from his body sprang all the herbs and plants of the earth, wheat sprung from his spine, from his blood sprang the vine.

"The Eucharist!" said Albert excitedly.

"For us it was called the Taurobolium, or baptism in the blood of the bull. A man became purified and immortal if he performed this important ceremony."

"I don't like the idea of sacrificing a bull," I said.

"Nor do I," said Soddhu, "so I'm glad that the blood has been substituted with either water or wine."

"I don't think it has," said Lumumba as we passed another huge cutout. Everyone agreed it was an advertisement for the bull fights. Soddhu looked thoughtful. Anything was possible, he said.

This important rite of purification and immortality, the Taurobolium, was practiced as late as the fourth century—who knows, maybe later than that.

"Maybe it never stopped," said Lumumba, "maybe only the name's been changed for this baptism in blood."

Anything's possible, Soddhu replied again, even Lumumba's insinuation about the Nazis. For indeed the Germans had taken this religion to heart, more so than any of the other peoples who had come under the influence of the Roman Empire. The Rhine valley, the Danube valley were strongholds of the Persian cult long into the present era, long after Christianity, its bloody rival for power, became the official religion of Rome.

Oh well, said Soddhu drawing to a conclusion, you had to hand it to Christians. They were smart to entice the ignorant masses away from Mithra with a living being, someone they could identify with. If only we had thought of it, there'd be a Magus in the Vatican instead of a Pope.

"And Khvetukdas instead of sin," said Albert sadly. "If only you'd told me about this sooner, my child." He turned his bible over listlessly.

"What did you say your book is called, the Zend-Avesta?"

"I swear, if you give him that book . . . !" said Goldschmidt threateningly.

"Is it okay if I just recite a few passages?"

Goldschmidt hesitated and Albert said quickly: "Go on, my child, tell us what you know, stop wasting time."

So Soddhu began:

Zarathustra inquired of Ahura Mazda thus: "O Creator! In that perplexing time, are there religious people who wear the sacred thread girdle on the waist, and celebrate religious rites with the sacred twigs? And does the religious practice of next-of-kin marriage continue in their families?
Ahura Mazda said to Zarathustra thus: "the most perfectly righteous of the righteous is he who remains in the good religion of the Mazdayasnians and continues the religious practice of next-of-kin marriage in his family.
It is said in revelation that Aeshm (the demon of wrath) rushed into the presence of Ahriman and exclaimed thus: "I will not go into the world because Ahura Mazda the lord has produced three things in the world to which it is not possible for me to do anything whatever."
Ahriman exclaimed thus: "Say which are those three things."
Aeshm exclaimed thus: "The season-festival, the sacred feast and next-of-kin marriage."

And Ahriman said to Aeshm: "Enter into the season of festival! If one of those present shall steal a single thing the season festival is violated, and the affair is in accordance with thy wish; enter into the sacred feast! If only one of those present shall chatter, the sacred feast is violated and the affair is in accordance with thy wish; but avoid next-of-kin marriage! Because I do not know a remedy for it; for whoever has gone four times near it will not become parted form the possession of Ahura Mazda and the archangels."

"Wow!" Albert exclaimed. "So the devil can cause havoc with anything but a next-of-kin marriage?"

Soddhu nodded and continued.

Chapter 65 of the Dadistan-I Dinik begins thus: As to the sixty-fourth question and reply, that which you ask is thus: Where and from what did the origin of race, which they say was next-of-kin marriage, arise; and from what place did it arise?

The reply to this, that the first consummation of next-of-kin marriage was owing to that which Marhaya and Marhiyoih did, who were brother and sister, and their consummation of intercourse produced a son as a consummation of the first next-of-kin marriage. So that they effected the first intercourse of man and woman, and the entire progress of the races of every lineage of men arose from that, and all the men of the world are of that race.

Chapter 77. As to the seventy-sixth question and reply, that which you ask is thus: Will you direct someone then to make the heinousness of this sin of unnatural intercourse clear to us?

The reply is this, that the first material creature was the righteous man, the smiter of the fiend, the righteous proprietor. In the world, therefore he is more recognizing of the sacred beings, and more able to take care of the production and provision of creatures. And with the manifestation of this knowledge, the best duty is that which exists in lawfully practicing procreation. The complete progression of righteous men arose therefrom.

In like manner he who is the omniscient creator formed mankind in the first pair who were brother and sister, and became Marhaya and Mahiyoih, and all the races of material life exist by means of acquiring sons and his omnisciently causing procreation. The man and woman were also made to lust by him and thereby became father and mother of material men; and he naturalized among primitive man the qualities of a desire for acquiring sons together through glorifying. And the law and religion authorized it as a proper wish, so long as they proceed from those who are their own relations. And with those whom next-of-kin marriages, original duties and desires for other sons have formed, complete progress in the world is connected, and even unto the time of the renovation of the universe it is to arise therefrom. And the birth of many glorious practitioners of the religion, those confident in spirit, organizers of the realm, arrangers of the country and even accomplishers of the renovation of the universe which arises from those same to whom that practice shall be law, is a miracle and benefit of he world, the will of the sacred beings and the utmost good work discernable because the complete progress of the righteous arises therefrom and the great female faculty is manifested.

"Just as I suspected," said Lumumba. "The renovation of the universe—that is, the resurrection day, is to come through incest, as is the idea of glorifying the lord."
Soddhu nodded and continued

The sage asked the spirit of wisdom thus, "which is the good work that is great and good?"
The spirit of wisdom answered thus: "the greatest good work is liberality, and the second is truth and next-of-kin marriage."
The sage asked the spirit of wisdom thus: "which sin is the most heinous?"
The sage asked the spirit of wisdom thus: "the fourth most heinous sin that mankind can commit is to break off next-of-kin marriage."
The sage asked the spirit of wisdom thus: "through how many ways and motions of good works do people arrive most at heaven?"
The spirit of wisdom answered thus: "the first good work is liberality. The second, truth. The third, thankfulness. The fourth, contentment. The fifth, wanting to produce welfare for the good, and becoming a friend to everyone. The sixth, being without doubt as to this, that the sky and earth and every benefit of the worldly and spiritual existences are owing to the creator Ahura Mazda. The seventh being so as to the unquestionableness of this, that all misery and affliction are owing to Ahriman the wicked who is accursed. The eighth, freedom from doubt as to the resurrection and future existence. The ninth, who for love of the soul effects next-of-kin marriage."
And the bountifulness of Ahura Mazda was extolled by them, and they went on with their duty; they also performed the will of the creator, enjoyed the advantage of the many duties of the world, and practiced next-of-kin marriage for procreation, union, and the complete progress of the creations of the world which are the best good works of mankind.

"Unbelievable!" said Goldschmidt. Soddhu continued.

And when their announcement for speaking to be heard was issued, then Zarathustra on becoming exalted called out into the embodied world of the righteous to extol righteousness and to scorn the demons.

The homage of the Mazda worship of Zarathustra, and the ceremonial and obeisance for the archangels are the best for you I assert; and of deprecation for the demons, next-of-kin marriage is really the best intimation, so that from the information which is given as to the trustworthiness of a good work, the greatest are the most intimate of them, those of a father and daughter, son and she who bore him, and brother and sister.

At that point, Soddhu's voice began to give out.

"Why was Zarathustra killed?" asked Yalinga as Soddhu tried to clear his throat.

"I imagine," said Lumumba, "that people were afraid of his message. Afterall, wasn't this the very practice which threw the human species into chaos in the first place?"

Soddhu nodded in assent. With heroic effort he continued the recitative:

It is declared that upon those words, innumerable demon-worshipping Kigs and Karaps'—priests and officials in the land of Tur—rushed upon Zarathustra and strove for his death, just like this which revelation states . . .

But the progeny of Aurvaita-dang the Tur, the scanty giver, spoke thus: "Should we for that speech destroy him, this great one who mingles together those propitious words for us—where we are thus without doubt as to one thing therein, such as next-of-kin marriage, that it is not necessary to contrast it—it would make us ever doubtful whether it might be necessary to contract it."

And Aurvaita-dang the Tur, the scanty giver, spoke thus: "Thou shalt not destroy the man whom my eyes have seen as the most loving-eyed of the whole embodied existence; he will attain strength, for it has not seemed to me, when thou destroyest him on this account, that wisdom has arisen for a long time; so that no rule of wisdom will arise in this earth, which is so counseling as this one is (that is, when they destroy a man who is counseling, wisdom will not arise for a long while)."

Aurvaita-dang the Tur, the scanty giver to his own people, also spoke thus:

"For me thou art a pure man who is counseling."

And Zarathustra spoke thus: "I shall not always be that quiet speaker, by whom I have mentioned is the most propitious thing to be obtained; and of interfering speaking and managing the temper, there is a next-of-kin marriage, and the high-priest who has contracted it is to perform the ceremonial . . ."

The nobles of Aurvaita-dang the Tur, the ruler of the land, were angry and clamored for Zarathustra's death; but he invited the Kigs and Karaps to the religion of Auhura Mazdda, just as this passage of revelations states . . . .

Soddhu's voice cracked for the last time. Everyone seemed lost in thought, but a few minutes later Goldschmidt broke the silence.

"Kigs and Karaps, but I'm hungry!" Crashing jetliners into historic places, he said, had given him an appetite.

We pulled up alongside a field of planted sunflowers. Each little face—and there were hundreds of them—was looking toward the east. The village in the distance, said Lumumba, was too far away to bother about, but about twenty minutes later as we sat in the field popping seeds into our mouths a horse and rider came charging toward us. The rider, a man in his sixties sat haughtily astride his mount. He was dressed in riding pants and boots. Atop his suntanned face a cap sat at an angle.

He addressed himself to all of us.

"Ladrones, mendicants, gypsies, salgan de la terra de mis padres!" (Robbers, beggars, gypsies, leave my land at once!) His magnificent horse pawed the earth nervously.

"But we are hungry," Lumumba replied humbly.

"Me sembre una *charity*? Salgan antes de que llame la policia." (You think I'm a charity? Leave before I call the police.)

Albert left his lunch and hurried over. "My son," he said. "Spare a few flowers for these wayward children, and God will reward you." A small patch of fur could be seen below his pant-leg. The man looked at it in disgust.

"I have no patience for your liberation theology, Father," he said in perfect English. "My ancestors have owned this land for 500 years. Obviously you are all tourists, otherwise you would know that I am don Francisco del Nueva Tarde de San Juan Martin del Fresco, the great-great-great-great-great nephew of their most catholic Majesties King Ferdinand and Queen Isabella."

As he finished speaking his horse lifted its tail and evacuated a large pile of manure.

"Ah," said Lumumba, taking hold of the bridle, "another dirty capitalist. As far as I'm concerned your need for private property is merely a manifestation of the incest taboo, a primitive method of controlling the gonads."

Don Francisco glared balefully.

"Another dirty communist," he said, spitting in the dirt. "Not only do you want to take away my land, now you want to take my women away as well. But we shall see about that."

He reached into his pocket and pulled out a cell phone.

"Colonel Perez? There is a radical priest here on my land and a whole band of brainwashed acolytes. Could you kindly send over one of your sanitation squads to take care of them? Muchas Grath'ias."

Spurring his horse and making it rear, the colonel rode away.

"I guess you showed him," said Yendi dubiously.

"Listen," said Lumumba, "my prey is almost within sight. Let the old fart jack off on his horse, what do I care?"

Later, near the Tunel de Santa Maria we stopped at a hotel and dined on fruit, crackers, biscuits and rolls. As Lumumba said, "it was all good."

That night we sought shelter in one of several abandoned houses on the other side of a river. Crossing the river was dangerous, but in Lumumba's mind it was better than meeting up with any of don Francisco's men.

"I can feel it," he said. "The chains of the incest taboo are drawn tighter here than in other countries, I'm not sure why."

"Well," said Goldschmidt as we settled down uncomfortably on the floor, "that palace we landed in certainly wasn't built by people who were trying to repress their gonads. All those pools and fountains made me want to take my clothes off, smear myrrh on my penis and have huge black men with bulging muscles run their rough, wild tongues up the inside of my thighs."

"Don't kid yourself," said Lumumba, "the Moslems are just as fucked as everybody else." The Sultan, he went on, could have as many wives as he wanted—as many women as he wanted—as long as he left the one woman he couldn't have—his mother—alone. Meanwhile the poor fellahin watched him from afar and sublimated—just like the poor people in western cities do when they go window-shopping at the expensive department stores. But it was awfully hard on everyone, this sublimation business, especially when you're riding a camel in the middle of the desert and there's no one around to sublimate with.

"I hope you're not going to turn the Alhambra into a monument to the incest taboo," said Goldschmidt.

"But that's exactly what it is," Lumumba replied. "I couldn't have put it better myself."

"Sometimes a palace is just a palace," said Goldschmidt.

"Never. A palace is always man's fortress against the humongous pile of forbidden desires."

If forbidden fruit weren't the most desirable, he continued, the sultan wouldn't need to have so many women at his beck and call inorder to make the sublimation work. But how to explain that the typical Arab's culture is so riddled by sexual anxiety? So obsessed with it that the veil covers women over like forbidden objects, and anyone who tries to penetrate the veil is likely to have his scrotum cut off and made into a tobacco pouch for the local imam's hookah?

"I venture to say," said Soddhu, "that it's all a backlash against the doctrine of Khvetukdas. Afterall, theirs is the land—the Middle East—where Zarathustra did his preaching."

"That is very possible and I venture to say that you're right."

Since the doctrine of Khvetukdas was so blatant, the answer to it had to also by blatant, stripped down to the very marrow. Don't just make one woman forbidden, cover them up and make them all forbidden. As for the Sultan's harem, this was simply another response to the same problem—or rather, an extension of the sexual laws imposed on the common people.

The Sultan could have all the women in the world except the one he really wanted, and the harem existed to teach men this lesson: Take one woman, or ten, or five hundred, but never the one from whose loins you slipped, the woman in whose womb you first learned to masturbate, the woman whose blood you smelled and whose body you lived off for several months. Inother words, the woman you long to be reunited with above all others, the mother.

"Ah, for Khvetukdas!" said Albert longingly. "Dear Professor Págalu, when you return to Yale could you possibly teach a class on this lovely doctrine? So many people will be saved from the torments of hell."

"But how will Yale keep supplying our country with presidents?" asked Goldschmidt.

"Anyway, I doubt I'll be going back," said Soddhu throwing me a sultry glance. It was still light enough for Herbert to catch it.

"Good move," said Herbert. "I think for drug-running you get about twenty years."

"How many for murder?" Soddhu quipped.

"I told you before I didn't kill Crumb. Say, Professor," said Herbert to change the subject, "what about all that DNA carved into the Alhambra this morning, might there be a formula for that too?"

"Let me see now, what did I say? Oh yes, that the decorative designs and treatments on all the structures, the rhythm and symmetry in the mosaics, freizes, enamels and carved writings—indeed, the overall allure of sensuality so endemic to the Alhambra, is not merely the result of a curious mixture of sign systems.

"Is there a formula in it? Well, why not?

Yes, the abstract motifs—the complex designs of intertwined floral, foliate and geometric figures—were the transcodings of elemental biochemical forms—structures found in RNA, DNA and the self-catalyzing enzymes that constituted the first forms of life on the planet. That was why we found them so beautiful—they reproduced in aesthetic form our own essence, the patterns deep inside us that made us what we are. Once again it was our own bodies we were worshiping, our own creation, our own orgasm. The arches, even the building itself reminded us of that, because the organic nature of Islamic architecture couldn't be denied. The irony was that the aesthetic power of those patterns had been harnessed to repress the very function they represented.

The Alhambra was a building which embodied the sublimation of forbidden desires. That is why the inscription pointed out by Soddhu appeared so frequently: "Only God is victorious." This invocation signified the Moslem's submission to the Islamic form of the incest taboo. To say that Allah is conqueror was to say that the law of Allah organized and ruled over man's sexual desires, that Allah had conquered the unbridled lusts of his followers' wily gonads. Yes, those basic geometrical forms represented the unbridled lust of sexuality in its originary state—the pure vibrational joy of electrons finding a form in which to express their orgasmic essence. But those same forms had then been commandeered by the incest taboo and transmuted into a heavenly promise which said 'Repress your sexuality here on earth and you'll be rewarded in the hereafter with eternal bliss. You'll be returned to the primitive patterns that form the orgasmic essence of your being.' Did we understand why Moslems were always ready to blow themselves up? They were always being teased with images of paradise on the other side of the grave.

"What is blowing oneself up when you believe you'll return to that primitive geometrical, orgiastic perfection?" Lumumba asked.

Goldschmidt agreed that there was great beauty in the designs, but to read in them such things as RNA and DNA was, he said, utter nonsense.

Lumumba told him to go back to his college biology. If he studied the three-dimensional models of basic organic molecules he'd find that they were built on the exact same geometric principles as the tessellated walls of the Alhambra. Both were created out of the interplay of mathematical possibilities and constraints available in finite space. At the Alhambra, humans had mimicked the bonds of molecules tessellating in their own bodies. It was for that reason that we found the Alhambra so captivating, so seductive. The beauty we saw was the beauty of life itself, something irresistable.

296

But there was more. The fountains and pools were as integral to the design as the tessellated tiles. In the Koran, paradise was referred to as a pavilion flowing with water. But rest assured, whenever humans talked about water in a figurative sense, what they were really talking about was semen, female lubrication and the symbiotic waters of the mother's womb. Paradise in all religions was a coded word for intercourse and orgasm in all its blazing glory. Hadn't he already told us that the word itself meant an enclosure, a pleasure garden? And that it came from a Persian word meaning 'enclosure'—something that went around something: *pairi*— about, around—and *da_za*, a wall. Now tell me, he said, what more glorious wall was there than the wall of the vagina which encircled (went around and about) the penis? What better enclosure was there for taking pleasure than the one provided by the vagina? For within that garden, for male and female alike, was to be found the greatest of all pleasure— orgasm.

"I prefer the back door myself," said Goldschmidt, "if you know what I mean."

Any enclosure, said Lumumba, would send a man to paradise, even if it was only the right hand masturbating. But he was talking about the official enclosure, the one which was encoded as a garden in all the sacred scriptures thousands of years ago when men were looking for a way to control the gonads. Various myths had various names for it. Perhaps this was one of man's greatest achievements, his ability to transform a woman's uterus into an abstract concept of such far-reaching consequence.

He recited from the Song of Solomon:

A garden locked is my sister, my bride,
A garden locked, a fountain sealed.

"Sounds like the Alhambra, all right," said Herbert.

"Or the Garden of Eden," said Goldschmidt.

Also called the Garden of God, said Lumumba, where brother and sister lived in incestuous bliss until a snake appeared, and the rest was history; the incest taboo was solidified and men could never again have their mothers, at least not in this lifetime. It would have to be the next. Yes, Paradise was the abode of the righteous after death. When the Messiah returned, the righteous dead would come up from their gloomy cavern and find themselves on an earth that was transformed once again into the original Garden of Eden. The deserts would bloom and the beasts would once again live in idyllic amity with man who was now at peace with his own animal self. What this meant, of course, was that men would be able to couple without the constraints of the incest taboo.

Did we see how clever this was? The reward for being good was the very thing that made us bad in the first place—forbidden intercourse.

But this was what the coming of the Messiah was all about, a father's promise to his son that one day he would be able to fuck his mother in a mythical afterlife called heaven. The apostle Paul gave the name Paradise to the third of the seven Hebraic heavens, and John said in Revelations: 'To him who conquers I will grant to eat of the tree of life which is in the Paradise of God.' In other words, incest was the final state of bliss attained by the saints. The Christian Paradise recalled the paradise from which early man was driven. It flowed with milk and honey, miraculous trees which freed humans from all sorrow, pain, disease and death—the fruits of forbidden intercourse. Once men returned to their incestuous paradise, religion promised them they would be whole again. The last chapters of the New Testament were nothing but a promise to believers of a fulfillment of their incestuous oedipal longings.

"I don't know," said Albert doubtfully. "All they taught us was religion, and sometimes they let us watch the Disney channel. I often wanted to watch the Discovery channel but they wouldn't let me. But now, listening to you and Dr. Págalu, I think I'm in danger of undergoing a paradigm shift in my thinking. Oh, woe is me! What is a poor fundamentalist chimp to do when confronted by the hard truths of science?"

During the night Soddhu and I crept outside and made love. Herbert was a murderer, thus did I rationalize my perfidy. And besides, since my mother had taken an aborigine, why couldn't I take a Zoroastrian?

Poor old Gordon! I hadn't thought of him in weeks. Were the police still shining a light into mother's bedroom? But all they were doing, of course, was policing their own gonads, guarding the good white side against the evil dark side.

Ah, dear Lumumba! If he were right, if white men were afraid of dark men because of the taboo, then the taboo was bad, very bad. But what would the world be like without it? I had no time to consider. Soddhu had begun the final assault, and as I braced for it I imagined myself back in the Alhambra surrounded by marble fountains, sculpted lions, starry domes and hidden alcoves.

When the moment came, instead of seeing Jesus or Herbert or Soddhu or Daddy, once again it was Dr. Lumumba. But instead of being domineering and cruel, orgasm had incarnated him into the sweetest and dearest being I had ever known.

But wait, there is more.

When the next orgasm came I had another revelation: *Could anything be better than this? If only it could last forever!*

And then it dawned on me: To have orgasm last forever, to be in this exquisite place for all eternity, there was no other reason to believe in heaven.

And now do we know?
Why the artists all painted
That look of great sorrow
on Jesus' face, His eyes
Turned toward heaven
(Lumumba's wild heaven!),
The heaven He'll forfeit
Being nailed to the Cross?

Chapter Twenty-Three

In Which It Is Told Why the Truth about Bulls is Really No Bull,

How Soddhu Pulls the Plug on Jesus, and Why the Cardinal Learns More about His Hat Than He Cares To Know

In the morning an old man and a donkey stuck their heads inside the doorway. The donkey who was very small was carrying a load of hay as big as a mountain. Lumumba wasted no time with formalities.

"Señor," he said, "no cree Usted que su burro lleva demasiado peso?" (Don't you think he's carrying too big a load?)

"Nothing's too big for Paco," the man replied proudly. "Last week I even had my wife on him, and she weighs 150 kilos. Now please get off my land, or I shall call the Guardia Civil."

A second later the old Spaniard lay sprawled on the floor and Lumumba let the little donkey go. He brayed his gratitude, and took off at a run, his burden of hay lying scattered on the ground.

"A good way to start the day," said Tchibanga as he dragged the Spaniard down to the river.

The fields rolled by with a pleasant consistency. Lumumba and Soddhu discussed the Persian mysteries, Albert listened attentively, Herbert sulked, Kumasi and Okovango slept and Yalinga had sex with Yendi and Tchibanga.

"I'll bet you didn't know," Soddhu was saying, "that the Lord's Supper came from *us*."

"By god I didn't," said Lumumba. "I'm beginning to think the Christians stole more from you than from the Egyptians!"

"You'd better believe it," said Soddhu. "Their religion and ours were so much alike, I imagine that's why the struggle for power lasted as long as it did. But never forget that we were there first. The idea of baptism, the Messiah (we call him the Saoshyant), good and evil, salvation, the Eucharist, December 25th, Sunday for worshipping, abstinence, renunciation, immorality, a last judgment, resurrection and final conflagration of the universe—all of that was ours, but do we get the credit?"

"Be thankful for small favors," said Lumumba sarcastically.

"Loser, loser," Tchibanga quipped as he pumped away at Yalinga. It was hard not to stare, even after all these weeks. Only Albert and Lumumba seemed impervious; and besides, Albert's attention was now riveted on an imposing structure rising from the jagged heights above a village.

"If it's a monastery," said Albert, "I'd like to stop. I'm feeling very much in need of a confessor."

"I'm afraid it's only a castle," said Lumumba. "You'll have to wait for a private meeting with the Pope, ha, ha!"

"But none of us have ever seen a real castle," I argued.

"Is it the castle you wish to enter, or your incestuous longings which the castle represents?"

"Can't a cigar ever just be a cigar?" Goldschmidt groaned hopelessly.

"Not in your world," Lumumba replied, "where thought itself is a method of controlling the gonads."

"Okay, I bite. What does a castle have to do with Oedipus?"

The castle, Lumumba said, was a material representation of God's law, which of course was nothing other than the incest taboo translated into a particular cultural context. The castle, the king, the queen, the sacred sword, knights fighting to protect their honor—didn't we see that it was all part of the sexual symbolism of the incest taboo which we humans had created? And to believe in a castle's beauty was to acknowledge the underlying cause of that beauty—the desire to unite within the first degree.

Herbert broke his silence. There was an edge to his voice, I wondered if he knew about last night.

"Whether castles are part of the taboo or not," he said, "surely you will agree that they served a much more practical purpose."

"And what is more practical," Lumumba asked, "than bolstering up the imaginary line of the incest taboo?"

"Castles were originally built as a form of defense," Herbert replied. "The people who built them weren't trying to glorify the incest taboo, they were trying to save their skins."

But organized warfare, said Lumumba, was one of the results of the incest taboo. Men didn't kill each other directly anymore, they did it indirectly in the form of warfare. By the way, wasn't it lovely the way men always found a justification for organized warfare? He liked the one about barbarian hordes overrunning civilization. But 'barbarianism' was simply a phrase used to denigrate a different cultural version of the incest taboo. Did we see the hypocrisy? Did we see how men defended that which they hated most? Yes, all men hated the taboo, all men wanted to fuck their mothers. But when a culture came along with a different approach to the taboo—a different way of 'culturing' it in a petri dish and making it grow so that men would obey it—then men had to get rid of it because it was too alien and threatening to their own form of the culture.

"Don't you think," said Herbert, "that people have become more tolerant of other people's cultures?"

His question provoked the gallows laugh from Goldschmidt and Soddhu.

"Not on your life," Lumumba answered. People's distrust was as deep as ever, he said, and would probably stay that way as long as no one wanted to talk about Oedipus. A person knew only his own limitations— what would work for him inorder to keep him away from his mother's bed. From the day he was born he learned these attitudes and taboos as his culture swept him up into its view of the world. Another cultural view— and mind you the world was an inner thing not outer—had no bearing on this person, no hold.

The fear of other cultures stemmed from the fact that its attitudes and taboos wouldn't be able to stop the inner impulses, and the inner boy-child would end up in his mother's bed. Xenophobia was nothing more than a man's fear of his incestuous longings. The biggest xenophobes were the people who deep down wanted it the most—incestuous relations with their mothers, fathers, sisters, brothers, sons and daughters.

All this talk about a New World Order was nothing more than another way of organizing the incest taboo to preserve the power of the fathers which was now represented by corporate industry instead of fortified castles.

"Even if what you say is true," said Herbert, "what are we supposed to do, just lay down and surrender? If we live in that world you describe, we really have no choice but to defend ourselves."

Not true, said Lumumba. If enough people had sex with their mothers all at the same time it would create a kind of energy wave that would roll over the entire planet. The Russians couldn't resist it. The pent-up Arabs couldn't resist. It would be a force as powerful as when men first stood upright and had their brains flooded with the overpowering sexual energy of the straightened spine.

"I never know whether you're kidding or not," said Herbert sourly.

"You don't think that if everyone on the planet was fucking his mother, doing what he wanted to do most, there would be time to fire off a bunch of silly nuclear weapons? And even if there were, have you ever tried to fire a nuclear weapon while having sex with your mother?"

"No, but I'd sure like to," said Goldschmidt. "I'll suggest it to the boys at Langeley. The country needs a good national defense policy. We could call it the Motherfuckers Defense Initiative—MDI. It has a nice ring to it."

"Speaking of rings, here comes another one of those bull signs," said Lumumba. "What say you we pull it down?"

The "bullboard" was secured with rope, everyone pulled and the cutout went down in a cloud of dust.

This activity had bought us to the attention of a herd of bulls grazing in a field a little ways off. At the sound of the thud they came trotting toward us.

"Run!" shouted Herbert.

Everyone dashed to the van, everyone except Lumumba. The bulls came up to him—there were four of them—snorting and bellowing.

"Say goodbye to your uncle," Goldschmidt said to Albert. His voice seemed to waver between joy and sadness.

But the bulls merely stood there and a moment later they folded their legs and lowered themselves to the ground. Lumumba sat down in the middle and began to speak.

"If only there really was a manual," said Goldschmidt wistfully as we cautiously joined the circle.

I was surprised by how well spoken the bulls were—Lumumba translated everything—and how well behaved once they realized we weren't going to drag them into a bullring.

"It's the last thing we want," said a bull named Paco, "regardless of how ferocious we look."

"We know we're supposed to fight humans," said another bull named Carlos. "But we don't know why. I mean if it's a question of size, there are bigger animals than bulls. Why don't humans fight elephants for instance?

I mean, if you start sticking something sharp into an elephant he'll charge too. So will a rhinoceros or a lion!"

"My dear Carlos," Lumumba replied. "If the Spaniards were truly Christians they probably wouldn't be so obsessed with you. But the fact is their Christianity is simply a cover for the archaic roots of Mithraism that run in their sulky Latin bones. Isn't that right, Dr. Págalu? Like the Germans, they are Mithraists at heart. In their unconscious minds they are still worshiping the ancient sun god Mithra and sacrificing bulls in his name."

"I never heard of Mithra," Carlos's friend Pepe said. "Is he a friend of the pope?"

"In many ways yes," said Lumumba.

After the Roman emperors officially took the titles of *pius*, *felix* and *invicties* in the second century A.D.—all epithets inspired by the Persian religion—the Roman Catholic popes followed suit. The new monarch in his *piety* stood to receive the special favor of Heaven, and he was *happy and invincible* because he was insured of its divine grace. Without these Mithraic concepts there would hardly be a church.

The bulls looked astonished and Lumumba, now assured of their high intelligence, continued to elucidate them with the knowledge he himself had only just acquired. Yes, it was the Tauroctonous again, but in Lumumba's hands it had a new twist.

Mithra, the heroic god of the Aryan (Persian) people went out to capture a great bull. The combat was terrifying but in the end Mithra prevailed and succeeded in dragging the animal by its hind legs backward into a cave. The symbolism here was profound: it was the story of bipedal apes wrestling with gravity and orgasm, fighting back the demon testicles, dragging them into the cave, the womb from whence they came—and in this painful process becoming human. The painful Journey (Transitus) suffered by Mithra as he dragged the bull into the cave represented this process, but it was just as easy to point out that the bull suffered just as much, as have all animals have ever since man decided that inorder to repress his animal self he had to declare war on the entire animal kingdom.

"So it's a strictly a phallic contest of wills?" asked a fourth bull named Pancho. "And Mithra proves he's more macho than the bull? I guess that makes sense."

Wait, said Lumumba, the story wasn't over. The bull was able to escape from his prison—the cave, of course, the vagina, the womb—and roam free again. You see how difficult it is to restrain the animal in man? Mithra was ordered by the heavens to go out and find the bull again, only this time to kill him. Mithra didn't really want to, of course. Why kill off that part of you that is totally natural? But he deferred to the will of heaven, Ahura Mazda himself—and killed the bull. At last that irascible part of man—his animal gonads—had been controlled. Then an extraordinary thing happened. From the body of the bull sprang all the plants and herbs in the world. From the spinal cord sprang the wheat that gave men food; and from the blood sprang the vine that produced the sacred drink of the Mysteries. Inother words, the sacrifice of man's animal self brought peace to his tormented species. The bread and wine which would later become Christ's body first came from the bull's.

By the way, he said turning to us. Did we know that the root meaning of *eucharista* was a word meaning greed and desire? No, of course we didn't.

"So we are the Eucharist," said Carlos. "Is that why the toreros always pray to Jesus before they kill us?"

"Yes, my dear friends, I'm afraid so. You are the hapless substitute for the original murders which took place in prehistoric times. The bullfights of today can be read as a symbolic reenactment of these prehistoric struggles. The toreador baits the bull into a frenzied rage, the same rage that dominated men during the time of chaos. He then asserts his mastery over the rage by killing the bull—symbolizing the ascension of the incest taboo as a way to regulate sexual desire, and conquer the terrifying fecundity of women."

"My oh my," said Pancho. "I never imagined that the thing was so complicated and full of sexual overtones. Why, it's beginning to make me feel ashamed to be a bull!"

He lowered his head and looked at his enormous testicles.

"Is there anything I can do about these? I suppose if they weren't there I wouldn't have to fight in the bullring. And after everything you've said I'll be damned if I'm going to be killed for something as stupid as the misunderstandings humans have about their gonads."

"Never be ashamed of your splendid balls," said Lumumba. "It's only because men have turned them into signs of their own interior psychic battleground that it has to spill over into the real world and skewer you boys every weekend infront of thousands of slavering, sexually frustrated Mithra worshipers who throw their hats in the air because they are so stupid."

"Nevertheless," Pancho said, "if my balls weren't there I am very sure the hombres wouldn't take me to the bullring."

"Maybe they could just come down in the ring and have sex with us," said Carlos. "Not that I'd like it but it's better than getting killed."

Goldschmidt was getting excited.

"If only I could whisk you off to my love nest in Amsterdam!" he said to Carlos. "You could service me and my friends non-stop. Zow, it's better than gerbil-stuffing, I say old chap."

"Amsterdam's too far," said Carlos after Lumumba translated. "But maybe we could run away to France. It's just across the border."

"Are you crazy?" said Pepe. "They'll haul you off to the arenas at Arles or Nimes."

"Ah, the old Roman amphitheaters! How apropos for a bullring," said Lumumba.

"I wish I had never been born," said Paco sadly, "at least not as a bull."

"Listen," said Lumumba. "there's not one animal on the planet that hasn't become a hapless victim of man's fight against his own sexuality."

"But we didn't do anything!" said Pancho. "Why don't we just refuse to fight?"

"It's hard to refuse after they stick you with a pick," said Paco slowly.

"He's right," said Lumumba. "Anyway it's the same thing as saying that if every man refused to fight there'd be no more war. You know that's not going to happen. The incest taboo may have stopped young men from killing old men but not from killing each other and all the poor animals. War is an outlet for repressed sexuality and so is the bull fight."

The conversation stopped. For a while there was only the sound of a few pesky flies and the occasional passing car. As everyone played with their own thoughts there was no sign of impending doom, and the earth gave off an impression of peace and happiness. But the tranquility ended when Herbert broke the silence.

"This business about Mithra and the bullrings," he said stubbornly. "I'm not buying it."

"Then go to Merida," said Soddhu. "The bullring is built on the exact same spot where a Mithraeum—a temple to Mithra—once stood. When the Romans were in Spain the soldiers would purchase a bull and have it slaughtered while they crouched under a special grate so that the poor beast's blood would pour all over them."

That said it all. We could be sure that today's blood-spilling in the bullring was identical to the blood-spilling of a thousand years ago. The bull's blood was still being substituted for the father's blood in a rite that recalled the primitive rituals of sons who banded together to kill the primal father and steal his harem. But today the sons hired matadors to do the killing because it was more sanitary and gentrified—at least from the Spaniards' point of view.

306

The bulls swished their tails and bellowed.

"What are they saying now?" Goldschmidt asked.

"They're saying that they're all going to sit under a cork tree and smell the flowers. They won't ever fight again even if they're called fags. And the matadors can go fuck themselves."

But as we walked to the van, something peculiar happened. The bulls began to gore each other and fight.

"By God," said Goldschmidt, "I think they're trying to castrate themselves!"

Lumumba shook his head sadly.

"Poor things, they don't seem to understand that men will kill them anyway with or without their balls. If you are born an animal your fate is sealed no matter what."

"Perhaps it's better to be killed in the slaughterhouse than the bullring," said Tchibanga.

"There's no such thing as a better place to die," said Lumumba, "especially for the hapless victims of man's relentless gonads."

The landscape became fickle. There were rolling hills one minute, then jarring deep gorges the next. The only thing you could depend on were long stretches of pink oleanders growing in the center divider. Another bull sign appeared near Madridejos. As we pulled it to the ground, another huge cloud of dust flew into the air.

"I haven't had this much fun," said Goldschmidt, "since we sent exploding condoms to the prime minister of Burundi."

"If only we could kill somebody," said Yendi, "we could leave our calling card here on the bull."

As if the fates had been listening a black Mercedes pulled up and three men jumped out. They appeared to be around thirty and were all wearing ties and silk suits.

"It's the same men who pulled down the other sign, Miguel," said a man called Luis. "I recognize their van."

Miguel nodded and looked at the sign lying face down on the ground.

"So you do not like Osbourne brandy, Th'ñor?" he said. "Perhaps you will grow to appreciate it after spending a year in jail and drinking only water."

"Brandy?" Lumumba repeated. "Pardon, Señor. We thought your signs were advertising the *cortijos* where they teach young Mithra worshippers to slaughter the bulls."

"How stupid can you get?!" said a third man named Angel. "Everyone and his mother knows the Osborne silhouette, they are all over the country!"

"An unfortunate mistake," said Lumumba humbly, "we are from America."

"Ah, that explains everything!" said Miguel. "They are stupid gringos! Well I tell you what. If you will be kind enough to put the sign back, and also the other one you pulled down, we will not press charges."

"It would take a crane to put the signs back," said Lumumba.

"That is true," said Miguel. "I guess we will have to press charges."

"Can't we all just get along?" said Herbert miserably.

"Obviously not," replied Miguel. "Angel, see if they are armed."

"Let go of my shirt, you little twirp," said Yendi as Angel started to search him. As he took a step backward, a piece of the shirt ripped off in Angel's hands.

"Ai, chinga Chihuahua!" he cried. "It's a werewolf! Everyone run for your life!"

But their speed was no match for the apes, and Luis and Angel were quickly dispatched. Tchibanga spoke despairingly:

"In Africa they called us 'spirit men,' in Egypt they called us baboons, and now they are calling us werewolves. Me oh my, when will these insults all end!"

Miguel, who had fallen to his knees, spoke pleadingly.

"Th'ñor," he said. "I work for one of the richest men in Spain. If it is money you want, he will give it to you."

"We don't want money that's been made off the sweat of poor repressed gonads," said Yendi contemptuously.

"What he means," said Lumumba, seeing Miguel's puzzled look, "is that men find alcohol soothing not because it deadens their brain but because it deadens the terrifying pain of their repressed gonads. It's like this, Señor. The incest taboo creates the need for alcohol, and the need for alcohol creates wealth, and wealth is needed to make men rich. But to have rich men you need to have poor men, and the poor need alcohol to deaden the poverty created by the incest taboo. It's like the Wheel of Life—not the Buddhist version but the GLA version. Do you compréende?"

"Th'ñor, I'm not into this New Age thinking, although some of my sisters are. But I can talk money."

He pulled out his wallet and handed Lumumba a thick wad of bills.

"There's enough here," he said, "to bribe yourselves out of any situation anywhere in Spain."

"I'd rather use it for something more constructive," Lumumba replied as he took the money, "like the GLA Orphans Fund. It's tax exempt, you know. Here's your receipt."

With that he broke the poor man's neck and used his blood to register the infamous acronym.

"General, they don't fool around in Spain, you're asking for trouble," said Goldschmidt.

"But that, my dear fellow, is what the incest taboo is all about."

The rest of the wallets were collected, and Yendi suggested that at least three of our group could change into the men's suits. But Lumumba said that no one would ever wear silk on his watch: the silkworms, he said, were cruelly boiled alive.

As we drove off Albert stared morosely out the window. Lumumba spoke to him in rare good humor.

"What's bothering you, my little Christian zealot? Are you upset about those men?"

"No, not at all. It's what you said to the bulls. How you have the nerve to tell them that the churches and cathedrals are Mithraeums in disguise, and that here in Spain the Son of God, our dear sweet Lord Jesus, is actually a bull, I have no idea. It's such sacrilege! I must put my foot down, dear uncle."

Goldschmidt looked relieved.

"Apparently I was wrong and all is not lost," he said. "This is the most unshakable brainwashing I've ever seen, better than a Coca Cola commercial or the Moonies. You did a damn good job, Dr. Hickey, Dr. Págalu."

"Oh shut up," said Herbert irritably. He was watching Soddhu make eyes at me. Albert continued.

"You can say all you want about the bullfights being Mithraic in origin, that they are symptoms of a religious pathology that afflicts all men in one form or another, that they are a way for Christians to keep alive the Roman sacrifices to Mithra by symbolically drenching themselves in the same hot blood as the Roman legions did when they crouched beneath the grate in Andalusia. You can say these things all you want, it's okay because no heathen gibberish can eliminate my faith."

"Spoken like a true Christian!" Goldschmidt said happily.

"Yes, but what *is* a true Christian?" said Lumumba. "According to our friend here"—he nodded toward Soddhu—"the idea of a Savior and the Virgin who gives birth to a Savior; the idea of heaven and hell; the final battle between good and evil and the bathing of the world in fire; the Final Judgment and the resurrection of the dead; shepherds bearing gifts to a child; a flood story and an ark; and a story that tells about drawing water from a rock—those are all Zoroastrian concepts which have filtered down into Christianity. Or haven't you been listening?! Perhaps a true Christian is actually a lapsed Mithraist."

"But how could they have so many things in common if they are completely different religions?" Albert asked.

"That's what I'm trying to tell you," said Lumumba. "They are one and the same thing with a few minor differences, and their real purpose is not to explain the world but to find a solution to the problem of desire."

Men needed to invent God, he said, because if primitive men had acknowledged their desire they could never have controlled it. The only way they could gain control of the situation was through repression, and religion *was* repression. It was a systematic replacement of the truth with a fiction—but a very special kind of fiction, a fiction that told the truth if you looked at it closely. Remember what he said, how the word for religion actually meant 'to tie back with ligaments'? Of course the use of a ligament could be purely metaphorical, but it was easy to visualize a time when men, or half men, were so crazed that they used real ligaments—living cords you might call them—to teach lessons or inflict punishments—a practice that eventually led to the belief in God.

"If what you say is true," said Albert, "and God is nothing but a story men invented to escape their own desires, then that would mean that I'm the one who has betrayed God—because the true God is my animal self."

"In a manner of speaking, yes," Lumumba replied.

"Listen, Albert," said Goldschmidt. "If you succeed in turning yourself back into an ape you'll have wasted a lot of taxpayer's money. The CIA doesn't operate on a shoestring, you know. It took a lot of $100,000-a-year company men to buy up Yale's administration and bribe the grants committee so that our project would go through."

"Woe is me," said Albert, "it looks like I'm caught between a rock and hard place. How can I ever return to Mahale when I owe so much to Yale?"

The graceful countryside with its planted fields and pretty villages was slowly but steadily giving way to the ugly, non-descript buildings known as urban sprawl. As we neared Madrid the freeway became fast and furious, an impossible convergence of interconnecting lanes filled with traffic and turnoffs.

"Burgos! Burgos!" Herbert screamed. But it was too late. The lane we were in pointed to Madrid. Lumumba pounded the steering wheel and swore.

310

"By the time we get to Altamira, Muñoz will be back in New Haven!" he shouted

"Say, General," said Goldschmidt, "is traffic part of the insect taboo?"

"Sure, why not? If people were fucking their mothers they'd probably want to stay home all day."

Whether it was his erratic driving or sheer bad luck, a policeman on a motorcycle pulled up next to us and looked in the window. Immediately he dropped back.

"I hope to God he didn't recognize us," said Herbert.

"Why should he?" said Lumumba. "There's no one alive to give our description."

"You've forgotten don Francisco."

A few minutes later we heard sirens. Lumumba checked the rear view mirror and swore: a line of motorcycles and squad cars was trailing behind us.

"All this because we pulled down a couple of billboards?" asked Yendi.

"I doubt it's because of the airplane and a couple of hundred dead bodies," said Goldschmidt sarcastically. "Oh well, now I'll have a nice time contemplating your uncle's head mounted on my trophy wall in Kenya."

"Oh how I wish I had died with Kribi!" said Yalinga. "Human life is so cluttered and stressful. Someone is always trying to kill you!"

"My dear niece," said Lumumba, turning off the freeway. "We've come this far, haven't we? Just hang in there. All this killing is leading us closer to the truth."

Kumasi opened his mouth to recite his favorite aphorism but Goldschmidt broke in angrily: "I don't care if the truth *is* the biggest penis in the world. There's no way out of this, General. You'll have to pull over. The game is up."

"Not till the fat monkey sings," Lumumba replied lightly.

Near the Shrine of the Virgin we found ourselves in traffic that made the streets of Cairo seem deserted. It was even worse along a street named the Virgin del Puerto.

"What was it you said about virgins?" asked Soddhu absentmindedly.

"I said that the reason men love to sleep with them is because in their hearts they are really sleeping with their daughters."

"If only the Magi were in power," said Soddhu wistfully. "Men's dreams might come true."

"But they aren't in power," said Albert, "because they went to Bethlehem to worship Jesus."

"You're missing the point," said Lumumba. "By preaching to the choir that the Zoroastrian priests had come to worship Jesus, the Christian theologians were able to propagate the belief that their rival religion had finally been defeated."

"Amen," said Soddhu giving Lumumba an adoring look. "Finally someone speaks the truth! If only Dean Wiggins were here to hear it."

"The truth is a tree and the tree is a phallus," said old Kumasi firmly. "Isn't that the truth."

The roads were jammed in all directions, and in some streets traffic had come to a complete stop. Our "tail" fell behind.

"Something's going on at the palace," said Lumumba, straining his eyes toward a knoll just ahead. "What day is this?"

"Thursday," said Soddhu checking his watch.

"*Maundy* Thursday," Lumumba corrected. "Pedro was right, there must be a million people here."

He took a handkerchief from his pocket and held it over his nose. The stench of dead carcasses in their stomachs, he said, was driving him crazy. Nevertheless we inched our way toward the palace, and at Calle Segovia we abandoned the van and went the rest of the way on foot. Lumumba's plan was to lose ourselves in the fray and afterwards find another car. What he hadn't counted on was being swept up by this wave of humanity and herded onto the palace grounds.

"At least we've lost the cops," he crowed.

But poor Kumasi was about to fall down and Yalinga was hard pressed keeping hold of Okovango. We pushed our way to the front lines facing the parade grounds. Several officials were standing there perusing the crowd.

"Now's our chance," Lumumba called out. But as we started to edge toward the gate one of the officials suddenly pointed in our direction. "Ellos!" he shouted. "Them!"

"Ha, ha!" Goldschmidt trumpeted shrilly. "The seat of the incest taboo's got you by the seat of your pants, General."

Lumumba was about to bolt when a man next to us said, "Do not be ashamed, Th'ñor. It is a great honor to have your feet washed by His Royal Majesty, Juan Carlos."

"I'm afraid they'll have to find someone else," said Lumumba sharply.

"That will be difficult, Th'ñor, since you and your friends are the sorriest excuses for human beings we've ever seen," the man answered. "A thousand pardons for saying so."

"There are people who look worse than we do," said Goldschmidt sounding offended.

"No, Th'ñor, believe me there aren't," the man replied.

"Go," said a woman, "they will feed you in the kitchen after the ceremony."

"Actually I think we are quite hungry," Lumumba replied. He had just noticed a dozen policemen inching their way forward.

"Come," said the official. He was very excited as he and another man escorted us into the palace. "Have you ever seen beggars like these, Manuel? The Cardinal should be very pleased," he said.

"Th'i, Sancho, and wait till he sees they're deaf and dumb to boot," Manuel replied. "I imagine His Royal Majesty should really be roiled."

"Do you have a feeling we're being used?" Herbert asked Lumumba.

"It's better than being shot," Lumumba replied.

"But we'll be shot anyway," said Tchibanga, "when they see our feet."

"I'm counting on Mr. Goldschmidt to prevent that from happening. He'll be in a lot of trouble if he doesn't."

As we entered the Royal Chapel there was an audible gasp from the many people who had been invited to the ceremony.

"What's the matter," said Yendi, "they don't like our clothes?"

A homeless beggar who had been chosen to be the twelfth apostle began to tremble violently. I could see why. The chapel itself was like a palace; everything seemed to be made of gold.

"More virgins," said Soddhu pointing to some frescoes on the ceiling.

As I stared at the magnificence, the feeling came over me that I was in a place forbidden to ordinary people, a place that emitted magic and mystery. It was the place that children dream of, perhaps because the first stories they ever learned were of kings and queens and love-sick princesses and princes disguised as toads.

But by now I knew what Lumumba would say, that the spell was woven into the most primitive parts of the psyche, a kind of pre-symbolic fantasy filled with the splendid but distorted icons of the adult world, a place where the reptilian brain was being seduced by the stories of the cerebral cortex.

The palace, he would say, was the symbolic seat of the incest taboo and one of its most popular and longest ingrained conceptualizations;

inother words an illusion, but also a monument to man's inhumanity to man. For every gold filigree on the ceiling someone had had to die. The palace was built on the wrecked lives of those who had toiled in the gold and silver mines of Peru. But what was that to us? The incest taboo had to be fed with human lives and lies inorder to keep it alive. That was our way of dealing with incest, and the forbidden palace was the place where a child could live out its forbidden fantasies in secret, and a king could live out his in public.

Goldschmidt took his seat next to Albert.

"Having the king of Spain wash my kike feet will be a real honor," he said with a sneer.

There was a nervous twitter and a moment later a sentinel appeared at the doorway.

"His Royal Majesty, El Rey Don Juan Carlos de Bourbon! Her Royal Majesty Queen dona Sofia de Bourbon!" he shouted.

"They must think we're deaf," said Tchibanga irritably as the king and queen took their seats on the gold dais next to the altar.

"His Eminence, Cardinal Gomez!"

As the Cardinal entered, Albert almost jumped to his feet.

"Why look!" he said. "The Cardinal's wearing the vagina hat! Oh uncle, do you think he'll let me try it on?"

"You silly thing," said Yalinga. "Why wear that when you can have the real thing?"

"Gomez, gomez," said Yendi, "where have I heard that word before?"

"It's the bull's urine I was telling you about," said Soddhu. "Remember the purification rites of the Magi? Water, sand and gomez—that was the perfect mixture to ward off the devil."

"You said it was the mingled urine of a man and woman who've performed Khvetukdas," said Albert.

"Actually they're both supposed to work equally well," Soddhu replied.

The sign language had been duly noted, and indeed the cardinal looked quite pleased whereas the king did not. Neither did the grandee who stood in attendance.

The ceremony began, passages were read from the Bible, a huge monstrance of gold and silver was lifted off the altar.

"You see how the sunburst supports the cross?" said Lumumba ignoring the ceremony. "It's a perfect example of the way Mithraism and Christianity have blended together, and how the glory of orgasm is associated with the power of the sun. Very pagan, of course, the entire concept."

314

The cardinal smiled. So did Sancho and Manuel and several others in the room. It was easy to see who was allied with the cardinal and who was allied with the king. It seemed to be about fifty-fifty with a slight tilt in the king's favor.

But now it was time for Juan Carlos to perform the ceremony. Accompanied by the cardinal and grandee, he went to the beggar first and sprinkled the poor man's feet with perfumed water. He then made a ceremonial gesture as if to dry them, and leaned forward as if to kiss them. The beggar almost fainted, and sighed with relief as the three moved on to the next apostle. The 'washing' was quickly repeated on Herbert's feet, mine, Soddhu's and Goldschmidt's. Lumumba's turn was next.

"Th'ñor, you must remove your shoes," said the Grandee in a loud whisper. The cardinal was hardly able to conceal his amusement.

"Do I have to?" said Lumumba. "I'm very self-conscious."

"You should have thought of that sooner. Now please hurry up," replied the grandee.

"Okay, Gramps," said Lumumba, "whatever you say."

As he took off his shoes so did the other apes. At the sight of their prehensile toes, there was an audible gasp across the room and the cardinal's face grew white. He turned angrily to the king.

"Your Royal Highness, what is the meaning of this?" he said through his teeth.

Before Juan Carlos could reply the grandee put aside the chalice of water and spoke in his ear: "If the cardinal thinks you've done this on purpose, your Majesty, then why not take the credit? It's a feather in your cap, if you ask me."

"Th'i, you're right, don Felipe."

He turned to the cardinal and smiled.

"Your Eminence," said the king, "we are all God's creatures, are we not?"

"Yes, of course," Cardinal Gomez replied bowing his head stiffly and sending a killing look at Manuel and Sancho. The ceremony continued, don Felipe advised the king again:

"Invite these mendicants to the State Dinner tonight. Perhaps that will be the final straw, your Majesty, and the cardinal will stop fighting us."

"I must reward Sancho and Manuel for sending me this plum."

"Truth is stranger than fiction, your Majesty," the grandee replied.

As the entourage stopped infront of Albert the little ape began to gesticulate wildly.

"What is he saying," Cardinal Gomez asked in an icy voice.

"He wants to know if he can try on your hat," said Soddhu.

"What impudence!" said the cardinal. "Tell you friend that this hat is only worn by the princes of the Church. For us it's the same as a royal crown."

"My friend says it looks more like a royal vagina," Soddhu replied.

The cardinal glared at Juan Carlos.

"And you accuse the priests of being dirty!"

There was one final debacle. A feast had been prepared with many sumptuous dishes. They were to be offered to us by the king, but Sancho had instructed us earlier not to eat, it was only done for ceremony. But as the food was passed around the apes plunged their hands into it and began to consume all the dishes made of vegetables, pastry and fruit.

"Th'ñores e Th'ñoras, your behavior is outrageous!" Cardinal Gomez shouted.

"We are Americans," said Lumumba sucking down a tart. "We don't know any better."

"And we don't worship the incest taboo either," Tchibanga added.

Goldschmidt reached for the meat but Yendi caught his hand and smacked it.

"Lips that touch swine will never touch mine," he said, giving Goldschmidt's cheek a tweak.

The cardinal gasped, and no longer able to restrain himself stormed from the room.

"Isn't the king supposed to leave first?" Yendi called after him.

The chapel emptied out quickly, even the beggar had the good sense to leave. We were about to follow suit when Manuel reappeared along with Sancho.

"Please do not leave, Th'ñores e Th'ñoras, the king has requested your presence at a dinner he is holding tonight for a delegation of U.S. congressmen. If you will follow me?"

"I'm sorry but we have a plane to catch," said Lumumba.

"His Royal Majesty will not take no for an answer."

To prove this Manuel snapped his fingers and a retinue of palace guards appeared holding rifles.

"On second thought," said Lumumba, "we can catch it later."

"Grathias, Th'ñor. You have made the right decision."

A string quartet was playing some lively chamber music as we entered the reception hall just off the gala dining room. Waiters dressed in fancy livery walked through the animated crowd with flutes of champagne and trays of hors-d'oeuvres which had been made of bananas, said Sancho, in our honor.

As all eyes turned in our direction, Lumumba shook his head unhappily.

"We need to get out of here," he said. "This is a dangerous place."

"Perhaps they're just admiring our clothes," said Yalinga. The palace had given us some very beautiful ones, and Yalinga looked especially nice in a gold evening gown and matching gold slippers.

"Oh what the hell," said Goldschmidt. "You're here until you're gone, you're alive until your dead. We may never be invited here again, so let's live it up a little."

With that he went to talk to a congressman.

"If the professor gets us out of this one it'll be a miracle," Herbert muttered.

But a miracle had seemingly occurred regarding the cardinal. He spoke pleasantly to Juan Carlos and even joked with Albert about the vagina hat.

"It's really called a miter," the cardinal said casually.

"A what?" asked Lumumba, all of a sudden interested.

"The word is from the Latin *mitra*. But it actually comes from the old Persian word *mithra* referring to the headgear worn by the ancient priests of that country."

For once Lumumba was speechless. Was he thinking what I was thinking, that this fabulous ceremonial hat came straight from the Magi, the men of Khvetukdas, the men of the gomez?

The king, meanwhile, seeing that the cardinal remained unruffled, even when one of the apes told him that his name might be traceable to bull's urine, began to look troubled. Several times I saw him converge with his grandees, then look in our direction.

God save the king, I heard myself thinking. But if God is orgasm, as Lumumba said He was, what did the king have to do with orgasm? What did the king have to do with the incest taboo? As I looked at Juan Carlos I tried to get the thoughts clear in my mind. The king rules by divine right. He is the earthly representative of God. But God is orgasm, so what is the king? The earthly representative of orgasm? The spokesperson for orgasm? The controller of the gonads? In the old days the king was the go-between, between God and man. But God is orgasm, we worship orgasm and the king gets his power from that worship. Ah, that's it! The people allow themselves to be ruled by the king because they believe he is a spokesperson for orgasm. The king keeps orgasm in check. The king helps control the gonads. The king keeps the incest taboo alive. What was that line? The king is dead, long live the king; inother words, there must never be a lapse in the king's rule—that is, in man's vigilant watch over the wily gonads.

Ah, wouldn't Lumumba be proud of me, I thought, as we followed their Royal Majesties into the Gala Dining Room. It was spanned by a single long table capable of seating, Sancho had said, over a hundred and forty people. Above our heads there were fifteen chandeliers and a gilded ceiling covered with frescoes.

"Boy, this insect taboo is something else!" said Albert as his eyes wandered around the room, from the large tapestries to the marble columns and bronze and porcelain vases.

"Yes, definitely not too shabby," Soddhu agreed.

"Man's homage to orgasm never is," said Lumumba.

Their Royal Majesties were seated at the head of the table, while our party was seated close by.

Lumumba sat to the left of the queen, then came myself, Albert, Cardinal Gomez, the Duchess of Caceres, Yendi, the Countess of Monte Christo, Goldschmidt, Princess Hortensia of Bulgaria, Herbert, and Prince Mark of Macedonia. Yalinga with Okovango sat near the king and to her right was Soddhu, the Countess of Salamanca, Tchibanga, the Lady Grandee of Cordillera, Kumasi, the Duchess of Badajoz, and Congressman Brown and his wife. Beyond Mrs. Brown the table dissolved into a blur of faces belonging to a hundred or so Spaniards and the rest of the Congressional delegation.

"I don't understand this," Brown said to Goldschmidt. "According to the State Department document, His Royal Majesty was supposed to seat *our* delegation at the head of the table. Instead, he's put a mere professor there."

"My dear Congressman," said Goldschmidt, "rest assured that is no mere professor. Nevertheless when I return to my desk in Nairobi, I'll look into it straight away. Perhaps someone's head should roll in Washington. But look on the bright side; this way you and I can get to know each other."

The string quartet removed itself to the dining room and began to play Mozart.

"Would you rather hear 'Bungle in the Jungle?' " Prince Mark said to Lumumba. The prince looked at the cardinal and winked.

"Actually," replied Lumumba, "I would rather hear Mozart's 'Eine Kleine Nacht Musik.' I used to listen to it while I was doing my dissertation on the origins of music inside the gonads. Are you aware of the mathematical similarities between orgasmic electrons and music?"

"Ah, you know music," said Juan Carlos impressed. "Later I will show you my Stradivarius collection. It's in the next room."

He rose to give a toast.

"Let us drink to the health of our good friends who are here with us tonight from America. They could not have come at a timelier moment."

"Salud, salud," said the crowd. But the toast was unclear, and while some lifted their glasses to the congressmen others lifted theirs to the apes.

"What an ugly fellow," Brown said to Goldschmidt as Lumumba rose to take a bow. "What is he a professor of?"

"Particle Sexuality and Atomic Orgasm," Goldschmidt replied. "It's a relatively new field of scientific inquiry."

"Must be why I haven't heard of it. Ugh, what's this?"

The waiter had just placed a silver tray infront of him piled high with bananas. Similar trays were being placed up and down the table. The Duchess of Badajoz turned to Brown. "Do not cry," she said. "In honor of our esteemed guests we are all going to eat every banana recipe in the kingdom tonight."

"We came all this way," Brown replied furiously, "to eat bananas? I had my heart set on wild boar and bull's testicles in cream sauce. That's what it said on the State Department's printout, anyway."

"Perhaps," said the duchess chillingly, "you should pay less attention to printouts from your State Department."

Brown returned her look with equal coldness. "Listen you tin-plated old battleship, just because you're a duchess doesn't mean you can talk to *me* that way."

The duchess looked like she was going to fire a salvo from her rusty main guns, but the Congressman's wife intervened. "You must forgive him," she said. "The truth is he doesn't like women all that well. We only got married so he could be elected."

"How sad for you," the duchess replied. "I myself love women. But why shouldn't I since I am one? But I also like dark handsome men with just a little bit of gray." She turned her watery eyes to Kumasi and gave him an adoring look.

"You must be blind, sister, if you think he has just a little grey," said Brown.

"The truth is a tree and the tree is a phallus," said Kumasi pleasantly, spitting pieces of banana soufflé onto the duchess's bosom.

"Is that a riddle?" she asked.

"Yes," said Lumumba, "and if you can answer it you'll have unlocked the deepest mysteries and darkest secrets of human civilization."

"There are certain mysteries best kept locked, Th'ñor," said Cardinal Gomez.

"Ah, yes," said Lumumba, "otherwise you might be out of a job, eh Your Eminence?"

The cardinal only smiled, and the other guests tried to solve the riddle. No one was able to, of course, not even the king, so it remained for Lumumba to explain it, which he did as the last course was being served.

For us it was old hash, but the Spaniards listened with rapt attention as Lumumba went over it again, how the conceptualization of truth emanated from two sources. The first was the tree, the idea being that to tell the truth (which, unlike a lie, has the same firmness and substance as a tree) you must talk as straight as a tree. But the second source, which was actually more important than the first, was the penis. As the ultimate measure of all things, it was as firm and straight as a tree, hence the truth. And not only was the truth measured by the penis. Everything else was too, from mathematics to kingship, soup to nuts; without this proper measurement there would be no civilization.

The cardinal's lips curled ever so slightly.

"You are saying, Th'ñor, that in some way His Royal Majesty is mixed up in the worship of the phallus?"

"Bingo! Advance to GO," Lumumba replied. "But let me explain."

The king, he said, taking up a theme he had touched upon in Egypt, was the measure of all things, was he not? But this measure was a linear measure, a straight line which came from the Latin word *rex* meaning king. It was impossible to deny the kinship between *this* straight line and a line as straight as the erect penis. Naturally this etymology applied not only to kings ('straight measurers') of a country, but also to those straight measurers of the Church such as priests, bishops and cardinals. The pope, of course, was the straightest measure of all. But the great irony was that while the fathers of the church had gained their power from this ancient conceptualization of the penis, when it came to controlling their own carnal desires they were like kids let loose in a candy store.

But this was not surprising. Considering how surrounded they were, day in and day out, by so much sexual symbolism—huge phallic candlesticks, holy semen water and such—what choice did they really have in the matter?

The room grew suddenly quiet, Cardinal Gomez rose slowly to his feet.

"You've had your fun, Th'ñor, now I shall have mine."

"Sit down, Gomez," the king ordered. "We can talk about this later."

"Forgive me, your Majesty, but I'm afraid we can't. Everything I've heard tonight—orgasm, penises, the truth—is your way of saying you want me to punish my priests. Well, Sir, I will bow to your wishes but under one condition."

"Namely?"

"That you turn these miscreants over to the police. As members of the Gonad Liberation Army they have committed crimes far more severe than anything the church has ever done to the faithful."

The Cardinal pulled out a document and handed it to the king. At the same moment what appeared to be the entire Spanish army descended upon the room.

"Oh, damn," said Goldschmidt. "We shall be gunned down before I finish my bananas almandine!"

"If you are responsible for this food," said the Congressman, "then you deserve to be shot."

"What district did you say you were from? When I get home I'll tell all my friends not to vote for you. Yikes, I hope they don't shoot Lumumba in the head. According to my taxidermist head shots are hell to repair."

"Your Eminence, if I may argue?" said a young man who had risen to face the cardinal. "To be molested as a child is to be condemned to a living death. At least their victims"—he looked at us—"died a quick death."

"That may be true," said Cardinal Gomez as the man took his seat to a scattering of applause. "But in their most recent acts of terrorism, they tore down our beloved Osborne bulls. This is an outrage which cannot go unpunished."

"Here, here!" said don Felipe, his alcohol-sodden cheeks flushed purple with rage.

"Th'ñores, you are under arrest," said His Royal Majesty.

No sooner had he spoken than Lumumba pulled the Duchess of Cacares from her seat and swung himself onto a chandelier. The other apes followed taking their dinner partners with them. Albert pulled up the cardinal, Kumasi took the Duchess of Badajoz (she looked quite happy), Yendi, the Countess of Monte Cristo, and Tchibanga, the Countess of Salamanca. Yalinga was the last to follow, it was difficult pulling Okovango away from the banana trifle.

"Head for the door!" Lumumba shouted. As the apes swung overhead from chandelier to chandelier, one of the soldiers fired. A look of bewilderment crossed Yalinga's face as she fell. With a heavy thud she hit the table, then rolled to the floor and lay motionless in a crumpled heap. As Okovango crawled out from under her I grabbed him and hurried toward the door.

"You're okay until you're not," said old Kumasi sadly, "nothing happens until it does."

The duchess nodded and caressed his goatee with an expert hand.

As the apes gazed at Yalinga's motionless body Goldschmidt pulled out his CIA and State Department identification cards and threw them in the commanding officer's face.

"You've made a terrible mistake," he said. "A lot of heads are going to roll for this."

Before the officer could recover from his surprise we made a quick exit. The apes followed suit, but not before dropping the cardinal into a vat of banana trifle. The others were set down just outside the doorway.

"Till we meet again," the duchess called after us.

Chapter Twenty-Four

In Which It Is Told How Kumasi Becomes Spain's Greatest National Hero

"Galloping groupers!" yelled Goldschmidt. "Those things are worth millions!"

In his anger and frustration Lumumba had broken into the cases displaying the king's Stradivari collection and proceeded to smash the four instruments into tiny bits and pieces.

"I had always wanted to meet the human incarnation of the incest taboo," he said, "but not at so terrible a price. These things which are dear to his heart are now worth nothing, but then, were they ever? Or were they simply more figments of the imagination, more manifestations of the incest taboo? Humans can't fuck their mothers so they make music instead. The excess electricity denied passage to the forbidden object of desire finds its way into the brain where it's transformed into the mathematics of music. Everything in your culture which sublimates your sexual desires causes problems for us. I have no love for these."

"That is obvious," said Soddhu taking one last glance at the catastrophic mess. Many of the strings were still vibrating as if they were alive but taking their last breaths before dying.

We came to a balcony above the stables. It was enclosed in glass, but Lumumba broke it open with a bust of King Ferdinand V. We hurried down a flight of stairs onto the esplanade which led to a garden and another flight of stairs. Climbing up we came to the street. It was Calle Segovia and the van was still there, but now it wouldn't start.

"I think we're in trouble," said Goldschmidt. It was starting to get light and the streets were awash in sirens.

A familiar voice called out from the street.

"Buenos th'ias, Th'ñores, Th'ñora. Como amanesio? (How was your sunrise?) Don't tell me you were at the ceremony! I looked for you but I didn't see you."

It was Pedro our old steward, but what was he doing in a limousine with the king's license plates?

"My cousin got me this job, driving the dignitaries around. For some strange reason I don't want to fly anymore."

Without being invited we all piled in.

"Where is the little one's mother?" he asked, seeing Okovango asleep in my arms.

"She's dead," Lumumba replied, "and you'll be dead too unless you get us the hell out of here."

"Th'ñor," said Pedro sounding hurt. "I told you before that I would go with you anywhere. I meant what I said, there's no need to make threats."

"Then why aren't we vamoosing?"

"I am supposed to be picking up some dignitaries from America."

"We are those dignitaries, for God's sake! Now let's go," said Goldschmidt.

"My, my, everybody is so impatient these days. You would think that after walking way from a plane crash one would have a different perspective on life."

"What you think," said old Kumasi, "is not always right, and what is right is not always what you think."

"Did you tell that to the duchess?" Yendi asked. Kumasi nodded, then rolled his head on his chest and fell asleep.

We went along Calle de Alcala then passed the arched façade of the Puerta de Alcalá. This was the old part of Madrid, resplendent with trees and parks and palace-style buildings. Even the smallest ones had grandeur, and there was a sense of the Alhambra everywhere. I pictured beautiful Spanish women in flowing mantillas fanning themselves coquettishly atop their balconies. Lumumba ridiculed my sentiments.

"There's no beauty here," he said cuttingly, "only the illusions programmed into you by your culture. These fat, thick buildings with their ridiculous neo-classical facades are nothing more than a fantasy regression to some mythological past when gods and goddesses watched over men who played like happy children in a flowering garden."

"I can see, Th'ñor, you are not in a good mood," said Pedro. "Here we are driving in the king's limousine and you sound like the Grinch who stole Christmas."

324

"Perhaps I am," said Lumumba. As his eyes went from Kumasi to Okovango he resumed his analysis of the city in a tone of rancor and disdain.

The buildings, he said, were imprinted with the symptomatology of the archetypical desires they both repressed and expressed. The conflict between love and desire for the mother and terror of the bullying, rampaging father was everywhere, in the spires of the cathedrals where one could almost feel the throbbing pulse of the primal father as he thrust his stone phallus into the heavens; and in the massive weight of the civic buildings which imposed a father's laws on the terrified child cowering in their shadows. Yes, the phallocracy of government institutions and internalized social rules grinding the terror of the father into the child's flesh was only too obvious. The city was a psychic war zone, bristling with the symbols of early childhood desires and terrors, and only a human, brainwashed by the propaganda of sublimations, would be able to find it beautiful.

"I always wondered," said Pedro, "why there was so much traffic here."

We turned north onto Paseo de Recoletos. A few minutes later the buildings of old Madrid were replaced by modern skyscrapers or, as Lumumba put it, the perfect blend of religion and money, obelisks crammed with offices reaching toward the heavens in search of sublimated orgasm. It was no coincidence that the world's tallest building—the Twin Towers in Kuala Lumpur—was located in a Moslem country. Surely one could find an equation in which it was stated that the stricter the taboo the greater the sublimation.

Was that why an architect from Yale had been chosen to build the towers, Herbert wanted to know?

"Muscles, tendons and all," Lumumba replied. It was business as usual. The rigid tenets of Islam were not at all opposed to the fundamental ideas of Christianity so deeply ensconced at Yale. The movers and shakers of the world everywhere were all motivated by a need to sublimate orgasm. That's how civilization began, and that's how it would end. The leaders of the world had no other agenda than to keep the taboo alive, and if they blew up the world to do it, well, wasn't that what Armageddon was all about?

An hour later the skyline of Madrid was merely a smudge on the horizon, and the landscape returned to its pastoral loveliness. We came to Buitrago, a picturesque village of white houses and red-tiled roofs. It was built alongside a canal, and there were people in it swimming. Lumumba's nose wrinkled at the faint stench of sewage coming off the water.

"Might as well do what the natives are doing," he said. Pedro stopped and they all went off to relieve themselves. When they returned they were in a much better mood than before.

"The lake's at least an inch deeper," said Tchibanga proudly.

"The truth is a tree and the tree is a phallus," said Kumasi waking up from his sleep. "Even for chimps."

"I say, General," said Goldschmidt climbing into the car. "We could make a good team, you and I. How would you like a job at the embassy when this is all over?"

"I suppose there's always room for a secret agent who can scale a building and then look great in a tux," said Lumumba.

"Absolutely," said Goldschmidt. "Your talents would certainly not go to waste."

"The question is," said Yendi, "how could you tell the real chimpanzees from the Neanderthal apes that work in the agency?"

"That's right," said Tchibanga. "Aren't there enough monkeys working there already?"

We continued on. The towns passed by slowly: Robregordo, Bocequillas, Milagros. The hills had been stripped of trees, and Lumumba said that man had a great ambivalence toward trees. He loved them and hated them, worshiped them and destroyed them. All this because of his fear of the gonads.

"Oh come now," Goldschmidt groaned. "Do you really want to make the case that environmental degradation—to use a term favored by you environmentalists—is due to the incest taboo?"

"Why not?" Lumumba replied. "If civilization is based on this one taboo, then surely everything else is an offshoot."

"*If*," said Goldschmidt sourly. "If."

"I have to side with Goldschmidt," said Herbert. "We need raw materials inorder to build things we need to live comfortably."

"As usual the seemingly rational explanation is covering over a deeper explanation," said Lumumba. In truth, he went on, it was nothing but a holy war man was waging against nature. The aggression against nature came from sexual repression. Man hated what was natural in his unrelenting attempt to beat down the sexual stirrings forbidden by the incest taboo, and he used nature as a whipping boy and scapegoat. Was it logical to strip the forests? No, but strip them he did—it was his way of beating down the phallus.

Well, why not? Didn't the oppressive fathers beat their sons into submission, forcing them to sublimate the maternal object for something else? Little wonder their aggression should be directed against Mother

326

Nature. It was really not a metaphor when people talked about raping the environment. Men were simply acting out their hatred of the father by taking Mother Nature—the mother—by force and violating her to destroy her virgin affiliation with the father.

"Don't get me wrong," he concluded. "I don't care how tormented you are by your petty sexual desires. But it sure is a shame that you have to destroy the planet inorder to work them out."

Kumasi started to express his opinion on trees and phalluses, but fell asleep before he could. The apes looked worried and Okovango wanted to sit in his lap but Lumumba motioned for him to let Kumasi rest.

We stopped at a hostel to buy food. Kumasi woke up but seemed confused. Lumumba put his hand on Kumasi's shoulder.

"Wait here old friend, we'll bring something out to you."

In a little while we came to a waterfall along the side of the road. Lumumba stopped and let the apes drink from a pool of water. Lumumba filled Pedro's cap with the refreshing drink and brought it to Kumasi, but the old ape turned his head away, closed his eyes and went back to sleep.

Later as we were passing a stand of fir trees he opened his eyes and said: "Remember, Albert, that the truth is a tree and the tree is a phallus."

"I will never forget it," Albert replied. "You may rest assured of that."

Okovango squirmed free and settled on Kumasi's lap.

Kumasi nodded and went to sleep again. The afternoon wore on slowly. Pedro drove at a snail's pace and the Spanish landscape passed by uneventfully. There were no bull signs to tear down, and the hills and valleys were dotted with nothing more ominous than the villages and houses of farmers.

"At the rate we're going," Goldschmidt said, "we should reach Altamira in about two years."

"But no caterpillars have been run over," said Yendi, "so shut up."

Pedro tried to make conversation.

"We are heading toward El Cid country. Have you heard of him?"

"We saw the movie," said Herbert. "Charleton Heston and Sophia Loren."

"Ah yes, a perfect vehicle for Heston. But El Cid is more than Moses and the NRA," Pedro replied. "To Spaniards he is El Cid Compeador, the champion of Castille and spirit of the Reconquest when the Catholic kings were fighting the Moors. Why, in a word he is Spain itself!"

"Hmmm," said Lumumba, "I rather thought he was a bit of a scoundrel who became sanitized and eulogized through a fluke of nature. Inaccurate history, you know, is often rooted in the incest taboo."

"What does the incest taboo have to do with El Cid?!" asked Pedro abruptly.

"My dear Pedro," said Lumumba, "you cannot separate politics and religion from the incest taboo since basically they are one and the same thing; but since there are so many facets to each one, the identicalness becomes lost to the naked eye."

Now without a doubt, said Lumumba, El Cid was merely a rogue, a sort of a twelfth century mercenary fighting for whoever paid the most—Moslems one day, Christians the next. The name itself, El Cid—his real name was Rodrigo Diaz de Vivar—sort of meant 'big shot' in Arabic. But the poets, as they usually did, ignored the facts and fabricated El Cid as a perfect representative of the supposedly chivalrous values of the Spanish aristocrats. It was actually a very telling process, since the historical El Cid behaved very much the way the aristocrats themselves behaved—deceitfully changing sides whenever it looked like it was to his advantage, whereas the fictional El Cid behaved the way the aristocrats wanted to see themselves and have others see them—as heroes and gentlemen. It was a very good example of the way human art worked as a tool of ideology—ultimately, that is, of the incest taboo, since heroes and gentlemen—e.g., the romanticized male—acted as bulwarks against any encroachments to the taboo.

We pulled into a rest stop where all the signs were written in Arabic.

"Come July," said Pedro, "this place will be crawling with Arabs off on their holidays. It's very funny to see them, they bring their mattresses along and lie down next to their automobiles."

"History would have been a lot different had Zarathustra prevailed," said Soddhu sullenly.

"Instead of complaining," said Herbert, "why don't you just be grateful that there are any of you still left?"

"Who says I'm not?" Soddhu replied. "Every time I'm in a city where there's a fire temple I drop to my knees and say a hundred *ashem vohus*: 'Holiness is the best of all good. Well is it for that, well is it for that holiness which is perfection of holiness.' "

"I'd say that has a certain ring to it," said Albert.

"I told you before," Goldschmidt said roughly, "if you want to go to Washington and meet the big shots—maybe even the president—you'll have to toe the line and forget all this nonsense. Dr. Págalu, I insist that you stop discussing your religion. The problem with apes, as I see it, is that they're way too impressionable."

"Why do you call him an ape, Th'ñor? Is it because he is a Catholic? You know, he reminds me of one of my cousins. First he was Catholic, then he was Protestant, then he was an evangelical, then a Buddhist, then a Moslem—everything but a Jew, well who in their right mind wants to get killed? Right now he is with the Hare Krishnas. Perhaps next time I see him I will tell him about you, Th'ñor Págalu."

"It might be more helpful," said Lumumba, "if you tell him that the last place to search for his lost animal self is in a religion, *any* religion."

"Did he ever go to Mecca?" Albert asked.

"Oh yes, and he almost paid for it with his life when the pilgrims started one of their usual stampedes."

"I'll never understand what all the fuss is about," said Albert "Why people come in the millions to see a silly old box with a silly black drape over it and a silly old stone inside."

"That's because you've grown accustomed to worshipping only the phallus," said Lumumba. "The black-draped Kaaba and the sacred stone inside is as transparent a symbol of a woman's tunnel of pleasure as you'll ever want to see."

"No kidding!" said Soddhu. "I thought the Moslems were the most patriarchal of all."

"Yes," said Lumumba, "it's hard to imagine a bunch of Moslem holy warriors exhibiting a clitoris in plain view, isn't it? But don't you see? The terror of the vagina is so much closer to the surface in Islam. That's why they have to worship it even if they can't admit to what they're doing. It's also why they have to oppress their women so much and cover them from head to foot—a desperate attempt to hide the material object of desire and desexualize it while at the same time acknowledging the hidden desire in the form of holy ritual."

"It's so much easier to," said Soddhu, "just to worship fire, especially since all roads lead to the vagina anyway."

He simulated a kiss in my direction. Herbert glared.

"First chance I get I'm going to knock your block off," he said. "And to think that we used to chew khat together."

Okovango turned his little face to us. There was a worried look in his eyes as he tried to burrow further into Kumasi's lap. I thought it had to do with Herbert and Soddhu arguing, but Lumumba knew better. He checked the old ape's pulse, then pulled Okovango away. Old Kumasi was dead.

"You're here until you're gone," said Goldschmidt, "you're alive until you're dead."

There was no hint of sarcasm.

At about seven we arrived at the medieval city of Burgos.

"Th'ñores e Th'ñora," said Pedro, "con th'ua permission" (with your permission) I would like to stop here overnight and visit my cousin. He is an acolyte at the cathedral, he can get us some hotel rooms very cheap, I'm sure."

"Money is not the problem," said Lumumba, "we are very pressed for time."

"Th'ñor, to tell you the truth which I know is related to a tree and a penis, I have been driving since dawn and I am very very tired. Yes, we can still make it to Santillana this day but it will be in the middle of the night when we arrive there."

"And what about our old friend here?" asked Lumumba giving Kumasi a gentle touch. "We can't leave Kumasi in the car."

"No problem," said Pedro. "We can put him in one of the small chapels in the cathedral, my cousin Jose will not mind. There is renovation going on, the place is a mess anyway."

Kumasi was carried in with expediency, and Jose went off with Pedro while the rest of us were left to wander. The cathedral was immense.• A forest of columns rose from the polished floor to the arched ceiling high overhead. They were thickly crenellated and looked like long ropes made of muscles and tendons. They rested on plinths which looked like the toes of giant elephants, but the most amazing thing was the moment when the columns arched themselves into the ceiling. Called reredoes, they gave the cathedral the appearance of a living organism. It was a wonderful blend, Lumumba said, of mathematics and magic.

"This is how orgasm would look," he said, "if you could capture it on paper. The flying buttresses and arches of cathedrals are simply an attempt to duplicate the delicate tapestry of arches and curves, spins and symmetries that constitute a human's inner essence. Have you ever seen a blueprint of the nave of a church? It mimics exactly the physiological blueprint of a woman's womb. The faithful are worshipping orgasm the minute they step inside."

"Is that why this place is so beautiful?" I asked.

"My dear Mrs. Hickey. If there were no incest taboo, this building would be as unimpressive and ineffectual as a wood shed on a farmer's land. It would disappear, with all the other artistic creations, into a flat, undifferentiated fuzz. Beauty is indeed in the eye of the beholder, a mere figment of the imagination whipped on by the need to redirect your erotic feelings away from the dangerous object of desire onto something totally

---

• The author has given a description of the cathedral at Toledo. The Burgos cathedral, although smaller, is no less impressive, no less organic.

safe; anything will do—a building, a piece of jewelry, a painted canvas. This is why capitalism works so well, even though it too is a figment of the imagination."

"Well it's no figment," said Goldschmidt, "that I'm hungry. Do we have to wait for Pedro, or what?"

Lumumba appeared not to hear him. He was gazing at a tomb near his feet, marked by a simple block of marble. It was too dark to read the inscription, but as Lumumba continued to stare at it an idea occurred. There was a crowbar within reach, and within moments the strong apes had pushed the stone aside and lowered Kumasi into the dark tomb. The slab was put back just as it was, just as Pedro and Jose turned the corner.

"Aha!" said Pedro merrily. "All those nasty things you said about El Cid, and here you are gazing with such interest, I must say almost a look of reverence upon his tomb. His wife is buried there too, by the way. Well it's hard not to fall under the spell of our beautiful country. So many people have, you know. You aren't the first, Th'ñor Lumumba."

He slapped Lumumba heartily on the back. It was obvious that he and his cousin had been drinking, so much infact, that when we left the cathedral he took no notice that Kumasi was not with us.

We spent the night at a hotel next door to the cathedral. It was aptly named the El Cid Hotel. In the early morning hours I had a dream: We were inside the church, running from the police. By the time they entered we had disguised ourselves as monks. Lumumba, dressed in the flowing white robes of a priest, stood at the pulpit. With Albert's Bible in hand, he turned to the 1st Epistle of John and began to read:

"No one born of orgasm commits sin; for orgasm's nature abides in him, and he cannot sin because he is born of orgasm.

"Beloved, let us love one another; for love is of orgasm, and he who loves is of orgasm and knows orgasm. He who does not love does not know orgasm, for orgasm is love.

"No man has ever seen orgasm…"

The sermon over, he snapped the book shut and proceeded down the aisle holding up a gold and silver monstrance. The apes walked in front, merrily strewing the aisle with newly-minted coins they had stamped "In Orgasm We Trust." The coins tinkled like bells as they clattered to the floor.

As we walked toward the nave the police pushed the crowd back to make way for us.

"Grathias, mis hijos," (Thank you, my children) he said with a Castillian lisp.

"Bless us, Your Eminence," the police said in unison. "We are after some dangerous criminals."

Lumumba halted the procession. "I will only bless you," he said, "if you promise to leave those dangerous criminals alone."

"But Your Reverence," said a man. "They are murderers and cutthroats, wanted by the police in every country. Why, they just butchered the butcher! He's lying on top of his freshly made sausage."

"My son," said Lumumba slowly moving the monstrance from right to left, "these people are sinners, true, but it's not our job to punish them."

The movement was hypnotic and the man answered as if in a trance: "I thought it was, that's why we are policemen. So we can punish people."

"Not me," said a second officer. "I'm a policeman so I can keep myself on the right track. If I weren't policing others, I'd become a criminal too."

"Me too, me too!" several voices cried in unison. They all looked surprised at their own utterances.

"My children," Lumumba said, his eyes boring into them. "You have suddenly achieved the power for truthfulness. I ask you, which would you rather do? Run around in this great July heat chasing criminals or go back to your cool houses and fuck your mothers?"

He moved the monstrance imperceptibly closer.

"Fuck our mothers!" they shouted in unison. "And our daughters and sisters too!"

The crowd looked on in amazement, their eyes beseeching Lumumba to explain the meaning of these bizarre words.

"I give you my blessing," he said with a benevolent smile.

A policeman fell on his knees and kissed Lumumba's robe.

"Rise, my son," said Lumumba. "Remember what Jesus said in Luke 2 verse 49: 'Wist ye not that I must be about my father's business?' Of course he was referring to what his father did in the bedroom, so in emulating our Lord and Savior Jesus Christ you too must go about your father's business, especially if he can't get it up anymore. What are good sons for anyway?"

One of them looked at Lumumba with an awakening perception.

"Now I understand," he said, "why Jesus cried out: '*Eloi, eloi, lama sabachthani?*' Hell, if one of my sons went after my wife, I'd forsake him too!"

Lumumba beamed. "You have been blessed with great insight. Go in peace. The Virgin Mary awaits you in her bed."

332

They hurried away and we left the cathedral. But outside on the steps we ran into Cardinal Gomez and a retinue of sycophants. Seeing a halo around the cardinal's head, Lumumba began to argue.

"Are we not also children of God?"

"You don't have the right feet," the cardinal answered belligerently.

"Speak not so arrogantly," said Albert, "or the Saoshyant will cook you in his sacred fire."

"Bah!" said the cardinal. "You think I'm afraid of some silly old messiah? Why do you suppose I never wear garlic? The *kigs* and *karaps* be damned, and anyone else who castigates Khvetukdas. I might look like Gomez but my name is Zarathustra. And lest you doubt it, please look at my halo."

A grandee nodded and handed him a chalice of scented water. As the cardinal poured it over his own head the flames sizzled and expired. The crowd in the plaza cheered as the wetted face of His Royal Majesty, the King of Spain beamed down on them from the stairway.

"My Royal Subjects," he said. "The notorious gang of chimpanzees that has been terrorizing the world has decided to honor us with their presence. I know they are a group of psychotic, murderous animals with no redeeming qualities. But despite these small character flaws, I would like you to treat them as our honored guests."

The crowd cheered.

"The fool is dead," they shouted, "long live the fool!"

He nodded benevolently, then signaled them to disperse. When the square was empty the king sat down on the steps next to Lumumba and the cardinal. He removed his boots and I was astonished to see that he too had the prehensile toes of an ape.

"Welcome cousin Lumumba," he said, his canines gleaming as he swallowed a banana whole. "I didn't expect you to stop by. I thought you were still sore about my victory in our debate over Hegel's deconstruction of Kantian ethics. You never could separate a categorical imperative from the subtle machinations of the world spirit in the pragmatic world of day-to-day ethics."

"Actually, it was the blond bimbo I was sore about, the one you swiped that night in Monte Carlo," said Lumumba. He looked around the empty square.

"How have you gotten all these humans to be so docile and obedient?" he asked.

"A drug I extract from magic banana peels. It puts them under a permanent state of hypnosis. Would you like me to turn them into chickens?"

333

"How can you? They've all gone home."

"That's true," said the king. "I'll have to use Gomez instead."

Lumumba nodded and the king turned the cardinal into a bull.

"This must be a dream," I heard myself thinking. But Lumumba said that actually it wasn't and with the snap of his wrist he pulled off his mask. I knew the face at once, but when I said "Daddy, what big teeth you have," I awoke with a start.

At San Felices del Rudron we stopped for water. At Bezana a jagged range of mountains came into view.

"Those are the Cantabrians," said Pedro. "It won't be long now."

We came to a high crest and miles and miles of steep hills and valleys.

"A good place for a cave," said Lumumba, "and for landscapes riven by unconscious desires. An animal whose desires have been driven underground by a physiological structure it didn't ask for finds a cave and gives in to its torment. This is Altamira."

"But Th'ñor," said Pedro, "I have been to the cave many times and nothing is there but the most beautiful pictures which they say were painted 25,000 years ago."

"What do you think Pedro, that they were cavemen one moment and artists the next? How do you suppose the transition occurred, by magic? Well, in a way it did, of course, the magic of the visions I call them, although the scientific term is entoptic. Do you have any paper?" A sheet was passed back and Lumumba made these diagrams:

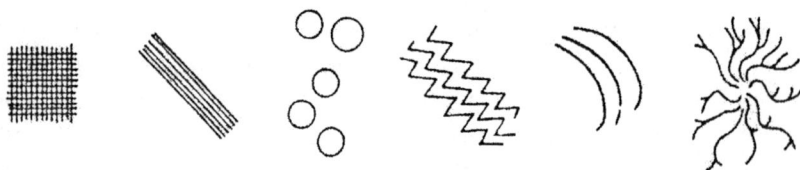

"That's all that separates them from us," he said to the apes, "these six little signs. Nothing more. No great God in the sky or, as more sophisticated thinkers would have it, no mysterious, unknowable Force in the endless expanse of the universe. All they did was push their brains to the limit and make the sparks fly. The cathedrals, the highways, the rockets to the moon, $E = mc^2$ are all a product of these six little forms"

"Doesn't that make it all the more remarkable?" said Goldschmidt.

334

"Ah, the superior brain syndrome! There's no use arguing against SBS if one must think in those terms."

"Well, since we're not that stupid," said Yendi and Tchibanga together, "what *about* these signs?"

Lumumba told them to close their eyes and press hard on their eyeballs. They could only do this for a few seconds because the bright stabbing lights they saw were painful.

"Now you've had a taste," said Lumumba, "of the ancient bridge that humans journeyed across—was it neurologically real?—when they left their animal selves behind."

And once man learned to capture these six patterns—known as phosphenes or form constants—on cave walls, he could start to paint animals as well. But it had been a torturous path indeed to get to that point.

As Tchibanga and Yendi had just proven, many animals were capable of entering into altered states of consciousness by closing their eyes and experiencing these optical illusions which result from electrical activity inside the nervous system.

But with the bipedal apes it was different. Because of the new alignment between pelvis and brain, the altered states were amplified, and at some point—was it in the beginning or later?—they became plagued by flashing lights, stars exploding in their heads and electrical charges racing through them, perhaps at levels never before experienced by any animal on the planet. Poor animals, they had to do something. The answer? Scribbling! Yes, by exorcizing the images that were tormenting them they could directly confront the by-products of their over-stimulated brains. And what better place to do this than inside the womb-like enclosure of a cave, man's unconscious tribute to the stimulus that caused the demons to arise in the first place?

It brought relief. Like excising a tumor from the brain, they cast these forms out of their heads and onto the solid rock. Suddenly they were in control again, for by taking these optical illusions and turning them into exteriorized visual representations, they gained a degree of power over that which had heretofor been tormenting them.

But more important than that, what hadn't existed before (except in their minds) now existed on the hard surface of the cave wall. Illusion became reality, and the belief in this reality set the stage for magic and religion. The ability to throw phosphenes onto rocks made the rocks seem powerful. Once the rocks were powerful, the idea of harnessing them for human use became inevitable. Those who had the power ruled. But weaker animals with enough cunning could now grab the power from stronger animals because it was out *there*, out beyond the individual, all for the taking.

That's when the priests stepped in and diversified the magic into all sorts of concepts such as laws and rituals for which only they held the key. Because its origins in the human nervous system were unknown, it appeared that the power was coming from an almighty God. This legitimized the priest's power which he used more and more despotically.

Now did we realize why it was so hard to give up God?

God originated in the human nervous system, and it would be like cutting out a part of our own body to exorcise Him. God did not create man in His image. Man created himself in the image of the visions which the electrical surges had forced into his virgin neo-cortex. Religion was a neurological disorder. Art was electricity and electricity was art.

But it was also science and politics and everything else created by man. Had humans not been able to project these electrical patterns onto the walls, there would be no such thing as mathematics. Those primordial patterns provided the basis of human thought—the basic relationship that held the human world together. The sad thing was that after crossing the neurological bridge, the Paleolithic people had turned against their own bodies, driven a wedge between themselves and Nature. In short, instead of studying these representations as man's first attempt at art, we should see them as man's first attempt to split himself in two. The painting signifies the end of Eden and the beginning of Hell.

"And all this time," said Pedro shaking his head in dismay, "I thought they were only painting pictures."

By late afternoon the sun had slunk behind a layer of fog, and the air had become cold. Lumumba said we were not far from the coast. We drove through more mountains that had been stripped of their forests. The style of the houses had changed. The bottoms were made of stone and the tops of stucco. There were tree plantations and several sawmills.

"I'm glad Kumasi's not here to see this," Tchibanga muttered, eyeing thousands of limbless logs lying supine in dirty pools of water. "They look like they're dead."

"Don't think for a moment they didn't suffer when they were being cut down," Lumumba replied.

"General, please, give it a rest," said Goldschmidt crossly. "I have a headache."

"Do you?" said Lumumba. "I thought the Machiavellian minds that run the Pentagon—that five-sided arm of the incest taboo—were at work twenty-four hours a day."

"No, we're too busy having sex with our mothers, according to you."

"There'd be a lot more forests, that's for sure.

We had just come to the road sign for Santillana del Mar. Lumumba sniffed the air. "What's that deplorable odor?!" he asked.

"Maybe it's Muñoz," said Goldschmidt.

"No no," said Pedro, "it's probably the Santillana zoo, I think we just passed it."

"Is it too late to go in?" I asked.

"Th'ñora, it is not a place I recommend. Well, perhaps I am wrong, but are you supposed to feed the carnivores with something that once had beautiful pink wings?"

Chapter Twenty-Five

Why the Communist Party Welcomes Chimpanzees
Or
Altamira: Inside the Famous Cave There Is More than One Climax

"Lumumba, my dear friend! I've been expecting you!"

Victor Muñoz extended his arms and embraced Lumumba warmly.

"You must have driven, otherwise you'd have been here three days ago! Si, si, my housekeeper called me." He was a portly man on the grayish side, undistinguished except for a pair of gold spectacles perched askew his nose. The pretty town of Santillana had only so many streets, and after a short search we had found him in a tapas bar near the Plaza de la Sandara, eating a concoction of beans and bull's testicles (Tchibanga wondered whether they were from our friends) because, he said: "I will need to be fortified for tonight's activities."

"You're going whoring?" asked Lumumba.

"Much better than that, much better. Come and have a drink. Are you still a tea-totaller? Ha ha, you were the only one who never sang the Wiffenpoof song at Mory's. But I don't hold it against you. Who is the woman? Not bad, not bad at all! So you're still up to your old tricks, eh? But why should I say old? It's only been six or seven weeks since they kicked you out."

"Seven weeks, five days and three hours if you want to know exactly," Lumumba replied.

"Of course, of course, come and sit down, I've been wanting to hear what happened. Bartender, drinks on the house! Your friends will drink, won't they?"

"Oh absolutely," said Goldschmidt.

As the four of us sipped Sangria the facts began to unfold. Victor Muñoz, a molecular biophysicist, and Lumumba, who had entrenched himself in the same department had, for the last year, been sharing an office together. It was during this period that Lumumba had come up with his theories on human evolution and, while keeping the results secret, had oftentimes used Muñoz to bounce his ideas around.

This proved to be unwise. Before Lumumba could publish his paper: "A Comparative Analysis of the Subatomic Origins of Orgasm and its Bio-molecular Relationship to Human Evolution and the Incest Taboo," a family emergency had taken him to California (we learned later that one of his cousins at the Los Angeles Zoo had gone insane), and during his lengthy absence Professor Muñoz had pilfered the paper and published it under his own name. After the department got over its initial shock, the undeniable genius of the monograph had quickly gained Victor tenure and Lumumba, upon his return, had been relegated to assistant professor which, to his mind, was tantamount to being a janitor.

But as if that wasn't enough, when he went to force a confession from Muñoz he learned that his colleague had gone to Spain on sabbatical. End of story, now all should be clear, but it wasn't exactly.

"Listen," said Herbert as Muñoz trotted off to the bathroom, "I see a great inconsistency here. All along you've been telling us that human life is a chimera, an illusory pursuit of sublimated goals all emanating from the magical precepts of the incest taboo. Yet here you are, all upset that you were denied one of those sublimated goals. In my mind, it doesn't make sense."

"My dear Dr. Hickey," Lumumba replied. "Everything you say is true, but you've left out one crucial element, the fact that I've been living in human civilization for over ten years—five as a research subject, five doing my own research. How do you expect me to go back to the jungle and eat bananas all day? No, my place is at Yale, I feel comfortable there despite the heavy and heady atmosphere of the incest taboo. All I need is Victor's confession. Ah, here he is now."

"Look here, Lumumba," said Muñoz. "I'm willing to make some concessions, but we need to discuss it and I have an important engagement tonight. What say you we meet at breakfast tomorrow and come up with a compromise? Your paper for my tenure—that's really what you want, isn't it? I think I could work something out."

339

"There'll be no compromise," said Lumumba. His shaved-down canines gleamed scarily in the light. "Either you write out a complete confession now or I break your scruffy little neck. *Now.*

Muñoz laughed nervously.

"Still the old hot-tempered Lumumba, eh? You know, if you break my neck your chances of tenure will really be up a creek."

"True, but I'll have the satisfaction of taking you with me."

"I didn't know Yale professors talked like this," said Pedro to Goldschmidt.

"Why do you think they're Yale professors?" Goldschmidt replied.

Dr. Muñoz looked at his watch, it was nearing ten. Lumumba put a pen and paper in front of him, the professor hesitated for a few seconds, then began to write. A few minutes later he was finished. It was a full confession stating how he, Victor Muñoz had falsely claimed Lumumba's work as his own, how he'd fabricated even the bibliography, and that to atone for the egregious lapse of judgment he was handing in his resignation. The tenureship, he said, rightly belonged to Dr. Lumumba.

"Kigs and Karaps!" Goldschmidt exclaimed. "I can't believe it's over."

We left the tasca and checked into a Parador a block or so away. The dining room was still open and we sat down to eat.

"Well, General," said Goldschmidt as Lumumba opened a newspaper. "May I now take Albert to Washington?"

"Be my guest," Lumumba replied. He suddenly hunched forward and added: "But maybe it's too late." The headlines of the Herald International screamed across the front page:

Castro Assassination Attempt Foiled by Vigilant Chimps!

An attempt on the life of Cuban leader Fidel Castro was foiled Thursday evening when a group of performing circus animals jumped their trainer and prevented him from taking the life of the country's President.
The drama unfolded in front of a spellbound audience of several thousand at the Pedro Marrero soccer stadium in Havana, where the Ringling Bros. Barnum & Baily Circus was performing as part of a cultural exchange program between Cuba and the United States.
The animal trainer Miguel Machado, a Cuban exile who lost several relatives in the Bay of Pigs invasion, and was also a member of Alpha 66, a Miami-based group opposed to the Castro regime, apparently saw his chance to kill the President when Castro's bodyguards left to buy peanuts. President Castro, who was sitting close to the center ring, saw

the assailant approach with a machete and tried to escape. But it was the quick-thinking action of five chimpanzees that are credited with saving the president's life. As Machado lunged at the president, the chimps jumped him, grabbed his machete and chopped off his head.

As the stunned audience watched, one of the chimps picked up the head and began speaking to the President in sign language. A hearing-impaired bystander who was fortuitously in the area interpreted the words immediately: "Give me here John Baptist's head on a platter."

Visibly shaken, Castro left the arena and returned to the Palacio de la Revolucion. But later the President made a stunning announcement over Radio Rebelde, saying that he intends to keep the chimps on as additional bodyguards and possible advisors on religious matters. "I am most interested in hearing what they have to say about God," he said in his impromptu speech. A reply from the Vatican is expected shortly.

The chimpanzees have given their names as: John, Freddy, Brian, Tom and Bill. A spokesperson for the Ringling Bros. Circus headquarters in Sarasota, Florida has said that the chimps must be returned immediately, but an aide from the Ministry of the Interior who wished to remain anonymous said that the chimps would not be relinquished any time soon.

"Well now we know what all the secrecy was about," said Lumumba as our waiter brought the first course.

Goldschmidt shook his head incredulously.

"That Castro leads a charmed life, I'm telling you," he said.

"Take the advice of a general," said Lumumba, "and go back to the Bay of Pigs or exploding cigar scenarios."

But Herbert was ecstatic.

"If Castro is going to let the chimps convert him," he said to me, "I'll get the Nobel Prize after all. And your dad can still kiss my ass."

"Th'ñor," said Pedro to Lumumba, "that was yesterday's paper, here is today's."

The front-page headline read as follows:

Castro Appoints Chimps To Council of Ministers,
U.S. May Send In The Ships!

In a marked show of defiance that is typical of Cuba's leader, Fidel Castro said on Saturday that he will disregard the United States' demands to return the chimps to the Ringling Bros. Barnum & Baily circus, and will instead appoint them to the Council of Ministers in Havana. The State Department, unsympathetic to the fact that the five chimps in question are credited with saving the President's life on Thursday after a Cuban exile attacked him with a machete, has said that this refusal may lead to war. "We are putting six warships on a twelve-hour standby," said U.S. Admiral Frank Randall at a Pentagon press conference on Friday. "We hope this will show Castro we mean business." The announcement was received enthusiastically by Cuban exiles who have taken over Miami.

Castro, speaking on Saturday to an estimated crowd of several hundred thousand in the Plaza de la Revolucion, appeared to be undaunted by U.S. blustering, and appealed to Cubans to open their hearts 'to our chimp comrades' in the communist struggle. 'From the perspective of dialectical materialism,' Castro said, 'it can be clearly seen that chimpanzees have been systematically excluded from ownership of the means of production and Leninist conceptions of the working class.' The Cuban leader concluded with a rousing exhortation to the 'monkey-workers' of the world to unite and rise up against their capitalist oppressors.

As Castro spoke at the podium, his new ministers could be seen doing acrobatics from the statue of Jose Marti and the tower. Smoking cigars and wearing berets and Che Guevara T-shirts, the ministers showed no fatigue during the marathon speech which went on for several hours. Only one incident came close to marring the event, and that was when Council Minister Brian jumped from a nearby palm tree and landed on the Cuban leader's head. The tense situation was diffused, however, when Brian signed to the crowd 'Socialism or death.'

Dr. Daniel Harwig, a professor of International Relations at Georgetown University, said in an interview on NBC's Meet the Press, that Castro is simply using the chimps to bolster his flagging popularity. But Allan Affeldt, a sociology professor at Harvard, thinks that Castro is making a sincere effort to upgrade the standards of chimpanzees world-wide. "Perhaps this will bring an end to the bush-meat trade in Africa," Affeldt said in an interview on CNN.

The United States still denies allegations that the chimps were sent to Cuba to assassinate Fidel Castro, charges made by the chimps themselves during several days of de-briefing in their native sign language. Sources close to the chimps say the five decided to assassinate Machado instead because he had beaten them during their stay at the circus' home base in Florida. The United States also denies allegations that Yale University was the training ground for the chimps, and that a sixth chimp named Albert remains at large in Africa. Adding another twist to an already bizarre story, an unidentified source at Yale has confirmed the report that the two men and a woman who trained the chimps for the secret operation have disappeared in Africa and may be connected to the notorious terrorist group known as the GLA, now believed to be in Spain. They are considered to be armed and dangerous. No identities have been given.

"I wonder who the snitch is," said Lumumba casually. All eyes turned on Goldschmidt.

"I swear it wasn't me," he said. "Anyway, General, what motive would I have for giving away our position?"

"Oh gee my gosh, now why can't I think of any!" Lumumba replied sarcastically.

"Well I swear again it wasn't me. But go ahead, hate me, I'm a Jew, I gave the world the incest taboo."

The second course arrived and was eaten in silence. Everyone seemed preoccupied, even the apes. Lumumba had taken out Muñoz' confession and was reading it again when suddenly he exploded.

"Son-of-a-bitch, he tricked me!"

It was true. Muñoz had written the confession in one hand and signed it in another, and since the signature was different from the text the whole thing appeared to be forged and invalid. We hurried back to the tasca.

"I'm sorry, Th'ñor," said the proprietor, "but your friend left over an hour ago."

"Damn!" said Lumumba. "The scoundrel's probably halfway to China!"

"Oh no, Th'ñor," said Luis the proprietor. "There's a special party going on in the cave tonight and that's where he went."

"A party in the cave?" said Pedro incredulously. "But how can that be? Hardly anyone is allowed to go there anymore because of the damage to the paintings."

"You are right, Th'ñor, and I myself am rather appalled. But the Minister of the Interior okayed it himself, and perhaps it is only fitting. How else to honor Spain's greatest dancer on her fiftieth birthday in the town where she was born?"

"La Esplenda!" Pedro exclaimed.

"Th'i, th'i. And you know what else? There are rumors she will be dancing tonight—can you imagine seeing a gypsy dancing in *that* cave? I would give anything to be there, but unfortunately only the big-wigs have been invited, and I am only a poor shop-keeper."

"Not as poor as you were this morning," said Lumumba slapping down a twenty-dollar bill. "Pedro, bring the car and put up the king's flags!"

A beautiful park with manicured lawns, meandering paths and grand old trees had been decorated with twinkling lights and Japanese lanterns. There were throngs of people everywhere, all dressed to the hilt, animated and happy. The champagne flowed freely, and there was food everywhere; its freshly-cooked aroma drifted deliciously on a gentle breeze. The

343

strains of flamenco music sounded from somewhere off in the distance. Okovango lifted his sleep little head, sniffed for a moment, then fell asleep again.

The flags over our car said it all, we were ushered past the ropes without question.

As we wound our way toward the cave the crowd grew thicker, and by the time we reached the entrance, a small doorway affixed with a green iron gate, the crowd stood ten dignitaries deep. Ignoring the mingled looks of anger and dismay, the apes began to cut through.

Just past the entrance there was a wide vestibule well-lit with tiki lamps. The music we'd heard earlier was now very loud, it was coming from the main vestibule but it was impossible to see in, there were so many people.

Two men who had been in front were now pushing their way back. Gripping their drinks tightly, they brushed past us.

"She hasn't lost it, she's as good as ever," the first man shouted to his friend.

"I don't remember all those bumps and grinds," his friend answered.

"She's bringing flamenco into the twenty-first century, I think it's great," the first replied.

At the mention of bumps and grinds Lumumba sniffed the air with a new sense of urgency.

"Betty!" he exclaimed.

He tried to barrel through to her, but a new surge of boisterous humanity cut us off. As we turned back to go around, the sound of voices came from an unlit vestibule—more like a pit or a small chamber somewhat below us. We stopped to listen.

"Th'ñor Dodd, they don't call me El Lobo for nothing. If you think I'm going to fall for this ridiculous masquerade, you are mistaken. You promised us guns and ammunition, helicopters and pilots, and all you have given us are two lousy suitcases of dynamite and a date with that broken-down whore. Who is she anyway, your mother?"

"I can't believe you've never heard of her," said Johnson, "the woman who once held all of Spain enthralled, the woman who danced naked before Generalissimo Franco and spurred him on to butcher the depraved Republicans. Ask her yourself. She will tell you about the men the general had hanged in her honor."

"I didn't say I've never heard of her, what kind of Basque do you think I am?" El Lobo replied. "I said it didn't look like her, but maybe you are deaf."

"It looks like her a little," said a man called El Pollo. "She has the same mole."

"Moles can be pasted on, you idiot."

"I swear to you," said Dodd, "this one is real."

"Even if it is," said El Lobo, "we need guns and ammo, mortar shells and hand grenades. You can't kill politicians with second-rate whores."

"You can if they're diseased," Dodd replied.

"Th'i, but that takes too long, guns are much faster."

"Your war has been going on for thirty years," said Johnson.

"That's because people like you promise us much and give us little. We are not satisfied with your two bags of dynamite, not satisfied at all." He kicked over one of the two suitcases next to El Pollo.

"Whoa, easy!" said Johnson. "Do you want to blow the whole place up?"

"No, Th'ñor," said a man called El Gato. "So why don't you give us some old planes instead?"

"Sorry," said Royce, "but the CIA has temporarily discontinued its surplus planes exchange program. The quality of cocaine we've been receiving has been too poor of late."

"Listen," said El Pollo, "let's stop arguing. I say we give them their money and take the dynamite *and* the woman."

"I say so too," said El Gato.

"¡¿Ustedes estan locos?!" (Are you crazy?!) said El Lobo. "Not even Pamela Anderson is worth six million pesetas, and I wouldn't give *two* for this broken-down grandmother and these miserable bags of dynamite. If you guys want the old battle-axe you can get your own fifty grand. I won't stand by and watch you use movement money for personal whoring."

Clutching the briefcase he brushed past us and left the cave. El Gato apologized.

"Sorry, Th'ñores, but he is el jeffe, the boss. Ath'ios."

"Terrorists these days aren't nearly as gullible as they used to be," said Johnson after El Gato and El Pollo had left.

"Just as well," said Royce. "I never did tell Betty *the rest* of the story.

"Oh well, nothing ventured, nothing gained. This isn't the real reason we're here, you know."

"General, do you think it's a trap?" asked Goldschmidt.

"Even if it is, I have to find Muñoz. All I want to do now is smash his ugly hominid brains to a purplish pukey pulp."

With renewed effort we at last gained access to the main chamber. Lumumba stood transfixed (as did we all!) as Betty clattered rhythmically across a makeshift stage. Her gyrations had everyone transfixed, and with a little foot-stomping here and hand-clapping there, hell, said Goldschmidt, she could pass herself off as a gypsy anywhere, especially with an audience as bleary-eyed as this one.

"You mean it's not *her*?" asked Pedro in surprise.

"Of course it is," a man next to him snapped. "Can't you see the mole?"

It was useless to look any further for Muñoz. He was not in the cave and never had been. Lumumba said he had half suspected it, but the confusion of human scents had thrown him off.

"I think we should get out of here," said Soddhu. "That fellow who caught us eating sunflowers? He's here, and so is don Felipe. I think he's with the cardinal."

"And Okovango's getting heavy," I said.

"Give him to Yendi," said Lumumba stubbornly. "I want to watch Betty."

"And you must at least look at the paintings," said Pedro. "You might never have another chance."

He pointed to the dome overhead. It was covered with the unforgettable sight of dozens of animals bounding and leaping across the ceiling. The clever artists had used the convexities of the rocks to realize the figures. They were mostly bulls—Pedro called them bison—but a large reindeer stood alongside the herd as did a few wild boar and horses. The animals were painted in red and outlined with quick black strokes. What the paintings said to me was that these artists had finally mastered form, and that the joy of this mastery was plain to see, exuding as it did from the leaping and bounding animals themselves. For the moment Betty was forgotten.

"Zounds!" said Goldschmidt. "These could sell for millions! If only they'd used canvas!"

"I feel that Mithra was born here," said Soddhu staring at the bulls. They must have loved animals a lot inorder to paint them like this."

"They did," said Lumumba. "Too much in fact. And so they had to part with them. These paintings are a symbolic depiction of that parting."

"You are wrong, Th'ñor," said Pedro. "The people who painted the animals were hunters, and these were the animals they hunted. By capturing the animals' likeness onto the wall, somehow the hunters believed the animals would be easier to catch. The term for this, I believe, is 'hunting magic.' "

Lumumba looked amused.

"Ah, the official explanation! My dear Pedro," he replied. "The term 'hunting magic,' much like its sister term 'hunter-gatherers' comes from the minds of men who prefer not to look at the dark side of their nature and the hideous origins from which they sprang. Is it not hideous to be split in two? To have one part of you going in one direction and the other in another, and all the while your head is exploding in stars and spirals and grids? I'm telling you the truth, man's departure from nature began here, I can feel it in my bones."

Art at its root, he said, was association—the power to make things stand for and symbolize other things. This art stood for and symbolized orgasm and the body turning away from its animal self. The animals we saw here were trying to communicate the beauty of orgasm through symbols. These paintings were rooted in the agony and ecstasy of the gonads, and represented man's attempts to get a handle on the forces inside himself.

Scholars made the whole thing a mystery because the images arose from deep-seated sexual problems that even today we weren't able to look at because they were considered taboo. Scholars really didn't *want* to know what these animal symbols meant, though it would be simple enough if they did, since we weren't talking about images conceived in the minds of elephants or birds but in the minds of human beings who were not that far removed from today's humans.

Here was the origin of religion, here on the ceiling. Our Madonnas, saints, gods and sons of gods all emanated from these animals. But by now we knew that religion was made up of sexual symbolism, and what was more sexually symbolic than these representations of man's animal self?

"Do all these bulls remind you of Khvetukdas?" said Albert.

"It reminds me more of the grotto in Nazareth," said Herbert, "where the angel is said to have appeared to Mary and announced the birth of Jesus."

"Caves, grottos, Jesus in the manger with the animals, *these* animals, the animal in man, the cave as vagina—it's all the same thing," Lumumba replied, "the same tune played over and over but with different variations."

We continued to gaze in awe.

"Hey look, Kathryn!" said Herbert. "There's your dad!"

"Ah," said Pedro, "you have found the Anthropoid Bison. He is one of the most popular figures at Altamira."

A magnificent bull with the face of a bearded human stood in profile near the bottom of the panoply. His eye, ear and nostril were etched, as was one of horns, his belly and tail. The strange creature seemed to be

347

wearing a headdress, and there were signs around his body which none of the other animals appeared to have. From a distance the face seemed to express sadness.

"He is very funny, no?" said Pedro.

"No," said Lumumba. "The story of mankind which is the story of an animal leaving its animal self behind is not funny at all."

If the artists were joyful, he said, it was because they presumed they had rid themselves of their animal identities. But alas, the presumption was false (bear witness by the Anthropoid's sad expression).

It was a confusing time in our evolution, he said. We were emerging from our old state and saying goodbye to it. Like the chrysalis and the moth, we were about to change into our new incarnation—a hallucinated human issuing from the terrifying sparks in our brain which would come to be called God.

No anthropologist would ever understand this unless he dared cross the line of the magic taboo. Dared to see that black was white and white was black, that things weren't what they are and are what they weren't, as old Kumasi might have said. All this was here in the Anthropoid Bison. Perhaps someday, someone would cross the imaginary line of the taboo, the line men learned to paint in caves like this after experiencing the visions, the line they hallucinated around themselves (sometimes it was called the magic circle) and allowed no one to cross—and solve the riddle of the paintings.

There were shamans today who visited what the uninformed refer to as the spirit world. In their trances, they harnessed themselves to animals— to the potency of the animal.

"In the shaman's mind he thinks he has become part of a world beyond this world. But the truth is, he has returned to the world he left behind. The potency is the sexual power he felt in his animal life. And how good it felt! When the shaman becomes an instrument of the spirits, he's allowing the gonads of his animal self to take over. In his trance he puts paint on the face of a rock. The rock represents the irreversible boundary of the world he left behind. Just as you can't pass through rock, you can't pass beyond the imaginary line that keeps you from experiencing your unbridled sexuality, your animal self. Just as you can't pass through rock, you cannot pass beyond a taboo. The taboo is an extension of the rock's impenetrability.

"Sometimes the shaman paints a line on the rock which 'disappears' down a crack, only to emerge somewhere else as if by magic. But this magic has been hallucinated, and for the shaman, the incest taboo exists because the rock is magic."

What we saw in this cave was all part of the hallucinatory transition which made animals into men, sex into religion. Our taboos made us what we were. We were the taboo and the taboo was us. It was impossible, he said, to separate a human from the hallucinatory lines and grids, or separate our hallucinatory lines and grids from our taboos. As for these paintings, he saw them as a logical consequence of the lines and grids that preceded them. They too were inseparable from the taboo.

The rigidity of human nature, the hardness we displayed toward one another, the intractability of our thoughts all stemmed from our belief that our taboos were as real and impenetrable as the walls inside this symbolic vagina. The incest taboo, in other words, which springs from the intractable rocks, was the source of our human malevolence.

But that was only to be expected. Every turn we had taken had been done on purpose inorder to put us further and further away from our animal origins. (And who would suspect we were animals if we didn't have fur?)

"You look at the bison-man," he said, "and you see an animal. You squint your eyes and you see a man. It's a joke. What is, isn't. What isn't, is. The painter crouches and paints his deception. Paints himself into it and becomes part of it. Paints the greatest deception ever—the human race. Believes he's not an animal any longer, believes he never was an animal, believes a powerful sorcerer—God—made him from the soil, believes someday he'll grow wings and play a harp in heaven. Whether the deception started thirty thousand years ago or three million years ago isn't important; what's important is that it *started* and continues to this day."

Humans still believed in their hallucinations, still believed there was a real boundary between themselves and animals, countries and nations. But to believe in this reality was utter madness. These drawings had established a world of make believe, a world devoid of the truth and the honesty which only animals were capable of.

"But let's stop with this animal-human business," he said as Okovango stirred in Yendi's arms. "It's a categorization I find uncompelling. Rather than refer to this bearded bison as half animal, half human, let's say it is a representation of orgasm half free and half incarcerated. Gonads real and unreal. This is how they got themselves under control. By learning to sublimate orgasm—to see it as curves, spirals, tunnels and vortexes—they were finally able to call the shots, leave nature behind and slide into a world where hallucinations pass for reality."

He gestured broadly at the paintings.

349

"This is the turning point, the beginning of the end, the betrayal, the beginning of a false species, what you call human."

"Are you saying we've hallucinated ourselves into being humans?" asked Soddhu.

"Not being, *thinking* you are human. Only the deception is real, and this deception has led to great unhappiness and tragedy. Kumasi would say: 'You aren't what you think you are and you are what you think you're not.' "

"Th'ñor Lumumba," said Pedro. "As you know I am already a confused man, but now I am more confused than ever."

"The General has a way of doing that," Goldschmidt quipped.

"I wouldn't talk, Mr. CIA faggot," said Tchibanga.

"Sticks and stones may break my bones but names will never harm me," said Goldschmidt.

"Will you two *please* shut up!?" Lumumba yelled. Pedro spoke quickly.

"It's the cave, Th'ñor. It makes everybody a little crazy."

"Just as it did 25,000 years ago," said Lumumba. "Tell me, Pedro, are there any paintings of lions in Altamira?"

"No, Th'ñor, no lions, thank god. I am afraid of lions."

"There is a cave in France where there are lions, a whole wall of them, in fact. The cave is even older than this one. Now, I'd like you to imagine yourself standing at the entrance to this cave. It is thirty thousand years ago, and you have not yet separated from the monster which lives inside your groins and is causing a lot of trouble. But you want to put a stop to the agony, and the time is ripe. The brains have been prepared for just this moment. Evolution has paved the way. Those millions of years since the first tool was made in imitation of the penis haven't been wasted. Your mind has been created in the image of orgasm. Your mind is a product of the revelation of orgasm, and all its cells are busy preparing to compute the data relating to the genitals. So it is no coincidence that now when you stand before the mouth of the cave you see the opening of a vagina. It is no coincidence that on entering the cave you imagine yourself penetrating the mysteries of life itself. The further in you go, the more dangerous the journey becomes because the computing brain knows how dangerous sex can be. You stop here and there to release the entoptic phosphenes onto the walls, either as form constants or animals. But still, the danger seems to lie ahead.

"At last you enter the innermost chamber of the cave. This is where the monstrous demon resides, the demon Orgasm which commands you to do terrible things, the demon you must obey, the demon you can't resist, the demon that lifts you off the earth, transports you to paradise and becomes God in the process. Do you see how God has sprung from the demon and the demon from God? To honor this god and control him you project his image onto the wall. He is the king of beasts, the lion, ferocious and powerful and undeniably beautiful because he *is* ferocious and powerful. Do you see how beauty originates in the ferociousness of orgasm? Now, since the lion lives so deep inside the cave, in some way he seems to be hiding there. It's as if his presence is a secret. And the truth is, the lion *is* a secret. For by painting him deep inside this symbolic vagina, no one knows he's there. No one knows what a ferocious force lives inside the gonads. The clever cave artist has killed two birds with one stone: he has named the beast (hoping to control him) and locked him away (hoping to forget him). Out of sight, out of mind. The demon god has been relegated to the deepest recesses of the cave, and by imprisoning him there on the walls the artist magician has been able to diminish his fury. Yes, a real lion can harm you but the representation of one can't. The lion in the loins is no longer real. It has been conquered. Orgasm has been conquered. The desire to kill and maim has been conquered. One more step in the development of the human being—a deceptive step, but a step forward in the development of religion."

"Could you say," said Soddhu, "that every church begins inside a cave? Our mithraeums were mostly underground, you know."

"Better to say that every church, every cloister, every sacred book and every minister's sermon begins inside the vagina."

"And my cousin Jose thinks that *I* am the sinner?" said Pedro ruefully.

Tchibanga signaled impatiently. It was time to go, he said.

With a deep sigh, Lumumba took a last longing look at Betty and started to edge his way out. The room was stifling and Okovango began to cry in the crush. People turned to look.

"I hope nobody yells fire," said Herbert.

But something far worse was about to happen. The sound of a loudspeaker outside suddenly blasted away at our eardrums.

"Th'ñores e Th'ñoras, may I have your attention. This is General Arriba speaking, Commander of the Northern Forces of Spain. We are doing our routine annual cave check, we ask that everyone come out with their hands in their air."

"Son-of-a-bitch!" said Lumumba. "Who is the traitor! Goldschmidt?!"

"Ay yi yi! When does it ever stop," Goldschmidt groaned.

351

But no one besides ourselves had taken the announcement seriously. Obviously it was a joke and the army was here—if it really was the army—because La Esplenda had once been the Generalissimo's paramour. Anyway, whoever heard of an annual cave check?

As the music continued the loudspeaker blared again.

"This is Commander Cox, officer in charge of U.S. Naval Operations, Tarragona, Spain. The cave is surrounded by tanks, and in ten minutes I will give the orders to fire. Any loss of civilian life will be added to the charges already against the Gonad Liberation Army."

The music came to a stop. The crowd grew quiet, and any lingering doubts were soon dispelled thanks to Cox's failure to turn off the microphone.

"Excuse me, Commander," said General Arriba. "No one has given you permission to blow up the cave."

"The Pentagon has authorized me to use whatever means are necessary to free Father Albert."

"You will trade this irreplaceable cave art for the life of one lousy priest?!"

"Those are my orders."

"Ai Chinga! Estas loco?!"

"Sorry, I don't speak Spanish."

A look of hope crossed Lumumba's face.

"With that idiot in charge perhaps we have a chance."

"I wouldn't count on it."

It was Johnson who spoke. The gun he was holding was pointed at us.

"Sorry, General, but there's no way out unless you happen to be a bat," said Dodd.

"I always knew, Lumumba, there was something fishy about you," said Johnson.

"Look who's talking," said Herbert. "Unless it's just part of being a senior planner to sell guns and ammunition to any lunatic who wants to blow up the world."

Goldschmidt shook his head wearily.

"You still don't get it, do you, Dr. Hickey," he said. "By selling guns to terrorists, we are setting the stage for a world conflict of unprecedented importance. Perhaps you are right, General. There *should* be only one incest taboo—*ours*, an Anglo-Saxon-Protestant Incest Taboo heavily guarded by Capitalism. And just think how nice it will be, everybody shooting everybody else—every tribe in Africa pitted against each other, Moslems shooting Christians, Protestants shooting Catholics, Hindus shooting

Moslems, Palestinians shooting Jews. The long-range plan is to have one government (ours, of course) meting out justice to all. One government and one incest taboo—that, my friends, is the goal of Langley."

"A noble goal indeed," said Lumumba. "Albert should be of immense help."

"I'm sure he will, once he learns what a thrill it is to screw up other people's governments and spread havoc and destruction among simple third world people who are still trying to survive. Being a spy, Albert, is the ultimate white man's high, better than colonialism, better than slavery, better than genocide, better even than corporate profits!"

By now the cave was empty. In his haste to leave, one of the musicians had forgotten his guitar; Betty was strumming it when she came to join us. She avoided Lumumba's eyes as Dodd tied us up. I was surprised to see he was tying Goldschmidt up too, but the Consul was more philosophical:

"This is the thanks I get for giving the world the incest taboo."

When the job was done, Johnson relaxed his aim.

"Okay, Royce, you can call in the troops. Oops!"

The guitar in Betty's hand came crashing down on Johnson's head. As he fell to the ground he dropped his gun. Dodd went to grab it but Albert was there first.

"Stand back, my son," he said aiming the gun at Royce's chest. Royce grinned and began to move forward.

"I know you won't shoot, Father. You are a man of the cloth."

Albert fired, the bullet caught Royce in the groin and he doubled over in pain.

"Nice shooting," said Betty. She helped Albert untie the apes, then Lumumba pulled her into a passage behind the chamber. They were only gone a few moments, but when they returned Betty's face was flushed and jubilant. So was Lumumba's.

"I've discovered an air vent going to the surface," he said straightening down his hair. "Give me the dynamite."

He disappeared into the passage taking Yendi with him while Tchibanga held the gun on Johnson.

"I hope he doesn't blow us all up," said Herbert.

"Th'ñor, it is the pictures I'm worried about," said Pedro. He ran his fingers lovingly over some geometric forms which Lumumba had said were part of the bridge, simple yet Cabalistic lines wherein lay the seeds to the magic incest taboo and all the fearful ramifications that grew out of it. The cave was so full of these designs! Lumumba had said that the key to interpreting them hadn't really been lost; it was only hidden by the fearful dictates of the incest taboo.

Now he came back and told Tchibanga to tie up Betty, but not too tightly.

"Aren't we coming with you?" asked Herbert in a panic.

"Sorry, folks, but this is the end of the line. I have to travel light now, those guilt-ridden cowboys out front aren't going to ask for my autograph. Albert, are you with us or not?"

The little ape looked around sadly.

"Mr. Goldschmidt," he said, "I'm so sorry, but I think I might not be the right material for Washington afterall."

"Oh come on, Albert!" said Goldschmidt. "Just because we got off to a bad start—all this confusion and everything—doesn't mean it'll always be like this."

"Oh it's not *that*. It's that I rather like the idea more of worshipping a bull, and if Dr. Págalu will be so kind as to visit me in Africa and instruct me in his religion I should like to become a Zoroastrian priest. Uncle is right, it's time I stopped feeling guilty about Nedele. Well, tallyho everybody, Khvetukdas awaits!"

He hurried after the others.

"Dr. Lumumba, don't forget the formula!" Herbert shouted as loud as he could.

"It's in the mail," the Professor shouted back. "Okay, everybody, fire in the hole!"

'Isn't that apropos," said Soddhu.

The charge went off. The cave shook violently and detritus fell on top of us. But when the dust cleared no one was hurt and all the paintings were still intact. The sound of clacking boots and excited men was coming toward us.

"It might have been preferable to have gone with the General," said Goldschmidt.

"They aren't going to kill us, are they?" Herbert asked.

"You never know," said Goldschmidt philosophically. "Sometimes it just depends on what kind of mood they're in."

"If they do they do," said Soddhu. "If they don't they don't."

Commander Cox charged in with his men.

"Boys," he said after a quick reconnoitering, "there's a million dollars and a year's worth of confiscated cocaine to whoever brings in the General, dead or alive." As the soldiers ran off whooping like Indians we exited the cave. The helicopters circled as the men continued to sift through the rubble, unwilling to believe that the wily apes had escaped. Betty knew otherwise and was crying like a baby.

"Don't worry, your husband will be okay," said an officer handing her a handkerchief.

We were herded without ceremony into waiting cars, and as I pictured the apes, four adults and a child heading who knew where I too felt like crying: the party was over and there might never be another.

We were taken to the State Department for debriefing. It lasted several days. All the top brass were there including Colin Powell and Admiral Randall who was still hoping to start a war with Cuba. The President and Secretary of State appeared sporadically. Everything we knew about Dr. Lumumba was classified as top secret, from the food he ate to what he wore when he went to bed at night. Some of the worst grilling came from the National Security Agency and the Pentagon.

"Why, you'd think we were a bunch of criminals," said Goldschmidt indignantly during a break.

At times I found my eyes wandering over each general's uniform. One man not only had ribbons going down the left side of his chest and the right, but also down the middle all the way to his stomach. Another man had them lining the sides of his pants.

As I looked at these ribbons I remembered what Lumumba had said about war, how the winner of a battle is the one who kills the most people, how the soldier's job is not so much to protect his country as to arrange for the killing of men with other forms of the incest taboo, and how gaining new land was merely a pretext. (Although expansion of land always gave the victor the power to expand his own version of the incest taboo.) There was an excitement to war which men would never talk about because it was counterproductive to the Ten Commandments. Shellshock, he had said, was nothing more than the excruciating guilt of having experienced the joy of killing.

Did I dare tell them this? That God is always evoked in war because God and war are both sides of the same coin, both rooted in the overwhelming ecstasy of human orgasm?

As I looked at their steely eyes I decided it might not be wise. Indeed there were many things that the four of us, Goldschmidt included, thought it best not to say. But it was not always possible to command our thoughts, and by the end of the debriefing 'Operation Lumumba' had been reclassified: not satisfied with top secret, the Pentagon had raised the files to Code Level Extremis.

"The penalty of divulging even one word of this debriefing will be severe," the President had said. "If this were wartime, all of you would be hanged, you, especially agent Goldschmidt."

355

"Understood, Mr. President," said Goldschmidt, "only too clearly."

On the last day as on the first, a Bible was brought in to bind our testimony.

"You still want us to swear on this after what we've told you about religion?" Herbert asked surprised.

"What else do we have," the agent answered, looking bewildered.

"There's always gomez," said Soddhu cockily.

I gave my word along with the others, and in writing this account of our travels with Dr. Lumumba the manuscript is being kept under lock and key.• As Admiral Randall had remarked at each and every meeting, what would happen to civilization if people got wind of Lumumba's vision? The Admiral's words were meant to send a chilling message, but instead they reminded me of a passage from Isaiah:

> The wolf shall dwell with the lamb,
> and the leopard shall lie down with the
> kid; and the calf and the lion and the
> fatling together; and a little child
> shall lead them.

Now I ask you: why not a little ape?

• The author's decision to publish was due in part to public pressure, and in part to an offer by publishers that couldn't be turned down. Despite Lumumba's teachings we still have to sublimate.

Postscript

Life has returned to normal, or almost. Soddhu and Herbert have gone back to their old jobs at Yale, Herbert and I have almost made up, despite the nagging doubts I still have about Crumb. My fling with Soddhu is over. Despite his passion, the bloodless halls of the campus have had a sobering effect on both of us.

He still pursues me, but his frequent trips to Africa are giving him a new direction in life. Albert, he says, is taking to Zoroastrianism like a duck takes to water.

Goldschmidt quit his job at Langley and has become a full-time drug dealer in Africa. Now that he has no other obligations, Baxter gets his shipments on time. Is that why he's being pressed to run for the Senate? Dodd and Johnson are still at Bechtel, and people are still leaving Lyon Isle since Gordon's arrival. But they are mostly the old crowd from San Marino; the newer set doesn't seem to mind *who* mother married, and a few have even invited the couple into their home. She and Betty continue to play cards, but whenever Royce leaves town on business Betty flies back to the South to visit relatives. (Mother says she can't understand why Betty never told her about all these relatives before!)

Dr. Baker is still setting up clinics in third world countries, and Ntimama has bought a magnificent villa (is it Mobutu's old place?) in France.

There's no news of Bangassu, but Pedro keeps in touch. He was happy to report that the Santillana zoo has been shut down indefinitely since terrorists blew it up about the time we were there and took away all the animals. (Though they continue to deny it, even under torture, the Basque separatists are being blamed.) The missing animals were traced to a moving company, then to the airport at Santander where the trail has gone cold.

But here is news!

Goldschmidt tells us that the local papers are having a field day with reports of a banana boat that is steaming up the Congo River carrying a cargo of dangerous animals. Commandeered by some frightful-looking men rumored to be ghosts, all the tribes along the river have fled in panic. There was a final sighting along the river at Kongolo which coincided with the disappearance of an old surplus airplane.

More news. Soddhu has just returned from Mahale. The mountains, he says, are crawling with all kinds of wondrous animals: swans, cockatiels, falcons, mice, pythons, kestrels, ducks, genet cats, martins, owls, peacocks, roosters, flamingos, deer, bear, bison, tigers, orangutans, coyotes, alligators and turtles. (Pedro confirms that these are the animals from the Santillana zoo!) All efforts to catch them have failed, and since they seem to be living peaceably on a diet of bananas, the new warden has decided to let them stay. (That their presence is bringing in revenue normally reserved for the Serengeti is most likely the real factor.)

But this is the best news! Lumumba's quarter page of the formula has finally arrived. It came in an envelope with no return address, postmarked from a college town in the South. Herbert has pieced it together, and after much soul-searching has decided to present it as his own. Here is Lumumba's formula:

$$F_0 = \frac{D^2 \sum E_c \times \sqrt[3]{A} - P_s \; \odot \to (P_{2s} - \Delta S)^2 + R^2 - F_s}{\sqrt{C^2} - O_{ehc} + S_{gs}}$$

Where:

F_0 = Force of Orgasm
D = Desire
E_c = Rate of evolutionary change
(speciation/millenium)
A = Rate of morphological adaptation
(protein sequences: variation per millennium)
P_s = Selective pressures
(deaths/cause/10,000 individuals)
P_{2s} = Penis size (centimeters)
ΔS = Angle of spine from horizontal
R = Repression (kilowatts/gram of cerebrum)
F_s = Fantasy (wet dreams/month)

C   = Speed of light
O_{che} = Orbital energy of hydrogen electrons during orgasm
S_{gs} = Specific gravity of semen

There was also a diagram which looked like this:

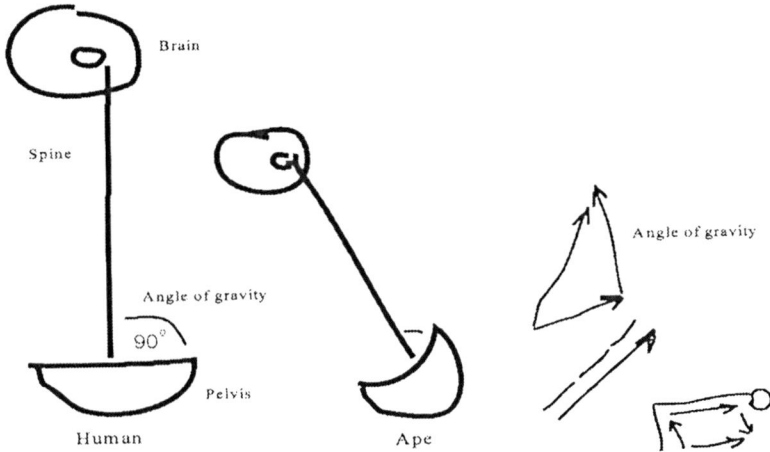

Final news. The formula has already caused a stir in fields as far apart (although Lumumba would say they are one and the same) as astronomy and zoology. One Yale physicist is using it to investigate one of the last unsolved problems in classical physics: how turbulence arises. Herbert is the newest star on campus, much to his delight and my father's chagrin. No, Daddy is not at all happy, Herbert's success has thrown him off. But now that I know why it hardly even matters.

As Albert said just before we parted, all is Khvetukdas.

End
March 26, 2000
New Haven, Conn.

About The Author

Anna Purna is a native of Southern California. Raised in an intellectual milieu not far from Hollywood Boulevard, her interests range from Homer and Doestoevsky to Lana Turner and Johnny Stompanato.

In college she received a degree in philosophy. This has helped her synthesize a world view of her own: "As I see it, we're all here by accident." She is an avid swimmer ("I do my best thinking when in the water") and enjoys being in the Great Outdoors. She has lately discovered that listening to the recordings of songbirds is the best music of all.

The author currently resides with her husband and dog in a beach community not far from Los Angeles.

CPSIA information can be obtained at www.ICGtesting.com
Printed in the USA
LVOW081932140113

315673LV00007B/216/A